The Total Sum

Ivan Winters

DEDICATION

To all those with whom I have had the honour to work. I may have
written the words, but from you came the knowledge, often, by its very
nature, unrecognised and unsung. Yours is the unspoken story that for
those who know, will always be remembered as the deeds of the truly
courageous.

CONTENTS

Chapter 1
1968

HMS Contest cut through the dark green water, a scar of phosphorescence slicing behind in the semi-darkness. The quiet thud of the engines beat the heaviness of the evening, the sound muffled in the enveloping cloak of the late April dusk. Above, the blue-black skies were already speckled with a thousand stars as billions more awaited the retreat of the orange streaked west fading into the indistinct Irish hills some miles off to port.

The water lay flat and still, the steady slash of the water slicing at the bow easing as the ship slowed and came to a brooding stillness.

On the bridge, the shaded eyes of a silent figure wrapped in a black overcoat and woollen hat studied the captain as he peered out onto the shadowed sea.

"This is it," said the captain turning to face the civilian, "this is the place."

To a casual observer, it was clear from the captain's flat delivery that the relationship between the two men extended no further than what was required for the task in hand. Business-like: Professionally detached. Commander Legge had been leery of the other man since he had stepped aboard the C class destroyer at HMNB Portsmouth. He had spent half a life in the Royal Navy, rising from Officer Cadet through the ranks to Commander, a rank always referred to as Captain on board his ship. Now his ship and his third command was the deadly grey warship of Her Britannic Majesty. A thousand years of history were represented by the epaulettes on his shoulders. A uniform resonating back to the times of ancient Kings; of Aelthred, of Saxon blood. Officers before him had served Henry VIII, had engaged the French in the battle of the Solent and raided Spanish ports under Elizabeth I. The Atlas had once been washed Empire pink by the efforts of commanders like Nelson and Exmouth. Royal Navy ships had engaged the enemy at Jutland, Heligoland and the North Atlantic. It was a noble record and one that led Captain Legge regard the shady secret world of men like the one standing before him with barely disguised disdain.

"This is the Beaufort Dyke?" asked the man, "You're sure?"

The Able Seaman on lookout glanced across at the Officer of the Watch who returned the look with a steady glare. Captain Legge did not flinch.

"The trench is almost forty miles long and two miles wide. 300 metres of Irish Sea lies below this welded hull - some of the deepest water around the British Isles. It would take a rare gift of inept naval navigation to avoid setting a 350-foot-long destroyer over it at some point Mr…ahm, Brown."

The man who identified himself as Brown grunted and turned back to face the darkness outside the glass. The Officer of the Watch smirked. The Able Seaman saw it and added to it his own inward scorn. The Captain was the Evenstar, the moral compass of the ship's universe. In questioning the master of the ship, Brown had assured the junior rating's everlasting contempt.

HMS Contest was reaching the end of her serviceable life and Captain Legge knew within a year or two she would be broken up or sold to a friendly power. New ships were coming on line and soon the vessel that had been home for Legge and his crew would be a forgotten relic of the post war years. The sea would reclaim her 1700-ton displacement and new technologies would leave behind the once impressive gunlaying equipment, the quadruple torpedo tubes and the analogue High Angle Fire Computer.

The destroyer was more to the men aboard her than the sum of her parts however. She was a living thing, security, familiarity, home - part of the fabric of their lives.

When Captain Legge had been told the manner of what was likely to be the ship's last mission, the sting of partaking in one of the murky stratagems of the intelligence services had left a sour taste in his mouth. Not that he had been told much. That the pale-faced man was to be afforded whatever aid he requested however had been made very plain.

"And Commander Legge," the Admiral had concluded a week

previously in his teak panelled office at Whitehall, "Mr, ahm..." he glanced again at the sheet on his desk, "... *Brown* will be on board to oversee the disposal. Unless there are unforeseen conditions which render this *impossible*, you are to comply with all of his requests. The job is called Operation Neptune. You now know what less than six people alive currently know. It will remain that way. Any questions?"

The tacit acknowledgement was that none was expected. He nodded to an aide who stepped over and opened the door.

"I shouldn't foresee any problems Commander," he said finally, reaching for the phone on his desk.

Commander Legge recognised an order when he heard one. He donned his cap and saluted. The Admiral lifted the handset.

"Lieutenant Balfour will show you the way out."

"I will need some time to prepare for disposal," said Brown. "I will not require help thank you."

The Captain nodded as the civilian left the bridge. The man had already visited the large crate strapped down onto the poop deck just above the fantail several times since they had sailed. Each time he had gone alone and without assistance. Whatever it was, it was clear that Mr Brown was not going to illuminate anyone with information as to its contents.

The captain pursed his lips and looked from the radar screen back out onto the languid waters. All was clear. There was no other vessel within ten miles. Brown could have all the secrecy he needed in his furtive dealings. The mission had been a simple one and the weather could scarcely have been better. The crate would be winched overboard and committed to the depths of the trench where lay countless tons of war materiel, dumped from the leftovers of two world wars. One more secret consignment would make no odds. There would be no issues.

The box was strapped onto the deck near the stern. Nothing about it afforded any information as to its contents. A plain five-foot square cube, its robust timber plank construction was held together with metal straps stretched tight and fastened down with heavy brass screws. Brown was hunkered down, beside it in the rising deck, making some final check as the captain and the first mate watched from the bridge.

"So, what now?" asked the mate, to whom little in substance or detail had been shared as to the nature of the mission.

"He winches the crate over the side," replied the captain, "and buries another sordid secret."

Brown insisted on being the only man on deck during the process. Apparently he had been given some instruction somewhere on the use of the specially fitted derrick. Had more capable hands been permitted to assist then the committal would doubtless have passed by without incident. Another small action would have passed without comment like so many of the myriad of unwritten events of cold war subterfuge.

Instead of lowering the crate to the surface of the water, Brown operated the release when the crate still had almost ten feet of salty air beneath its timber planks. It was far enough for the slight swell to rock the cable into a pendulum arc that allowed the box to collide with the armoured steel hull on its fall. Just enough to damage the crate. Just enough to jar the vials within.

Brown was surprised by the violence of the splash, but he could not see the damage to the metal strapping nor the contortion within the inner packaging. He rebuked himself for his carelessness, but that was all. Otherwise the job was complete and the evidence was gone. His superiors would be pleased and international relations remained as before. He returned to the bridge and succinctly reported to the captain that the business for which he had come was finished. The captain nodded to the helmsman, delivered the required speed and bearings and looked out into the darkness. All in all, it had been a brief enough operation; already a past event, nothing of particular significance and the days to come would bear no record of it ever having taken place.

As the throbbing warship pulled way into the gloom, the engines pulsating in the oily waters, the wake behind settled over the tomb below leaving behind an ominous eerie silence. From where the crate had descended into the depths, a single bright green bubble rose, its phosphorescent sphere breaching the surface and releasing the merest trace of unnamed gas without witness or observation. Many years would pass before a human being would pass over the exact spot again.

Chapter 2
North Channel

As close to invisibility as a man can get is out at sea, at night, in a fibreglass kayak. Metal ships many miles away shine as bright blips on the radar screens of modern vessels, but no radar yet in service can pick out a man paddling in the dark in a small plastic vessel at wave height.

Not that any man in his right mind would be half way between the Galloway coast and County Antrim in a thirteen-foot-long kayak at night unless he had a very powerful reason to be there.

The man was eighteen and he had left Portpatrick six hours earlier on a bearing for a Northern Irish port called Donaghadee. He was in a kayak, though he called it a canoe, not being the sort of young man to use words too punctiliously where commoner ones sufficed.

It was an argument that found him where he was. An argument with a friend who told him it was utterly impossible to paddle to Ireland and back in one day. Being young and seeing every risk as an opportunity, he naturally had taken the statement as a personal challenge. Had he been a little older, wiser or simply less spontaneous, he might have remained in Dumfries and let the argument remain academic, but that was simply not in his nature. Without reference to tide tables or expert advice, he simply strapped the kayak onto the roof of his old Nissan saloon and headed off to the Galloway coast. His plan consisted of paddling to Donaghadee, buying a local Newspaper to prove he had been, and then returning.

That he had remembered a lifejacket was no credit to his planning. There happened to be one he had stashed in the hull and he only donned it as a casual afterthought as he pushed the fibreglass craft out onto the stony beach at Portpatrick. An hour out onto the abnormally tranquil water, he congratulated himself on his luck with the weather while at the same time mildly reprimanding himself for having brought neither food nor water.

"Aye, well, I'll get something on the other side," he reassured himself aloud, while his inner voice quietly asked a more pertinent question.

"Do you not think Finlay," said the voice, using his surname as it most often did, "that two o'clock in the afternoon's a little late in the day to be setting out to cross the Irish Sea?"

It was only because of the descending gloom that he saw the weakly flickering lights. The darkness had fallen like a shroud and fear followed hard on its heels. He had realised halfway to County Down that he would never make the journey and despite himself, had taken the inner voice's counsel to return. He had been paddling for eight hours before he finally surrendered. So low down on the water, the Irish coast had been next to impossible to discern and now only the Galloway hills were dimly visible to the East. The lights were cottages and farmhouses twinkling far off on the Scottish uplands. With a goal to strike for, he struck for the almost imperceptible glimmering, caring little whether he landed at Cairnryan or Kirkudbright. Solid ground of any name was all he desperately longed to reach. The eerie silence was broken only by the sluicing of his paddles in the oily water, an alien sound that increased his sense of utter helpless isolation.

It was then that he saw it, his mind failing to decipher what his eyes were recording. It was so surreal that his heart gave an almost audible thud as he suddenly saw a ghostly light flicker below the surface three metres in front of and under the bow of his canoe. He ceased paddling and struggled to contain the waves of disorientating fear washing over him, gripping at his chest and scattering his thoughts like starlings from a stubble field.

Sitting in the little craft, bobbing alone in the darkness, he involuntarily dropped his hands and stared. From below his kayak a yellow glow flashed and spread fingers of light out into the deep waters. Before his mind could structure some idea of what was happening there was a sudden violent effervescence bursting up from below the hull and he was immediately capsized and plunged into the boiling waters.

Chapter 3
Anya Nevotslova

Anya Nevotslova looked out into the bitter sub-arctic of the Kola Peninsula. Inside it was warm, the double-skinned thermal lined metal a barrier to the sub zero winds whipping needles of ice and hurling them with mindless glacial fury against the Institute's embattled outpost. Inside the remote complex, the two hundred and twenty-two scientists and their military escort were the only human beings within five hundred square kilometres of frozen waste. The bitter landscape of icy enmity scoured by howling, wailing squalls was as alien to any warm and living thing as it was possible to imagine. That humanity could exist in such conditions was a tribute to the drive and determination of people driven by a relentless passion to push the boundaries of knowledge and discovery. People like the hardy alumni of the Arkhangelsk State Technical University. In a world dominated usually by men, men toughened by state military service, Anya was distinctly conspicuous. She was slight in build, quiet in demeanour, keeping herself distanced from the unsophisticated and too often hard drinking scientists of the institute. In Arkhangelsk she specialised in metallurgy and technical alloys, coming consistently top of her class in every discipline.

A month before her arrival at the outpost, Anya had been summoned into the office of the director of the engineering faculty. To be called before the inscrutable inspection of Viktor Karmonov was not an invite to be sought out voluntarily. Although in his mid eighties, he looked twenty years younger and bore a rugged face as if cut from weathered granite. His entire character was surrounded by an aura of understated menace. Standing in the same room with the man was like being in a locked cage with a sleeping wolf. A sleeping wolf with one eye surreptitiously ajar.

Karmonov was one of the socialist Elite, a political commissar during the Chairmanship of Nikita Khrushchev. To that man, Karmonov's very existence had depended; nonetheless he modelled his life on another. Years had passed since the vindictiveness of the mindless cosmos had wrenched open a swollen blood vessel in the head of a small stocky man in a dacha in Volynskoe. That head had belonged to the great Joseph Stalin and in that moment Mother Russia had lost its soul. That the soul lost was truly a lost soul in the redemptive sense was not a thought that could ever cross the mind of Viktor Karmonov. Stalin was his boyhood hero. In 1945 as the Nazis slaughtered the defenders of Stalingrad, they were themselves butchered in return by the vengeful armies of a man who would go on to slaughter 30 million of his own people. Into that hell the infant Karmonov was born. Delivered into the filth of the underground sewers of a city brutalised by indescribable violence, his mother had less than an hour to grasp her son before bleeding to death. His soldier father was last seen leading a charge with Molotov cocktails against a Panzer battalion of Tiger tanks. He never returned. It was young Khrushchev the commissar whose intervention saved the child's life and gave the child's name as a forecast of outcome. To survive such a beginning and live through the complex deadly intrigues of Stalin's purges, ending up in a position as head of faculty said much about the man. Loyalties were nothing to him. Like a chameleon, he would be whatever he was needed to be and no price was too much for him to extract from the lives of others if it was to the preservation and elevation of Viktor Karmonov.

"So," he said, a sheaf of papers in one hand and a paper knife turning over in the fingers of the other. "You are Anya Nevotslova."
It wasn't a question. Neither was it a simple statement. Without looking up at the girl standing in front of him, Karmonov delivered the words like an accusation. She hesitated, unsure whether or not a reply was expected. Uncertainly she remained silent as the man slowly took off his thin glasses, set the papers on the dark wooden table in front of him and purposefully placed the paper knife on top. He looked up for the first time since she had entered the room and set a heavy finger across his chin. Anya noticed that the two middle fingers were missing. An old scar above his left eye made it look as though one eye was partially closed. He studied the pale face of the girl before him.
"The daughter of *comrade* doctor Boris Nevotslov."

Evidently she had guessed right. Karmonov had not been asking her a question. He said the word *comrade* with the slightest suggestion of a smirk before his face returned to its expressionless steel. This time he paused, looking with a steady expectation at her, boring a hole into her eyes.

"Yes, comrade," she stammered. "My father told me he… he was, he served with you in Afghanistan." She nervously pushed back an errant strand of blonde hair that had escaped its clip.

"Did he now?" His gaze remained fixed to her face. "Though perhaps he told you more than that?"

Anya's father had indeed. He had told her about the man who was more dangerous than the murderous *Mujahedeen*, a man afraid of nothing and feared by all. She knew from her father's testimony that Viktor Karmonov was brutal. A man totally amoral, whose cold atheistic god was worshipped at the temple of self-elevation and personal empowerment.

"Not… not really sir," she lied, reverting to a title once regarded as anti-communist; a label used by the decadent west. But the USSR was long gone; Anya was a child of *Glasnost* and *Perestroika*. Men like Karmonov were survivors of the old dispensation. Men who still held on to formidable and ominously indefinite powers.

"I was younger when he was… when he died," she added.

"The former Commissar's eyes narrowed at Anya's slip. She had been going to say that her father was killed. In all but name, put to a slow death by the state. Back from Afghanistan a broken, sick man and without time for proper recovery, assigned to work in a metallurgic research station in Novosibirsk. Anya remembered the infrequent trips home, where each time she saw less of the father she loved, and more of a man haunted by demons he would articulate to no-one. The months with him at Arkhangelsk were the best days of her life, days continually spent at his side, absorbing all she could from her beloved *papa*. Her mind wandered to the bright birch forests. But there had been another. Another who had also held her heart. His remembered face, smiling and alive, shimmered momentarily before her until it was suddenly wrenched away by the rasp of the Director's voice.

"Nonetheless," the guttural voice interjected - a searching eye fixed on her face - "here you are and specialising in the very discipline in which your father was, how shall we say… uniquely qualified?" He picked up the papers again, setting the paper knife to one side. Opening a drawer in the desk, he slid the file in and shut the drawer purposefully.

He raised his eyes slowly from the desk and cast a long cold look at the girl before him. There was no suggestion of imminent words. He simply studied Anya as if she were a mark on the wall. Whether he was looking at her or through her in some incomprehensible observation, Anya could not tell. The silence grew thick and almost unbearable. To speak would have been an outrage. To remain silent was like she was being tested and failing all the more as each second ticked by.

Suddenly, in a single fluid movement he raised his heavy hands and placed them like objects on the desk. Palms down, old scars telling unknown stories across their backs. He locked her eyes with his. Eyes flat and impenetrable.

"Ilyich Gasparov will arrange your transport from Severomorsk," he said, the silence suddenly broken. "From there you will be escorted onward to your placement where it will be explained to you just what kind of work they require a metallurgist for. I'm sure you will find it enlightening."

Again, the trace of a smirk as his face dropped to engage another set of papers to his left. Correctly, Anya conjectured that her interview was over and with a murmured 'thank-you', left the room.

Four weeks later Anya found herself on the Kola Peninsula. The journey from Arkhangelsk had been long and freezing, aboard a battered ice-breaker bound for Murmansk. The steel hull of the vessel had been buffeted by arctic squalls as soon as it left the relative peace of the White Sea and entered the violence of the Barents Sea. Four hundred and fifty wind whipped, wave beaten miles later, the ship hauled due south into the Kol'skiy Inlet and sailed for another day before finally tying up at a protected harbour just south of Severomorsk. There stores and passengers were disgorged into a frozen world of wind-driven snow and ice. At the dock she was met by a military captain of few words who bundled her into a drab green saloon driven by another soldier. After a short drive across the docks, broken only by the captain's directions to his driver, she was put on a small boat and ferried across the channel. On the western side she was met by another officer - a duplicate of the first in his fur cap and jacket, and taken to a tracked military truck, its engine rumbling and fuming on the snow-covered ground. Inside, several other passengers were huddled in their furs, apparently strangers to one another, heads bowed to conserve as much warmth as possible in the unheated compartment. What followed was the worst journey of her life. If the trip across the Barents Sea had been bad, the next twelve hours was a struggle of strained survival as the semi-rigid vehicle bumped and heaved across one hundred and fifty gut-wrenching, freezing kilometres of the seemingly trackless wasteland of the Kola Peninsula's northern arctic tundra.

By the time they arrived at the massive complex, an incongruous contradiction of strange buildings in the frozen alien landscape, Anya was longing for the almost balmy air of Arkhangelsk.

~~~~~

"The *Kolskaya* Superdeep is why you are here."

Gasparov was speaking to the new personnel who had joined the project. He was a thin, wiry man, thick close-cropped black hair set over dark eyebrows and a long narrow nose.

"Some of you, Averin, Liminov, are here because we need further, ahm, mining expertise."

Two large men, at the back nodded to one another and the others as the small group turned to see to whom the names belonged.

"Rogov, Chemeris, Yashkin – Mineralogy and Petrology." Again, they were acknowledged by the rest of the group as one by one each man began to discover who his colleagues were. Gasparov listed some other names, giving their field of expertise before coming to Anya.

"Anya Nevotslova, as one of only three female staff is our metallurgist and will be working with me." Anya looked with greater interest at the speaker, wondering what kind of a man he would prove to be. So far, from his speech and delivery, he appeared self-possessed with an air of deliberate authority. Gasparov was evidently finishing and Anya refocused her attention on his words.

"So that, colleagues, is us all. The personnel you are supplementing have been working here, sworn to total secrecy for the last eighteen months. Every single person, including labourers, electricians, cooks, mechanics and so forth, like yourselves, are under the same restriction. This is a military facility and we are under military orders. I am sure you are aware of the consequences of that particular distinction."

He paused, looking around the room, and apparently satisfied that his meaning was understood, continued.

"Most of you have no real idea what we are doing here. However, you will be assigned to your work stations where the head of your specialism will explain our enterprise to the degree you are required to know. Apart from the head of project whom you have all already met, the work we do here is not to be discussed with another human being outside of this room."

Anya glanced briefly around the room and saw other pensive faces doing the same. There was no impression of anyone being any more informed into the secretive operation at the facility than herself. Somehow or other Karmonov had left her with the impression that it was some kind of a mining operation, possibly involving precious metals extraction. In hindsight, he had been so vague that it could have been any one of a million things. The conjecture had been all of her own creation. Nothing she had heard so far vindicated or denied anything and now for the first time she realised just how little she knew about why she was here at all.

Chapter 4
The Awakening

The light above his bed began as a blur and gradually sharpened into an identifiable object. It was a fluorescent tube. More, it was a flush-mounted strip light and its soft glow illuminated the pale green walls of a room roughly fifteen feet by twelve. Lying on his back, he looked without comprehension at the square panels on the suspended ceiling then tilted his head to the left. A window. No curtains. Vertical blinds, slightly ajar with the shapes of buildings outside framing a grey sky. Inside the room, a small high table with a jug of water and an empty glass. Beside and behind his head, wires, tubes. Some kind of a support with something flashing on it. A light. Green.

Now a noise. It was a buzzing. On, off, on again. The rasping annoyed him, but only mildly so. Here he was. He was in bed, a single white blanket covering him. The pillows were fresh. He could feel their starchiness as he turned his head.

Where was he?

Who was he?

Outside the room several people, nurses, doctors and some in business suits stood in the corridor.

"And you mean to say this man has been in a coma for all this time?"

"Yes, it has been a deep unconsciousness without response to the varied stimuli we have provided thus far," Doctor Jamieson replied. The new Chief Executive of Glasgow Royal Infirmary had fired out the question with a curtness close to ignorance. The consequence was that the doctor took an immediate dislike to him. He hoped he would not be the kind of man who would make a habit of visiting the wards. With hospitals reduced by government interference and financial expediency to the levels of businesses, managers like the hawkish Mr Standish were able to present themselves in ground once the hallowed sanctity of the untainted practitioners of medicine. Without deference or recognition to the depth and scale of learning and expertise that consultants like Mr Jamieson had worked a lifetime to achieve, Standish's very presence reeked of self-importance and delusional superiority.

"Have you any idea how much this kind of thing costs?" he demanded.

"Actually, we don't call them *things*, Mr Standish," replied Samuel Jamieson in a carefully measured voice, "we call them patients, or more accurately, people."

Inside the room the man could see the dim outlines of people on the other side of the obscured glass of the door. The rasping continued in his ear. He turned to his right and saw a screen. It had jagged lines moving across it. The green flashing light beside him was suddenly matched by another above the door. He put his arms onto the mattress either side of his body and attempted to push himself up. The screen on his right began beeping. Despite his efforts, the man lay heavy, immoveable upon the bed. A wave of exhaustion surged over him as his head fell back into the pillow. Outside there was a noise.

As the group stood and talked outside the room, one of the nurses found her attention seized by a light flashing above the patient's door. She looked to the surgeon and then back at the light. It was still flashing.

"Excuse me," she said and quietly moved away. The Chief Executive continued oblivious, elucidating some financial imperative or other to the consultant surgeon. Doctor Jamieson turned and watched the young nurse disappear into the side ward. The monologue of Standish became a suddenly distant background irrelevance as his eyes fixed onto the flashing light. He opened his mouth to speak but was interrupted by the wide-eyed nurse suddenly reappearing at the door. She caught the steely eye of the surgeon.

"He's awake!" she gasped.

Standish suddenly knew instinctively that no matter how persuaded he was of his own primacy, at that moment he became an irrelevancy to the medical staff he had been upbraiding. Like a disappearing vapour, they left him standing with his managers in the corridor. He had become an instant redundancy and the assault on his pride was an almost physical crushing.

Inside the side ward the man watched as several people appeared at the bottom of the bed. A nurse – two nurses. A man in a white coat, a doctor? The man adjusted his glasses and spoke.

"My name is Mr Jamieson," he said. "I am a doctor. Do you know where you are?"

The man on the bed looked at the nurses. They were looking from the doctor to him. One moved to the bedside to his left and did something to the controls beneath the screen.

"No, I… I… no, I don't know…have I had an accident or…?"

Or what? What was happening? Nothing made any sense. He was totally devoid of any frame of reference. Nothing to indicate normality or removal from it. Limbo.

"This is Glasgow Royal Infirmary," continued the doctor. "Yes, you've had a bit of an accident. You've been… asleep for some time, but things will soon begin to clear for you I'm sure. How do you feel, are you in any pain at all?"

"I don't, no, I don't think…no, I feel… empty. I feel empty."

The nurse beside him reached over and touched his head with her palm. She smiled at him. He attempted a smile in return, but it was as if his face was stiffened and all he managed was a faint grimace.

"Am I very sick?" he asked, turning back to the doctor. "How long have I been asleep?"

"No, not very sick," replied Mr Jamieson. "We think you may have had a head injury of some kind, but now that you are conscious and back with us, I'm quite sure you will soon be on the mend." He too smiled and glanced at the folder in his hands.

"Conscious? Oh. Was I unconscious for long?" The nurse beside the doctor shot him a curiously nervous glance as the doctor cleared his throat.

"Yes, well, quite some time. You have been unreceptive for several… for quite some time, yes. You see…" The doctor cleared his throat and steeled his eyes. "You have just awakened and things will undoubtedly seem strange. Don't worry though, as I said, you're over it now and you'll soon be your old self. I am sure of it."

The man lay still as he took in this new information. After a second or two he looked back up at the doctor.

"Mr Jamieson?"

"Yes?"

"I don't know who I am. I don't know… what is my name?"

"Mmm… yes, well, as I say, don't worry about that. Coming out of a…

a prolonged sleep period isn't an instant thing. Some things will take a little time. For now, we're pleased that you're able to talk and ask questions. Rest now and we'll talk again later. I'm sure you would appreciate something to eat, mmm?"

The doctor went to leave but suddenly the patient spoke again.

"How long was I asleep?"

"Sorry?"

"How long was I asleep, was it a… was it a coma?"

Mr Jamieson hesitated before answering. He removed his glasses and glanced out of the window before turning back to face the man on the bed, his eyes searching his own, a face anxious and earnest.

"Yes. You have been comatose. You have just awakened from a coma."

Ordinarily Detective Inspector McGregor would have tasked his sergeant or one of the constables. After all, it was only a missing persons file, but he had a favour to return and despite his rank, sending someone else to fulfil it wasn't an option. He scratched a few notes on his pad and reached for his coat.

"I'm heading over to Glasgow Royal Infirmary Jim," he said as he passed by the open door of his sergeant's office. "Favour for a friend. Missing person, should be back before lunch."

"No bother Jack," nodded the sergeant using the name everyone bar his mother called John McGregor, "want me to come along?"

"Naw," dismissed the inspector, "you've enough on your plate this morning. Don't expect it'll be much of a trip anyway. See you in a bit."

Jack made his way out to the car park recalling the phone call the night before. Would he mind calling over about a man who had awakened from a coma. Maybe assist in determining his identity? It seemed an odd request, but whatever Doctor Jamison's request might be, Jack would do his best to support him. That he still had his precious Helen was down to him. Her life had hung on the balance for days but the doctor's super-human effort of surgical expertise and rugged commitment had been almost overwhelming. If there was one man on the planet Jack McGregor would never refuse it was Robert Jamison.

Missing Persons was the bottomless pit in police work. The Bottomless Pit and the Slough of Despond. It seemed that Glasgow had hundreds of adult males who had absconded, opted out of society or simply disappeared without trace. Or, at least, without caring to leave one. The streets abounded with lives unravelling from complexities simply too big to deal with any more. One of the untouchables - the price they were willing to pay for whatever freedom was found in the anonymity of Glasgow's cold pavements and city-stained alleyways. His experience told him this would just be one more who had awakened in a hospital bed. Still, there was always the possibility of resolving one more obscure personal mystery. And who knew, the patient himself might be forthcoming and provide all the detail that was required. He swung out onto Dobbie's Loan and headed west. He would be there in five minutes.

The patient meanwhile was finding very little forthcoming. Any concentrated thought he attempted seemed to come up against a wall of fog that blurred and obfuscated his efforts. Beyond that he was in a hospital bed and was apparently recovering from some kind of an accident, nothing else suggested itself to him in the way of further detail. Not knowing anything about himself, especially not knowing his own name was a vacuous horror – an annihilation of his very identity. Primal existence. Brute being. That he should *be* somebody he knew could only be true, but the utter anonymity of the person he occupied was as empty as a house devoid of anything but blank walls. No hint of a previous inhabitant – no clue to a past.
"I have had a life," he muttered in a whispered lament. "I am someone!"

Inspector McGregor's wait outside Mr Jamieson's office was not long, but in the two or three minutes he waited, he took in his surroundings as the pretty red-hair tapped on her keyboard. It was a thing he invariably found himself doing anytime he was somewhere new. He noted the light green of the walls, the pine framed scenes of heather covered mountains, the freshness of new carpet and the stain on the secretary's sleeve cuff. An inch-long sliver of masking tape ran along the skirting board – the room had been recently painted. The stain on the secretary's sleeve was light green. She had brushed against the wet paint - very recent redecoration. She wore a sacred heart ring on her left hand – she was Catholic. A map of Glasgow poked out of her black glossy handbag at her feet – unlikely to be a local. Perhaps the scenes in the paintings reminded her of home. A highland girl down in the big city. With hair that colour and ring, possibly an Appin Stewart, a MacGregor or even a MacDonald? No engagement ring. Not yet, though a silver heart pendant around her slender white neck was possibly a gift from someone special.

The phone on her desk tinkled and she picked it up.

"Yes, he's just arrived, I'll send him right in Mr Jamieson," she said, smiling across at the inspector as she spoke in a distinctly north Scottish accent.

Setting the phone down, she arose to open the door as Jack stood up to follow her.

Robert Jamieson was already on his feet and half way across his office as he entered through the opened door.

"Inspector McGregor, so sorry, I shouldn't have kept you waiting!" exclaimed the consultant and he proffered his hand. "Thanks you so much for coming and giving up your precious time!"

Jack shook off the comment with a shake of his head.

"No, no, not at all. If there's anything I can do to help, it will be my privilege."

Mr Jamieson offered his visitor a seat in a comfortable leather recliner as he himself sat back casually against the edge of his desk.

"And how is Mrs McGregor? Well, I trust?"

"Very well – *excellently* well thanks to you. We can never thank you enough for…"

"Nonsense, just doing my job," dismissed the surgeon with a wave of his hand, "only doing what they pay me to do. I merely put things back in the right place. Healing comes from a place far above my ability. I am delighted to have been of some little help. Delighted that she is doing well, delighted for you both." He lifted a folder off his desk as he spoke and began pulling out sheets of paper.

"I'll not waste your time inspector, I have a rather interesting case, and I feel sure you might be able to help."

"I'm not so sure," replied his guest, "you may have placed too much faith in *my* abilities!"

"Not at all, not at all," exclaimed the surgeon, "But let me explain first. As I told you on the phone, I have a patient who has just awoken from a coma – you are familiar with the nature of a coma?"

"I could suffer a refresher," suggested Jack with a smile, "First aid is the height of my medical knowledge!"

The doctor smiled as set the papers on the desk behind him and pressed the tips of his fingers together.

"A coma is a state of unconsciousness. It can last anything from six or seven hours to several years in rare and extreme cases. The principle determinant is that the patient cannot be awakened."

"Pain? Shock treatment?" queried the policeman.

"No, neither. They will not respond to any external stimuli; not light nor sound - not even pain. It is not like sleep – there are no cycles of wakefulness - no voluntary actions. A deeply comatose patient is entirely unable to consciously move, speak, feel or hear."

"I thought some patients reported having been aware of what was happening around them during their coma?"

"So rare as to be discounted, and certainly never in a deep coma such as our patient has undergone. It is much more complex than just a profound sleep. It is almost a kind of neurological death. You see, to maintain consciousness, two important neurological components must function. The first is the cerebral cortex..."

"This is getting a bit beyond my First Aid syllabus," interrupted Jack, "is that the bottom part of the brain?"

"Not quite, it's the grey matter - the outer layer if you like, of the brain. You are thinking of the second component, a structure located in the brainstem, known as the reticular activating system. Injury to either or both of these is enough to cause a patient to experience a coma."

"So your man has had a head injury?"

"Well now, that's one area where our patient's diagnosis diverges from we might expect to find. We have never determined any evidence of a direct head trauma – though admittedly other factors can bring about a comatose state."

"Like alcohol?" the inspector sighed, "Glasgow has no shortage of that particular problem."

The consultant nodded in agreement. "Yes, alcoholism has been known leave its victims in temporal coma but so equally can a stroke, or even highly uncontrolled diabetes."

"So you think your patient could be in a coma for one of these other reasons then? A diabetic?"

"Unlikely. To be perfectly candid with you inspector, he doesn't really fit into any of the boxes."

Inspector McGregor scribbled a few notes in his pad, which he had fished out of his pocket during the conversation.

"How does he not fit?"

The consultant pulled out some sheets from the folder beside him on the desk.

"These are printouts of his brain's electrical activity," he said passing two of the sheets across the room. "Normally a comatose patient has lower activity than someone conscious and as you see from the first sheet here, his was barely perceptible."

The inspector studied the rows of slightly fluctuating lines and nodded. "Not that I know what I'm looking at, but this line doesn't seem to be doing much."

"We measure comatose patients on a scale. Coincidentally, it is known as the Glasgow Coma Scale, anything below eight is deeply comatose. This man rarely got above a two."

"Oh. And that is rare?"

"If he had been on a life support machine we'd have turned it off."

"So, how did he come around?"

"Quite suddenly. Despite popular depictions, comatose patients generally re-enter consciousness very gradually. This is another unusual component."

"And how is he now?"

Mr Jamieson passed over the second scan. "This was his brain activity just before I contacted you."

The inspector studied the sheet. This time there was no line at all.

"Shouldn't there be a wavy line or something?"

"There should be, but there isn't. Do you know why?"

Inspector McGregor looked up.

"Because his activity since he awoke is so far beyond the scale, we have nothing capable of recording it. Our equipment is too sensitive. An electrician's multi-meter would be more use. I have no idea what is going on but there is more neural electricity pulsing in that man's head than should be possible to survive. It's like connecting our probes to the mains."

In his room, the patient was reading a book he had found in the back of the locker. Probably left behind by the previous occupant and missed by the cleaners. The one in his hand was one of two books he had discovered in the locker, the second he had set on the bed.

"The Collected Poems of Robert Burns." He didn't know if it was something he liked or not so he opened it and found it easy enough reading.

Within two hours he had read the entire contents, including the lengthy prologue and editor's notes. Words from the pages were dancing around inside his head.

"And fare-thee-weel, my only Luve!" he said aloud, *"And fare-thee-weel, a while! And I will come again, my Luve, Tho' 'twere ten thousand mile!"*

"I *will* come again," he repeated slowly, and the strangeness of his own voice, along with the pathos of the poem was a haunting, intangible 'otherness' introduced into the confines of the room.

He set down the book and lifted the other from the bed. For some moments he stared at it before opening it. He hadn't read much when something made him look up. Before him, a figure appeared standing in the doorway.

He was a man in his early forties, a suit and tie and a look of natural authority.

"I'm not catching you at a bad moment?" he said simply as he took a step in.

The patient shook his head. "No, no, just reading." He set the book beside the other onto the bedside table and looked up at the visitor.

"The name's Jack," said the visitor putting out his hand, "Mr Jamieson asked me to call in, if that's O.K. with you?"

"No, nice to see you, I... do you know me?" asked the patient suddenly.

"No, sorry, only calling in a professional capacity, I'm a detective with the Strathclyde Police. Thought we might chat, maybe I could ask a few questions?"

"I see. Yes, ask away, though I might not be much help."

The inspector gave a short laugh as he pulled up a chair beside the bed. He didn't want to intimidate the man; a similar or slightly lower eye level could often reduce inevitable tensions

"With any luck I might be able to help you a little. I'm told you've been in a coma?"

"Yes, oddest sensation. Like I'm in a dream, but awake. Nothing seems... real?"

"I'm sure it does all seem very strange. Do you know how long you were unconscious?"

"No. It only occurred to me this morning that I haven't been told that yet." A thought suddenly occurred to him, "Do you?"

The policeman shook his head. "No, though I think it has been a considerable time."

"I meant to ask but I… well, maybe I didn't feel quite prepared for what the answer might be. I think it's more than hours – days, weeks even."

"Can you recall anything about yourself, anything at all?"

The younger man gave a wry laugh. "I don't even know what age I am," he said. "I looked in the mirror, twenty-six? Twenty-seven? Who knows?"

Jack McGregor studied the face before him. Dark brown hair – clean complexion, around six feet tall. Mid twenties seemed about right.

"Can you remember your name?"

"Sorry, sounds stupid, but I've really no idea."

"Your accent, West coast, but I'm not thinking Glaswegian?"

"I don't know, I'm sorry – I know this is Glasgow, but the nurse told me that."

"Definitely not Edinburgh," said Jack as much to himself as the patient, "and in all likelihood no further North."

"Don't the police have records for people like me?" asked the patient suddenly, "I mean, someone must be missing me; family, friends?"

"Aye, we have any amount of files with people who have been reported missing, though I'm trying to narrow it down a bit. Have you any images of places you can conjure up? School, workplace?"

"No, nothing. Work. I suppose I had a job – no idea what it might be. Can't have been that good at it if no-one's missing me though."

"Not at all. Could be you're self-employed. Plasterer, painter – any number of occupations where your disappearance might not raise suspicions. Let's see though – are you up for a bit of work?"

The patient nodded so Inspector McGregor continued. "This might sound odd, but let's try some images. I'll say a word or a phrase and you tell me what you see in your head, you understand?"

"Just describe how I imagine it?"

"That's the idea. So, if I say, picture the nurse you first saw when you awoke, what do you see?"

"Small, pretty, large eyes, an upside-down watch in her left breast pocket, fair hair, will I go on?"

"No, that's good. Try this. House. Now what do you see?"

"A house, ahm… a roof, front door, a garden, four windows, curtains"

"Here's another. Primary school."

"Oh, I don't know, children playing, a teacher at a desk. A playground, children writing, schoolbags."

"That's O.K. Here's another. Car accident."

"Two cars crashed into one another, ahmm… a tree with a car in it, a car crashed into a wall, someone lying against a steering wheel…"

Inspector McGregor continued for a few minutes, sometimes using single words, sometimes phrases. He made notes in his pad as he listened, but if the patient hoped he was coming up with something encouraging, he would have been disappointed. The replies he was being given were generic – nothing particular. He was operating entirely from imagination rather than recall. When given a word, he would look off to his right when replying. Jack knew that if reaching for visual recall into memories, people would almost always look upward to the left. Constructed images would take the eyes to the right. The first question had been a reference to test if he was a majority left looker or a rare righter. The patient looked to his left on the first reply. Every other he looked right. None of the questions apart from the first initiated a memory response.

"Anything?" enquired the patient.

"It was just a mental exercise," Jack lied, "hopefully enough to start something rolling in your head. I wasn't expecting any answers so soon." He rose from his seat and put away his pen. He had promised the consultant we would not tire the patient overly.

"So, you'll be back again Inspector McGregor?"

"Very likely. I'll get a search started in our Missing Persons department. Hopefully too, you will begin to recall things. With a bit of luck on our side we'll have this sorted quite quickly."

After promising that he would keep in touch, Inspector McGregor excused himself and a few minutes later rejoined Mr Jamieson.

"So, anything?" asked the doctor taking off his glasses.

Jack McGregor shook his head. "Nothing. I'm sorry. He really is blank isn't he? I'll open a file on him when I get back and get a thorough search started. One thing though – how far back do I need to go? It's long, isn't it?"

Mr Jamieson turned his glasses between his thumb and forefinger.

"Let me answer that by first of all giving you some information I had not shared with you in our earlier conversation. That young man's appearance is in every way indistinguishable from when he was first admitted inspector. I mean, exactly the same. His hair hasn't grown – his fingernails have not required any clipping. These irregularities and others equally unusual are factors in why I asked you to speak to him before informing you as to the duration of his coma. I did not want to cloud your initial assessment with the, what shall I say, *abnormalities* of the case?"

"Abnormalities? I'm not sure I understand – are you saying he has only been unconscious for a short period then?"

"That is precisely what I am *not* saying inspector. There this mystery plunges into depths I am still trying to gauge. You see, to supply you with the answer to your question? - Eleven. That young man has just awakened from a coma of at least eleven years!"

In the car park, Jack sat in his car for a minute or two before starting it. That a man could suddenly awaken from an eleven-year long coma presented all kinds of unimagined consequences. To awaken into a world strange and unknown, an alien in a parallel universe with no other alternative to return to. Knowing no one, familiar with nothing, no sense of personal history, your own name a mystery? It was almost impossible to envisage. Clipping in his seatbelt, he turned the key as his car came alive. Driving out of the hospital car park and moving up through the gears, he felt a faint unease in the background of his mind. Something indistinct, a vague nagging in his head about the conversation in the ward. Some remark, a phrase? He couldn't pin it down.

Back in the station, his sergeant was still in his office.

"Back already boss?" he called as Jack passed his door. He was still at the same desk where Jack had left him, the pile of folders in front of him seemingly undiminished in scale.

"Are you welded to that seat? I've been away an hour and a half."

"Time flies when you are having fun," quipped the sergeant. "The weekend D.O.R's are what every sergeant lives for. Did you know Kenny McGrath hit another barman with that wooden leg of his?"

"At least he knows his name," said Jack, coming into the office and perching on the edge of the desk. "I've just been with a man who has awakened from eleven years in a coma and if you told him he was Scotland's first man on the moon, he'd have no reason to disbelieve you."

"Eleven years? Who is he?"

"Who knows? He certainly doesn't. Here Jim, do you think you could pull out all the missing persons over the last, say, twelve years – no, make it fifteen. Those Duty Officer Reports can wait."

Jim looked at the files on the desk and imagined how much higher twenty years of Missing Persons would be.

"Will do Inspector McGregor sir!" he said with exaggerated deference.

"What did you say?" replied Jack suddenly.

"Will do?"

"No, Inspector McGregor, you called me Inspector McGregor."

"Uh… yes…? Because you are? Had you forgotten?" The sergeant squinted up at Jack with a quizzical look.

"No, what I mean is, that's it! Something has been nagging me since I left the hospital. That's what it was. I intentionally gave only my first name to the man – trying to be less officious, I suppose. As I was leaving, he asked me if I was coming back."

The sergeant scratched the back of his neck. "What's so odd about that?"

"Because he used my surname – the surname I hadn't told him. He called me Inspector McGregor. Now how the devil did he know that?!"

Chapter 5
Kola

Gasparov looked at Anya Nevotslova with such dispassionate regard that the girl could read nothing whatsoever from his expressionless eyes. Under the cold detachment of his steady stare, she wished now that she had not asked the question.

"You are here because we want you here," Gasparov eventually replied in words so drawn out that it was several statements in one. "If you need to know more than that, you will be told."

Anya deliberated for a moment whether to leave it at that, but eventually her curiosity won out over her fear.

"My specialism is in rare earths," she said, "I had thought that there would be an opportunity here to research or even…"

Gasparov interrupted by raising his hand, his palm toward her.

"On this station, our work is only possible if regulated by discipline and a willingness to…" he paused and locked his cold blue eyes onto Anya's. "…*cooperate*. I fully expect that you can do that?"

The raised intonation on the last word may have sounded like a question, but Anya knew that it was not. She nodded and said nothing. Gasparov seemed to study her for a moment.

"This is not a place for someone like you," he began. "It brings… complications. But you are here because your presence is required on The Project. The Project is why we are all here."

Anya found her voice again and dared to ask another question.

"But I don't even know what the project is. Shouldn't I at least know something?"

"We none of us are independent agents," Gasparov replied. He turned to go. "Know this, Anya Nevotslova. Mother Russia has survived the treachery of her enemies by her children who have surrendered their own interests for hers. You would do well to remember that."

Anya stood in the laboratory ruminating on the conversation when the door opened again and three men strode in.

"Ha!" grinned the taller of the three, "I told you she'd be here. Look for a metallurgist and you'll find her somewhere near a microscope!

The three were Rogov, Chemeris, and Yashkin. Chemeris was the speaker. Of the three he was usually the first to be heard, his attitude often cheerier and of less gravity than that of his two colleagues.

"Have you seen Gasparov?" He continued, looking around the lab as he spoke.

Anya nodded. "He was here ten minutes ago. Just letting me know my place in the world."

"I wish he would tell us," complained the short and dark Yashkin, his sturdy appearance proclaiming his Mongolian ancestry. "That's a full week we've been here and I've yet to get any real directive." His distinctive voice was clipped with 'r's that rolled off his tongue like bullets.

"Not that I care much," shrugged Chemeris, "I'll be getting twice what I was getting with *Rosneft*, not to mention the free lodging and as much free food as I can eat. Who cares if I get it for playing chess all day?"

"You don't *play* chess," answered the monotone drawl of Rogov. "You *lose* chess." His usual immovable features altered by a barely perceptible twinkle in his eye, the millisecond of mirth making it clear who he lost *to*.

Chemeris shrugged. "No shame in losing to a machine, especially one that has all the charisma of a rock."

It was true. Rogov was indeed a dispassionate man. Inscrutable and hard to read, his great advantage was that his outward deficit of expression he shared equally with everyone. If he was unreadable, he was unreadable to all. For all that, Chemeris and Yashkin gravitated to his company. He may not have said much, but in some inexplicable way, it was becoming understood that he was the leader of the little group; that within him resided a nascent authority the others somehow lacked.

Anya looked out of the small triple glazed window, across the frigid waste punctuated in the foreground by frozen buildings and the large derrick of the drilling rig behind.

"I remember something about the borehole from a long time ago," she said as much to herself as to the three standing in a semi-circle behind her. "It was the deepest anyone had ever penetrated into the earth's crust. '*Uralmash*' they called the rig. It got to over 12,000 metres before it was called off."

Yashkin and Chemeris glanced at one another. Rogov quietly watched Anya as she turned to face them.

"The space race was demanding more and more roubles," said Chemeris, "So we dug a hole. Why throw more money into a pit?"

"Perhaps it was more than just a pit," Anya responded.

Rogov raised an eye toward her slight figure. "You speak as if you have some knowledge of this - some *personal* knowledge?"

Anya looked back toward the rig. "My father worked here – not for long I don't think, but he was here." She ran the fingers of her left hand over the surface of the lab bench in front of her as if to caress some fragile remnant of the past. Her sentence sounded unfinished, but she said nothing more and silently turned and gazed out toward the snow whipped scene beyond the reinforced double-glazed window.

"Well, I for one am curious," said Yashkin, breaking the pensive atmosphere. "We, or at least, I, thought we were coming to help look for oil."

"Twelve kilometres below the surface? Hardly likely I should have thought," commented Chemeris.

"Maybe Gasparov is a firmly entrenched abiotic origin proponent," said Yashkin, "a lot of these old *Sovietski's* are. In fact, not just the Russians."

"What do you mean?" asked Chemeris, his eyes narrowing. Yashkin had used the word 'Russian' with no particular affection. Having native Mongolian Tartar blood infused with the unstated superiority of Genghis Khan and his descendents, he saw no reason to reverence those whom he regarded as rude vodka drinking oligarchs west of the Volga.

"The Swedish have been placing bets for years on the abiotic oil hypothesis," replied Yashin, "Stockholm's top chemist has been publishing for years on its viability. For a time, the theory stood shoulder to shoulder with the Fossil fuel hypothesis. In fact, in my early years at university in Ulan Bator, it was the preferred proposition. I'm still not quite decided myself."

"Perhaps you are not," commented Rogov flicking a glance in Yashkin's direction, "but most would say the Americans and British won that argument years ago?"

The others were silent for a moment. Rogov was, after all the specialist in minerals.

Yashkin shrugged. "So, maybe not, though oil can be manufactured from minerals in the laboratory."

"Synthesis by definition is not authenticity," replied Rogov dryly.

"Let's see what our metallurgist thinks," suggested Chemeris who was warming to the debate. He nodded toward Anya. "Mineralogist – Metallurgist, it's not that different."

Rogov sat back quietly on the lab table as much as a gesture of approval for Anya to speak. Chemeris folded his large fingers into a clasp across his chest. Yashkin pushed back a loose strand of blonde hair and waited. All three looked at Anya.

"Well, I hardly know..."

"But you know the theory," prompted Rogov. Anya pushed back a stray strand of blond hair. Rogov's prompting made her feel that she was being tested. As if he was quietly assessing her.

"Well, yes I know some of it. It goes that that crude oil is the result of natural geological processes, not biological ones. Mostly it has been disregarded, certainly by the West, as you said."

"So, you say it's not true then?" asked Yashkin.

"Maybe not, but then again, it's not pseudo-science either," said Anya, warming to the subject. "The theory is sound enough. As far as I understand it, carbon residing in the magma beneath the Earth's crust reacts when coming in contact with hydrogen to form methane and a whole variety of other, mostly alkaline hydrocarbons."

"And the required catalyst?" prodded Rogov, like a schoolteacher coaxing his pupils.

"Other rock and minerals might be sufficient. Rare earths possibly. There would also have to be the presence of tremendous heat and pressure, but at the depths at which the hypothesis dictates the processes occur, that wouldn't be a problem. In fact, the counter argument against biological processes invoke the depth. Abiotic proponents argue that oil is sometimes found far below any strata that vegetative matter could to have descended to. There are other required factors, but as far as I know it, those are the basic assumptions. Actually, there is some experimental evidence that such mineral derived oil has regenerated in deep wells that were pumped out years before."

"Seepage?" This time it was Chemeris.

"Probably, though Mendeleev was able to repeat the process in laboratory conditions, just like Yashkin says. Also, using the same theory enabled Soviet exploration teams discover several larger deposits – the South Khylchuyu and Sakhalin II fields for example. All very persuasive if you're an abiotic enthusiast. You all know this anyway." She blushed slightly and gave a small nervous laugh. "Listen to me," she said. "Lecturing of what I do not know to experts in the field!"

Rogov waived away her embarrassment. "Not at all comrade sister. We are all specialists, but that does not mean we are omniscient." He briefly glanced in the direction of his two colleagues. "Well, these two *kozels* aren't anyway."

Chemeris the Mongolian squinted at Rogov for a moment, "Who are you calling a goat, comrade? At least a goat has a personality."

Yashkin merely shrugged. "And listen to our great patriot. 'Comrade sister' indeed!"

"So, our little Anya is not just a pretty little flower," observed Chemeris, unclasping his hands and standing up. He looked around. "We're drilling for oil then?" He said it, but like the others, he was sure that was the one thing they were most likely not doing at Uralmash.

Rogov's expression did not change. His face was not the canvas for his thoughts.

"Whatever the case," he said after a moment. "We will all have to keep our wits about us, Anya included. This place is no place for fools or the talk of fools."

After they had gone, Anya felt strangely unsettled. In one way, she was glad for the company of the men who seemed to share with her in a common disquiet. At the same time, she felt as if she had undergone some kind of a test – an inquisition. A test she had no idea whether or not she had passed.

Time passed more quickly at the station than Anya had expected. If Gasparov had been threatening her with his reference to idleness, he needn't have bothered, she found herself so busy that the vague blur distinguishing the day from the night at the high northern latitude on the Kola Peninsula merged together into an endless semi-twilight world of work and study. The Project's many interconnected buildings consisted not only of laboratories, living quarters, engineering and mechanical facilities, but also a remarkably modern and comprehensive library. During the day, she would work in the laboratory, carrying out analysis and chemical trials on the samples brought to her by Chemeris or Yashkin. A week after their conversation, work for all of them had suddenly come like a flood and from having had time to speculate at their functions, all was now business and constant deadlines. They would deliver drilling bores, ice clinging to the fur-lined hoods of their heavily insulated work clothes. Rogov rarely appeared, preferring to spend as much time at the rig as he could. His was an intense existence. A man as much at home with the machines as his fellow man.

"He's barely human," grunted Chemeris after Anya had asked after him one shadowless afternoon. "Spends hours hunched over the rig, or picking through the spoil heaps. Writing continually in that indecipherable little notebook of his. You'd think they were hauling gold out of that endless pit rather than the slime and grit it actually is. Minerals, hah! Fancy name for mud."

Anya only smiled back. The samples she had been given were ones most likely to contain metal based elements and if Rogov was finding fascination in his study of the cores brought up from the deepest bore hole ever made into the Earth, she too was starting to find traces that were beginning to intrigue her own line of professional interest. A small voice at the back of her mind however would occasionally trouble her. It was like being at a cocktail party when amidst all the chatter a barely seen stranger glides by in the noise and laughter and, in passing, whispers a half-heard question in your ear and disappears without trace of where he went. The operation, at one time wound down at Kola due to the massive costs, had been re-started and with it all the trappings of limitless funding. Russia was proud of its science and engineering, but at the end of the day, billions of roubles just to bore a very, very deep hole?

But it was a quiet unease and the busyness and sheer interest of her role allowed it very little time for deeper participation in her daily agenda.

Rogov stepped out into the freezing spindrift. Wind whipped at the edges of his heavy fur-lined hood laying a circlet of white around his face. He grasped the guideline pegged out on steel uprights that ran from building to building. To be caught in a whiteout in the Kola Peninsula was a gamble the arctic won too many times to challenge. He made his way across the familiar one hundred metres to the angular rig enclosure and pulled open the heavy steel door, stamping the snow off his feet once inside. The rig building had a heating system of a kind, but with the necessary vents and requirements for the drilling, whatever heat was generated by the rudimentary system was lost to the elements before any of the human inhabitants felt any benefit. Taking off his fur-lined parka was not an option if his teeth were to stay attached to his jaws. He was unable to work using the thick gloves he wore when outside but he slipped on the woollen ones he kept for his labours at the rig. In the building, the grinding whine of the drill dominated all other sounds within, but before he made his way across to his bench, something made him look out of one of the tiny porthole shaped windows cut into the walls of the structure. Not for the first time he felt as much as heard the dull rumble of a heavy vehicle crawling ponderously over the permafrost. There were others working around the drill, but he appeared to be the only one who took an interest. And why would anyone take notice? Even had they heard over the noise of the drill, heavy vehicles were continually rumbling and working around the site. It was turmoil of action at times, more like a building site than a scientific drilling base. He cast his eyes around the lit interior of the base; everyone was busy with their work. Stealing another look out into the semi- darkness of the whiteout, he stared into the swirling flakes. A movement on his peripheral vision was gone before he could be sure it was even there. To anyone else, there was nothing unusual, nothing out of the ordinary. But Rogov wasn't anyone else. Rogov had a mind that never slept, noted every abnormality and registered any anomaly that flickered on the steady line of uniformity. The drill rig was the farthest building West on the base; the only points beyond being several large spoil heaps. Dumpers would make regular visits out there to spill out unwanted mud and slag from the borehole. Those vehicles he often heard, their gears whining and engines straining on the outward journey but with their drivers gunning the empty trucks on the return journeys. So what was different about the rumbling he heard outside the window now? What was it about the other times he had heard the same noise? He turned to his workbench and began reading his last sample recording. It was as he was adjusting a slider on his scales that the answer suddenly silently slipped unceremoniously into his mind and instinctively he knew it was right.

Chapter 6
Gone

Inspector McGregor was at his desk writing out rosters when his sergeant poked his head in through the open door.

"Call from your friend at the Royal a few minutes ago boss," he said. "Tried putting it through but you were on a call. Asked if you could call back when you're free?"

Jack nodded and scratched an eyebrow with a bent finger.

"Aye, I'll do that, thanks Jim," he replied, making a note on his desk notebook before going back to the job in hand.

When he called half an hour later, Doctor Jamieson was unavailable. He made a note to call by on the way home, it wasn't out of his way, and since his visit to the young man with the missing memory, he'd had a couple of questions he wanted to ask his friend the doctor anyway.

As it would happen, Doctor Jamieson had just sat down at his own desk when his secretary told him he had a visitor. He was tired, but when he heard who it was, he shelved the 'I'm unavailable at present' standard reply for such times and asked that the inspector be ushered in.

"Jack!" smiled Robert Jamieson as the police officer entered. "What a coincidence. I was looking for you earlier today!" He motioned toward a seat at the side of his desk and pulled it out for his guest.

"Aye, sorry, I missed your call – thought I'd call by on the way home on the off chance I'd catch you at your desk."

"Hah!" exclaimed the doctor, "This is the first I've been at it today believe it or not – things have been somewhat frantic since this morning."

"You know," smiled his friend, "I've observed that about jobs in the public sector."

"How's that?"

"Well, you either have a job where the work is scarce and you fill the days in twiddling pencils, or you end up with one where you are worked like an absolute mule. I should have become a traffic warden in Kircudbright. Work will be the end of one of us one of these sweet days!"

Doctor Jamieson laughed and nodded. They had talked about the pressure of their individual careers before and neither envied the other.

"So, how is work Jack, I hope you are not overdoing it?"

Jack dismissed the caution with a wave of his hand as he pulled a small notebook out of his inside jacket pocket with the other. "Actually, before you called I had been going to contact you myself. It's about that young lad that came out of the coma a couple of weeks ago. I've a couple of questions I'd like to ask you about him. And if I could possibly get to speak to him again too I'd appreciate it."

"Oh... so you weren't told then?" replied the doctor with a slightly quizzical frown.

"Told? Told what?"

"He's gone. Left this morning wearing clothes the hospital had provided him."

"Gone?" queried the inspector.

"Slipped out at visiting time. A nurse saw him in the corridor and wrongly assumed he was visiting the lavatory. Walked right out and disappeared. It's why I had called."

Jack sat back in his chair and tuned the notebook over in his hands.

"How long ago was that?"

The doctor pursed his lips for a second. "It would have been about 10.30 this morning?"

Jack pushed his shirtsleeve back over his watch. "Mmmm. Had he any money? Did he take anything else with him?"

"I don't think so," replied Doctor Jamieson as he pushed his chair back and began to stand, "but let's just take a look will we? As far as I know, the same staff is on the ward."

As they headed down to the wards, something Jack had meant to ask came to mind.

"You never did tell me how it came to be that the patient was admitted in the first place?"

The doctor held open the double doors into the wards for the policeman.

"Ah, yes, I may have missed that. He was left at A&E reception."

"*Left?* How do you mean?"

"Just that. Someone left him. The receptionist told us at the time that someone had half carried him in and then left immediately without speaking."

CCTV?"

The doctor shook his head. We use it to prevent assault on our staff, not record the admissions. I suppose no one at the time thought so much as look at it, let alone save it. A&E is a busy place Jack."

A young nurse was passing by the empty wardroom as the two men approached.

"Ah, nurse McKinstry isn't it?" said Doctor Jamieson. The slim girl paused and Jack noticed her cheeks blush slightly as the surgeon addressed her.

"Yes sir. Can I help you sir?"

"Our escapee," asked Doctor Jamieson," we'd like to take a look at his room. Is it still as he left it this morning?"

The policeman watched as the nurse's face redden a little more.

"Oh... yes... we, I haven't, I mean..."

"Don't worry," interrupted Jack sensing her embarrassment. "We just want to see if he left any clues behind."

The surgeon seemed to suddenly realise his misunderstood inference.

"And of course it was no one's fault nurse. Certainly not yours. We can't run a hospital like a prison. Though, if we did, you would be the prettiest prison guard I ever saw!" he laughed.

"No - I mean thank you sir," she replied, a smile of clear relief sweeping across her face.

Inspector McGregor smiled within himself. It was strange, the nervousness some people had of higher authority. He saw it himself with the constables, particularly the newer ones on station. He never felt as if he were an intimidating person himself, had no desire to be so, but at times he could see from junior police officers a tightening of the jaw, a stiffening of backs as he entered a room. On one particular morning briefing, he had slapped his hands together after a few minutes and told the tense room of probationers to, "Lighten up. No one is going to shoot you!"

He might as well have told them he was about to do that very thing.

They almost jumped out of their seats with his clap. After a few nervous laughs, everyone pretended to be casual as the tension multiplied two-fold. Some things just needed time and experience.

The three looked around the room. It was empty except for the bed and the drawer unit, the monitors having been removed a week earlier.

Jack ran his fingers over the white bed linen. "Did he have a pair of shoes, or just hospital slippers?"

The nurse, who Jack had determined was probably a student nurse in her first or second year, nodded.

"Yes, we had found him pair of shoes. A nice pair of brown leather brogues actually. We keep a room with clothes patients sometimes leave, or donate you know, for those in need?"

"And he made no mention of leaving – no clue that he had somewhere to go?"

The nurse slowly shook her head, thinking. "No sir. Nothing. He would chat to whoever was on duty – he was very nice actually, but he seemed, well, peaceable, considering everything, if you know what I mean."

"I had a notebook provided for him," said Doctor Jamieson. "In case he remembered anything. Sometimes on awakening after a sleep, the mind can retain some of the processes it has been running through. The brain often uses sleep to do a bit of 'file management'."

"Do you still have the notebook?" Jack asked, looking at both the doctor and the nurse. By way of an answer, the nurse opened the top drawer of the cabinet beside the bed. It was empty apart from the book of Robert Burns' poems.

"A moment," said Jack as the nurse went to return the drawer. He pulled it out full and then looked in the cabinet below.

"Interesting," he mumbled as much to himself as the others.

"How's that?" asked Doctor Jamieson. "Is there something there?"

"No - it's what isn't there, "replied the policeman. "And I'm guessing he took it with him."

Doctor Jamieson glanced at the nurse who shook her head unknowingly in return. He had no idea himself and he waited for Jack to explain.

"Unless the staff have removed it, which I imagine highly unlikely. I noticed he had it in his hand when I first came." He looked back at the other two with eyebrows ever so slightly raised.

"Placed there as it is in hundreds of thousands of other hospital drawers and hotel rooms across the world?" He could tell from the light on Nurse McKinstry's face that she had got it.

"That's right," he said. "For some reason our mystery man has made off with the Gideon's Bible."

It was a small enough piece of information Jack knew. But it was information and where none other existed, every scrap would count.

"I'll need to speak to whoever is in charge of hospital security," said Jack, as he shook hands with the surgeon. Somehow, the transition from an investigation of a missing memory to a missing person took him back into more familiar ground where there were well-practised procedures to follow. It might have been a move back rather than forward, but ironically it had moved him onto a starting square where he felt more in control.

"Thank you," said Doctor Jamieson, as Jack made his excuses to leave. "If you find out anything, or I can answer any questions, please let me know. I hate the idea of that young man out and alone, lost in a world a stranger to him. It is critical that he needs to be here where we can help as much as we can."

"If we find him, or any information, you'll be the first to know Robert," replied Jack, turning and leaving through the double doors of the ward.

Doctor Jamieson smiled to himself as he made his way back to his office. Countless times he had encouraged Jack McGregor to call him by his first name. It was only now, as he assumed his role as investigator that it had fallen off his tongue without so much as a moment's hesitation. He hummed tunelessly to himself as he strode along the corridor. Yes, Inspector McGregor had the bit between his teeth. "No better man – no better man." It was only on the repeat of the words that he realised he had said it aloud.

Chapter 7
Jan Mayen

"So, let's talk about this island then, eh?"

The speaker was Sir Simon Montague, one-time special advisor to the Cabinet Office, now head of MI5. The venue was the third floor in Thames House, headquarters of MI5. Properly called Security Services, they were known as 'Box' by affiliated agencies by reason of the simple fact that their P.O. address was Box 500. The meeting consisted of a small knot of half a dozen individuals. They sat around a large mahogany oval table for the briefing, their portfolios representing their own particular interested bureaus. Box kept the pulse on the beating hearts of a great many potential threats, running pre-emptive threat analysis's on the real, the spurious and the imagined risk to the United Kingdom, its friends and partners. Sometimes the pulse even belonged to those friends and partners.

The man to whom Sir Simon had addressed the statement opened a manila folder and took out some documents. He was dressed in a typically smart charcoal grey pinstripe business suit, aged mid-fifties but looked younger, a man who evidently kept himself in good shape. His name was Jonas Smythe and he had arrived that morning from his office on Thomas Heftyes gate, which, being a street in Oslo was also the location of the British Embassy to Norway.

"Perhaps the room would appreciate a few quick details about Jan Mayen before anything else sir?" He guessed he was probably the only man in the room who had heard of the place, and reckoned most could do with the primer. He was wrong on his first assumption, but correct on his second.

Sir Simon nodded graciously and Smythe folded his long fingers together.

"Jan Mayen island is an island some 400 miles North East of Iceland,

300 from Greenland and furthest from Norway whose island it is. It is bleak. As far as any inhabitants go, only personnel engaged by the Norwegian Armed Forces live there. They operate the LORAN-C transmitter base there."

"Sorry," interrupted a voice across the table, "LORAN-C?"

"Apologies old man," said Smythe, pulling a loose sheet out from the folder. "Long Range Radio. Basically, LORAN-C is a low-frequency land-based radio navigation system. It's been about a while but has certain benefits."

"I thought we were all on GPS now?" asked another.

"Yes, but I believe, and I'm no expert, but I believe one significant benefit is that is *not* GPS. There are occasions when, well," he took time to frame his words, "...occasions when it is expedient not having to rely solely on *satellite* navigation." Most in the room understood his inference. The Americans provided almost all of the European and non-previously-soviet satellite navigation. It was during operation Desert Storm that they demonstrated their ability to discreetly alter transmission data, which made the Iraqi battle field GPS useless. That they could do the same with anyone else using the same data hardly required elucidating. "If you have the requisite receiver," continued Smythe, "it is an accurate means to know your position at sea or in the air. Apparently it's very hard to intercept or interfere with."

The room seemed satisfied with that, so he continued.

"Apart from the military there are also a handful of meteorologists from the Norwegian Meteorological Institute on Jan Mayen. Two dozen souls at most. Bit of a God-forsaken place actually. No trees, no vegetation, in fact, all the island has to offer is hard grey gravel."

"I spent a long wet winter in Belfast years ago," said a man called Reid. "Sounds similar." The room laughed. Belfast on a good day could be the Belle of the North, but on a wet grey March, the land of the political trench warfare could drain the heart and soul out of a man longing for the warm tree-lined fields of Kent.

"Trust me, Ulster is the Bahamas compared to Jan Mayen," continued Smythe. "Every day of the year on Mayen is gloomy, grey, cloudy sunless and cold. Summer the temperature barely scrapes in low single figures above zero."

"Have you been there Jonas?" asked the man called Reid. "You sound like you've more than just briefed yourself."

Smythe shook his head. "No, I have not, and I'm sure we shall come to that later. Meanwhile, you'll want to know why any of this is important. Events have unfolded around that island over the last few months that have alarmed the Norwegians to such an extent that the *Etterretningstjenesten* – The Norwegian Intelligence Service – has, let us say, opened a channel of certain communications that they had previously been sharing with Vauxhall House."

"MI6? I haven't heard anything about this!" exclaimed a broad faced man sitting to the other side of Sir Simon. Alex Harker-Bell, although a Section Five man, had worked in MI6 for a couple of years before settling on a long illustrious career with Security Services. It was acknowledged that he still had close affiliations with ex-colleagues there.

Sir Simon set a hand on Harker-Bell's shoulder. "No, no-one has old man. It has all been very, well, *awkward?*"

"Because of the military involvement, Vauxhall House has kept its cards close to its chest on this one," added Jonas Smythe. "Nonetheless, NIS is concerned. They want this tight – very tight."

"And they are worried MI6 are not as… *circumspect* at present as one might earnestly hope?" added Sir Simon, a gentle smile directed apologetically toward the older man.

There was a quiet shuffling around the room. No one needed to be told of the sensitivities that were currently beleaguering Military Intelligence. Accusations had even been made from across The Pond that there was a leak in London and the finger was pointed in the direction of the Albert Embankment and SIS.

"So whatever happens next in this briefing gentlemen," said Sir Simon underscoring his intent by dragging his finger across the desk in front of him, "this place alone will be where it will be heard. Those present in this room today are the only ones who are being briefed on this situation. It will remain that way. Without divergence from that fact." He suddenly smiled in his uniquely warm manner that could so easily obscure the weight of his intent. "But then, I hardly need to say that."

"So, what *is* the problem exactly?" growled Alex Harker-Bell. "We're hardly here to discuss geography or radio sets."

"It concerns certain *irregularities* on the island. Irregularities that for particular and specific reasons require investigations from, ahm... *non*-Norwegians." replied Jonas, glancing up at his boss.

Sir Simon carefully set down the pen he had been holding before speaking. "It appears that there have been certain geological abnormalities on Mayen," he said. "We have been made aware of a highly classified report from a Norwegian meteorologist working on Mayen of such import that he framed a highly alarming statement to his superiors in Oslo. His reports do not lend toward a natural cause, but due to the nature of what he detailed, it has raised significant unease in high places - very high places. We need to know more."

"Why not ask him then?" suggested another voice. Desmond Reid was a Security Services Senior Scientist, his background and expertise being the reason why he was included in the group.

Jonas Smythe turned and faced his colleague. "Therein lies one of the problems," he said. "He was in a road traffic accident. Unfortunately, it was a fatal one."

"Oh," said Reid pausing to think before adding, "Ask the line managers he reported to then?"

Sir Simon looked at Jonas before turning to Desmond and the rest of the room. "Both men have disappeared completely. NIS have pulled out all the stops, but they seem to have simply vanished. No trace, nothing."

A hand from the back of the table rose slightly. A man whose silence had rendered him almost unseen up to this point leaned forward with a hand set palm down on the table. He looked around thirty and was clean-shaven with a military cut of short black hair. Behind his suit lurked an evidently toned and muscular frame.

"*Where* was the road traffic accident?"

It was Smythe who took the question. "Interesting you should ask that Jon. On Jan Mayen. Drove off a cliff... apparently."

"Suicide?"

"Unlikely. He was less than a year married, a child on the way. Everything to live for."

Sir Simon lifted the pen again and rolled it between his thumb and forefinger. "In any case, suffice to say, we need eyes-on. A landing - feet on the ground." He looked toward the old Navy man. "Alex, this is where Commodore Legge might be of assistance?" He looked in the direction of the man who had been silently sitting to the side of Harker-Bell and gave a nod.

Commodore Legge had come reluctantly to the meeting. He was not in a place where he felt comfortable and in fact was only there since his old colleague and friend Alex had asked. That, and the fact that just before arriving he had been handed a note from the Admiralty that he was to fully comply with any request asked of him.

"If I can be of professional help, I shall. Though I can hardly imagine how." He said simply, addressing the room in general.

"Let me be so bold as to inform the room that you, Commodore, have actually been on Jan Mayen?" said Sir Simon innocently.

All eyes in the room suddenly turned to the tall Commodore, his jaw muscles tightening as he narrowed his eyes slightly at Sir Simon.

"Not personally," Commodore Legge replied.

"No, but you did land a party of marines there some years ago I believe?"

Legge looked briefly around the room. "I was under the impression that that incident was classified information Sir Simon."

"Ah yes, but one does not get any more classified a place than this room Commodore," he smiled back benignly. "If I remember correctly, at that time you were merely creating a trail of confusion - putting the Ruskies off the track as it were, eh ?" The Navy man could only listen as the MI5 man spoke with apparent knowledge of events he had never spoken of to another human being.

"This is somewhat different," continued the senior Security Services man, "We need a man who can land a party on that same island but under more challenging conditions, in a less... *regular* approach."

Commodore Legge found himself like a man suddenly awakening in the middle of a shoreless sea. Suddenly he found himself with no clear direction and, like the swimmer, no context to inform him which way to strike for solid ground. The volume of what was not being said in the room was deafening.

"It was challenging enough," he heard himself say. "There is really only one bay that allows a safe approach for a larger vessel, and that is dependent on the time of year. I know very few men who could safely bring a sizeable ship in to any other location on that place."

"Nonetheless, if we were to organize some kind of an unannounced visit, I imagine it would be within your capacity to assist, to provide someone who could perform a jolly dicey piece of seamanship, if so required by Her Majesty?"

It was less a question than a statement from Sir Simon Montague. A statement heavy with expectations of assumed, unarguable consent. The Commodore found himself skilfully manoeuvred into a position devoid of options.

"I have always endeavoured to carry out any orders required of me."

He said without embroidery.

"Splendid," smiled Sir Simon. "The Admiralty informed us that there was no-one else so well qualified as yourself. That at least is a source of some comfort in what may prove to be quite an intricate game of chess."

"Jan Mayen plays very few games," interjected the Commodore. "And when she plays, she plays for keeps."

A couple of throats around the room cleared at the Navy man's comment but Sir Simon merely smiled benignly at the Commodore.

"Yes, indeed, quite."

There followed further discussion for some time where smaller details, timings, even finances were arranged, but if Michael Legge thought he would be appraised of further information on the exact nature of what was happening on Jan Mayen, he was to be mistaken. Perhaps if he had been present right to the end, he might have heard more, but at one point Sir Simon made a profuse apology.

"Gracious me Commodore. My sincere apologies. Your time is a priceless commodity and I am spending it like a reprobate prodigal. You will have important issues to attend to I'm sure. Please let us know when you have your man eh? Thank you so much for your time and enthusiasm for our... ahm...*project?*"

It was only as he paused outside in the panelled corridor that Commodore Legge realised he had been politely expelled from the room. Before he had time to fully consider the implication of that, the door opened again and the man who had queried the death of the meteorologist exited.

"Commodore," he said, a genuinely warm smile spreading across his rugged face, "Glad you're still here sir. I can never find my way out of this maze. Do you mind?"

"I'm not sure I'll be much help," replied Legge, "I'm not exactly a regular visitor myself."

"Ah yes, but as a Navy man, we'll never get quite lost with you leading the way Commodore. If the worst comes to the worst, you can pull a sextant from your case, or just follow the stars."

The man spoke with such an easy and open manner that the older man had to smile back.

"I sincerely hope we aren't going to be wandering about in these interminable corridors till the sun sets, Mr...?" The Commodore realised that he had not picked up the man's name and felt slightly wrong-footed.

"Oh, sorry sir," said the dark haired man, "Lander – but please, just call me Jon. I think the lift is at the bottom of this corridor. Or did you park in the multi-story?"

"I came on the Tube Mr..., ahm... Jon," said Legge who wished now that he had taken more time to take in his surroundings as he and Alex had caught up on old times on the way in. "Lander?" he added as a question. "Any relation to *Stephen* Lander?"

"Ex head of MI5? Not that I'm aware of sir. If I was we might know a little more of what this business is all about though, eh?" He gave a conspiratorial wink and Legge found it hard not to give a genuine chuckle in response.

They took the lift to the first floor where he found himself steered along by his new-found friend until they passed a cafeteria.

"Fancy a quick coffee Commodore?" asked Lander, "unless you're pressed for time? Personally, a latté and a muffin in Thames House has to be a perk worth availing of now we're here eh?"

Commodore Legge went to defer but suddenly thought to himself, why not? The man seemed genuine enough and was certainly engaging. He had half an hour or so and the thought of a coffee was quite an appealing one.

"You know, I never was one for the cloak and dagger side of things," explained Legge as the conversation continued. The younger man nodded in an understanding kind of way over his coffee as the Commodore went on. "Something dishonest about it. Ignoble. Now running a ship, a destroyer, a carrier – that requires such intense clarity of thought and purity of command. There's something almost reverent about it."

"Reverent?" asked Lander, an eyebrow raised slightly the remark.

"It's a life outside passing societal fads and intrigues. A regular rhythm of tradition and history. The captain's essential quality - to be able to clearly and succinctly press his will onto a thousand men with razor sharp precision. Where idle points of view or argument can mean disaster. The unspoken, but undeniable truth that a vessel floats only by extreme and unequivocal integrity on seas dispassionately intent on crushing it into its cruel wilful depths. The crew, not a number of independent self-centred individuals, but a living, pulsing machine whose unthinking obedience to command alone ensures the survival of all. There is no place for subterfuge on a ship Mr Lander. And when it is brought aboard, it is an unstable, dangerous passenger."

"Unfortunately not everything is quite so above-board, nor so ship-shape and Bristol-fashion in my world, Commodore," said Lander with a semi-apologetic smile. "I wish it were. Trust, honour, integrity. Rare and precious commodities. Rare enough that some will trade in blood for them."

"I should have thought that such things are not for sale," added Legge, his eyes examining the eyes on the other side of the table.

"For the appearance of such things, there are powerful people in powerful places who would sell their souls for them," replied Lander, his eyes remaining fastened on the other. "And the lives of countless others."

"So, what part do you play then Mr Lander?"

Lander gave a mirthless laugh. "My part? Good question." He hesitated for a moment before adding, "I suppose my part is to uncover the deceit of the one and lessen the cost of the other."

Legge, despite himself, warmed to the man. Even if he dwelt in the shadow lands he detested, there was a genuineness about him that was likeable. In a tough spot, when nothing could be certain, he might be a man who could be trusted.

"I am a Commodore of the Royal Navy Lander," he said, "and I know they gave me the apparent respect that rank requires, but it seems to me, that whatever is going on in that room, I was very much the odd man out. I'm not quite used to that if I'm honest."

He hadn't meant to confess his feelings to the younger and presumably more junior man, but he felt he was someone to whom he could earth the tension he had been experiencing since his being press-ganged into the meeting. Unused to being on the back-foot, he nonetheless felt there were deeper waters than the ones they had dragged him over. Waters of which he had been told little.

Jon Lander looked up at the senior naval man. "I think I understand sir. You know yourself, your men, your ship. You plot your course and anything unexpected you deal with, but even then it's on terms you understand. Thames House types are men who deal in a different set of cards altogether. They have to play games where there are no rules but where playing the wrong card can end badly." He paused in thought for a moment before adding, "'badly' hardly being the word to describe the consequences.'"

"Life and death at sea is not a game Lander. I sometimes think there are men who imagine trading in men's lives is just that; some kind of huge game."

Lander took another sip from his cup and pressed a finger to his temple. "Sun Tzu said *The supreme art of war is to subdue the enemy without fighting'*. That's more the territory I'm accustomed to. When types like upstairs fail, then types like you have to bring in the heavy machinery, the men. And you remember what Stalin said then: *'The death of one man is a tragedy – the death of a million is a statistic'*."

"Sometimes a show of force can prevent an escalation," said Legge, who resented the idea that his vocation in life could be associated with mass killing.

"Indeed," admitted Lander, "that can indeed sometimes be the case. But to prevent the need for force at all is where the trick lies, is it not?"

"So where exactly do you lie in all of this?" asked Legge. "You're not Navy obviously, not Air Force. You sound like you had some kind of military background, but I don't get the impression that's your field now. You seemed comfortable up there, yet, you're not a Security Service pen pusher either. I can't quite place you Lander."

"You are an impressive man Commodore. For someone who says he sees only the straight and narrow, you've got a nose for the bushes. I'm ex-Regiment. That's the military side, almost impossible to hide that. They like a few of us types around – men who can follow orders. But they want men who go further than that. Men who know when the time is to know what the orders are when they haven't been told them. I'm the man they get when the man they need can't, or *won't* do the job."

Legge studied the man opposite. He supposed there were situations when the only way to get a thing done was to act in a way that stretched the rules. There was that time in Belize he recalled. He had had to stretch the strictly protocol because there was simply no other way. Perhaps men like Lander were men who allowed men like him the luxury of being able to act within the rules. Perhaps he was over precious at times about the virtue of his own position.

"I knew a man called Stonebraker," laughed Lander suddenly. "Eustace, his first name was. Imagine calling your son that? Of course all he got was Useless. We served in the regiment together. Was anything but useless. A ruddy good man." He frowned as some past memory crossed his vision. With the faintest hint of a sigh, he continued. "Anyway, on his first parade the sergeant major was walking down his line of recruits, bawling and screaming – as sergeant majors do. He would stop at each man, ask his surname and then humiliate him. 'My name is Sergeant Major Stone!' he would yell into each man's face, 'Stone by name, stone by nature. Unlucky for you, you useless bunch of miscreants.' Then he would demand his name with his nose six inches from the poor sod's and roar it back at him. 'Milliken? What kind of a stupid name is that? You're a pansy Milliken! A ruddy pansy!' And so he went down the line."

Legge listened and smiled. Breaking men before making them. A tradition as old as the army.

"Anyway, he comes to old Useless and does the same thing. Course, he mumbles back some incomprehensible reply so that the sergeant major sticks his moustache not two inches from his face and screams at him. 'Sergeant Major Stone asked your name... boy!' And he says it. 'Stonebraker sir.'

Legge, despite himself, gave a loud laugh. "Ouch! I think I might have opted for Smith."

Lander laughed back. "Yes, that would have been one option. Anyway, everyone else laughed. That was a mistake. We paid for that several times over. Except for Useless. Old Sergeant Major took a shine to him. Renamed him, but didn't pick on him any more than the rest of us."

"Renamed him?"

"Shoeshine. Once he got that, Stonebraker was gone. Not even sure his wife knew his name till she saw the marriage certificate she was signing. Funny that."

They laughed over the story and Legge shared some of his own. The conversation became easy and the afternoon one of the more relaxed Commodore Legge had enjoyed for quite some time.

"Is Lander aware of Operation Re-Start?" asked Alex Harker-Bell in the veneered walls of the briefing room. The others in the room turned to Sir Simon Montague as he carefully placed his silver pen onto the writing desk before him. Not all in the room were aware of the programme and Harker-Bell's ignorance of that fact led to a presumption that made Sir Simon's lips to purse in irritation.

"When he needs to know, he will find that out for himself."

It was Jonas Smyth's voice that replied, a quick glance having been made first toward his superior.

"Yes, yes," continued Harker-Bell, his eyes still on the head of MI5, "but it seems to me the man will find it odd that we never mentioned it when he becomes aware of its existence."

Sir Simon lifted the pen again and gave it a short twist that rolled out the nib.

"Alex old man, give a man a blank sheet and you give him creative freedom. Lander is an artist. Where his strength lies is in independent action. Best not to colour in parts of the picture that may only distract from the aim of the mission." He looked directly at the M16 man. "Need to know and all that, eh?"

Harker-Bell gave a quiet grunt and sat back. Smyth turned to Desmond Reid, for whom Operation Re-Start was something he knew he was not privy to. Reid was long enough in his position to know that security revolved around the least possible people knowing the least possible.

"Desmond," said Jonas, "Jon will probably need a bit of your expertise further not the road. I should expect a call from him if I were you."

"Facilitate him," added Sir Simon, "you'll have a clean sheet on this one."

Desmond Reid understood and made a mental note. This was going to be a big one.

"I like you Lander," said Legge at last. "I'm not sure I might like whatever exactly it is you do, but you seem a man to be trusted."

Lander finished his coffee and noiselessly set the mug back on the beech table. "It seems to me I'm going to be asked to go to Jan Mayen," he said thoughtfully. "Three murders – for that's what they were, don't appear to make that visit a carefree proposition. If I'm correct, then I shall be asked to go ashore unannounced and as you have deduced already, by a manner that will carry some risk. From what I gather already, the Norwegian Intelligence will officially have no involvement. Anything goes awry and they'll want iron cast deniability on this one. Unofficially? Who knows? The *Etterretningstjenesten* are shrewd operators and you can be sure they'll have eyes and ears somewhere. Whatever the case, I would surely appreciate that the seaward side of things will be handled by someone who is as professional and competent as they come."

Legge nodded slowly as he folded his muffin wrapper into a small rectangle. "I guarantee you this Jon Lander. You will have my best men alongside you if this kicks off. I will ensure that nothing flaps in the wind on my side of things, even if that means I have to go myself."

They both of them knew that was unlikely, but nonetheless Lander put his hand across the table. More than a handshake, it was a pledge. The word of two men. Two different men, but two men for whom their word, once given, had an indissoluble currency in the world of shifting values.

Chapter 8
Donaghadee

He took a few jobs here and there. For six months he worked as a labourer in a farm outside Penrith. He was a quick learner, needing only to be shown anything once to be proficient at it almost immediately. He enjoyed his days on the land. The farmer's fields were above the Old London Road and looked down West across the wide valley and the thin line of the M6 and the Northern mainline to the Cumbrian Mountains. On most days Blencathra, High Street and Helvellyn shook their lofty manes in the clouds twenty miles away. On a clear day the sparkle of the Irish Sea was visible like a distant dancing silver serpent.

He went by the name of Finn. He still had no recollection of his name, but Finn seemed to resonate and he stuck with that. He had told the farmer he had left Scotland to see around a bit and quite quickly the Lancashire man saw that Scotland was all the poorer for it. The man did well anything required of him – better than well, he did it efficiently and with a heart and a half. Labouring seemed a waste of his talents. When the rear bearing on the PTO shaft of his Massey Ferguson split in two, he offered to fix it if the parts were provided.
"Are you a mechanic then?" he asked the young man.
"No, but it's not like it's rocket science," he had replied simply. The older man took the chance and within two hours using what tools there were in the shed, the tractor was up and running again.
"The diesel pump could do with a service at some stage too," he informed the farmer as he cleaned his hands with an oily rag. "Save you a bit of diesel if we do that."
"We? Diesel injector pumps are a bit different to changing a bearing lad," smiled the farmer. "That's a job for the professionals. Five

hundred pounds would scarcely look at it."

That night Finn stripped the pump and took it to the kitchen table of the cottage he lived in at the farm.

In the morning when the farmer prepared for the usual churning over and belching of smoke he was shocked when it immediately thudded into life with barely a wisp from the exhaust. Later, he spoke to Finn as he was preparing salt licks for the Swaledales on the fell.

"Oh, I hope it's going all right. I was a bit tired last night and didn't get the chance to test it."

"You didn't get the...? Lad, it's running as quiet as the wife's motor car. Whatever did you do?"

Finn didn't see the need to explain how he had stripped the thing down to each constituent part, cleaning and rebuilding all night. Several gaskets had been dozed and he had remanufactured new ones from some gasket paper in the shed as well as rubber cut from an old bicycle tube. Part of the pump seemed an inefficient way of doing things. He modified the vacuum bellows and altered some operating pressures within the pump. Had he had more equipment and time, he reckoned he could have made several improvements to the design. He had also removed the three injectors and serviced them. As he had told himself, it was hardly rocket science.

A week or two later the farmer put a proposition to the young man.

"Finn, I have a brother in law in Ireland and things have got hard for him of late."

"How's that Mr Kitching?" asked Finn.

"His son, my nephew, died last just before you came here. Lovely lad. Meningitis, and him only twenty-two."

"Oh, I'm sorry."

"Aye. But what with the farm being bigger than one man can handle, and the cost of the funeral and that, Tom is finding it hard, and my sister – well, she's fit for nothing as yet."

"You're wondering if I could help?"

"You're not the sort of lad a man can surprise much Finn," said the farmer, pushing back his cap. "The dear Lord knows I could do with you here, but his need being so great, I just wondered..."

Finn shrugged. Why not? As far as he knew he had never been in Ireland before and it would be a new experience. Everything was a new experience come to that.

Donaghadee was in Northern Ireland, so he was still in the U.K. and the ferry journey required no passport or I.D. which was just as well since he had nothing of the kind. The farmer had driven him the 130 miles to Stranraer where a regular ferry service ran to Belfast. Once again the farmer heaped his thanks on Finn.

"Thank you again Lad. The missus says you're a saint. I think you're not so bad myself," he smiled. "But watch old Tom now, Being an Ulsterman he's not easy to please. I think you'll surprise him mind."

Belfast had long shaken off its reputation as the Beirut of the North portrayed for so many long years in the media. Shiny new buildings and roads were in evidence everywhere and as he was driven out of the city by Mr Kitching's brother in law, the sun glinted off the Lagan beneath the bridge and the performance halls at the waterfront.

"Belfast looks like a really nice city," commented Finn as they headed east and out towards the countryside. Unlike Glasgow, it came quickly.

Tom McCracken was still a man in mourning, but he made the effort.

"A different place to how it was. I'm no in it much ye understaun, but it is lookin' well now ye say that right enough." He cast a surreptitious eye at the young man as he looked out of the window. In the last difficult months, fate had turned against him, scorning his hopes. He needed help to run the farm but had lost the will to look for it. What glimmer of light he had left he had directed toward his wife whose misery threatened to take her into perpetual night. He gave a silent sigh as he changed through the gears.

They made small chat as they drove over the hills surrounding Belfast Lough and down through a couple of small towns arriving at the McCracken farm about an hour after walking off the ferry.

"This is the farm," said Tom simply. "I've an annex to the rear. Sure, bring in your things and get settled. Anne will have supper for us at nine."

The annex was an extension to the main house. It had its own entrance door leading to the yard and came complete with four rooms, a small kitchen, bathroom, a bedroom and a reasonable sized living room. Finn looked around approvingly at the clean and tidy rooms. A bunch of fresh wild flowers sat in a vase in the middle of a pine table in the main room. Everywhere smelled fresh and clean. He was impressed. He would be comfortable here.

"Twas the mother in law we built if for. Been empty now a couple of years since she passed on, but Anne keeps it nice don't ye think?"

"I do," smiled Finn. "It looks fantastic. Thank you Mr McCracken."

The older man found a sudden warmth at Finn's genuine appreciation. "No, thank you son. You come with a great recommendation and James, being an Englishman is hard to please." Finn simply smiled and nodded back.

"Oh, by the way, if ye're wonderin' what this is for," he said, pointing at a camping gas cooker sitting on a low shelf at the back window, "the electric supply out here can be a bit off and on betimes. If that happens we leave this so you can always boil a bit o' water for a cup of tea. There's candles in the cupboard above."

As he shut the door behind him he turned and looked at Finn. "Remember, supper in the big house in ten minutes? Don't knock, the door's always open, but call me Mr McCracken again and I'll throw you out of it. Tom it is, eh?" For the first time since he met him, Finn caught the faintest hint of a smile.

Life at the McCracken farm was hard physical work. Unlike Penrith, where sheep were the main focus along with a small beef herd, the farm outside Donaghadee was centred around dairy and started early in the morning. The day began at four in the morning with the first batch of Holsteins in the parlour before five. Tom found that he only needed to show Finn the run of things once and he was almost immediately competent. Within a week he had picked up the rhythm of the farm and he fell to whatever needed done without complaint, never needing to be shown anything twice and even undertaking certain tasks without having been asked. He ran the milking parlour like an old hand and intuitively seemed to know the foibles of each of the herd as they were threaded into the gates. Not only had he a way with the animals but had a rare talent with the machinery of the parlour and found little to challenge him in its operation.

The working week had long hours but Finn had no problem with that. He had nowhere else to be and besides, Tom paid him an honest wage on top of free accommodation and three meals a day. For the stage Finn felt himself at, it suited him just fine. He had thinking to do and at night in the annex that is what he did.

Within a fortnight the gloom of the days ahead began to lighten for

Tom, though he hardly yet began to realise it. His mind was so taken with worry for his wife's mental health that there was little room for other reflection.

One evening he glanced across at his wife. She had taken up reading again and sat with a People's Friend on her lap as both of them warmed before the large Aga stove in the working kitchen. They had other rooms in the house, but like most farms, they were kept for special occasions and the kitchen parlour was where most of the living was done. The memories of the special occasion that the front sitting room had last been used for made it difficult to even go there. Eight months had passed since their world had crumbled and grey day after grey day had ticked by with interminable slowness and pointlessness of purpose. Finn brought a change in atmosphere. It was imperceptible at first but watching Anne turn the pages and read what was on them, Tom McCracken began to hope.

Suddenly his wife set down the magazine and looked directly at her husband.

"You know, I was thinking. I don't even know Finn's second name."

It was a turning point. Where nothing had held any interest, suddenly she seemed to see Finn for the first time and even began to initiate conversations with him. It appeared from his conversation that he had no family and was oddly vague about his past and upbringing. Except that he came from Glasgow and was looking for a new life, she learned little more. She shrugged. He seemed such a nice lad. If she and Tom could help him, they could do that. He must have had a mother. Perhaps he had lost her. A son without a mother. She, a mother without a son.

As she turned the bacon on the pan, Anne looked across at the table where the two men sat at their breakfast. Finn was not Andrew. She wasn't about to fool herself. He was not some kind of changeling replacement, but he could have a future that her son could not. He appeared to have no one else in the world and here she was, spare and useless. It did not have to be that way and in that moment she unconsciously reset her sail into a different wind.

On Sunday mornings the McCrackens would set off for church service. It was on Finn's third week that Tom appeared at his door and, scratching self-consciously behind his neck, told Finn he was heading out.

"Only, as the missus asked me to ask ye son, if it suits, you'd be welcome to come along."

"To church?"

"Aye, well, but just if you're wantin'. I'm no forcin' ye or that."

Finn shrugged. He wasn't planning on anything else and it wasn't like the television was much of an attraction. He mostly listened to radio anyway.

"Yeah, I'll just grab a coat?"

The journey only took five minutes; the Presbyterian church was in the town and was barely three miles away. Finn had only been in the town once or twice since he had arrived in the Province and on this bright and sunny Sunday morning it looked bright and cheerful. Tom parked in front of the church and the three of them made their way across the road to the tall sandstone building, its spire dominating the main street. They were met at the top of the worn steps by the minister who was shaking hands and exchanging short welcomes to each of the members as they arrived.

"Ah, Tom and Anne. So glad to see you this morning," he said, even as he glanced toward the stranger they had brought.

"This is Finn we told you about," offered Anne. "He came with us this morning."

Finn looked up. There was stating the obvious, but Anne said it with almost a hint of pleased possessiveness in her voice that made Finn smile at the warmth of her claim.

"Ah, good to meet you Finn. I'm Alastair Boyd," said the minister, a broad open smile upon his face and a large honest hand immediately grasping Finn's. He looked about forty with some streaks of silver just beginning on the hair on the sides of his head. Others parishioners were behind the McCracken's and their guest, so he set his other big hand on Finn's back. "You'll not rush away at the end Finn? You'll have to tell me about yourself."

Finn enjoyed the service. He found himself knowing not only the tunes, but the words to the hymns. It was an increasingly common phenomenon to the young man – finding that he had an intimate knowledge of a variety of subjects, the acquisition of which he could not explain. When it came to the sermon, Finn found Alastair Boyd an engaging orator, quoting not only from the Bible, but using illustrative quotes from Dostoyevsky, Larkin and Marlowe. Looking around the congregation, Finn guessed his audience may have found some of his posits challenging their minds and thinking more than they might normally expect in a small rural Presbyterian church, but Finn found it all fascinating.

True to his word, the minister sought Finn out before he and the McCracken's headed home for dinner.

"You'll maybe get a chance to call around some evening you're free?" he suggested, glancing across at Tom as he spoke to Finn.

"Yes, well, I would like to but..."

Tom caught the meaning of the minister's glance and spoke up.

"Sure you're finished before seven most nights Finn, and three on a Friday. I'll take you around to the manse if it's a lift you're needing."

"No need Tom. If you're happy enough Finn, and you're not busy at something, I could collect you on Friday and you could have dinner with us?"

Finn was more than happy and somewhat surprised when that Friday Alastair Boyd arrived at the McCracken farm on a motorcycle, a spare helmet slung over an arm.

"Too good a night for the car," he explained simply without asking Finn if he had any issues with riding pillion on a Triumph Tiger. Finn put on the proffered helmet and perching on the rear of the big bike, the two of them burbled down the lane and off to the manse.

The minister's wife had the table set as they growled up the driveway to the manse and waved them in from the front window. Inside, their three small daughters were busying about, helping their mother and smiling coyly as their new guest pulled off his helmet.

"Ruth, meet the young man Tom and Anne have told us so much about," said Alastair introducing his passenger to his wife.

"Finn, isn't that right?" asked the fair haired woman as her girls peered up from behind her.

As Finn affirmed her question, her husband leaned forward and lifted up the smallest of his daughters who giggled and laughed in his arms.

"And this is Rosie, and my other two princesses, Emily and Rachel – though unfortunately, he winked, "the cat took their tongues and they can't speak anymore. Oh well, so sad."

"But we *can* speak daddy," said the tallest, who was Emily, "mummy just told us we had to be polite."

"Yeth," said the other, "and not to thstare at the man," she added, staring at Finn.

After the meal, and after quite a bit of giggling and staring, the girls skipped off into the kitchen to help their mother tidy up as their father invited Finn into his study.

The room was almost as large as the dining room, but was lined floor to ceiling with bulging bookshelves with a couple of other freestanding shelves sitting either side of a large oak desk. Apart from the desk chair, two well worn padded leather Tudor recliners sat around a small coffee table. The minister showed Finn to one as he took the other. As he took his seat, Ruth appeared with a tray.

"Coffee or tea?" she asked with a warm smile.

"Oh, whatever the Reverend Boyd is having," replied Finn, "thank you!"

"*Reverend* Boyd?" she laughed, "Alastair, whatever is the *Reverend* Boyd having, whoever *he* may be?"

"Alastair," grinned the minister, "I just get Alastair," he said. "Any hopes I ever had of enjoying the honourable and elevated position of Presbyterian respectability were dashed the first day I met that girl." He smiled broadly at his wife as she playfully ruffled his hair.

"Don't let my Alastair fool you Finn, he might have as many degrees as a thermometer and be able to drone on all night with his interminable babblings, but really, if it wasn't for me, he'd just be a boring old bookworm, isn't that right dear?" She laughed again; an engaging and infectious laugh and Finn found himself having to check himself from joining in.

As she left, Alastair shook his head. "She is right you know. Ruth is everything I'm not; funny, witty and such fun to be with. Keeps my feet on the ground."

Finn admired their relationship and felt a small pang akin to envy. The family seemed so happy, so comfortable in their skins whilst he was still trying to adapt to being a man without a past. A solitary ship in a solitary sea.

They chatted about a lot of things. Motorcycles, mechanics, history, living in Northern Ireland, what it was like being a minister, a father, a husband. Finn talked about life on a Cumbrian farm, the fells he had walked, the endless lights threading their courses along the valley on the M6 at night. They discussed ethics, morality, individual responsibility, shared values. They spoke of grand subjects and small things too. Favourite foods, TV or radio programmes. An hour sped past without either noticing it. To his delight and surprise, Alastair found the younger man conversant on almost any subject that interested him, and for the first time since receiving and accepting the call to serve in the small community, he found someone his equal intellectually. At least his equal. When he explained his fascination with Alvin Plantigna's Modal Ontological Argument, Finn grasped it immediately and without being told, saw that it led to a world analysis of statements about possibility and necessity. Since his couple of years lecturing at Union Theological College, Alastair Boyd had not immersed himself with such enjoyment in a conversation.

As the light began to darken into descending dusk, the minister turned on a couple of desk lamps and turned to Finn.

"I hope you don't mind me mentioning it, but I couldn't help but noticing your singing in the service last Sunday," said the minister.

"It was that bad?" grimaced Finn.

"Oh no, not at all. What I meant was, you seemed to sing every word without needing to look at the hymnbook. Quite a feat." He eyed his guest with an interested eye.

It was a strange question, not one Finn was expecting, and he was unsure exactly how to answer. Since he had left the hospital in Glasgow, he had lived quietly, never sharing with another human being any of his internal turmoil and the endless questioning of his own mind.

"I have a good memory," he answered. He knew it was lame and he could see Alastair Boyd consider it.

"Tom was saying you are a bit of an expert in most things," he said. "Reckoned you were a bit of a genius actually."

"What, me?" exclaimed Finn. "Hardly. I just..." Alastair watched Finn struggle with some kind of inward indecision before continuing. "I just *know* things," he said eventually. "If I think hard enough, I'll know."

It was an odd thing to say and the older man pondered a moment before speaking again.

"If you ever want to chat again Finn, and about anything that is in your mind," he said slowly and purposefully, "nothing leaves this study. Nothing. There are some who find that helpful, and if you are one of them and feel you can trust me, I will always be available. I really enjoyed your company and conversation, but if it's listening you need,

it's onc thing I can do well."
Finn looked up and studied the other's face for a moment. There was a candid honesty there that quietly spoke of integrity and understanding. "Thanks," he said, "I might just take you up on that sometime."
And inside himself, he felt an assurance that he would.

Chapter 9
Materials

"There is something not right with this place," said Yashkin suddenly. "I don't know what, but something is not right."

Chemeris cocked an eye toward the stocky figure and glanced at Rogov. Rogov, as implacable as ever, said nothing and continued writing in his small notepad as if no one had spoken. The three men were together after the day shift, having met in their shared room rather than the communal hall.

"Like what?" asked Chemeris, turning back toward Yashkin. The swarthy Mongolian ran his fingers through his wiry hair and shrugged.

"So, we've bored a hole 9 inches wide a third of the way through the Baltic continental crust. Today the drill bit is 14 kilometres down. For what it matters, no one has ever been this deep."

"So what's your problem?"

"*Why*, is my problem."

"Since when did *Matushka Rossiya* ever explain herself to her children?" remarked Chemeris carelessly. "The food's good, my room is warm and the money is even better. Why complain?"

Yashkin grunted and put his broad hands into his pockets.

"Digging a hole? For what? The Federation is broken, the Black Sea fleet Navy lies rusting in Sevastopol and defunct nuclear reactors are leaking like sieves all over the steppes. Mother Russia has barely two roubles to rub together, and what are we doing? Spending millions on a hole and making piles of dirt. Even the Americans knew when to give up. Something's not right." He sat down and went silent. Yashkin rarely took centre stage and he had unsettled himself with his brief outburst.

"It's more than dirt," said Rogov suddenly.

"Did the silent one speak, or have you taken up ventriloquism

Yashkin?" asked Chemeris winking at the Mongolian.

Rogov set down his notebook, closed it on the table and turned to face the other two.

"7 kilometres down there should have been a transition from granite to basalt. The Mohorovičić discontinuity should be present at that depth, but instead of the expected transition, something changed within the granite itself. Samples brought up show it utterly fractured and completely saturated with water. Not just water, but immense concentrations of hydrogen gas. The mud extracted at 10 kilometres down is boiling with it. Hydrogen and something else. But not just dirt."

"You see," said Chemeris, looking to Yashkin, "Rogov says it's more than dirt, so no need to be worried."

Having spoken, Rogov returned to his reticence, quietly returned to his notebook and resumed scratching indecipherable scribbles on its grey lined pages.

Chemeris turned and reached a bottle out of a cupboard above his bed. "Maybe we're drilling for vodka," he grinned, pulling out three small glasses. "It certainly isn't for oil. Just as well, we can't drink oil. This," he added handing out two glasses to his friends, "this we can."

They sat drinking, reading, writing for some time and as the alcohol began to loosen his reserve, Yashkin spoke again.

"Perhaps I should ask Gasparov," he said with the hint of a slur in his voice. "If anyone knows what we're supposed to be doing here, it will be him."

Rogov's response was instant. "No," he said, turning abruptly. "Perhaps you should not. That is the very thing you should *not* do."

Yashkin looked intently at Chemeris who returned his puzzled gaze with a furtive, silencing motion of his hand. Rogov missed the movement and as he studied at his two comrades, closed his pad.

"Why we are boring, and for what I do not know. Whatever the case, this is not the time for any of us to be asking careless questions."

Chemeris shrugged in mock unconcern. "Well that's that cleared up then," he said.

In reply, Rogov stood up and slipped his notebook into an inside pocket of his jacket. He walked to the door and opened it. He looked out, turned, slid the door almost shut and addressed Chemeris and Yashkin in a quiet voice.

"It may be more than dirt, but I didn't say there was no need to be worried." With that, he walked out, closing the door behind him.

"Is it just me, or was that an intense Rogov moment?" asked Chemeris.

Yashkin responded by fixing a silent probing eye on the bigger man.

It was a look to which Chemeris found he had had no reply.

Anya was working on samples in her laboratory. Below her microscope was a sliver of a greenish material, the nature of which had occupied her for some days. Just as she adjusted the slide under the light, a knock at the door caused her to give a start. Looking up, she watched as Ilyich Gasparov entered, turning to close the door behind himself. For some reason she could not explain, she silently pulled a sheet of notepaper over the exposed sample on the cluttered desk in the moment his face was away from her. She quietly returned to the microscope as he came forward, positioning himself close, but slightly behind Anya so that she had to turn around to see him.

"So, how is your work proceeding Anya Nevotslova?" he demanded in his thick, dispassionately guttural voice.

Anya stammered slightly as she replied.

"Oh, hello sir... y-you startled me, sorry, my lab is a bit of a mess."

"Yes, it is."

He looked around the lab with cold, knife-edged eyes. Not knowing what else to do, she turned back to the microscope, making small pointless adjustments to the settings. She returned and found he had not moved. His eyes however, slowly scanned the room as if searching for something - recording its contents, his gaze prowling the room as a wolf in an empty sheep pen.

Anya waited a moment for the thin faced man to say something more, but there was only silence. Brooding, suspicious silence. Nervously she tried to decide whether to speak or not. His menacing presence silently smouldered in the room. Why did he stand like that? Was she supposed to say something? As she nervously rehearsed her choices, his eyes suddenly fixed directly on hers. His stare almost palpably bored through her retinas to probe the open-eyed exposure of her barely disguised panic. She was about to involuntarily stammer some incomprehensible thought when his grip detached and he turned to the items on the table just behind her. Loosened from his piercing stranglehold, she turned and regarded the items spread-eagled on its surface. Tweezers, aluminium rules, small glass bottles. Isopropyl

alcohol, acetone, cotton buds, scalpels, small piles of rock and dirt. In the centre, the sheet of notepaper blatantly veiling the strange green sample beneath. She nervously turned back to her microscope, anxious and fearful without knowing why. She had incurred the sharpness of his tongue before and had no desire to have his masked derision repeated. She saw nothing as she stared down onto the reticule. Did he want to ask about the samples? Should she say that she was finding the work interesting? '*Interesting*?' What was she thinking? As the seconds ticked by, her thoughts were interrupted by a faint click behind her. Her hands involuntarily gripped the control knobs on the microscope. Two or three more interminably long seconds dragged by until, her chest tightening and her forehead beginning to glisten in a cold clamminess, she turned to break the threatening silence.
He was gone.

She stood, her mouth slightly open, pointless words still lying unuttered on her tongue. The click had been the door as the enigmatic head of the Kolskaya Superdeep Project had wordlessly left the room. On the table beside her the paper with which she had veiled the sample lay, undisturbed and unmoved. What was he looking for? Why did she feel as if she had something to hide? She uncovered the sample on the table and looked at its odd green fluorescence. What it was she had not yet determined. Had Gasparov asked she would have had to admit her ignorance. Perhaps it was just not having an answer for the mysterious material that had caused her to recklessly conceal it before the one man whose very aura demanded disclosure of all.

Rogov turned a corner and saw the unmistakeable back of Gasparov disappear down the corridor. He paused for a second and then looked at the door on his left. The metallurgy lab was the abode of the young Nevotslova. Thinking for a moment, he looked up the corridor again and seeing all was clear, knocked the door.
Anya gave a start as the door at which she was still staring suddenly responded with two short knocks. He was back! Whatever words had been waiting to be said were gone now and she could only wait for Gasparov to enter and torment her again with his inscrutable, obtuse, or worse, silent interrogations. She would be accused of incompetence, ineptitude, of obfuscation.

Rogov entered and found himself looking straight into the white face of the young scientist.

"Sorry, I knocked - but I didn't hear a reply," he began. Seeing her expression, he added with a frown of concern, "Are you feeling well Anya Nevotslova?"

Anya let out the breath she had been holding and as her chest began to untighten, smiled back at the safe and robust shape of Rogov.

"Oh, Rogov, it is you! I thought it was... no matter. I am glad it is you."

Rogov nodded slowly. She had thought he was Gasparov.

"I was passing. I knocked your door on an impulse. Perhaps you are busy?" He cast his eyes around the lab. Every flat surface was covered in untidy piles of rock and sand. "You look busy."

Anya caught the direction of his gaze. "Oh, yes, but, I am glad you called. I... I..."

"Perhaps Ilyich Gasparov's company is not an easy one to accommodate I think?"

Anya gave a small start.

"No," said Rogov, "I have not been speaking with the head of the Kolskaya Superdeep Project, I saw him leave your room just now. He did not see me." A covert, barely perceptible smile wrinkled the edge of his mouth. "He likes to keep us on our toes, no?"

Anya loosened and her shoulders relaxed. She had not realized just how raised and tight they were. The atmosphere in the room almost immediately drained much of its electric tension.

"He frightens me; I don't know why. Makes me feel... I don't know, foolish... small."

"It is how he works. A skill, an artifice. How he commands his game of control. Do not let it unsettle you. He will be tormenting someone else even now."

Anya found the older man's self-assurance comforting. Yes, she had been under a few minutes of Gasparov's scrutiny, but perhaps she had passed whatever test he had been putting her under. Or maybe he had succeeded in what he had set out to do. Leave his mark of authority as a shackle on her mind. She pushed back a stray lock of hair from her eyes and followed Rogov's very different gaze around her lab. The bore she had been working on had intrigued her. Without having formulated the intention in her head, she had inexplicably hidden it from

Gasparov. Perhaps it was simply his comportment that unsettled her, but Rogov was a different man. She turned it over in her mind and could find no logical reason as to why she might not elicit his help. Before she had fully decided, she heard her voice speaking.

"I have been struggling with some of the deeper samples," she said, her very expression brightening as she spoke. "I wondered... perhaps you could help?" She revealed the unnamed sample below the notepaper on the desk. These are samples I received a couple of days ago. I've made slides. I was actually working on them when Gasparov made his... his call." She smiled wryly.

"And what did he think?" asked Rogov, "Did he give an opinion?"

"No, I... ahm, no, he never looked at them," Anya flustered. "I have some ideas, but you are a mineralogist," she continued quickly, "you might have seen this before. Perhaps you would take a look?"

"If you like," said Rogov as Anya turned back to her microscope and began adjusting the controls.

"These were from the 14,000 metre bores," she said, peering down the ocular. "Would you like to take a look?"

She moved aside and Rogov stepped forward to bend over the eyepieces. His focus was slightly different from Anya's younger eyes but after he had reset the dial, he studied the sample below the lights.

The semi-translucent material was a greenish blue and appeared to have veins running irregular patterns through its structure. Rogov narrowed his eyes and increased the magnification by switching the lenses.

"The colour made me think of some kind of copper intrusion," said Anya, "but it has very low conductivity. I do think there is some magnesium present though."

"Yes," Rogov replied, still fixed to the microscope, "it does appear to have some kind of metallic content, but it also appears to be mineral in composition, no?"

"You think it has crystalline structure? I wasn't sure. I was experimenting with it being a rare earth, but nothing I can think of seems to coincide with its properties.""

"Yes," replied Rogov, "Though it would remind me of Forsterite or some magnesium iron silicate. Any iron present?"

"No, I tested it for that," Anya replied.

Rogov drew back from the eyepieces and rubbed a thick finger across his lower lip.

"Water content?"

"Ridiculously high. From 14,000 metres!" Rogov merely nodded. It was further evidence of the abnormalities they had been finding already. That water had continued a further two kilometres was simply astounding. Had it been anyone else Rogov might have queried her finding but Anya Nevotslova had already impressed him with the depth, accuracy and variety of her knowledge. She may have been young but she had a head on her shoulders. Instead he simply nodded hesitantly. He looked back at the sample for a few moments, paused again and appeared to ponder something before speaking. When he did, what he said put Anya off balance.

"Do you know why you were chosen?"

"Sorry?"

"Why Viktor Karmonov selected Anya Nevotslova, daughter of *Doktor nauk,* Boris Nevotslov to come to this place."

"I... You knew my father?"

Rogov studied the girl before him. The same eyes, the way she tilted her head.

"As a man would know any colossus of his field." He paused again and after a moment, lifted a sample of the unknown material from off the table. A mind sharp and inquisitive. There were many highly competent scientists at the Kola, but from the outset Rogov had seen in the diminutive girl a light just that shade brighter. Tonnes of rock and she had filtered out a few ounces.

"I should like to study this further sister – if that is not inconvenient?"

"No, please, I have what I need," replied Anya, feeling oddly disquieted over the unexpected mention of her father. She would have said more, asked what Rogov knew about her father, but as she searched for words to frame her questions, Rogov slipped the sample into his jacket pocket and turned to leave.

At the doorway he hesitated as if deliberating over something.

"I think..." he said, and then paused for a second. "I think it would be wise to be careful, Anya Nevotslova."

After he left, Anya remained staring at the closed door. Rogov had not mentioned before that he knew her father. Why not? Rogov was not like Gasparov. Gasparov left an atmosphere of threat and indirect if not actual intimidation behind him. Rogov seemed to be a man secure in his own skin. A man with a natural assurance - a demeanour that reassured the others with his air of quiet self-control. Something had changed. His parting words inferred there were things he was not saying. She would be careful. If something was unsettling Rogov, then that was reason enough.

~~~~~~~

Outside, conditions in the freezing Kola began to deteriorate. As the barometer fell, a hard, brutal wind fell upon the station, driving before it huge flurries of snow. Thick drifts rapidly formed on every prominence of natural or man-made geology. The darkness exacerbated the bitterness of the wind, a wind driven by the violence of its northern arctic origins. Humanity, the alien in the environment sheltered behind the insulated walls of the project buildings. As the squalls angrily prowled the wailing night, those within occupied themselves at work, occasionally glancing into the whirring darkness when a particularly violent gust beat against the plexi-glass windows or hammered hard and demandingly on the steel walls.

A thousand miles away in the Arkhangelsk State Technical University, Viktor Karmonov presided over a small group of select individuals. They sat in comfortable chairs, seated around a leather covered table in the centre of his private office. Each person had a manila folder set in front of him. Various items from the folders were spread about on the black patina of the leather surface. The door was locked. The discussion was deliberate, concise. There was a direction of travel in the subject at hand. Someone overhearing might say it was conspiratorial – the men in the room would have disagreed. They would have called it patriotic. An exchange of national necessity. At that moment they were deliberating on a telephone conversation Karmonov had shared with them.

The day before he had spoken with Ilyich Gasparov. From that conversation, made over an encrypted line, it was becoming self-evident that the time was drawing nearer when the small group of people behind The Program would be in a position to present to the Duma an irreversible state of affairs that could leave no alternative but acceptance. A *fait accompli*. The greatest acts in history belonged to those who were prepared to carry them out, even if that necessitated violent, brutal action. He was a man who saw with visionary clarity what needed done. He reviled the gutless hand-wringing of cosseted fools. Spineless, grey and indecisive men who had never had to crawl through the entrails of friends and comrades to achieve victory almost as bitter as defeat. Men who failed to understand that no peace ever came about without the requirement of blood.

The world had changed when the Americans had revealed the secrets of Los Alamos by the events at Hiroshima and Nagasaki back in 1945. What Karmonov and his small intensely committed group of true patriots to Mother Russia had almost birthed into existence would have even greater implications. One thing they agreed was certain: the bitter years of retreat and regression would end. The Europeans, the British and especially the Americans would beg like little puppies before the might of the Eastern Bear, awakened and alive from her long hibernation.

Despite the confidence of their aims and the robustness of security surrounding their activities, there were still issues outstanding. Sensitivities that needed, if not addressed, at least, assured. The days when the USSR could withhold from its own people knowledge of the Americans' successful landing on the moon - even for years after the event, were long gone. The world had shrunk, borders were porous lines of demarcation and international communications were open to the masses in a way that not even Stalin, with all of his mighty grip on power, could have controlled.

"Still no sign of awareness from the Americans?" asked a large, heavily browed man across the table from Karmonov. His dark, brooding presence almost matched that of the man he addressed. Almost, but not quite. Karmonov shook his head.

"There is nothing that intimates any knowledge whatsoever," he growled in response. "Comrade Geim, inform the room of the latest foreign satellite reconnaissance we have so far."

It was as much a command as a request. Although the powerful men in the room saw themselves as equals, not many would have demurred from the unspoken consensus that Karmonov was more equal than the others.

"Their satellites pass at the same times," replied a wiry man with round rimmed glasses to the right of Karmonov. "Orbital latitudes remain far south of North Kola. Our intelligence has indicated no request for orbital inclination change on their Mentor bypasses..."

"*Mentor?*" queried a voice to Geim's.

Geim peered over his glasses at the room. "Mentor replaces the

Magnum serics which, you will recall, the Americans launched from their Discovery shuttle in 85. This newer version is the CIA's Advanced Orion Satellite. They have deluded themselves to believe we are unaware of it. With side-scanning radar, it might have the capacity to probe the operation, but nothing so far suggests they have attempted to do so."

"It would seem comrades," interrupted Karmonov, "that the Kola Superdeep has done its work as we had hoped."

The heavily browed man whose name was Igor Gurevich nodded in apparent satisfaction. "To hide in full view where no-one thinks to look," he grinned.

Karmonov took out a sheet of paper from his folder as the rest nodded in satisfaction with Gurevich's statement.

"There is however, one other issue that has been highlighted by our agent in London." The others suddenly looked up. Karmonov rarely mentioned where the sources reported from, and despite the complete security and mutual trust of all present, such an overt disclosure was immediately unsettling.

"It is nothing that has not already been dealt with," said Karmonov, immediately sensing the disquiet, "but we should all of us be aware of every... development."

It was a statement that Karmonov and the others knew was far from true. Even in such a cohesive group as were gathered in the room, there were things – certain *actions* that needed done that were not always explained in detail. Occurrences that, if not in an individual's defined remit, were best to have little explicit knowledge of. Deniability was a useful tool, hard to set aside.

"The Norwegians are straying close to displaying an interest."

"The *Norwegians?*" exclaimed a grim-faced man directly opposite Geim. "*Zhest!* What do you mean the Norwegians?"

Karmonov eyed the man across the room and then slowly scanned the others as if mentally imposing calmness by pure force of will.

"There was some event, subterranean, that aroused, if not suspicion, an unhealthy curiosity. A science station on Jan Mayen."

"What are the Norwegians doing on that God-forsaken rock?" asked Gurevich for the others.

"Vulcan studies," replied Karmonov. "There is a dead volcano on the island with access to deep sub strata. They have been pottering about there for years. The usual fascination of environmental change with which the West seems continually obsessed. In any case, one or two of the scientists detected unusual sounds whilst deep in a dry fissure. It aroused their curiosity. Our source got word. The problem was eliminated. We will have no more concern from the Norwegians. Nonetheless, it is my view that it highlights the fact that even if it happens by accident, we should move before The Program has any danger whatsoever of detection."

There was no-one in the room who had the slightest qualm about what methods might have been employed in the silencing of any nascent threat to their program. The news however that there was any kind of a threat in the first place was, whilst not unexpected at some point, sobering in that it had appeared at all.

As they finished their clandestine meeting, all were agreed that while caution and secrecy were still critical, the time at which their hand should be played was more imminent than they had previously gauged.

And that, thought Karmonov, was of all outcomes, the one most pleasing.

There was one part of the conversation with Gasparov however, that Karmonov had failed to share with the others. He had his reasons and some of those were personal.

"What of the girl?" he had asked Gasparov toward the end of the conversation. "Has she shown any potential... value?"

The encryption on the line accentuated the nasal intonation of Gasparov's reply.

"She is highly motivated, just as you said she would be, comrade," his voice grated down the line. "I have ensured she receives the bores you directed. She certainly appears to be applying herself with zeal to the task."

"Good," said Karmonov. "If she shows the slightest preoccupation in any singular sample examination, I must know immediately, you understand me?"

Gasparov did understand and marked the request. To fail Karmonov was not a desirable option, especially when his requests were more in the order of a command.

~~~~~~~~~~

Rogov's specialism was minerals- best of all the rare and the singularly uncommon. All of his life he had spent in ever decreasing spirals, whittling his way down into the very nature of the object of his studies.

He had a strange knack for spotting the unusual – an ability to disregard the obvious and hone in on vague shadows – subtleties that were often the key to aiding identification. That kindred ability he had seen in Anya. It was rare in someone as young as she and he knew that one day she would be a leader in her field. As soon as he had seen her sample, it had gripped him far more than he had allowed himself to show. The mineral, if mineral it was, was like nothing he had ever seen, and yet something about it was familiar – like an ethereal and indistinct memory, the more he tried to recall the more it receded from his grasp. Anya had mentioned rare earths. Possibly it was that that had alerted him. Like Anya, rare earths were of particular interest to him. In fact, many rare-earth elements were quite plentiful within the Earth's crust. Cerium for example, though a rare earth, was far more abundant than copper. Others however, were hard to find. Gadolinite was a mineral composed of rare earths and found solely in a small village in Sweden. Some he had never seen. Natural Promethium for example. It was rare – extremely so. He knew however that it was radioactive and in his lab it would be a simple matter of testing the sample Anya had given him for radioactivity.

As he turned the sample over in his cotton gloved hands however, something about it caught his eye. Holding a powerful fibre-optic light behind the sliver of material, his eyebrows raised as he saw the greenish hue change colour in his hand. It began to fluoresce in a pallid pink and then to a dark blue. With the light still illuminating it from behind, it returned to green before repeating the cycle. Setting it down onto white paper, he turned off the light and watched as the mineral sat innocently unchanging. Whatever it was, strong light seemed to cause some kind of a photosensitive change within its structure. He placed it below his own microscope with a 50x magnification. Again, it sat below the lens with that odd greenish hue. The lights of the microscope brought about no effect. He leaned over, switched on the fibre optic flexible and directed its powerful light once again onto the material. Immediately it again began to fluoresce and repeat the pink, blue, green cycle. He decided to try something different. He clamped the end of the flexible light to the microscope sample cradle and turned the knob of the fibre optic to infra-red. The material sat impassive below the light. He turned on the ultra violet component to see if that would show anything. Suddenly and without warning, the room burst into a riotous circus of mad dancing light. He leapt backwards, shielding his eyes as the brightness blinded him and he grasped wildly for the off switch on the fibre optic light source. The light from the sample was now spinning around the room in colours and intensity that struck a sudden feral excitement into Rogov. Groping blindly, he found the switch and just as immediately as the circus of light and colour had commenced, it ceased. The room fell into relative darkness and Rogov half sat, half fell onto his stool.

He placed his hands onto the table, one either side of the microscope and opened his eyes. He muttered a prayer of thanks: everything was in focus and his sight seemed normal.

He could hear the raised beat of his heart in his ears as he struggled to comprehend what it was that this was below his microscope. With quiet determination he immediately began to organise a series of further tests. First, he went to his lab door and locked it. Why precisely he would need to do that he did not rationalise, but he did not want to be interrupted for the next hour or so and he made that reason enough. Just as he turned back to his desk, the door knocked. Covering the sample, he returned to the door, unlocked it and prepared to address Gasparov. It was Anya. She was excited, breathless almost, a light in her eyes.

"I've been playing with light spectrums!" she exclaimed. "I've just had the just had the most incredible reaction!"

Chapter 10
Phenomenon.

Finn looked around the room. There were a lot more people present that he had imagined would attend. Down in the first row sat Tom McCracken. Beside him sat Ruth, Alastair Boyd's wife. Beside her were the two eldest daughters, Emily & Ruth, while Rosie sat on her knee, already looking like she was about to fall asleep. Up on the stage were three teams, three people behind each table.

It had been a week of events run by the local council with proceeds going to a local charity set up to provide financial assistance for young families who had lost a loved one to cancer. Tonight was a quiz. The preliminary rounds had weeded out the weaker contestants and now the final was down to the last three teams.

Alastair Boyd had managed to wangle Finn into agreeing to take part and so he found himself where he was, in a team of three with two other surviving teams spread across the stage in the Presbyterian Church Hall. The third member of their team was Anne McCracken. Many people smiled with warmth and genuine pleasure to see Anne who had risen above the tide of her debilitating grief so recently. That she was able to appear in public and even to laugh and smile was attributed by many to the young man at her side.

The quiz was straightforward enough, team questions, different categories, followed by questions in general knowledge to team individuals and finally a 'first finger to the buzzer' round.

The team led by Alastair quickly went into the lead, and the village, knowing that their minister was a man of wide and informed knowledge, expected no less. In second place, and giving a good account of themselves, the team captained by the local primary school headmaster, pressed hard on their heels.

It was when the final two rounds came into play though that the show truly began.

"Each of you will now have forty-five seconds to answer as many questions as you can," explained the Alderman - the quizmaster of the evening.

On average each person got asked about six questions. When the minister and the school master had finished their rounds, each had added five points to their respective teams and the difference between first and second place was a mere two points. The two men had been judged by the audience to be the stars of the show.

Had been, until Finn's round.

When Finn was asked his questions, he answered almost all without the apparent activity of having to consider the answer before replying. In most he replied even before the questioner had completed his questions. When the bell marked the end of his round the Alderman gave a low whistle.

"Well done Finn, you answered all nine questions correctly!"

As the room applauded energetically, the quizmaster moved to the final round.

"First hand to the buzzer gets to answer the question. Two points for each correct answer, one point deducted for each incorrect one given."

He looked around the tables and the room fell to hushed quietness. At the back of the hall a girl giggled and her mother, several rows in front, glared back at the young lad sitting close beside her. He replied with a silly grin on his face.

"Geography: Name the capitals of the following countries. Each country will constitute a question."

The teams set their respective hands next to their buzzers.

"Angola."

A buzzer sounded. It was Finn.

"Finn?"

"Luanda."

"Correct. Canada?"

Again, the buzzer sounded immediately. Again it was Finn.

"Finn again?"

"Ottowa."

So it went on. Finn's hand was on the buzzer before anyone else managed to get to theirs and at the last question of the round, Finn was, to the delight of the awestruck audience, once again the man with his finger on the buzzer. The capital required belonged to Chad. Finn supplied N'Djamena. As an answer it was, of course, correct.

So it continued, the last three rounds were Popular Music, General knowledge and History, but it made no difference. Only one hand belonging to only one contestant pressed his buzzer first. Thirty-two questions. Sixty-four points. All to Alastair Boyd's team. All answered by Finn.

The room burst into rapturous applause. The villagers knew when they'd been given a good show, and this one had been worth every penny of the entrance fee. It wasn't that the other contestants didn't know many of the answers, but they were up against a man who knew them all.

The Alderman shook his head in semi disbelief.

"I believe this young man could tell me where and when I was born!"

Suddenly Finn's voice interrupted the polite laughs.

"Royal Victoria Hospital, Ward Six, 8:35am on Saturday the 4th of June 1960," he replied.

There was a second of quietness broken by loud guffaws of spontaneous laughter from the room at Finn's perfectly timed humour. As if he could know such a thing!

Finn stiffened, smiled back, and lost for anything else to do, folded his arms out of the way of the buzzer and onto his lap.

Alastair Boyd noticed however that not everyone was laughing. The Alderman was staring at Finn, mouth slightly ajar and a look of curious bewilderment on his face.

Later the prizes were given out to polite applause. Polite up to the point where the Boyd team stepped forward. Tables were thumped, feet banged off the wooden floors and cheers erupted for the hero of the hour. Afterward supper was served and during and after the sandwiches and tea, Finn was approached by two dozen different people and congratulated heartily.

Finally, contestants and audience began to filter out the main doors toward homes and hearths. The evening was over and judged to be a tremendous success.

Tom and Anne waited for Finn as he and Alastair chatted outside the hall.

"Well, I'll head on now," said Finn, "Tom and Anne will be keen to get home. I think this is the latest I've ever seen them up." He smiled and shook the minister's hand. "And thanks, it was a bit of fun."

"I was talking to Jim Corrie," said Alastair. "You were correct. About his birthday I mean." He gave a knowing smile. "But you knew you were right, didn't you?" He studied the younger man's face and saw that he too was right.

"He reckons you must be his number one fan," he added with a wink. "Can't for the life of him work out how you knew the exact *time* though." He gave a laugh and then suddenly added. "But I'm thinking you just knew. It's like you said. You *just know things*, wasn't that it?"

Finn looked into the face of the older man. A few seconds of silence passed between them.

"Are you about tomorrow?" Finn finally asked.

Alastair Boyd nodded. "Anytime after two," he said.

Anne had elected to take the rear seat, insisting on allowing Finn the conquering hero to sit in the front with Tom.

Anne beamed and chatted animatedly the whole way home. Not only had she been on the winning team, but Finn, *her boy* had stolen the show. She had enjoyed the evening, meeting up with old friends. Laughing again. Not cornered into a place of having to repeatedly thank people for their continual kindnesses and promised prayers. She felt *alive* again.

She was also as proud of Finn as if she were his own mother.

She could not know that a day was fast approaching that would change all that. When the door in the annex in the McCracken farmhouse would no longer swing to the comings and goings of the young man who had brought such light into her life.

As he drove back to the farm, the lights of the car illuminating the hedges and fields in the surrounding darkness, Tom occasionally shot Finn a curious look. In one night he was reminded that the young man on the seat next to him was as much an enigma as the day he had picked him up at the airport. Just when you think you know someone, it turns out, you don't really know them at all.

~ ~ ~ ~ ~ ~ ~ ~ ~ ~ ~ ~ ~ ~ ~

Saturday found Finn once again in Alastair Boyd's study. Ruth and the girls were out. Alastair made them both a coffee as they sat back in the Tudor leather chairs in the book-lined room.

"You told me before that you had a good memory?" asked the older of the two. "Not one question wrong was an impressive, though I suppose, not impossible record."
"They weren't the toughest questions in the world to be honest," shrugged Finn between sips of his coffee. It was hot and he had to blow on it to cool it a little.
"Perhaps not, but still." He paused before speaking again. "It was the birthday that got me," he said. "Not many people know the actual time of their birth. James Corrie told me he wouldn't have known himself, except that, by coincidence, he had had reason to need his birth certificate that very day. Finding the birthday of a public figure might not be the most difficult of tasks – though why anyone would bother would beg the question – but to know the very time of birth? You said you had a good memory? It must be a very unique memory."
Finn set down his coffee and eyed the other man. With his elbows on the arms of his chair he clasped his hands together and set his chin on top.
"My memory doesn't go back far actually," he said finally. "Not even a year."
The Presbyterian minister's puzzled expression was all that was required to encourage Finn to continue.
"All of my life that I can trace goes back as far as awakening in a Glasgow hospital. My first recollection was the appearing of blurred lights, then I found myself in a room. A ward. I had no idea what I was doing there – how I got there. Worse, I had no idea who I was. You call me Finn, but that was a name I grasped at; plucked from the ether. It seemed to sit better than most others I could think of."
"Weren't the doctors able to help? They must surely have passed you some information."
"They knew as much as I. They even brought in a detective inspector. He tried to invoke some recall, but it was as if there was nothing to remember."
"So they just let you go? Just like that?"

Finn shook his head. He looked out the window. A goldfinch flashed by and settled on the branch of a cherry tree. As Finn looked out through the glass, Alastair waited for him to continue. "No," he said after a few moments, "I left of my own accord. I suppose you could say, I slipped away."

Alastair Boyd took the meaning. "So the hospital has no idea where you went? Was that wise?"

"Wisdom had little to do with it. Leaving was... a necessity."

Alastair wondered at the statement, but was unsure whether to dig deeper in that direction.

"Do you think it was a coma?"

Finn nodded. "Eleven years they said. Maybe it was that that freaked me out, but I couldn't stay. I don't know how to explain this, but it wasn't safe. I wasn't safe – not in a city anyway. Not in a public hospital. Something told me I needed to disappear."

"With nothing but the clothes you stood in." It was a statement, not a question. Nonetheless, Finn responded by reaching into his jacket pocket.

"Not quite. I had this – *took* this." He had a dog-eared Gideon's Bible in his hand.

Alastair's eyebrows involuntarily raised. "And in my position, I'm bound to hope you've been reading it?"

"Some, though I hardly need to."

It was a disappointing answer to hear from the young man who had apparently been enjoying the services and hymns. The minister's face must have betrayed him, for Finn waved a dismissive hand and quickly added another sentence.

"I mean, because I know it all."

"You *know* it all?" Alastair's face took on another different expression. His face was having a changeable afternoon.

Finn looked serious as he replied. "Every word." He passed the bible across the room. "Try me."

The other took the proffered Gideon's and held it for a moment, studying his companion for a few seconds. Finn steadily returned the gaze.

"Well," he said, "Ahm... Genesis Chapter One?"

Finn sighed. "No, I'm serious. Pick a page, any page, give me a line – say, a word so many letters in."

Again, the minister hesitated, but then, with a resigned sigh of his own, opened the bible.

"Page twelve hundred. Column one - third line - third word."

"*Crowd,*" said Finn after a moment's concentration. "Another."

Alastair looked up. The word under his finger was 'crowd'.

Alastair flicked back in the pages. "Page, ahm, page five hundred and eighty-eight – last word on second column."

"*Him,*" responded Finn after no more than a couple of seconds. "Book of Job, Job himself speaking, '*Yet in my flesh will I see God, I myself will see Him.*'"

The minister narrowed his eyes. How was Finn doing this?

At Finn's prompting he tried a couple more. It was all he needed to realise there was something extraordinary happening.

"You must have perfect photographic memory recall!" he said in as even a tone as he could. It wasn't easy.

Finn pointed to the bookshelf behind the somewhat stunned minister. "Take a book of your choosing, do the same thing."

Alastair, his interest now immensely sparked, stretched back and pulled out the first spine he could reach. It was a green hardback, an old book, '*In the Steps of St Paul*' by H.V. Morton.

"Page one hundred and ten, third line, third word."

"Is that the first edition?"

"Ah... yes," mumbled Alastair after checking the first page.

"*Cyprus,*" replied Finn, again after only a second or two's thought. "From a sentence, '*The beauty of Cyprus is a perfect blend of mountain and plain.*'"

The older man stopped at that, stared at the page before him, then back at Finn. It was hard to process what was happening. Trickery? But how? There were no mirrors. Finn could not possibly see the page.

"Hang on a minute," said Alastair. He got up and stooped down to retrieve a large book on a lower shelf on a bookcase at the other side of the window. Remaining at the far side of the room, he stood; his back to the bookcase.

"*Encyclopaedia of Ireland – Gill & MacMillan.* What's the last topic on page four hundred and thirty-seven?"

"*The Giant's Causeway,*" said Finn with a look of determination on his face, "though whether or not I've ever been there, I have no idea."

Alastair glanced down at the tome in his hands. Finn was, as he now beginning to expect, correct.

"I would say that you have perfected some kind of trick, quite apart from the fact I cannot possibly see how. I don't believe you would attempt to make a fool of me."

Finn shook his head. "You are the only person to whom I have revealed this... ability. I suppose I need someone to trust. Someone who might be able to help?"

"I hardly know...have you always had a phenomenal memory?"

"I don't know. If I think, I just know the answer. When I was in Penrith I was able to take apart engines as if I'd been doing nothing else all my life. At first that encouraged me because I thought I was uncovering clues of my past – who I was. But it was the same with the animals. I knew all the procedures of milking, calving, feeding. So then I imagined that the inference was that I must have had a past that included engineering and farming – not that unusual I supposed. I still had no idea that there was anything particularly odd about the variation of knowledge I seemed to possess. On Friday afternoon I was in town - and having time on my hands, I joined the local library. I began taking back books to the farm to occupy myself at night. It was then that I discovered that whatever I read, there was almost nothing in them I did not know. I couldn't explain it, but I could close my eyes and recite pages I had not yet seen. Naturally, it occurred to me that that could hardly be normal, so I kept it to myself."

"I've read of savants who could perform apparently superhuman tasks of memory," said Alastair suddenly remembering something. "I read a book about memory not so long ago, 'Moonwalking with Einstein' I think it was. An American chap, Kim Peek, if I remember correctly. He had an amazing capacity to recall huge amounts of information. He would read and memorize books word for word. Thousands of them. In fact, he could read a book in about an hour and remember it all. He was supposed to be able to read one page with one eye while the other eye read the opposite page simultaneously. I remember reading that he had memorized near enough all of the editions ever printed of the Reader's Digest. In fact, in public exhibitions he would do what you've just done – supply the words of given pages and lines in any edition."

"You think I'm a savant?"

Alastair considered the question for a moment. He had to admit Finn displayed none of the associated traits or typical indicators of savant-like behaviour. Savants normally displayed mental abnormalities, debilities in other areas. Finn appeared normal in every other way.

Just then a thought occurred to him. He went over to his desk and lifted a brown leather-backed journal. There was something he could test. Concealing the journal behind a copy of *The Presbyterian Herald*, he looked up at Finn through narrowed eyes, then opened the soft leather back.

"See how you do with this," he said. He began to read.

"As G.K.Chesterton wrote in his book, The Everlasting Man, "A dead thing can go with the stream, but only a living thing can go against it." So the act of faith is an exercise of strength, not of weakness. To believe is not to surrender to the capricious flow of popular consensus, but to dare to defy it. The man or woman who fails to think is more likely in the preserve of the faithless, seldom of those who, whilst acting in faith, determine to go against the crowd approval of agnosticism whilst using all the faculties of intellect God gave them."

He looked up and waited. Finn looked back and said nothing. A few pregnant seconds passed and Alastair, about to declare a fallibility in the phenomena Finn had presented, was suddenly silenced.

"Very good," Finn said. "Your congregation will enjoy that address in the morning."

The minister stood inert, confounded. Finn carried on.

"That would be your own writing. Your own notebook of sermons. Just before you move to quote John Lennox in further support of Chesterton's proposition?"

Alastair remained silent; trying hard to rationalise. It made no sense. Perhaps, in the wildest of improbabilities. Finn could have seen and memorized more books than were ever before imagined possible, but no-one apart from himself had ever seen his own hand-written notes for the morning. He had only finished them before lunch.

Finn broke the silence.

"So this is my secret, the weight in my dreams. An enigma shrouded in a veil I cannot see through. Why do I know so much and yet know so *little?*"

Finn stayed a little longer, during which time the conversation batted around his possible origins as well as his future plans. Apart from the obvious fact that he had a Scottish accent, there was almost no other information Finn could supply.

"It's not a very defined accent though, it?" asked Alastair. "I mean, not a particular region I'm familiar with anyway. Not that I'd be an expert."

"The detective, Jack McGregor, he said it wasn't Glaswegian. Thought it might be west coast - Argyll possibly. Obviously I've looked on maps and studied place names - tried to find somewhere with a familiar ring to it."

"Nothing?"

"No," sighed Finn. "It's almost as if everything prior to awakening in the ward was wiped - deleted."

"But you must have a past," said Alastair, "even if you don't remember it. A school, friends, parents who have lost a son. What about an advert in a Scottish newspaper?"

"How do you mean?"

"I mean place one. State that you are looking for your family. Send a photo, tell a little of the background, give contact details. It's an interesting story, I'm sure you'd find newspapers willing publish it. Someone out there knows you."

Finn shook his head. "No, I can't exactly explain it, but every time I consider that kind of thing - opening to a wider audience, alarm bells ring in my head. Like I hinted before, keeping out of the public eye just seems... I don't know... just seems important somehow."

As the days ahead would unfold, the intervention of the Alderman was to instigate an event that neither of the two in the study that Saturday afternoon expected.

Chapter 11
Shipwreck

It was a land of gravel. Grey and sullen. Jan Mayen Island was like a rejected piece of the world, cast out in seas little known and less visited by humanity, a sliver of inhospitable mist-shrouded shale stranded between Greenland and Iceland, with its back to its absent parent, Norway. A place almost devoid of humanity, it was bounded by 80 miles of harbourless coast, refusing seaborne suitors with a shoulder cold and unapproachable. The interior was a practically road-less moonscape eerily filled with the sounds of vagrant winds prowling over barren rocks. Nonetheless, huddled inland there persevered a small handful of hardy individuals employed by the Norwegian Armed Forces and the Norwegian Meteorological Institute. Barely two dozen people, set adrift through the gale-whipped snows of the winter months. The military's sole given purpose; to operate and maintain the LORAN-C base. Adjacent to it, the meteorological station staffed by a grand total of three civilians, augmented by two of the military base's personnel. The soldiers were there ostensibly to give assistance to the demands of working in such a harsh environment, an environment that cared nothing for what manner of human being it was trying to kill. Both facilities were five kilometres away from Jan Mayen's single settlement, *Olonkinbyen* - the City of Olonkin. A day's work over, all of the personnel would retreat down from the wastes to the urban metropolis of six thermal-lined aluminium huts. As if to torment the inhabitants with the temptation of escape, Mayen's one unpaved airstrip lay within sight of the low-roofed settlement, or would do so on the rare days where visibility extended beyond a hundred metres.

Overall responsibility and administration of the island fell upon the epaulettes of the station commander of the Norwegian Defence Logistics Organisation, a sub-section of the Norwegian Armed Forces.

Not many applied for the role and the current incumbent, Kommandør Henrik Jensen, was not sure himself that he had.

Apart from the daily regime of the functions requiring oversight on the island, the commander had little distraction in his duties. For all of the military and civil personnel, the tasks required a huge commitment of time, technical knowhow and experience, but the low grey clouds and sunless days had the effect of adding monotony to jobs that could too quickly become onerous and repetitive.

In such an environment, any small event would invariably be heightened in its impact to a society deficient in the normal diversions.

So it was that when a man was found alive in a small yacht washed onto the dark gravel of the west coast near *Nordlaguna* - the northern of the two lagoons on the island - all attention was directed to the wreck and its single survivor.

The story of his survival was remarkable in the extreme. Had he not had the presence of mind to send a flare up from the carcass of his beached vessel, he may have lain there, undetected until the sea reached out and pulled him back into its cruel depths. By an incredible stroke of luck, one of the soldiers, *Oversersjant* Ari Bjørnson was on a solo hike of the west coast during a couple of days rest period and saw the flicker in the clouds near the lagoon. Fortunately the sergeant, first class, was also an army medic and was able to attend to the man he had single-handedly supported, dragged and finally carried 12 kilometres back to Olonkin City.

"So has he spoken yet?" asked *Kommandør* Jensen as Ari exited the medical surgery where the yachtsman had been sedated and left sleeping in a cot. The commander was as interested as anyone else in the newest addition to their number, and after the tragic death of the senior meteorologist some months before in an inexplicable suicide, he was determined that no one else was about to die on his watch.

"Nothing coherent since I got him here sir," replied the muscular, blonde-haired Norwegian. "When I found him he wasn't in great shape, but he was able to tell me he was a single-handed sailor. Thankfully no one else to worry about. I've him on an intravenous saline and electrolyte drip. I've also given him something to sedate him for 24hours. He'll need as much rest as he can get."

"What is a man doing up on a small boat at these latitudes, especially at this time of year?" asked the commander. "I wouldn't want to be out there in a frigate."

"From what I was able to make out from barely coherent sentences, he lost his rudder, mast and electrics in a storm off Orkney almost two weeks ago. Lucky he made landfall at all, he had jury-rigged some kind of a sail but he was absolutely at the mercy of the wind."

The commander shook his head in amazement. "He's a lucky man," he said, looking at the surgery door. "Hitting Jan Mayen in the middle of those vast seas out there was almost a miracle. That it was Ari Bjørnson that found him, was another."

Ari gave a grin; a Norwegian's Viking grin which could be hard to differentiate between a smile or an intent to dismember the recipient. Jensen returned the Nordic smile and slapped his sergeant first class on his broad and solid back. "You're a big man Bjørnson," he said, suddenly serious, "but how on earth did you ever drag, carry, whatever you did, a full grown man over 12 kilometres of the world's most inhospitable terrain?"

Ari shook his head. "Not that big a man sir," he said. "To be honest, I thought I wouldn't make it, I've never been so physically exhausted in my life."

The commander nodded with understanding. "You need rest sergeant," he replied. "Take yourself off to your bunk. We can manage without you at the station until tomorrow's shift."

"Thank you sir," sighed Ari, "I appreciate it. A few hours sleep and I'll be back to normal."

"Report to me in the morning," said the commander as he turned to go. He was a compassionate man, but he also had a radio and meteorological station to maintain and every member of his team had his defined role.

Life on the island, though busy with the multitude of tasks that required attention, was also one of isolation. The commander looked at the calendar on the wall of his living quarters. There was a grand total of eight scheduled flights to the island each year. The weather was so unpredictably foul that as often as not, the Royal Norwegian Air Force C-130 would be forced to turn back to Bodø without landing. The island's gravel airstrip lacked instrument landing transponders and pilots needed good visibility to put down. On those occasions the frustration for those on the ground, having waited eight to nine weeks for supplies, would be expressed in exasperated curses. Unseen in the low thick clouds above, the Hercules would fade away, flying the two hours back to the mainland without having put a wheel down on an island they could not see.

Henrik Jensen marked the next flight on the calendar. Six weeks if they were lucky. He wondered how their visitor would react to being told he was here for a while. He also realised he did not yet know his name or nationality. He assumed English; it seemed men out alone on the ocean in small yachts inevitably were.

He was Scottish. From Ullapool on Scotland's North Western coast. He sat opposite himself and Ari and looked in remarkably good health for a man who had been through such an ordeal. A quarter had been found for him in an empty civilian hut and it was there that Jensen sat with his sergeant as the man answered the commander's questions. His name was Donald Sutherland but looked as much unlike his famous actor counterpart as was possible to be. He was probably a little under six foot, lithe, but solid looking; He had short black close cut hair and his carriage and skin colour bore witness to a life lived out of doors.

"If my sergeant had not seen your flare it would have been, as you English say, a very different kettle of fish," said the commander. He had trained at Sandhurst and had picked up a few of the odd British idioms while he was there.

"Aye, true, the English do say that," replied the visitor, "but so do us Scots. I can hardly tell you how thankful I am to be alive. I can never ever thank you enough for saving my life."

Jensen smiled inwardly. He had forgotten the sensitivities of the four national identities of the British. The Welsh, Scottish, and Northern Irish in particular seemed to think that someone calling them English was going out of his way to offend. In reality, the rest of the world was unaware of the difference and even less cared.

He had set out from Ullapool to sail to Stornaway on Harris, the islands of the Outer Hebrides. He should have done it in a day, but in a violent, screaming squall that suddenly attacked from the South West, the yacht collided with something hard and metallic - he guessed a partially submerged shipping container lying in wait below the unforgiving green waters. The hull was breached, while the squall almost capsized his boat, breaking the mast and destroying his wireless and GPS. He had fitted anti-capsize lift bags the previous season and they kept him afloat while three-story waves pounded the hull for three days and nights. All the while he was driven further and further north until he began to lose hope of any respite. Much of his food was lost or spoiled and he lived mostly on cold baked beans and brackish water. There was a day of calm in which he was able to make basic repairs to the rudder and erect a spinnaker sheet on the broken mast stump. On the sixth day he spotted the Faroes far off to starboard, but was unable to make any headway east as the jury-rigged sail and rudimentary rudder would not endure robust tacking into the wind. Instead he was steadily driven north by the relentless gale.

When at last he was blown toward the rocky coast of Jan Mayen, he despaired that all was lost. Miraculously he made landfall but, weakened and exhausted, believed he would perish on the unknown shores of an island whose name he did not know. He had one flare left - he had used the others during the storm in desperate unanswered hope. He had fired that last flare during a break in the mist whilst on the beach without much prospect that there was even anyone to see it.

"You are an incredibly fortunate man Donald Sutherland," said the commander after the sailor had finished the story of his stranding. "*Oversersjant* Ari Bjørnson, unlike normal human beings, seems to find some kind of perverse pleasure clambering over this godforsaken rock. That he happened to be where he was, when he was, was a million to one chance."

The man called Donald gave a shiver. He ran his hand along the wooden arm of his chair as if finding reassurance in something tangible and real, something that proved he was indeed alive and on solid ground.

"You'll want to contact home," added the commander. "We can patch you through to a U.K. telephone number. There's a handset in my office when you're ready. There will be people worried about you. You were headed to Stornoway?"

"Aye, I was, but I'd no plans to lodge there. I usually sleep on the boat. I'd planned to see a bit of the place, take a few photographs. I sell to a picture library that specialises in outdoor activities, sailing, skiing and the sort."

In the course of the conversation the commander learned that the Scot was a loner. His only relative with whom he had contact was his mother, who lived, like him in Ullapool. He himself was rarely there but he was keen to let his mother know he was well.

"Though she'll no be worrying much," he said ruefully. "I've maybe no been as attentive a son as I ought to be. She'll no think it strange that I haven't called I'm afraid. Aye, I'd like to make that call, thanks."

During the call, Donald asked for Sergeant Bjørnson. Mrs Sutherland had asked to speak to her son's rescuer. Over the line, she expressed her immense thanks that her son had been saved. The commander could overhear her tears as she thanked his sergeant for all he had done. Ari, in his usual dismissive manner, assured the elderly woman that it was nothing. Her son was in good hands and all was well.

Jensen also ensured that the British Embassy in Oslo was contacted. They made contact with the appropriate authorities but it was left to the Norwegians to facilitate the first part of Donald Sutherland's repatriation. The next flight to the island would take him to Bodø from where he would be forwarded on to Oslo and thence to Aberdeen.

When it was pointed out to the sailor that it would be at least six weeks before that could happen, he was pragmatic. A man who has come back from the dead is in no position to complain that his life has not simply recommenced like a restart on a video game. He was determined, he said, to help out whilst on Mayen with whatever he could do; nothing would be too menial or demanding.

In the meantime, Jensen organised one of the island's two Mercedes G-Wagens to head overland to the wreck site to attempt a salvage of any of Donald's belongings. Although he asked to go along, he accepted the commander's decision to stay as he was judged by Ari to be too weak from his ordeal.

Although he could obviously not participate in any of the military's activities on the island, Commander Jensen agreed to inquiring from the civilian meteorologists if there were any duties he could assist them with. He also insisted his new arrival take four or five days to recuperate before thinking of doing anything physical.

"Lars is a good man," advised the commander. "I'll have a word with him and see if he can use an extra pair of hands. If anyone can find something to occupy your time with us, it will be him."

A few days later, true to his word, the commander took Sutherland, along with Ari, up to the weather station. Entering the building, they shook the snow off their boots and removed their parkas before proceeding through the second set of doors. A man there awaited them.

Like most of the Norwegians, Lars Guldberg was sturdily put together, not as big as Ari, but with the same Nordic features shaped from a life carved out of the North Atlantic fjords.

"Lars Guldberg, Senior Meteorologist," he said, thrusting out a rugged hand to Lander. The grip was strong, and piercing blue eyes scanned the man who had been introduced to him as Donald. He continued to grip the other's hand as his eyes narrowed into some kind of inspection of authenticity.

"Good to meet you Lars," said Donald, his own eyes fixed on the Norwegian's with an equal return of intensity. "A senior meteorologist was just what I needed about a week ago."

Guldberg's face made it clear that the statement was not fully understood. The yachtsman continued.

"Someone who could have told me to stay in harbour and not be so feckless as to head out into weather that had every malevolent intent to wrestle me to the bottom of the sea, along the shattered remains of my boat."

"I do not think a man who could sail single-handed into the South Greenland Sea could be as *'feckless'* as you put it, as he pretends to be," said the scientist suddenly smiling. "And with a grip like that, I think the wrestle would have been a hard one."

The two men were still fiercely gripping one another's hands, hands whose knuckles were both white with the force either had been gradually increasing as they spoke. They suddenly let go and both gave their respective hands a shake.

Lars Guldberg laughed and slapped Donald Sutherland on the back.

"I like you," he said. "We will get on well together."

"Well," said Jensen, "now that you passed Lars' little test that he likes to inflict on the innocent, I think I can leave you in his hands." He winked at his scientist. "Well now Lars. First man I haven't seen squirm with your little party piece?"

"I thought I would go easy on this one," lied the meteorologist, "Besides, I'll need him to be able to handle a brush. Some people think that walking in a pile of snow into my lab is appropriate just because they have the title *Kommandør*!"

Lars and his scientists took the yachtsman under their wing, and after giving him a tour of their laboratories, introduced him to the practical duties of daily snow-clearing and general tidying. He fitted in well, during the day assisting in the countless tasks of maintenance and odd-jobs inside and outside of the station while retiring in the evening down to the living quarters where he got to know some of the other military stationed on the island. After a few days the novelty of his company wore off and he found himself being treated more as just another of the team rather than a complete stranger. Stranger or not, all had to contend together with the bleakness and snowy greyness that was Jan Mayen.

Amazingly, Sutherland's cameras had survived the wrecking. He had a medium format and a Nikon professional digital SLR. Both, plus lenses had been in a waterproof Peli case and seemed none the worse for wear. Donald explained that he believed film was still superior to pixels in capturing the hues and moods of light in landscape photography. As it happened he had a booklet in his case of samples of his work. The staff at the weather station were impressed. He had taken photographs around Skye and Mull the month before he left for Stornoway. Even as 7"x5" photographs, they were stunning.

The details of their new visitor, how he ended up wrecked on their shores and his background as an iterant yachtsman/wanderer/landscape photographer were soon known to everyone as for a few days he became the centre of attention and interest.

"He seems an O.K. kind of guy, but I don't know how people like him do it," commented one of the soldiers as they sat around a table in the canteen playing cards one evening. "Where does the money come from? Yachts are expensive, all those sails and fancy equipment. What about food? Everyone has to eat."

"Ya, but not everyone eats as much as you do Erik!" snorted one of the others.

"Very funny Anders," replied the first soldier. "If you ask me, sailing single-handed is mad anyway. What normal person would want to be out on the sea on his own, miles from anywhere, from friends and family?"

"So welcome to Jan Mayen," said another soldier with a wry grin as he set down his card.

"You know what I mean," objected Erik turning around. "Crazy to set out in a storm if you ask me. An expensive mistake. He'll not be a boat owner again."

"Says our expert, Mr Fridjof Nansen himself!" Anders countered. "Correct me if I'm wrong, but isn't there a thing called *insurance?*"

"That man doesn't need to worry much about money," added a new voice. It was Ari. He'd just entered the room and caught the tail end of the conversation. He spun one of the chairs round and sat, leaning his arms on its back. "Our Mr Sutherland is a man of means apparently. Made his money in computing - sold up and left the rat race. Nice if you can do it."

"Not if you're drowned in the Greenland Sea it isn't," dismissed Erik.

"So how did you find that out?" asked Anders.

"I asked him."

"You asked him? What? 'Hi, my name's Ari Bjørnson. How come you're rich?'"

The others laughed and the affable Ari along with them. "Not quite Anders. He kept slipping out of consciousness on our hike back to the base." The others simply nodded. They knew what Ari had done, it wasn't just a hike and the sailor had been half carried by Bjørnson the Bear.

"So I kept him talking, asked him questions."

"Kept him alive," interrupted Anders in appreciation of Ari's feat. The rest of the men murmured their approval.

"Yes, well, anyway, he told me his story."

Ari passed on what he had learned. The Scotsman had left Edinburgh after making his money and had retired to the quiet town of Ullapool. After his father died, he brought his mother up to live with him. He very soon found he needed something to do and so he bought a boat and began sailing all around Europe. The West coast of Scotland though was always his favourite haunt. He wasn't married and had no steady girlfriend. A man who kept himself to himself.

After a while the conversation turned to other things and the laughter increased as the evening drew on. Money was won and lost, stupid jokes were cracked and everyone disparaged in turn. Jan Mayen was a small community, but as far as the military that night were concerned, there were worse postings in the world. Warmer, sunnier, yes; but maybe Jan Mayen actually wasn't so bad for all that.

One hundred nautical miles to the West the captain of HMS Albion nodded in approval. His Communication and Information Systems Specialist's report was good. The CISS had picked up the encrypted burst from their 'package'. The coded message of the three words, 'blue on white' told him that the insertion and 'rescue' had gone according to plan. It almost surprised him. He gave a slight grimace as he thought of his outburst some weeks earlier at the naval base on the South coast of England.

"Launch a wrecked yacht with a man aboard two miles off one of the most hazardous coasts in the world? Are you serious sir?"
Commodore Legge had arrived unannounced at Devonport HMNB where the captain was inspecting a routine repair to his ship. Seeking him out, the Commodore had brought the captain into a private office at the base.
"Captain Currie, I have a task needing done," he had said in his usual distinct clipped tone. "What I am about to ask you to do is hazardous, make no mistake about it, but it is also classified. You will know why you are where I am going to ask you to go. You will be the only one on your ship who shall. That is no easy thing to achieve. How you do that is down to you. Many aspects of how you perform this prospective mission is likewise, your responsibility. Before I detail it however, I want to know if I have selected the man who *can* do it."
Both men had known it was a rhetorical, if not impossible question. Currie was being asked to decide on something of which he as yet knew practically nothing.
His initial response when he had heard some of the detail had been unfeigned scepticism. Captain Currie was renowned among his peers for his razor-sharp and incisive mind. He also was a man who seemed unperturbed in expressing genuine misgivings to superiors. It was this very frankness Commodore Legge liked in the man. He reminded him of himself when he was a young captain. Commanders of naval ships at sea demanded men of independent inquiring intellect and Legge considered there to be a scarcity of them in positions of effective command. Many rose through the ranks by being what was required of them rather than being the gut-driven, independently-minded leaders of men. There was something about the nonconformist, singularly motivated man, who, whilst uncomfortable in company, difficult in conversation, passionately aimed to win his battles. Others simply aimed to survive. Sometimes the two had to be incompatible. Captain Currie had the authenticity he sought. The man for the job. The man for *this* job.

"Sir," Currie had asked, "with the greatest respect, HMS Albion is an LPD, I am the captain of a 22knot floating dock - are you sure you've picked the right ship, the right man?"

Commodore Legge smiled to himself. The weight of command was a heavy thing, and being surrounded by acquiescing junior officers only increased the uncertainties dogging the burden. Men with unsheathed opinions like Currie were knives that reduced the fog, clarified decision making by their courage to question.

"A Landing Platform Dock is exactly the right ship Captain, and whether or not you are the right man is down to you, not me."

"Jan Mayen sir?" questioned the younger man, "I've heard of it, never been there of course, isn't it Norwegian? I could be mistaken of course sir, but as far as I'm aware it lacks any adequate harbour."

"It lacks any harbour at all captain. In fact, of all its coasts, the western approaches are the most dangerous – treacherous actually."

"You sound like you know it sir."

Commodore Legge nodded. "I have had... occasion to handle a ship in its waters." He stiffened. So what of my request?

Currie knew that there was no request. Being asked was merely a device. He was being ordered. Not that it made any difference. *Impossible* was a stranger to the vocabulary of Captain Currie of the Her Majesty's Royal Navy.

For Legge, he had left the base with a strange sense of *déjà vu*. Years before he had been ordered to do something not so dissimilar. It had rankled at the time. The young captain doubtless would feel the same. A peculiar thing, how age and experience brings a man to be authorising the very thing oppugned in his youth. He had made one capitulation however to his younger self's past objections. He had given Captain Currie Lander's real name. It was the one thing that had always troubled him; that his trust should be questioned. He did not doubt Captain Currie's.

So it was that two weeks later, as he read the transcript, out in the Greenland Sea, 100 miles off the mauling rocks of Jan Mayen, Captain Currie felt an immense sense of satisfaction. This ship of his, this crew of his had done the impossible. The yacht which they had transported and launched was a suicidal act, or an act of murder. The thin skinned balloon-like floats that they had attached to keep Lander's vessel afloat were to be burst and disposed of by the man himself once he had managed to navigate the yacht onto the one spit of beach where landing might be possible. He then had to get off in a breaking undertow. The yacht had to remain for at least for long enough for the personnel on Mayen to get eyes on it. Before that the 'rescue' had to be coordinated without suspicion. It was an incredible ask. Incredibly, it seemed to have worked.

He turned to his CISS who was standing dutifully to the rear of the bridge.

"I need you to send an encrypted message to Commodore Legge. Three words. *Package in place.*"

"So, now you are from Scotland?" asked Ari. "I was not expecting that."

"One of my old pals from the regiment died," explained Jon Lander, as he and Ari took a walk along the eastern side of the narrow isthmus joining *Nord-Jan* to the smaller *Sor-Jan,* the southern part of the island.

Overall the island was shaped like a spoon, the handle at the south with the north dominated by the Beerenberg volcano. The ground beneath their feet was gravel with breakouts of mossy clumps of tundra-like hard grasses.

"He was in Afghan' doing charity work. We served together out there when we were in the regiment. Don just fell in love with the people - so he went back - thought he could make a difference. One Monday morning the Taliban set off a massive car bomb in Kabul central market. He was there buying food for some of the orphans he was working with. He was just in the wrong place at the wrong time. I had to break the news to his mother. She's a tough woman, agreed to conceal the death of her son for a few weeks so that I could assume his identity. People ask her how Don's doing and she smiles and tells them he's doing great while he's lying in some refrigerator in a morgue in Salisbury. Mrs Sutherland is one of this world's true heroes. Anyway, Don being from Scotland, I became Scottish."

Ari nodded slowly. "It is always the families who suffer the most. The medals, I think, are pinned on the wrong chests."

Lander gave a wan smile. "Ari my old friend, we are getting morose again. Tell me, how's the story being taken?"

"Good," said Ari. "I don't think anyone from Henrik Jensen down have any doubts about the story. The yacht was very convincing. Mrs Sutherland's thanks on the satellite telephone too. Also, someone found an article about her son's shipwreck on an online version of a small Scottish newspaper."

Jon Lander nodded approval of the successful decoys. "If they dig deep enough, they'll also find traces of Don's old computer business he ran before returning to Afghanistan." He stopped walking suddenly. "So, first part over, we'll need to moving on to the next stage."

The *Oversersjant* turned and looked steadily at Lander.

"Have your people told you how that works?"

Lander shook his head. "Security Services and the NIS were a bit vague on that. All I know is you are to be the only man I can trust. I could have told them that in any case."

"Jensen is a good man Jon. He has put Beerenburg off limits until he is granted the extra personnel he's been requesting."

"Extra personnel?"

Ari sighed. "I think Henrik Jensen feels responsible in some way for the recent death - you heard about it?"

Jon nodded. "Yes, it's partly why I'm here." He made a mental note. Ari had obviously not been fully informed on the brief.

"I think he feels that had he more men, he could have made it a standard protocol that no one be permitted to be out driving in a place like this on his own. Jan Mayen can alter a man's mood, too much time on his own isn't healthy here."

"So you believe he committed suicide?"

Ari started. "Johannsen might have been a civilian Jon, but he was a good man!" Ari's spoke with irritation in his voice, almost anger. He leaned forward and spoke the words as if they were bullets, stabbing the air with a stocky finger. "He went out that day to Beerenburg to check something. Whatever else happened, he did not kill himself. Didn't they let you read my report?"

"I read it Ari. No one doubted the veracity of your report. If they did, I wouldn't be here."

Bjørnson leaned back, the irritation fading. He turned and looked far out over the throbbing sea as wheeling gulls punctuated the sky with their forlorn cries. Lander knew his friend was about the most equal tempered Norwegian in a nation which majored in the virtue. This had affected him.

"It's got something to do with that volcano," he said quietly after a few moment's silence. "Johannsen became preoccupied with it."

"Did he mention anything to you?"

Ari shook his head. "We weren't particular friends Jon, but anyone would admire his tenacity, his fairness, the dedication he showed to his staff and his work. He was a good man and someone saw fit to kill him."

"Ari, I need access to the shaft in Beerenburg," said Jon bluntly.

Ari shook his head. "The Commander has the entrance locked. He ordered the other civilians to cease work on their research there. They weren't too pleased about it either. Lars Gulberg is married to that job of his. Putting the volcano off limits put him into days of depression." He paused for a moment. "Guldberg and Johannsen were close you know. Always running little projects together, talking interminably in the rest room, sheets of paper spread out on the table. Two mad scientists digging holes in the ground and wondering why we weren't all standing around in awe."

"He seems to be consumed by his work," suggested Lander. "Only that the station is closed in the evenings, I think he would spend every hour in his lab or deciphering readings from his meteorological apparatus."

"Ya, He has taken over Johannsen's role and I think he sees his failure to continue the work there as a failure to his friend. "

"He comes across as a decent sort of a man."

"Yes, for a civilian," the Norwegian grinned. "Nothing too fragile about him though. I like him myself, even if he continually drones on and on about isobars and pressure fronts like they were the world's most fascinating topics."

"Takes all sorts," laughed Lander. "The sort that sent me here however -" he added with more seriousness, "- that sort needs me to get into Beerenburg."

"I told you Jon, Henrik is adamant on that score."

"Nonetheless I will somehow need access - and an alibi to explain my absence on the station for 12 hours. For that I'm going to need your help."

Ari Bjørnson nodded slowly.

"A few days yet Jon," he said finally. "You need to be seen to recover more before you are out and about on your own. It's one thing cleaning test tubes, quite another to be found tramping around Mayen on your own." He suddenly stopped and gave a frown. "What am I saying? *I* need more recovery time." He gave his Lander an accusatory look.

"Was I really supposed to carry you just so much from the beach?!"
Lander laughed. "Ari old man, to have come this far and have someone
spot us through a pair of binoculars skipping through the moss would
have ripped the lid off before I'd even got started.

"Ya, well, the *Etterretningstjenesten* didn't conscript me to be a nursemaid,
so next time, it can be your turn my English friend."

Chapter 12
Recollections

Images swam through his dreams - flashes of light - water - darkness. Finn knew he was dreaming, or at least, knew he was not in the world of the awake.

His eyes were tight shut against the unseen menace. He could feel a rising fear and knew that it would lead to terror. He could not breathe, must not breathe, and yet every fibre of his being cried out in urgent demand that he succumb. The crushing pain in his chest was an unspeakable agony shouting that he open his mouth and give in to the unbearable urge. Now the fear was like a hand grasping his heart, a hand, cold and hard as steel, grasping, squeezing. At last he could do nothing else but inhale with an energy that could burst lungs. Burning, pain beyond belief, pain indescribable, unspeakable. He screamed, his eyes suddenly and terrifyingly open in horror and blinding shock.

Green, flashing green and yellow and blue. Not air was it that he inhaled, but burning liquid. This was death. Not any death. This was the death of the damned. Then all was black.

He thought he had awoken. A face loomed in shadows and light. A man. A man leaning over him with something in his hands. His face looked concerned. He was concerned about him. He gave a slight smile and put a cool hand on his forehead. "*Pozhaluysta, spat'*," he said, his voice far away. "Sleep now."

He heard his own voice, rasping, hoarse. "Where... where am I?"

"You are safe. Now you must rest. Sleep now." He leaned over and Finn felt his arm raised. A needle. Darkness descended.

Finn awoke. His temple was damp with sweat. He pushed himself up in his bed and pulled the sheets away from his upper body. The sheets were wet with his perspiration; the room was in darkness. He was breathing hard and he could hear the beating of his heart through his chest. Outside a cock crowed. A dog far away barked.

For a long time he sat upright, his back against the headboard. It took him a minute or two as his head cleared. Controlling himself, he took long slow breaths until his heart quietened. He closed his eyes and tried to remember the details of the nightmare. He had been lying on a bed, recovering, but it was not in Glasgow, not in Scotland. The man spoke in a thick foreign accent, German – no, further East - Polish, Russian. He had looked like some kind of doctor, but what was the room? There had been pipes everywhere, running along the walls, over the ceiling. Everything was grey, metallic. And there was a constant hum, a thrumming. There was more of the dream, but already it was becoming a fading forgotten phantasm. The more he grasped at it, the more it dissolved like a will' o' the wisp, a mist evaporating before his eyes.

Finn pushed himself back under the sheets and thought. Was it just a nightmare? Just dreams? No, he was sure it was more, they were memories; the more he considered it, the more he was convinced. But if so, what kind of experience, what terror was it that lay in those images? And if they were memories, did he really want to recollect them? He knew the answer to that question before he asked it. Whatever had happened, he needed to know. He had to know.

Anne McCracken took the call. Had it been her husband, he might have been slower to acquiesce to the request, but Anne was proud of her boy and so she beamed down the phone and told the Alderman she was sure it was a wonderful opportunity.

"I'm not so sure," said Tom when he came in first from the morning milking. "Though he'll be in for tea in ten minutes and you can tell him yourself." Anne dismissed her husband's reticence and finished buttering the scones. Her Finn was a wonder and everyone deserved to know it.

"I don't know," said Finn as Anne explained the arrangement. "I'm not that great in the public, I'd just as soon get on with my work and let others get their faces in the paper."

"Och," exclaimed Mrs McCracken, "sure weren't you brilliant at the quiz. Anyway, it's just for the local paper. A wee photo of our Finn in the Donaghadee News section of The Chronicle would be lovely. I would be so proud!"

Finn winced at Tom when the photographer arrived with Alderman Bryce. The councillor was all business and bluster, Wasn't Finn a great asset on Tom's farm? Didn't he do such a great job about the place? He was amazing, he was brilliant, he was such a great fellow. Here, I'll stand here, let me just place my hand on Finn's shoulder. What about one shaking hands? To the photographer as he took notes; "B.r.y.c.e, with a 'y', no 'i'."

Then it was over, they were gone and Tom turned at his wife.

"So much for that," he frowned. "That was just 'Alderman Bryce appears in the paper again'. These politicians are all the same. It's all about publicity and gettin' their own mugs in the headlines."

"Never worry Mr McCracken," said Finn with a slight laugh. "The photographer guy looked liked he'd been dragged here against his will. It'll probably never make the paper anyway."

It did. It made the paper the following Thursday. However, it did not appear, as promised in the local village events section. It was on the front page.

Anne was delighted. When the men came in for their lunch, she had the paper propped up on the milk jug.

"Look!" she said, her face brightly excited. "Look at our famous Finn all over the front page!"

Tom picked up the paper. The entire width of the front page had the headline 'The Man Who Knows Everything'. Below that were a few lines about the village quiz and a note to turn to page three. Tom peeled back the page. There, taking up a much smaller part of the page, the story continued below a photograph of a smiling Mr Bryce, his arm on the shoulder of a stiff looking Finn, his face adorned with a wan grin. He showed it to the younger man who grimaced at the photograph.

"I look like someone who's just been shot at and missed," sighed Finn.

"You look handsome," grinned Anne. "Did you read what they said about you?" Finn folded the paper so he didn't have to look back at himself and read.

"Alderman Bryce recently revealed to The Chronicle, a man with an extraordinary ability to recall any fact. 'I saw in him something maybe others had missed,' said Mr Bryce."

"What? *He* saw in him...?" stuttered Tom, almost gagging on the tea he had poured himself.

"Never mind that Tom," interrupted Anne. "Read on Finn."

Finn looked up - Anne's face brooked no argument.

"I am humbled to say that he has personally confided in me his amazing abilities. What I can say though is that he is a man probably unique in the United Kingdom, a scientific marvel who can relate the details of life and history as good as any encyclopaedia and with perfect recall. A living wonder living among us."

"You see," enthused the excited woman. "Our Finn, a living wonder!"

"I told him his date of birth and now I'm a marvel?" dismissed Finn. "I don't remember the personal *tête a tête* either."

"Hardly just his date of birth," mumbled Tom. He cast a studied eye at Finn and then waved a hoary hand. "Aye, but is that man ever full of himself!"

"He's a politician," smiled Finn. "I suppose that's what they do. I wish he had left me out of it though."

Tom gave a dismissive grumble. "Well, anyhows, as like as not that's him has got his bit o' publicity and you'll hear no more about it. Ye'll hardly complain son."

Anne frowned. Finn gave a laugh. "No, I prefer a quiet life Mr McCracken. That's just about as much as I ever want to appear in a newspaper!"

Anne took the paper and set it on a stool beside the Aga stove. "Well, I thought it was lovely," she pouted, "and all this gabbling is letting the stew get cold. So hurry up so I can get you out of my kitchen to clean up the mess of your boots."

A few days later, in Broadcasting House in Belfast, the host for 'Hello Ulster' on BBC Radio Northern Ireland was reading out items from that week's local papers on his show. It was a thing he did every Friday morning in his two-hour slot. Picking out humorous or odd little items, he would intersperse them through the music and highlight the local idiosyncrasies of which the Irish were so happy to mock in themselves.

"And finally, here's one from the Newtownards Chronicle," he said in his usual boisterous and cheerful manner. "Apparently there is a farmer down in the Low Country who is able to answer any question you ask him. It seems he can recite any fact, even knowing the intimate details of people he has never met." He shared a knowing laugh into the microphone. "I hope he never meets my wife!"

It would have stopped there, except that the station was being listened to that very morning by the editor of the national paper, *The Daily Telegraph*, who was in Belfast on business. For some reason the article piqued his interest and he noted the name of the local paper and filed it away in his inquisitively voluminous head.

A week or so later it resurfaced in the newspapers man's head. The paper was running a weekly feature on British eccentrics, savants and rare cases of people with unique abilities. He tasked a young reporter to find out more and pass it on to the journalist heading the feature. A few calls soon connected the reporter to the farm outside Donaghadee. Tom had called into the house from the yard to turn off the oven as instructed by Anne before she had headed out to post a letter. Finn was four fields away repairing fencing. He was disgruntled to learn he was talking to an English reporter.

"We've already said all there is tae say," he grunted, "and Finn's busy just now."

"I understand," replied the reporter, "We were fairly sure it was a rather exaggerated report anyway. How could anyone know everything? My sincere apologies for wasting your time." He might have been fairly new to the game, but the young and ambitious man already had an astute grasp of character.

"Says who that anybody exaggerated anything? Finn has a brain a boy like you would die for son."

"It's been claimed there is no question he cannot answer?" probed the reporter. Without giving time for the farmer to reply, he suddenly diverted into other questions. He kept this up for a minute or two before returning to the subject of Finn's prodigious knowledge. By now Tom was struggling to keep up.

"Our Finn knows the words in every book as was ever writ," he boasted in reply. "A genius is what he is, and him as can't hardly say who he is." He had no sooner said it than he remembered he had promised never to pass that information on to another living soul. He and the reverend Boyd had been chatting one afternoon and some details the minister had discussed Tom had said he would keep to himself.

"He doesn't know who he is? Isn't he your son, Mr...?"

"McCracken," filled in Tom, regretting he was still hearing himself speak. "No, look, this stuff... it's sort of private information son." He felt hemmed in and looked for a way out. "I've cattle tae feed and I have tae go. Thank you for calling, but I'd just as soon ye didn't feel the need tae call again, if you don't mind me saying."

"Not at all sir," replied the reassuring voice from the other end of the phone. "Thank you for your time. Again, apologies for taking so much of it. Goodbye sir."

With that the line returned to a dialling tone and Tom replaced the handset on the cradle. He was annoyed, irritated and at odds with himself. He looked at the phone and suddenly remembered the oven. Dashing into the kitchen he quickly turned off the dial and tried to dismiss the faint smell of burning. He was sure whatever it was Anne was cooking would be fine. And so too would the conversation with the newspaper man. He hadn't said that much, and hadn't he got rid of him? Anyway, it wasn't like he had said anything much, certainly nothing that was going to do any harm.

That night, Finn lay on his back on top of his bed. It was late, though he had yet to get out of his work clothes. The lights of the house had been extinguished, the McCrackens having retired earlier to bed. He lay, thinking through the events that had brought him to where he was. As he repeated his internal cross-examinations of the meagre memories that had flashed across his mind, a movement suddenly caught the corner of his eye. Outside, in the darkness a shadow moved in the shed opposite his room. A light from within spilled its yellow fingers weakly though a partly open door onto the stony yard. Again, Finn caught something move. Who would be there at this time of night? He slid off the bed, silently opened the outer door and slipped out across the stillness of the yard. Opening the door, he stepped in and was suddenly side on to Tom McCracken who was working at something on a wall of the byre. The man gave a start as he turned and saw the figure suddenly appear to his right.

"Finn!" he exclaimed wide eyed. "I thought ye had gone tae bed son."

"Sorry Mr McCracken, I mean, Tom - I saw movement and thought I'd better check it out."

"Aye," said Tom, "Tis a good lad y'are." He studied Finn for a moment as if weighing something up in his mind and then back at the wall where there appeared to be some kind of opening.

"Son, ye're a man as can be trusted – I know y'are." He paused again, as if engaging in some kind of internal debate. Evidently a side was taken as he looked up and spoke again.

"I'm going tae tell ye a thing only three people knows. Myself, Anne and..." he faltered for a moment and Finn knew he had been about to add his deceased son. "Aye, aye... well, three as did know. Three again when I tell ye my boy." He turned to the wall. "This here is an old chimney flue."

Finn saw now that the rectangular hole in the wall was set within a steel frame, the opening about the size of a shoebox.

"This shed would hae been the original cottage on the farm before the big house was built and it was turned into a shed for the calves," explained Tom. "The chimney and fireplace is long gone but when I unscrew these old bolts and remove the iron front, the old soot box is still here and it makes a powerful place tae hide things."

Finn nodded, understanding that Tom was sharing a trust.

"I hae no faith in them banks. Oh, we use them, but this is where Anne and I hide what is our own business, should times ever get bad as times do in this life." He reached in and to the left.

"Look here son." Finn moved up to the side of the older man and looked into the exposed soot box.

"Not a body would think o' lookin' in a place like this. In to the back here and round the corner is where I keep this box. Anne and I keep some money in here. Our own money that is no' depending on some man at the bank to allow us tae withdraw. Money; and a couple of other wee things that are safer out here and Anne doesn't need to come across, the way things are." Without opening the tin rectangular box, he placed it back in its hidey-hole.

"So, should anything happen, you know, tae Anne or me, well - now you know son." He sighed as he replaced the rusty nuts. "And I'm glad ye know. Tis a weight of my mind, having someone else a man can trust."

Finishing the job, he turned and placed his big rough hands on Finn's shoulders. "Anne would give her life for ye Finn." He hesitated for a moment and then continued, "I might even myself, for what you've done for my lass." Suddenly, and without warning, he pulled Finn toward himself, flinging his strong arms around him and holding him tightly against his chest, bowing his head on Finn's shoulder.

Finn tenderly put an arm around the old man's back as he felt the farmer's chest heave with low, quiet sobs.

"I never knowed it could be so hard," he said in a broken voice. "My only son - my only son."

Chapter 13
Experiments

It was radioactive. Not dangerously so, but enough to cause Rogov and Anya sufficient concern to take precautions. Now clad in lead aprons, the two scientists were carrying out a series of non-destructive tests on the sample before them.

"I had thought it might be promethium," said Rogov without embellishment. Anya waited a moment before speaking.

"Which would explain the radioactivity," she added, considering his statement. "But you think now that it is not?"

"Natural Promethium is exceedingly scarce, though it can be synthesised by bombarding uranium-235 with thermal neutrons to produce promethium-147."

"Synthesised?"

"That we can be sure it is not, and if not, then not natural promethium either."

"Because of the structure?"

"Because of its structure, yes, and its strange reaction to ultra-violet light."

Which seems to point to crystalline origins?" suggested Anya.

"Yes... but, I wonder," said Rogov, rubbing a thick finger across his brow. "Have you heard of the Tenham meteorite?"

"New Zealand?" she tried.

"Australia. Western Queensland. Found in the late 1800's. Many people saw it fall and so fragments were recovered very soon afterwards. Chondritic meteorites are extremely rare and contain some of the oldest and most primitive materials of the universe. For the first time a mineral, later to be called Ringwoodite was detected in sufficient quantities to be adequately analysed. But you know this perhaps?"

Anya nodded. "Ringwoodite. Yes, I remember. Named after the

Australian scientist who found it?"

Rogov nodded approvingly. "From the presence of it in the meteorite, he posited that it was present in large quantities deep in the Earth's mantle."

"But never actually found any?"

Rogov nodded in affirmation. "I was part of a project team that studied the findings he had published in the scientific journals. His conjecture was that it formed at high temperatures and pressures of the Earth's mantle somewhere around 600km down."

"But this is from the 14km drill."

"I know," said Rogov. "Perhaps he was wrong."

"Perhaps it is not Ringwoodite," added Anya.

"Perhaps it is not," said Rogov, peering down the microscope. "But we have to start somewhere."

"I think," said Anya, her brow furrowed as she interrogated her own memory, "Ringwoodite is able to contain hydroxide ions within its structure?"

Rogov spared one of his rare smiles. "You play with me little sister Anya. You defer to me as one with greater knowledge when your own is no less."

Anya just perceptibly reddened. "I have much to learn. I know so little."

"The words of a true scientist. When we think we know what is to be known, we prove that we know nothing at all." He straightened. "Non-terrestrial mineralogy is a particular interest of mine," he explained, "but I have never seen Ringwoodite. That may still be the case, but whatever this sample of yours is, I do not think it is anything that has been seen by many people. Possibly not any."

Anya turned a scalpel in her hand. "And yet we do not inform anyone?" she questioned hesitantly.

Rogov slowly shook his head. "Not yet. No, not yet Anya Nevotslova." Again he gave her an enigmatic look that intimated he was withholding some unspoken information. "In the meantime, if it is polymorphic, and I think it is, then we test it for pyroxenes. Also, as you suggest, for hydroxide ions."

Days passed, the drill outside continued to bore relentlessly into the earth below as men, wrapped in layers of clothing that made them look like ponderous bears, moved heavily through the bitter, biting snows between the buildings. The light, when it broke through the gloom, was short lived and pallid while all the time the base's heavy trucks trundled continuously across the site and into the bleakness of the dark tundra beyond.

Chemeris finished his shift and returned to the accommodation block. He stamped the snow off his heavy boots and began the lengthy process of undressing in the changing foyer set off to one side of the air lock doors. Yashkin was not far behind and the door opened and closed again as he too entered and began to unzip and peel off his layers. He glanced down the corridor before continuing to free himself from his heavy parka and leggings.

"I tell you, this is not about oil, abiotic or otherwise," he hissed at Chemeris. "I said it before and now I am sure. Perhaps if we were at a more favourable site, but whatever we are drilling for, oil is not it. What we are doing is not even rational."

Chemeris shrugged. "Since when did the motherland ever require her sons to be rational Yashkin? She craves the obedience, the *love* of her children. Does she ever explain her intentions? Does the great *babushka* even know herself?" He set his boots into the drying racks. "We are Russian, my dear comrade Yashkin. Doing as we are told is what we do. And I for one will do it as long as it puts food on my table and a roof over my head. *Matushka Rossiya* is an old woman who has lived so long she has forgotten who she is. Meanwhile she broods over us like a big hen. Our mother, our lover and our inquisitress all at the same time."

"So Rogov knows something," whispered the Mongolian. He shot another look along the corridor. "He said as much. We need to talk about this with him."

"Good luck with that," grinned Chemeris. "He has found his long lost daughter and has forgotten about his old friends, Chemeris and Yashkin."

"Rogov has no friends," dismissed Yashkin, "only lesser beings in a world where he walks alone and high above all others."

Chemeris stopped lacing his track shoes and looked at his friend.

"That is hard. He is not the life and soul of the party my friend, but neither is he as cold as you make him sound."

Yashkin conceded with a tilt of his head. "Well, perhaps not, but I would still like to talk with him."

"And we shall. Tonight we will open a bottle of vodka together and celebrate my birthday. Just like old times."

"It is your birthday?" Yashkin looked puzzled.

"Not exactly today – in a few months' time, but we can still celebrate it. Why waste a whole birthday on one little day each year eh?" He slapped his colleague on the back and with a loud chuckle, led him down the corridor.

Rogov was in the canteen at teatime. Among all the noise of men laughing and chatting, Chemeris and Yashkin found him sitting on his own at a table near a Plexiglas window. He was reading one of several books he had spread out on the table around his meal.

"And where is your *malenkaya doch* tonight old father?" quipped Chemeris as the two of them sat down opposite Rogov.

"Little daughter?" repeated Rogov with a slight frown on his normally impassive face.

"Anya," said Chemeris smiling. "You take her from us so you can adopt her and take her home to your dacha. You know it is usual to find a wife before the child. But then, why would Rogov do the usual when the unusual is his usual, eh?" He laughed at his own joke. Rogov evidently did not share the humour.

"She is a highly talented scientist with highly interesting ideas. Perhaps you should spend more time with her yourself."

"What is this you are reading?" interrupted Yashkin, who was flicking through the books in front of him. "Steven Jacobsen? I did not know we were taking our education from the Americans now?"

"American, British, German, Russian. Nationality means nothing. Facts care nothing for the mere geographic location of birth."

"These are recent papers," said Chemeris who had picked up a journal. "I did not know we could get these."

"If a man does not visit the project library, how would that man know what he could, or could not get?"

Chemeris merely shrugged at the reply and replaced the journal.

"I... *we* would like to speak with you Rogov," said Yashkin, holding him in a fixed stare.

Rogov nodded slowly, understanding the meaning. "Yes, but not here."

"Then where? In our room?"

"No," said Rogov. "Not there. At the end of tomorrow's shift. Before coming back to the accommodation bock, meet me, both of you, in the machine store behind the truck garage." His firm instruction elicited no defection.

"Well, that will be comfortable," sighed Chemeris with a mock shiver.

"No, that will be *safe*," said Rogov almost under his breath, his lips barely moving.

Yashkin and Chemeris looked at one another, then back at Rogov. Chemeris gave a nod and grinned. Rogov was not smiling.

Gasparov sat in his office, one hand resting on the telephone sitting on his desk. The index finger on the other hand tapped the table as he thought. He had a simple view of humanity. The world consisted of three types of people. Those he despised, those he respected and those who he had yet to commit to one of the first two categories. The first category was to all intents and purposes the general population of the planet. Gasparov scorned his own species and held it responsible as a single entity for all that was twisted and bitter within his own soul. The second category was small, possibly inhabited by less than a dozen or so people. At the top of that list was Viktor Karmonov.

Most people imagined Karmonov was simply the head of the State Technical University in Arkhangelsk. That, of course, was Karmonov's intention and only a very few, only a trusted inner circle knew anything other than that. He had woven a Machiavellian lace of untraceable threads around himself, and like a spider lurking in shadows, he watched and waited. Waited while others spent themselves in the endless rise and collapse of ambition and the relentless wrestle for power. Karmonov had patiently waited, gently steering events with an almost undetectable hand. A hand latent in the invisible darkness but quietly controlling the unconscious assistance of others. Every nation had men like Karmonov. Men who were the real power behind the façade of governments.

Conscious of Karmonov's latency, if not the detail of power he had access to, Gasparov meanwhile sat silent as his desk. One hand turned a pen through his thin fingers, the other still poised on the telephone, his deliberation still circling around the old commissar. The orders were clear. He was to contact Arkhangelsk if any particular interest was generated in the samples provided to the Nevotslova girl. She had very quickly settled into her post and seemed interested in whatever she was set to do. It was clear from his observation of her behaviour that she had some misplaced faith in an imagined virtue of single-minded attention to scientific objectivity. He smirked to himself. It was another of those constructs that separated those who wielded power from those whose destiny was to be the tool of those in possession of it. However, did the girl's interest invoke a requirement to contact Arkhangelsk? What about the stocky scientist with the thin blonde hair - Rogov? Had he taken an interest in the younger girl? He was old enough to be her father. Or was he interested in her work? Was that reason enough to bother Karmonov? He had said "any particular interest." He ruminated for a few moments more. He slowly removed his hand from the telephone. No, Karmonov was not a man to risk irritating. His displeasure was too hazardous to countenance bending towards himself.

Nonetheless, Ilyich Gasparov pondered the reasons for Karmonov's seeming preoccupation with the young scientist's observations. The daughter of Doktor Boris Nevotslov. Gasparov's thin cold lips twisted in a smile like a tortured piece of wire stretched below his long, angular nose. Karmonov had not flinched when decisions needed made about the Nevotslov issue. Nevotslov; another fool who believed in virtue - in humanity. Gasparov's lips twisted into an even more convoluted scar. Humanity was a torrid swelter of rage and lies, of deceit and double-crossing. Sheep like Nevotslov were prey for the strong, for the men who were prepared to take the horns of the altar and challenge the silent gods. Men like Karmonov. Men who imposed their will by brute strength of character. Men who could be respected. That camp was the side Gasparov had every intention of being on when it was all over. He rose from his desk, sliding his pen into his jacket pocket. He would wait until he had evidence of something more substantial to report; information that would elicit Karmonov's approval, the approval that was the drug Gasparov unconsciously craved most of all.

Rogov pondered the journal in his hand. He had gone to the room he shared with Chemeris and Yashkin. They did not follow and he suspected they had retired to the bar. Vodka was cheap at the station and even though it was rationed to prevent unproductive drunkenness, doubtless they would not return until they had received the full of their daily allocation. He swung his legs off the bed and headed out of the room. He had been thinking about something he had read in one of the journals and he could not get it out of his head. He grabbed his coat, making sure the keys to the mineralogy lab were in the pocket.

Chapter 14
The Depth of a Mountain

Finn was dreaming again. This time he knew he was dreaming. Like a man watching events in the street through a cafe window, people passing, talking, cars stopping at lights, doors opening and closing in the shops opposite, he was able to watch, but not affect the clamour of images.

People were speaking. People talking among themselves. They were dressed as if they might be doctors, medical staff and they were in animated conversation. The dream informed him he was their subject, but frustratingly, he could not make out what is was that was being said. Not that the words were indistinct - he could hear the words, but was unable to understand them. The observer Finn recognised that it was because the language was not English. Like before, the words were harsh - Slavic. Russian. Finn the participant tried to raise himself off the bed but found he was held down by straps. His head hurt and when he raised a hand to his temple he found wires attached, tubes running into parts of his body.

The light hurt his eyes, he tried to get the attention of the doctors, but there were arguing now and seemed not to notice the movements of the patient on the bed. Outside of the dreamer, Finn saw that the room was a cabin. The cabin of a vessel. There were no portholes, no external light and there was very little room. Finn the dreamer lay on a thin mattress, held by straps that seemed more to stabilise, than arrest him. He was hooked up to a couple of intravenous drips with monitors in the wall, recording lines and numbers. Giving up his struggle, Finn tried to get the attention of the men, and they were all men, at the side of the bed. One suddenly seemed to notice the movement and turned to stare at Finn. Finn in the dream said something and then recoiled as the man's mouth fell open as his eyes widened. Finn shouted something, a long sentence, and another of the gowned men instantly grabbed a knife. The third man, the tallest of the three, immediately placed himself between the knife wielder and Finn while grabbing the other's wrist. There was a brief struggle and the knife fell to the metal floor. The defender and the shocked man pushed the would-be attacker out of the cabin door and shut it.

"You are safe," said the taller man in strongly accented English. He hesitated for a moment before speaking again. "Do you know where you are?"

Oversersjant Ari Bjørnson listened as Jon Lander explained his aim.

"I need to get *into* the mountain Ari." he said, his eye fixed on the big Norwegian. He did not immediately reply but instead looked steadily at the Englishman for a few moments.

"I still think you should wait Jon," he said finally, "or until the Commander authorises its reopening. Getting in is not going to be easy."

"Nothing that is worth doing is, Ari," replied Lander. "And in any case time is not a luxury I have much of the way things are."

Ari slowly nodded. "If that is your judgement and you are determined to go, then we should prepare for going," he said, shifting in his seat and making to stand.

Lander shook his head and motioned with his hand for Bjørnson to keep his seat. "Sorry Ari, I need you here to cover for me. You go missing and I may as well wave a red flag."

Ari went to protest, but after a moment's thought, appeared to see the logic. Jon was sure he would. On Jan Mayen everyone was accounted for. In one of humanity's most remote and desolate outposts, solitariness was, of all things, the hardest thing to attain. Being unseen in a group of a thousand was hard to avoid, accomplishing the same amongst less than thirty souls was a feat almost impossible to achieve.

Bjørnson spread his hands across his thighs. "I can cover you for five or six hours Jon, no more."

"I need at least ten."

"Ten hours? How can I...?"

"If I don't show before that," interrupted Lander, "you can let Jensen in on it."

The bigger man shook his head resignedly. "I'll try, but if I have to wait that long Jensen will have worked it out himself. He's a sharp man."
Lander bounced a hard knuckle off the other's knee. "And if he's as good a man as you say he is, nothing lost, eh?"

There were no dogs on Jan Mayen, and had there been, they probably would not have heard the man who passed into the darkness from the lights at Olonkinbyen a few hours later. Lander made his way silently through the shadows of the prefabricated buildings until he was on the trail leading north toward Beerenburg. He was dressed almost entirely in black, a black woollen hat on his head and a small dark rucksack tightly strapped to his back. He passed the 5000ft long airfield; *Janmayenfield*, keeping well to one side of its open ground. There were no stars and no light from the moon as above, unseen clouds closeted the tundra in a silent darkness. He knew he could only risk a light when he was well away from the station but the trail at this point was just visible below his feet. The mountain lay north about nine or ten miles distant, but on the way he would pass a huddle of huts called The Metten where Ari had assured him an all weather quad lay garaged and ready for use in emergencies. To get there he had three or four miles to cover and with every minute counting, the man militarily fit through years of hard physical discipline, settled into a steady trot, a pace he could keep up for hours. He estimated he would be at the quad in thirty minutes or so. From there the quad would have him on the mountain half an hour after that.
The silence, thick and oppressive seemed almost offended at his passing, offering nothing but a sullen hush. No birds, no sound of lap of waves on the beach two hundred metres away in the murky blackness. The night, still and aloof and used to no other company than its own for generations, was disturbed by the quiet patter of Lander's rhythmic footfall. It protested the presence of one who dared to invade its remote kingdom by drawing in all the closer, quietening every breath taken in the cold air. A kingdom of cold dark night.
Lander's pale green light played on the hard grasses and rocky outcrops, giving just enough illumination to check his compass and keep on the rising track. Ari had given him the directions by which he could find the way to the Metten. When he came upon the huts thirty-three minutes after leaving Olonkinbeyen, he almost ran into the wall

of the nearest hut, so dark was the night. Naturally nothing was locked. There were only three small huts, two of which were attached, the smaller proving to be the small garage where the quad lay silent in the darkness. It started easily enough, and closing the wooden doors behind him, he was soon rolling over the rough ground, headed north toward the invisible brooding volcano. Even the burble of the exhaust seemed muted in the tangible blackness of the night. He didn't risk using the lights of the machine, continuing on using his green filtered head torch. It made for slower progress than he would have liked, but soon he was he climbing up the slopes of the Beerenburg, following the thin track that Ari had pointed out on a map some hours earlier. Forty-five minutes after leaving the small huts at the Metten, the track came to an end and he was at the mine entrance bored into the mountain.

The top of the volcano was still a couple of hundred feet higher, but it was from this point that a cavern ran down into the heart of Beerenburg and where the Norwegian scientists had up to lately been quietly conducting their experiments. There were no bushes or shrubs where he could conceal the quad, instead he took it a hundred metres off the track and parked it up next to a large boulder. Back at the cave entrance, a steel door blocked the way, but Lander started work with small tools from his rucksack and within ten minutes had the chain removed from the gateway. Slipping inside the doors, he pulled them behind himself and turned to face the descending cavern floor. The cave was bored at a five-degree angle, running down toward the heart of the mountain. Underneath his feet, the floor was compacted gravel and the sound of his footsteps was amplified by the hard smooth walls six feet either side of him. Heavy cables ran down both walls, he had seen a louvered door near the entrance which he guessed had facilitated a generator or electrical switch room. He had only progressed a hundred feet or so when he stopped and made a decision. He turned and jogged back to the entrance. He really had no idea how far he was going to have to go down the cave tunnel and though it would compromise his stealth, the quad would allow him to proceed much faster.

If his footsteps had been disconcertingly loud, the engine of the quad became a growling roar in the confines of the narrow passageway. He reconciled himself with the knowledge that the entrance had been sealed, it was half two in the morning, the site was out of bounds and no one, save Ari had any inkling he was here.

Nonetheless, his eyes darted around in the shadows beyond the quad's lights as he sped down the descending path. In a few minutes he came to a large space where the cave opened out into darkness concealing the size of the void he had entered. He stopped the quad, silenced the motor and got off. The lights from the quad lit up what Lander could now see was a vertical shaft, and he had stopped on a wide ledge overlooking it. It was rough and unmachined, though the rock seemed smooth, glassy almost. Suddenly it dawned on him what it was he was looking at. He had come to the central vent of the old volcano. In the brief that Jonas Smyth had given back on the MI5 building on the banks of the Thames, he had been told that the volcano was for all practical purposes, extinct. When he had queried what 'practical purposes' meant, Smyth had admitted that it had last erupted in 1970, depositing another one and a half square miles of land on Mayen during the four weeks it lasted. Reassuring him that it was quiet now, he added, somewhat dismissively, Jon had thought, that there had also been eruptions in 1973 and 1985, but they were much smaller affairs. He had at the time, privately reflected on the fact that people who are not planning to be anywhere near a hazard, are quite content in confidently assuring its complete safety to those whom they have directed towards it.

The ledge, which was about ten feet wide, ran like a shelf around the inside circumference of the main vent. Directing the quad onto the ledge, Lander turned left and followed the cables which still ran along the solid rock. About a third of the way along the cables disappeared into a dark opening on his left. As he followed, the lights from the quad illuminated the darkness, revealing another, secondary vent. Instead of rising as a secondary escape for volcanic magma might be expected to do, this tunnel, smaller than the first, led down and away from the central shaft. The floor gave signs of regular traffic, and Lander, reassured by finding things as he had been briefed thus far, settled down for what he was beginning to think, could yet be a considerable distance.

The tunnel led inexorably downwards. It turned and snaked in parts, in other sections it straightened and just kept on going down. After descending for almost half an hour, the way was suddenly truncated by a divide. How deep he was at this point he could only guess, but there was a marked rise in temperature and he briefly wondered if it was something he ought to have expected or not. Of the branch ahead, one way continued downwards, another to the left ran a few feet to a set of heavy blue steel doors. Getting off the quad, Lander found they were not locked. He stepped in and turned on his head torch. He appeared to be a huge room – so huge that his bright torch only partially illuminated the void. He turned to the wall beside himself and found a bank of switches. Flicking them on, he blinked as banks of powerful overhead lights dismissed the darkness in a swathe of cold hard light. His eyes involuntarily widened in incredulity. It was no natural cavern, but a room as big as a football pitch and packed floor to ceiling with machines; screens, keyboards, computers and blinking lights. It was some kind of massive laboratory. Lander looked around himself. He did not know what equipment volcanologists required to study their subject, but he was sure the enormous amount of technology before him was vastly more than the discipline should have commanded.

Morning broke over Jan Mayen in its usual demeanour – cold, desultory and begrudging. Life around the base at Olonkin City slowly came to terms with facing another gravel-grey few hours of resentful daylight as men yawned and spilled out of their beds onto cold concrete floors.

Breakfast was a shared event in the mess hall and as is the wont of military men all over the world, the soldiers unintentionally congregated together, the civilian staff drifting in later to yawn their way over their *frokost* - breakfasts of open sandwiches filled with meat cuts, spreads and cheese.

As Ari made his way over to the serving hatch to fill his coffee cup, the Commander entered the canteen and stood behind him.

"*Got Morgen* Oversersjant," he said. "Where is your friend this morning?"

"Good morning sir," Ari replied casually. "I don't know," he added. "Still asleep I would say. He is still recovering from his ordeal. Being English he is probably waiting for the birds to sing before he rises."

"Ya. He will wait a while for a blackbird's song on Mayen," smiled Jensen. "You will sit with me for breakfast?"

"He seems to have recovered well, your friend?" asked the commander.

"Ya, he is doing very well sir."

"I have a question," asked Jensen, fixing an eye on his subordinate. He waited until Ari replied.

"Sir?"

"I do not think I have seen such resilience in a non military man - or at least, not that kind of resilience."

It was not a question and Bjørnson simply nodded in agreement. He expected the question was still to come.

"And his bearing; it has a certain, *confidence* to it, do you not think?"

"I suppose that might come being a man used to being on his own, pitting himself against the elements."

"Of course," agreed Jensen, "but men like him are not so many. I have found that there are generally two paths on which such a man is found. The first is a rarely trodden one, the rare exception, the one in a million man born wholly at ease in his own skin by some unique fluke in his genes. The other is... well, the other is found on the path a man like you has trodden, Oversersjant."

"Like me?"

"A man who has been made who he is by military training, action in the field and, shall we say, certain *specialist* instruction?"

Bjørnson looked back into the face of the base commander and wondered just what he knew. He suspected all he had said was simply guesswork and conjecture, possibly even just casual speculation, but if so, it was all danger-close to the target.

Suddenly the commander leaned forward and looked directly into Ari's face. For a moment he said nothing and hesitated as if he were weighing some important decision in his head.

"He should be careful, Oversersjant," he said eventually. His voice was quiet, almost a whisper so that Ari had to listen carefully to catch each word. There were others in the canteen but there was no chance of the commander being overheard. Various men in the room were occupied in table conversations and to an observer, the commander and his junior officer were engaged in nothing different.

Bjørnson tried to comprehend what the meaning of the words were that had been whispered across the table. Was Jensen passing on a warning, or playing some game with him? He held the gaze of the other and struggled to find a suitable reply. A moment later the senior officer spoke again in the same conspiratorial tones.

"Do you know why we have a station on Jan Mayen, Bjørnson?"

"Well, sir... we maintain the LORAN-C... and the weather station, the scientists..."

Jensen interrupted with a flick of his hand. "What I am about to tell you I only tell you because I know who you are and why you are here." He moved slightly forward in his chair. "But now I will tell you why your country is here."

Chapter 15
Flight

Karmonov held the phone close to his lips. "Good. You know what to do. How you do it is of no interest to me. Inform me when it is completed."

He replaced the phone onto the cradle with careful precision. Nevotslov's intrigue had finally been hunted down. Karmonov had always known that it would. The West was no place for hiding anything. Time, he had always known, would bring the man to light. Time, and men placed in the right positions.

The critical phase of The Program had begun. It was imperative that any threat to it be eliminated. There could be no loose ends, no *unknowns* to endanger the next stages.

He thought back to those days after the arrest. It had taken a while to break Nevotslov. That he would finally succumb was not in doubt, but even Karmonov had been surprised at how long and to what degree of agony the fool had been prepared to endure. Truly, the human will was an impressive force. A pity that such a one had to choose to defy the inevitable. The human will was strong, but bodies were all the same – at some point the flesh would always collapse and cry out for release. The trick was to offer that oblivion and then withhold it. Keeping the man on the very precipice of death, the very worst kind of death. This was the secret entrance through the hardened walls of the will.

And once he had confessed? Karmonov's lip curled into a cruel twist. Then offer him hope of life but deliver instead a pointless, bitter end. But not too fast.

Finn opened his eyes. What had awakened him? Something had, of that he was sure. Without thinking why, he slid out of bed and quickly pulled on his trousers and a thick jumper. Pausing only to pull on his work boots, he made his way silently out into the shadows of the yard. A look at the night sky told him it was early in the morning – two or three o'clock. Something was not right. It was a moonless night, the only dim light coming from the single forty-watt bulb that was always left on in the milking parlour. In the dark winter nights, it gave an aiming point when going out to start the early morning milking. Instinctively he knew this time it was not simply Tom McCracken visiting his secret cache.

Finn had not turned on lights in his room before he left, using only the pale green illumination from his electric bedside clock to dress. Now in the yard, he pressed himself against a shadowed wall and listened. There was no sound except the occasional quiet rustle from the cowshed where some cows lay with their newborn calves. Though they were over twenty metres away and unseen, he could hear their steamy breaths in the stalls. Silently Finn slipped around the side of the house and crossed in the darkness toward the grain silo. From there he was able to slip around the rear of the cowshed and into a small patch of overgrown garden with some trees and bushes. Keeping low, he noiselessly made his way to the boundary hedge from where he could look back into the yard and have an overall view of the house. The lit window from the parlour was now out of his view, but its pallid light was just enough to give a faint and grainy illumination to the yard and house.

Silence. From here even the restless cattle could not be heard. He waited, hardly knowing why, yet certain that there was something amiss. An intent was at loose in the brooding stillness. A malevolence.

He watched, using the edges of his vision, knowing that there the eye's photoreceptors had much higher sensitivity to low light, albeit in grainy monochrome. Suddenly he thought he saw a movement to the far side of the house. He held his breath and concentrated his vision on the area where the movement had been. It was then that he smelt the gas.

Although the McCrackens had oil fired heating which was fed from a large oil container at the back of the house, there was a small LPG gas tank at the gable end which fuelled the gas fire in the front room. Anne McCracken liked an open fire, but when they had renovated their farmhouse some years previously and installed the oil heating, the open fire became redundant. As a compromise Tom had got a coal lookalike fire fitted which used the gas to power the flames in the hearth. Finn could only imagine the gas was escaping from that tank and the obvious thing would have been to make his way to it and turn off the valve.

That was precisely his intention, but just as he rose from his lair, he saw the definite shape of a person move up to the slightly ajar kitchen window and throw in an object. Frozen for a second, half crouching, half standing, his heart jumped as he saw that the object was on fire. Shaking himself out of his inactivity, he ran forward just as the windows of the farmhouse exploded outward in a massive fireball of blinding flame. Finn was thrown backward into the hedge where he lay stunned for a few seconds, his ears ringing with the blast of the explosion. Shaking himself, he struggled to his feet, re-orientated himself and stared aghast at the scene before him. Behind shattered glass, rooms were ablaze within the house. Suddenly the realisation that the McCrackens were in that burning house came like a kick to his stomach. Without a second's further thought, he leapt across the yard and plunged into the kitchen door which lay open and twisted on its hinges from the force of the explosion. As soon as he entered the burning parlour he could see that any progress that way was impossible, everything in the room was alight and the heat was absolutely unbearable. Their bedroom window! He could run out, around the house and get straight to Tom and Anne through their bedroom window! Running out into the yard he suddenly ran into something that struck him with such violence that he spun and collapsed onto the yard floor. A second later he heard what he somehow knew was the mechanical double-click of an automatic pistol being cocked. A shadowy arm thrust in his direction and took aim. Spinning on the ground, Finn rammed into the man's legs, causing him to fall forward even as the deafening report from the gun exploded in the violence of the struggle. Suddenly he was on top of Finn, strong arms grappling with his throat. Instinctively Finn rammed his knee into his assailant, catching him directly on his stomach, causing his grip to loosen briefly, but enough for Finn to grab and pull away the choking hands. There was a guttural grunt as his unknown assailant threw a fist at the young man. It connected painfully into his neck and Finn spun to get away. There was nowhere to run and suddenly he saw the still open door to his flat, light from the flames within spilling out into the yard two or three metres away. Without thinking, Finn threw himself into the burning room only to find the man, his features now visible from the flames, right behind him, the pistol pointed at his head.

"Die!" he spat.

"No!" yelled Finn as he ducked and swung his right fist with all of his might into the man's brutish face.

The man fell back, temporarily stunned. In that second Finn struck again and this time missed but connected with the man's arm, knocking the pistol flying back out of the open door.

He recovered and was on Finn immediately, muscled arms trying to wrap around his neck even as Finn could almost hear the killer's cold purposes screaming death into his mind.

But Finn was no weakling. He had worked hard on the farm. Hard work and good food had conditioned him into someone to be reckoned with and he had no intention of dying unknown at the hands of an unknown murderer. Reaching backward he managed to get a grip on the other's neck and, pulling his head into the rear of his own, snapped the back of his head into the face behind him. The man did not let go, but he could tell by his grunt that the blow had hurt. He repeated the action, jerking his head repeatedly back into the face behind which could not avoid the hits, held as it was by Finn's arm. It was too much, suddenly the choking grip loosened enough for a brief second. It was all he needed. Finn grabbed the man's hand and twisted back with all of his might. At the same time, he spun round, slamming the other hand into the big man's ribs with such ferocity that Finn was sure he must have caused damage. Still holding the man's wrist, Finn smashed his elbow into his face while at the same time spinning around the man so that now Finn was behind him, his own arm now in a choke hold around a muscled neck. The man was fumbling around his feet for something, and almost too late, Finn caught the glint of a cruel knife he had managed to pull from a boot. He slashed wildly, but connected with Finns' upper arm. Finn gasped as the knife tore through the flesh and he let go, leaping back to stand, his back to the open door facing the killer who got himself turned and made to lunge at Finn.

All during the fight, the apartment was blazing with fire, the flames having spread to engulfing almost the entire room. Just as the man poised to dive forward at Finn, there was a tremendous explosion as the butane gas cylinder powering the camping cooker which sat near the rear window suddenly exploded, blasting Finn out like a rag through the door into the stony yard. The entire annex was now a fully developed fire and by the time Finn got his senses together and struggled back again onto his feet, he saw with horror that the rest of the house too was a blazing inferno. Being a typical farmhouse, the rear door led into the yard. A second's glance told Finn there was no way that rear parlour door could be entered again. Flames were dancing out of the broken door and lapping two metres up the wall outside.

The front door, which faced the main garden and which was actually around the back of the working part of the house, was seldom, if ever used. Finn staggered as he tried to get around, having to push through an overgrown hedge that blocked the path at that side of the building. When he got there, he was shocked to see that the gas cylinder which fed Anne's gas fire had been ripped from its place and hurled through the window. The room inside was flaming as clearly the pressure release valve on the cylinder was operating, spewing gas into the inferno around it. He saw the cylinder suddenly expand as the heated steel failed and instinctively, Finn ducked. In that moment the second cylinder explosion of the night detonated within the building. As if in slow motion, Finn saw the roof lift at least a metre, collapse back onto the wall plates, and then crash on down into the conflagration that had been the home of Tom and Anne McCracken.

Finn watched dumbfounded, shock reeling through his mind, the sight before him an unbelievable violence to his every sense. As realisation crashed into his mind of the burning tragedy and his utter powerlessness to stop it all, he reeled with the horror of such pointless murder. Tears welled in his reddened eyes as he lay hopelessly in the wet grass of the orange flickered darkness. He was too late. He had not saved his friends. Their home had become their tomb.

How long he lay in the grass, his head in his hands, bleak and hopeless tears streaming down his face, his mind a disconnected convolution of competing emotions, he hardly knew. It was probably no more than five or ten minutes, but when he eventually collected himself, he made a painful circuit back to the yard side of the house. It was then he heard the sirens. Turning round, he looked over the fields to the roads beyond and saw the iridescent blue flashes of an emergency response coming his way. Clearly someone in distant farmhouses had seen the flames and alerted the Fire Service. As he turned again to look at the fiery ruin behind him, his foot stumbled on a metallic object. He stooped and lifting it up, looked at the automatic pistol in his hand. It was a Makarov 9x18 PB pistol, complete with a fitted suppressor.

Involuntarily he hooked his index finger around the magazine floor plate and disengaged the latch. The magazine easily slid into his hand. The copper metal jacketed bullets glinted in the light from the flames. Pressing it back into the grip, he immediately felt an irrational disgust with himself for knowing such detail at such a time. The lights were drawing closer, less than a mile away now. Further behind, more lights. Ambulance... police? He looked at the gun in his hand and back at the approaching lights. Before him three grotesquely burnt bodies would eventually be recovered. Multiple scenarios suggested themselves to his quickly thinking mind. Somehow he knew most of them were not good for him. He looked back at the house of two people who had become dear to him. He was overcome with an overpowering urge to flee. But he could not run, not from this scene. Not from this tragedy. People who had cared for him more than anyone he knew lay horrifically dead in their innocence metres from his sunken shoulders. *Innocence.* The word jarred in his mind. That was it. The innocent had suffered - been *murdered* because of some secret within himself. Others would die if he did not. *He* was the menace, the threat to the innocent. The sirens were loud now; he could hear the sound of the racing engines. He thought of the body of the unknown killer in his apartment. If he were not here, it would be identified as his. An unexpected memory of the kindly faced old farmer crossed his inner thoughts – the moments, so suddenly dear and precious now of his tender embrace in the night of his heart-broken sobs. He turned and looked at the cow shed across the yard. At the top of the lane he could see the fire engines sweep in off the road. Making a decision, he sprung into the shed and began unscrewing the four bolts off the soot box cover. As the sirens wailed into the yard, Finn moved to the back door of the shed, a box under his arm. He took one last look behind him, then turning silently into the darkness, the man who did not know who he was slipped into the flickering shadows and disappeared.

Chapter 16
Revelations

"This world as we know it has become critically dependent like no generation before it. Do you know on what that dependence lies, Oversersjant?"

Henrik Jensen was speaking, his voice barely audible over the hubbub of the room.

"Oil, I suppose," answered Ari Bjørnson as if it were an obvious answer. Jensen shook his head slowly.

"Nei, *information*. Specifically, information maintained within computer servers throughout the world. Massive amounts of information stored mainly on magnetic discs. Hundreds of thousands, if not millions of zettabytes of data. A figure so huge and so interconnected that it would be impossible to recover if lost. The total sum of the information age Ari. Think of it. Hospitals, transport, flight systems, universities, government, communication, military. The very operation of our cities and the capacity of agriculture to function and the systems to manage and control the hugely complex systems we have created to distribute food and power to huge populations. The loss of our web of information technology would drive civilisation back to the pre-industrial age."

Ari was listening, but he decided to act innocently unaware of any connection of his officer's disclosure concerning the island or their place on it.

"Sir, I appreciate your explanation in such hypothetical scenarios, but even if such an apocalyptic event were possible in a war – what would Jan Mayen have to do with it?"

"No one mentioned a war, Bjørnson, and this is not a hypothetical conjecture. I have told you of an actual event."

Ari felt the increasing tension as his officer drew closer to admitting the reality that was the purpose of Jan Mayen.

"An actual event? This has happened? But, I don't understand?"

"I am speaking of an event that will almost certainly take place in the near future. An event which the Norwegian and United Kingdom governments, alone among all others, are desperately trying to mitigate against. Together they have poured hundreds of millions of dollars, sequestered from secret military funding into this island. Into the Beerenburg."

"But sir," asked Ari, deciding to place more trust than he had originally intended in his commander, "What can research within a mountain achieve?"

"Are you familiar with the Carrington Event?"

Ari had certain information as to what truly lay within the deep confines of the mountain's fastness. Information so secret, he had been forbidden by the NIS to even reveal it to his friend Jon Lander. He knew about the colossal data systems installed and maintained by a tiny handful of men who were sworn to absolute secrecy as to its existence. But now the senior officer on Jan Mayen's weather station was disclosing to him information even he did not know. Jensen was a constant surprise. This *Carrington Event* was something of which Ari had not heard and his blank look was reply enough.

"I will tell you Oversersjant. And when I have told you, I think I will be ensuring that your friend knows." Ari gave an almost imperceptible nod of admission. Jensen continued. "But there will be more to this than computer resilience and I.T." Ari could not help his eyebrows make an involuntary and minute flicker. Jensen saw it. He paused and leaned so close that the two men were almost touching. "Johannsen found something else."

It was much later, over an hour or more that Ari still sat at the canteen table. Jensen had left and he remained, his mind churning over the new data, thinking, examining in his mind the implications of what Jensen had told him. He slowly and methodically began cross examining what he knew of each person on the island. Who they were, why they were here, what he had observed about their actions and behaviour after the recent events that had necessitated the arrival of the British agent. For the first time, Ari found himself considering the trustworthiness of his commander. Why would he share such detail with him? Yes, Jensen had clearly identified that his Oversersjant was more than he had claimed. Almost certainly he now knew he was a member of the Etterretningstjenesten. But it had still been a risk for him to share secret information. Had he been ordered to? By whom? The NIS, the British? He shook his head. No, that didn't work. Jensen was deeply concerned and needed someone to know. So, why not tell his superiors? What if Jensen was himself the killer? What if all along it was he who should have been in their crosshairs? He shook his head again. No, Jensen was more than concerned. He was afraid.

"So, where is your friend Ari?" It was Erik, one of the other soldiers on the base who called across the tables to Bjørnson. Ari was still digesting the information Jensen had so surreptitiously passed on that at first he did not hear the question.

"Hey, Ari, did the *Kommandør* tell you so many secrets that you won't talk to us now?" The table laughed and Ari suddenly dragged himself from his thoughts. The others had been playing cards and the game now over, had seen Bjørnson sitting on his own.

"Too good for us now," added Anders with an exaggerated sigh. "That's the trouble with officers, always thinking up secret plans to beast their men."

"You got that right you most reprehensible piece of uselessness that I ever saw draped in the cloth of Harald the fifth's uniform!" exclaimed Ari, lying back against his chair. He gave a wide grin and the rest laughed uproariously at the expense of Ari's sartorial remarks. He got up and joined the others at their table.

"So, what are you layabouts doing lounging about here anyway?"

"Nothing, as usual," replied one of the others, "I don't know why we get rest hours on this forsaken rock anyway. It's not like there's anything to do."

"Where's your friend?" asked Erik suddenly.

"My friend?"

"The Britisher. We were hoping he might show us some of his photos. Remind us what life is like out in the actual world."

"He must be in his room," said Ari dismissively. "He's hardly my friend just because I found him on a beach."

"And carried him here all on your own," added Erik. "He at least owes you something." The others murmured in agreement.

"Any one of you would have done the same thing. It was nothing so special."

"It was lucky you having been out there at just the right time," stated Anders. "Almost unbelievable."

Ari glanced with an affected lock of unconcern at his inquisitors. Were they just idle questions?

"Ya, well, I'm just a lucky guy. Maybe next time someone else runs ashore on this frozen rock, one of you will get to drag him across six or seven miles nearly breaking your back in the process. We'll see how lucky you feel then."

The men laughed at that, but Erik wasn't finished.

"I haven't seen him all day."

"Like I said, he must be in his room."

"He's not," Erik responded. "I knocked earlier. When he didn't answer I took a look in. His door wasn't locked. His bed was untouched."

"Just as well he wasn't there then eh? Invading a man's privacy."

"I told you. We wanted to see his photographs." Erik's eyes narrowed almost imperceptibly as Ari maintained his composure.

"He'll be around somewhere," said Ari with a wave of his hand. "You know these English. Eccentrics to a man."

"I thought you said he was Scottish," challenged Erik, cocking an eye at his officer.

At that moment the door to the canteen flew open. A couple of figures filled its frame.

"Flamin' right I am!" one exclaimed, standing erect and angry. "And the next man as calls me a Sassenach will hae me to deal with!"

It was Lander. Lars Guldberg stood behind him. Ari tried not to look shocked.

"And who was the Norsky poking about in my room?"

Erik suddenly looked like a child caught with his hand in the biscuit tin. "We wanted to invite you to join us," he protested weakly, "and show us some of your photographs."

"Aye, well," said Lander, his tone suddenly modifying. "I was back at the wreckage beach. Looking for any more of my stuff that might have washed up. I had a case of old photographs. Family and that. Lars here helped me look. No use though. I suppose I'll just have to accept they're all gone now."

Lars and Lander made their way over to the table where the others sat and pulled over two chairs.

"I found this though," Lars said, holding up a long white spike. It was a narwhal's tusk. Being among fellow Norwegians, he did not feel the need to identify what it was.

"It was a lucky beach my friend," he added, slapping Lander on his back. "It is why you were saved. You should have this for a good luck charm. Though it might also be my payment for driving you back to the base."

"Keep it Lars, though if anyone else feels the need to go rummaging about in my room, I may ask for it back to stick it somewhere no' intended for such things to go!"

Again the men laughed and a few beers later, the banter warmed as men, as men will do, mocked one another and made fun of every small idiosyncrasy they could find. By the time they were finished the night was late into the small hours and one by one each made his way back to quarters.

Ari was lying on his back on his cot when the door gave a quiet knock. The door opened and Jon slipped in.

Ari threw his feet off the bed as Lander sat on a chair beside the bedside table.

"Thought you might still be awake," he whispered. "Any trouble while I was away?"

"Not trouble. But, hey, what happened with you? How come Lars found you at the west beach? Where's the quad?"

"The quad's fine, it's back in its hut at the Metten."

"I've been lying here trying to work out how you and Lars met at night where you did. Now maybe you can shed a bit of light on that?"

"I wasn't lying when I said I went to look for something. I buried my Glock there, and I crossed over to check up on it after having left off the quad."

Ari nodded. Of course Lander would have come armed. That he felt he needed to check up on it was however, significant.

"Lars was there just before me. I saw the lights of the jeep arriving as I was crossing the island. I headed north, then came back down the shore and made to have stumbled across him."

"So what was Lars doing?"

"He said he was heading up to pick up samples from the *Sørbreen* glacier that he had left from earlier drillings. Climate change studies he's been doing."

"I suppose," nodded Ari. "He didn't think it odd to see you wandering about like a lost guillemot?"

"If he did, he didn't mention it. He gave me a hand to look for the photographs that didn't exist."

Lander grinned at Bjørnson and the big Norwegian shook his head.

"You need to me more careful my English friend. Lady luck has a way of running out on a man when he least expects it. One day a narwhal's tusk, the next ..." he made a slashing motion across his neck.

Jon turned around to check the door and moved closer on his chair to Ari.

"More to the point, do you know what is buried in that mountain?"

Ari did and took the time to explain to the Englishman what Jensen had told him the night before.

"Do you know the real purpose of the Norwegian interest in Jan Mayen?" he began.

"If it has something to do with an array of computers greater than any installation I thought possible, then I'm listening Ari. I'm thinking you are going to tell me it has little to do with the study of the weather."

As he awaited the reply, Lander tried to read his colleague's eyes, guessing he was about to be made sensible to information of a highly classified nature.

"Are you familiar with the Carrington Event?"

Lander's blank look was reply enough.

"Oh, the weather station work is real enough, but it hardly merits much of a military presence. There's the LORAN-C of course but that's hardly a state secret. I'm not supposed to know, and apart from Jensen and his small party of specialist scientists, ostensibly meteorologists – probably less than a couple of dozen human beings on the planet know what Norway is future proofing against."

"Future proofing?" Lander was fascinated, but aware that overtly zealous curiosity in the field of covert operations was one way of finding out nothing. Ari was his friend, but he was a Norwegian first, loyal to his country and the consummate professional of the *Etterretningstjenesten*.

"I know little enough about it and I'm no scientist, but it seems your country and ours have been working on a project to protect vital governmental I.T. and critical digital information from a catastrophic event - the Carrington Event. I knew about the facility; I hadn't known about the doomsday scenario."

Jon Lander was suddenly aware that there were things in his London briefing that he had not been told. Possibly things of which he ought to have had knowledge. Nonetheless a display of absolute ignorance did not occur to him as being the most intelligent response.

"Doomsday scenario?" he queried.

"Some kind of electrical disturbance caused by the sun years ago, " explained Ari "Jensen told me that scientists believe that we are bound to have one hit the earth sometime in the future, and if so, it will probably fry the world's computers. Only the UK and Norway are seriously preparing for it by replicating our nations' data systems deep underground, protected by miles of rock from a cosmic cataclysmic event."

"That explains part of what I found Ari," but not all." He thought for a moment, processing the new information and allying it to what he had seen. Suddenly he turned his head. "Why did Jensen tell you this now – unless he suspects you already knew some of it?" He paused for a moment before continuing. "Does Jensen know you are NIS?"

"Yes, I'm fairly certain he has worked that out."

"Can we trust him?"

"I think so... yes, I think he is safe."

"Have you seen the installation yourself?"

"No," said Ari, shaking his head, "I knew it was there, I knew it had something to do with massive data resilience, but it was Jensen who told me about the rationale for its existence. Why would someone resort to murder over it though? Something there does not ring true."

Lander mulled over the details Bjørnson had told him. London had not fully briefed him, but he knew that Security Services had given him a single mission and they tended to pass on only what the operative needed to know that was specific to that goal. They would have known he would have discovered the installation in the course of his investigations and probably withdrew from leading him down a false alleyway. They may well have had a point.

"You know that it goes deep, very deep?"

"Jensen said over a mile."

"Deeper Ari. The shaft leads to the data room but continues beyond and down. When I left the installation I followed it on down until I began to think I might not have the fuel to return. Deep below the data chamber is another, not as large, but fitted with what I can only imagine is some kind of acoustic detection equipment."

"Acoustic?" queried Bjørnson. "You think in connection with vulcan studies?"

"I don't know, but I found this."

It was a white lab jacket. Blood-stained, a clear bullet hole through the left breast.

"At point-blank range," added Ari, taking the jacket from Lander. "Burn marks on the cotton at the entrance point."

"And I found this too." Lander produced from the backpack from which he had brought the coat, a small spiral-bound jotter. "My Norwegian isn't quite up to deciphering this scribble," he said, "it seems to concern audio recordings."

Ari began reading the spidery writing. He read for a few minutes before looking up.

"Where did you find this?"

"I only found it by chance. I had fumbled my torch and as I stooped to pick it up, the light glinted off the notebook's spiral end. It was below a set of filing drawers. It appeared to have been hidden there."

Ari tapped the page of the jotter. "Reading this, it has nothing to do with the data resilience programme. I don't even think it is concerned with the volcano," he added. "There is a lot of detail on audio levels and frequencies, but here, listen to this. The page is noted the 13th of September. *We have installed the microphone into the bores. At this depth the sounds are unmistakeable. No one doubts it now.'* They seem to have been investigating some noise they found unusual."

"Not wanting to tell anyone their job, but I'd have thought deep underground vibrations would be wholly consistent with deep earth tremors under a sleeping volcano."

"Ya, but listen to this. *'The same repeated metallic noises lasting several hours. Definitely deep below us but oddly pulsing at regular intervals. Johannsen is convinced it is human in origin, but that is impossible.'"*

The two men looked up from the notebook. It was a startling statement. The team of scientists had detected noises that so interested, or even alarmed them, that they had temporarily suspended their key purposes to investigate them. That they had gone to the trouble of drilling bores into which they had suspended acoustic microphones, underlined their concerns.

"Jensen must have known about this," Jon said with sudden realisation. "He was in overall charge of the installation. He must have facilitated their deviation into exploring deeper." He paused in thought. "Ari, Henrik Jensen is either complicit in the murders, or he is in great danger!"

Chapter 17
Deathly Cold

Anya was working at the sample when Rogov entered her lab.

"You should not leave your door open," said Rogov as he shut it behind himself. Anya went to speak, but Rogov was already speaking again as he drew up beside her.

"Have you seen this article?" he said, presenting the journal. Any looked at it and shook her head.

"But this is in English."

"Yes, it is *The Scientific American*. The library at the station is unusually current in scientific journals."

"Unusually?"

"We are in Kola, one of the most inaccessible places in the world, and in receipt of international journals within a couple of weeks of their publication. I think that is not usual, though I am not complaining. And look at this." He pointed to an article on the pages of the journal.

"My English is not so good," confessed Anya, "I speak a little, but it would take me time to read this."

Rogov sat down on a stool at the lab table and pointed to a small photo of a man in a white lab coat at the top left of the page.

"This man, Jacobson - from an American University in a place called Evanston, Illinois - this is his peer-review. He claims that a reservoir of water three times the volume of all the oceans on earth has been discovered beneath the Earth's surface."

Anya's eyebrows raised in surprise. "What?"

"Let me read you this," continued Rogov. He pointed to a paragraph on the small print and began to read.

"The evidence is clear. Water has actually been hidden in Ringwoodite in the earth's mantle, some 700 kilometres down."

Anya gasped. "Ringwoodite!" She lifted a sample of the rock she and Rogov had been examining from the lab table beside her. "So, you are thinking...?

"*Nyet.* I simply find this highly intriguing. This man points out that most modern geology presents the current hypothesis that Earth's water originated from comets that have struck the planet in eons past, but he claims his team's discovery strongly points to the suggestion that the oceans in fact have gradually made their way up from the interior of primitive Earth."

Anya pushed a strand of hair away from her face and leaned back against the table. "Is this simple sensationalism from some American seeking fame do you think?"

"I do not think so," said Rogov slowly shaking his head. I have read this man before. He is the author many scholarly publications and is well respected within the scientific community. He used over 2000 seismometers to study seismic returns generated by hundreds of earthquakes over several years. As the waves transferred throughout Earth's interior, including the core, he states that his team used a computer model demonstrating that the only way these results make sense is if they have travelled through many kilometres of water."

"But this cannot be right, can it?" queried Anya, who found the article as perplexing as her fellow scientist.

"I am not sure," said Rogov, "but he measured the speed of the waves at different depths and distinguished by that which types of rocks the waves were passing through. Jacobson actually grew synthetic Ringwoodite in his lab to test his hypothesis by exerting extreme pressure and temperature identical to those 700 kilometres down."

"But 700 kilometres? The article makes it sound as if samples were recovered from that depth. That would be impossible!"

"Perhaps not," mused Rogov. "It could be the Americans have been able to recover the rock from deep volcanic eruptions. They have been studying the pyroclastic flows from the Mount St Helen's eruption in 1980 now for many years. Perhaps this is related."

"Could it be," began Anya, "could it be that our particular sample, if it is Ringwoodite, or something blended with Ringwoodite, has been forced up through the crust where we have been able to recover it in the Uralmash rig?"

"It could be. Just why it should react as it does with ultra-violet-light is beyond my science, but we need to decide soon if we reveal our findings to Gasparov."

"But you had said..."

"I know," Rogov interrupted, "but if we defer much longer and inform him later, it will bring undoubted repercussions as to why he was not informed immediately. If we decide to withhold our discovery altogether – we might be fooling ourselves if we think we are fooling him. I would not be surprised if he already suspects there is something we are not telling him. In that case, I would not limit the extent to which he would be prepared to go to make an example of a recalcitrant scientist or two."

"So, what do you suggest?"

"That you inform him you have found a core-sample which you are having trouble identifying. Ask him if you can consult externally."

"He will ask to see it," replied Anya.

"And when he does, you should show him a sample. He will almost certainly ask for it."

Anya's face fell in an expression of deflation. The discovery had excited her and the thought of no longer being able to work on it was a serious disappointment to her.

"But give him this," said Rogov with the merest hint of a smile. "It should take him off the scent for a while."

Anya took a whitish piece of material from Rogov's hand. It was a small sliver of glinting blue-white material, less than two centimetres in length, and flaky in texture.

"What is it? asked Anya.

"I thought it was ignimbrite - not uncommon to find after a volcanic event. I wondered at that since it came from some of the deep core samples. I've been playing about with it for a while. It only occurred to me what it actually was some days ago."

"Igneous by the look of it," Anya said, looking closer. "What's the glint in it?"

"Ah, yes, that's what had me scratching my head. When we extracted the drill, the very odd time I found this clinging to the tip. We are so deep now that our projections of the expected temperatures are collapsing like so much guesswork. Instead of the expected 100 °C, we are finding temperatures of over 300 °C. At this depth the drill bit can no longer work and the diamond detaches and is forced by the immense pressure behind it into the Boron shaft behind. This is the material formed from the sludge, compressed, heated and forming this layering. The glint is diamond dust. It will give Gasparov something to report back on and a few days without him breathing down our necks."

After Rogov had left, explaining he had an appointment to keep, it occurred to Anya that her fellow scientist had revealed some presumptions about the Kola director. For some reason Gasparov had an interest in her work and what she might come across in her examinations. Rogov seemed to know something about that and was making considerable efforts to conceal her discovery from him. So, what might Gasparov be looking for, and if it was related to the Ringwoodite-like mineral, why would Rogov want to keep it from him? She pondered her own reaction when Gasparov had come in to her lab. She had hidden it from his view without knowing why - and now she wondered at that.

Chemeris had agreed to meet Yashkin at the cold-weather changing lobby just inside the airlock. Fifteen minutes had passed and he began to doubt himself. Rogov had said to meet them at the machine store behind the truck garage. He and Yashkin had then agreed to meet here first and go out in the elements together – it was always safer to travel in pairs in an environment that had a single-minded intent on killing a man. Yashkin had left the bar to speak to someone and had promised to meet him here fifteen minutes ago. Or was it at the truck garage with Rogov? Vodka had a way of making things hard to concentrate on and he had had enough to blur his memory of the arrangements.
Ten minutes later he peered out through the Plexiglas into the swirling darkness.
"*Tipichnyy*! he exclaimed under his breath. "Now I'm going to have to traipse out there on my own. Why couldn't he just have waited?"
Donning the heavy fur-lined winter kit and boots took a few minutes. In that time he'd hoped Yashkin would have appeared. It was a pity he hadn't, Chemeris grinned to himself. He'd put together some good old fashioned Russian swear words into sentences that would have melted the snow all the way across to the truck shed. Still, he could pass them on once he saw the Mongolian midget stamping his feet in the cold beside the freezing corrugated tin.

Stepping outside, the freezing wind violently whipped the breath from his lungs. It was something that always came as a shock, the sheer severity of the temperature drop on setting out from the accommodation block. Chemeris gripped the guide rope firmly with his gloved hand and made his way across the snow swept ground, glad that he had double clipped the straps across the neck of his fur-lined hood. Reaching the metal doors of the drill facilities, he heaved them open and plunged inside, slamming them shut behind him. It was no warmer in the large working buildings, but at least he was out of the wind. The truck garage was through the maintenance shed and out across a second yard. The drill rig was a separate facility further out again to the left of that. As he gripped the line that led across the second yard, he heard a noise and stopped. Ahead in the darkness, he caught the lights of a truck faintly flickering in the swirling snow a couple of hundred metres to the north. It struck him as unusual, but not enough for him to contemplate why a vehicle would be out this late. The rear of the truck shed was hidden from the main accommodation block, not only because it was behind the maintenance shed, but also due to it facing into the tundra, away from all the other buildings. Whatever Rogov had so say, he had chosen a spot where they had no prospect of being seen by anyone in any other part of the complex. Arriving at the agreed spot, Chemeris gave a sigh. So much for being late, neither of his colleagues was here yet. He stamped his boots in the cold. He would give them five minutes. He thought back to the warmth of the bar and the vodka that he knew he probably drank too much of. *Like every other Russian*, he grinned to himself.

Whether it was the cold, or the effects of the vodka wearing off, for the first time Chemeris began to wonder at Rogov's behaviour of late. Never one to engage in casual conversation, he had all the same, been more circumspect, less willing to say anything of particular interest. He remembered the time Yashkin had, out of frustration declared that he had been going to quiz Gasparov. Rogov's reaction had startled them both at the time – in a manner completely out of character. Chemeris shrugged. Oh well, if this secret rendezvous had anything to do with that, all the better. Yashkin might thrive on cloak and dagger conspiracies, Chemeris just wanted an easy life. He shivered. It occurred to him that Rogov was a precise man; he would have been here if this was the right place to be. He thought hard. It was tonight he had asked to meet, wasn't it? Behind the truck shed? As much as for something to do rather than stand like an idiot in the dark, Chemeris took a few steps out toward one of the gravel tracks. The place was criss-crossed with stone and gravel roadways. In the winter everywhere was rock solid, but in the brief summer months, the tundra could become a quagmire and so stone roads allowed the machinery and vehicles to go about their business without churning through seas of mud and mire. He stamped his way out and back again to the steel wall of the shed. He waited a minute and repeated the journey. It was as he glanced up the track on his second walk out that he saw something dark lying on the roadway perhaps 80 metres distant. He peered through the drift in the darkness and then took a few more steps closer, trying to define what lay in the middle of the track.

Rogov, on leaving Anya, had made his way to the cold weather changing room. On the way he had to pass through the recreation area with the bar and games machines. It was there that he saw Gasparov. Others sat around in small groups; Mikael Averin, Sergei Liminov, a half dozen others.

Gasparov was sitting by himself at a small table and looked directly at Rogov as he entered the room. Putting his hand up, he beckoned Rogov to his table. Knowing that such a gesture was always a summons rather than a request, Rogov nodded and joined him at his table. Without being asked, he sat down. Standing would have intimated he had somewhere else to be and it was not a line of thought he had any interest in Gasparov considering.

"You are going somewhere comrade Rogov?" asked Ilyich Gasparov. He peered down the length of his narrow nose at the mineralogist as if sighting a rifle on an unsuspecting deer.

Rogov gave his head a nonchalant shake. "Just coming to see if anyone was here. Today is my rest day." A delay with Gasparov would interfere with the rendezvous with Yashkin and Chemeris, but he could not risk showing anxiety in any way.

"Perhaps you were looking for your pet metallurgist?" questioned the wiry project head. "There seems to be a certain - shall we say - *fondness* in that direction?" He gave what might have been a smirk, but it left his mouth and crossed the table as an unpleasant leering sneer.

"If you are referring to Anya Nevotslova comrade Gasparov, no, I was not looking for her. In fact, I was speaking to her a few minutes ago and she appeared well. She would be honoured at your concern."

Gasparov gave a dismissive swipe in the air with his hand. "I care nothing, but I cannot pretend not to be surprised at you comrade. You are not a young man."

"I did not know that an older man cannot admire those younger than himself comrade."

"That depends on what you mean by admire." Gasparov's look disgusted Rogov. It was almost pornographic in intent.

"I can help you there then. Indeed, I am *fond*, as you say - as I would be of any young scientist showing such enthusiasm and intelligence. I have always believed such attributes should be encouraged for Mother Russia, and in that respect, I am fond of her, and *admire* her motivation." He returned Gasparov's direct stare. "Very like her father in many respects, you do not think?"

Gasparov folded his arms and sat back in his chair.

"I had forgotten you were acquainted with Boris Nevotslov," Gasparov lied. He sat forward slightly. "I hope she is not like him in his choice of friends."

Rogov knew that a conversation with Gasparov was always a game of chess. In all of his time at Kola, he had played the vacillating amateur, playing defensive moves in response to Gasparov's attacks. A challenge to the fortress of Gasparov's self-assurance was not a risk Rogov had so far taken. Now he weighed the moment and decided to advance a tentative attack himself.

"*Doktor* Nevotslov had many friends comrade. I believe Viktor Karmonov was one of them."

A knight had been brought into play. Rogov waited to see how Gasparov would respond.

Gasparov's expression did not change. He stared implacably into the face of the scientist facing him.

"*Friend* is a strong word Rogov. It infers an equality of thought." He unfolded his arms. "Comrade Karmonov has few peers. Fewer still who share his insight."

Gasparov's scorn was a tangible presence in the room. Fools like Rogov knew nothing. Infants dipping their toes at the edge of the shore and thinking thereby that they had explored oceans. Puppets unaware of their strings.

Rogov nodded slowly and moved his knight back to safety.

"Forgive me comrade. It was too casual a remark. Perhaps I can offer my chief a drink?"

Gasparov pushed back his chair and rose from the table. He did not grace Rogov's offer with a reply. "This project is cursed by a lack of capability from its personnel. We all have our place, our part to play; that I must manage with such meagre resources is mine." He turned to leave and then paused. "I hope that you are not ignorant of yours." With that, he turned and left the room.

Rogov waited at his table. That Gasparov could unexpectedly return was a possibility he could not ignore. As he waited he pondered what he had learned. It was a risk to have come so close to sparring with the man, but he had thought the risk worth the reward. It was clear that Gasparov had an interest in Anya that vindicated his warning to her. He had also revealed a regard for Karmonov that indicated something beyond the expected deference to rank.

Determining after a couple of minutes that Gasparov was unlikely to return to the recreation hall, Rogov made to cross the room to the changing room. Suddenly the door burst open and Chemeris appeared in the far doorway, his eyes wide in distress, steam rising from his clothes. He was carrying a man on his back.

"Help me!" he exclaimed before collapsing onto the floor.

Chapter 18
Voice from the Grave.

"The tragedy at McCracken's farm three nights ago has deeply affected us all. The loss of three people - magnified by such awful circumstances... it is hard to accept."

Alastair Boyd, the minister at the Presbyterian Church was speaking on the Sunday morning following the fire at the McCracken's house. He was finding it difficult to read the words of his own sermon as his eyes kept welling up, blurring the notes on the lectern before him. He looked up and instead addressed the silent congregation without aid of written words.

"We talk of terms like broken-hearted," he began, "but I suppose that until this week many of us never really knew the depth to which such brokenness could take us. I speak for myself, and I know many, many others here, feel the same. Words seem so inadequate, so ill equipped to express the sadness that crushes our hearts like a dead weight; pitiless, merciless."

He stopped and looked into the bleak faces before him. No smiles, no blithe and happy expressions returned. All was forlorn and grey, like gazing on a landscape of ashen burned out homes. Before him were faces drawn in shades of hopelessness, an entire community grieving and the minister knew that they saw in his face a reflection of their own.

"For any who have somehow missed the terrible news, a tragic fire at the McCracken's in the early hours of Wednesday morning has taken the lives of Tom and Anne and their farmhand, Finn. The funeral has been delayed until Tuesday morning as fire investigators have spent some time in determining the cause. I have been in contact with the Fire Service and it would appear that there was a gas explosion. The fire spread rapidly and none of our friends had time to escape the building."

Heads were bowed as he recited what information he knew. There were a few achingly strained sighs and quiet tears, but apart from that, the church was deadly silent.

"We are a Christian community and as such we believe in a hope beyond the heartache that so suddenly invades our lives," said the minister with some determined doggedness in his voice. "If we have invested all of our hope, all of our expectations in this passing, painful world, we are not a community of faith. Remember the Apostle Paul's words to the little church in Corinth. *'If only for this life we have hope in Christ, we are to be pitied more than all men.'* This has been a bitter blow, especially when this couple, who had so recently lost an only son, had begun to live again, have hope again with the arrival of their new farmhand. Finn had brought a new light into Anne's eyes and the return of a smile to Tom's face which for so long had been a vacant stare, so long absent. But I know from personal conversations with Tom and Anne that their ultimate hope lay in their solid faith in God. Tom told me, shortly after their son so tragically lost his life in the accident, that they did not blame God. In fact, knowing that God Himself knew what it was to have a Son die, helped them trust Him all the more. Every night the two of them would read the little verse at the top of their stairs before going to bed. It was 1st Peter 5:7. *'Casting all your cares on Him, for He careth for you.'*"

Alastair looked around his silent congregation. They looked back with a hunger for comfort and reassurance. He spread his hands across the lectern.

"It is my intention to do as they had learned through bitter experience. I urge you to do the same. Take your burdened hearts and give them to the One Who carries our burdens. Cast your care on Him and He has promised that He will care for us all. We could explore and scrutinise why such things happen, have an intellectual exercise into pain and suffering, why God allows such tragedy, and perhaps someday we will consider such things. Today is not that day. Today we grieve. Today we weep. Today we cast our cares on Him."

Alastair Boyd spoke for a few more minutes, but he had the wisdom to know that enough had been said. They sang a final hymn together and then closed in prayer. Afterward, standing at the door he spoke to each of his congregation as they filed out. It was solemn, none of the usual good-natured chat and remarks that passed between the pastor and his parishioners, but there was a reality to the handshakes and blessings. Some gave him a quiet hug, some held his hand and could hardly let go. Others whispered a quiet thanks and Alastair knew that somehow, quietly and unseen, God had been present that morning, and that had made all the difference.

The funeral passed on the Tuesday with similar solemnity. Tom and Anne were well regarded within the close-knit farming community and the deaths being so tragic, people wanted to show their sympathy. So many came that the church could not hold all the mourners. The overflow of neighbours and friends stood in the street with speakers relayed outside and it was as if the whole town had silently bowed its collective head, brought to a halt the normal passage of time and quietly grieved together.

Later that night, when all that had been said had been said and the world slowly resumed its turning, the minister and his wife sat silently at home, each quiet in their own thoughts. The girls were in bed and Ruth glanced at her husband. She had seen him officiate at many funerals but seldom had she seen him return so taciturn. Being the wife of a minister came with requirements for the role that had to be learned from experience. She knew that when her man had receded into windless seas of inward reflection, it was either the time to shake him out of it and fill his sails with everyday tittle-tattle or just to let him be. Ruth had the gift of an innate wisdom to sometimes allow him time to struggle with his thoughts until his mists of melancholy had been broken through and he would return having left a weight on some unseen shore.

It was in this shared silence that suddenly Alastair looked up.

"Did you hear something?"

Ruth had been reading and had not. "No, was it one of the children?"

"No, it was outside, I thought..." he stood up and peered into the darkness in the back yard.

"Probably the dog," suggested his wife.

"The dog's in the shed tonight," replied Alastair, "seemed a bit cold." He moved to the wall and turned out the lights to allow him a better view outside. "You didn't hear anything?"

Ruth shook her head and observed her husband. It wasn't like him to be so concerned about an unusual noise. The tragic circumstances of the McCracken fire were probably heightening his senses.

"Take a look if you want dear, but I'm sure it's nothing."

"Aye, I'll just take a quick look about, though I'm sure you're right honey."

He lifted a torch at the back door and flicked it on as he stepped into the cold darkness. Outside all was quiet and the only noise was the indistinct occasional flap of a loose corrugated sheet on the work shed that he was always forgetting to nail down. He swept the light across the yard – nothing. He was about to return to the house when he decided just to take a short walk to the road and back to clear his head. He turned the corner of the house and made his way along the painted silver path made by the light of his torch. The damp tarmac shone like black Moroccan leather as he wandered to the front gate. As he neared the roadway, lights rose over the brow of the hill to his far left. A car's headlights, the car invisible behind its illumination whistled by and then quickly faded into silence as the vehicle disappeared into the night. All was quiet again and he stood looking back at the manse, its outline only faintly discerned by light from the rear room falling onto the back yard beyond and out of view.

After standing for a few minutes, not really concentrating on any particular pattern of thought, he sighed and returned up the drive. Just as he had passed between the gable of the house and his car, the light from the torch caught something he hadn't noticed on the way down. It was set on the low wall that ran around a low flower border at the edge of the property. He walked over and saw a box sitting. An old wooden box. He looked at it for a moment and then looked around. He could have sworn it hadn't been there when he had swept the yard with his torch. It certainly hadn't been there during daylight.

"What that you have?" asked Ruth, looking up from her book as her husband returned into the room. He was carrying something under his arm and had a curious look on his face.

"It's not yours then?" he asked, setting it down into the low table beside him.

"Mine? No, I don't have an old wooden box, and it's not any of the girls' either. Where did you find that?"

"Sitting on the flower-bed wall beside the car. Funny, I didn't notice it until I came back from a wander to the front gate and back." He scratched an eyebrow and pulled on his reading glasses.

"How on earth did it get there? Is there anything in it?" his wife asked curiously. "It does look quite old."

"Let's see," replied Alastair, flipping back the latch and pushing back the lid on its hinges.

He looked in and was quiet for a moment. "Oh," he said.

Ruth got up and knelt beside her husband, looking at the contents revealed. "Papers? And, is that *money*?"

"A lot of money," nodded her husband. He lifted a thick wad of twenty pound notes. There was more below. "There must be several thousand pounds in here – and letters..." He paused as he opened some old brown envelopes. "Photographs," he exclaimed.

"But that's, that's..." stammered Ruth.

"The McCracken's boy," finished her husband. "And here is his birth certificate and..." he hesitated as he looked at another document, "...and this is his death certificate."

Ruth and Alastair looked at one another uncomprehendingly. There were other things. School reports, a postcard to his parents from a school trip, some childish drawings, a driving licence, personal records of a life cut short.

Alastair reverently set the items he had lifted back into the box. "Now is not the time to go through all this I think," he said slowly, tapping the lid lightly. "Maybe in the morning. I'll probably need to let the police know too now I think about it." He looked again and his wife's bewildered face, his own none the less so. "I don't understand this," he said, "I don't understand this at all."

Ruth was asleep as Alastair lay awake in bed beside her. His mind was a whirr of activity, conjectures and speculations contesting with one another for acceptance and none quite making the case for a persuasive resolution. Slipping out of bed, he silently padded down to the kitchen for a glass of water. The box sat beside his chair where he had left it, and although he had not intended to examine it again until the following morning, nonetheless the intrigue of the thing caused him to sit down and draw it up onto his knees. Opening it revealed again the money, the envelopes and the personal items. Leafing through the contents, he came across a book, in fact, a dog-eared, well used Gideon's Bible. He would have replaced it in the box with the assumption that it was Tom and Anne's son's bible, when his interest was piqued by a piece of paper sitting out proud from the leaves.

Opening the bible, he removed the note and placed the opened book upside-down on his lap. He unfolded the piece of paper; it revealed a few hand-written words.

'A.B. I can't put you in danger. Insp McGregor – Jack - I'm beginning to remember. I wish it wasn't like this. I'm sorry. F.' There was a gap and then another line had been added. *'I had to borrow some. He would have understood.'*

Alastair pondered the words. An odd note to place within a bible. He turned the bible over and as he reflected on what he had read, noticed where in the text the note had been placed. It was the book of Job, page five hundred and eighty-eight. A phrase was underlined in pencil. *'Yet in my flesh will I see God, I myself will see Him.'* He could feel the hairs rising on the back of his neck as he looked again at the bible which he now realised had an odd familiarity. He quickly returned to the note. *McGregor? Inspector McGregor?* He quickly lifted the Gideon's again and flicked through to the front leaf. *'Glasgow Royal Infirmary – please do not remove'* was printed in faded ink on its yellowed inner cover. He could feel the tension in his chest as he began to join the undeniable dots. A.B. Alastair Boyd? F. *Finn?* It was impossible. Just when he thought he had the dots drawn in the only order possible, he saw a picture that could not be, that simply could not be.

Chapter 19
New Shores

Finn looked out at the port of Saint Nazaire. As the primary French port on the Atlantic coast, everywhere was a hive of industry as ships of all sizes awaited their turn to disgorge their cargoes. Derricks lined the wharfs and jetties with long low ships attached as if by umbilical cord. Bulkier RoRo's were docked at terminals, lorries loading and unloading containers within which was stored the requirements of consumerism that drove the economy of the modern world. The shipyards of Chantiers de l'Atlantique spread their cranes above the horizon, ships in partial construction being birthed in the docks below. The freighter that Finn had boarded at Warrenpoint in Northern Ireland however was not docking anywhere near at hand. A cargo of timber and fertiliser was awaiting her at the port of Nantes some thirty miles inland along the Loire estuary. Below the decks of the coaster *Niamh*, a load of road salt lay destined for that port from where it was being transported north to Belgium by rail. It was a destination that suited Finn's plans, such as they were. Passing under the huge spans of the Saint Nazaire cabled-tied road bridge that linked the huge port to Saint Brevine le Pins on the southern side, Finn thought back to his last few days and his flight from the town where he had been so briefly happy. His heart literally ached as he remembered the couple who had unquestioningly accepted him as their own. A couple whose deaths were his responsibility. They should be alive, alive at their farm with their friends and memories while instead it was he who lived. He who lived without friends and with memories that offered nothing but bleak hopelessness. Tom and Anne were innocents treated like the guilty while he was the guilty without knowing why.

He fingered the passport in his hand. It was not his own, but the image of the young man staring back at him was a close resemblance. Not for the first time, it occurred to Finn that Tom and Anne had never spoken their son's name, but there it was on the passport before him. Andrew Tom McCracken. He looked into the face of the man whose identity he now carried, the young man whose death had brought such pain to the couple whose death brought so much pain to him. An inner voice derided him, mocked him and assured him that his pain was well deserved. He had known not to form close friendships, to avoid community, to stay away from relationships. Nonetheless he had allowed himself to find a place in his heart and thereby had signed the death warrants of the humble farmers from the small Irish town.

Boarding the freighter at Warrenpoint had seemed an obvious route of escape. Rather than the larger ports of Belfast or Larne, few questions were asked. He was a young man travelling to Europe and some of the ships bound for the continent had places for the few who were content to bunk up in rough cabins for a price that was cheap but useful enough to a skipper of a small coaster. He had taken over a thousand pounds from Tom's chest but he knew that he would not have objected. Several times Tom had had asked Finn about his personal finances, offering him a loan for a car for example. Finn had always politely refused. He would repay the sum of course; probably send it to the Presbyterian minister with whom he had left the remainder and the chest itself. Along with the money he had saved from his wages, he had enough to assist him in getting further along a road that was only dimly beginning to suggest itself below his feet.

He watched the terracotta roofs on the southern bank inch by the rusty hull of the Niamh. France – far from Glasgow, Penrith and Donaghadee. Far from friends, from James Kitching and his wife, far from Alastair Boyd, Ruth and their girls.

He had lain awake under the stars on the two nights he spent in the open on his journey to Warrenpoint. The man at the farm was an assassin, that much was clear. Finn had no doubt that he was the intended target; there was no mistaken identity on the part of the killer. He had gone over every detail of the night of the fire. Presumably the intention had been to murder them all as they lay asleep. His wakening had complicated matters. The Makarov pistol he had wrestled from his would-be killer was hidden in a rucksack he had bought in a charity shop in Newry. He had fled in the clothes he was wearing and he had bought more in the same shop. It was all cash and no receipts, leaving nothing of a paper trail for others to follow. Somehow he knew there would be others. It would take a day or two, but when no word returned to the agent's handlers, the alarm would be out. Agent. He considered the term he had used. The man had only spoken one or two words as they fought, but they were heavily accented. Latvian, Ukrainian, possibly Russian. Someone wanted him dead, someone far away. He considered his abnormal abilities. He knew so much, yet other areas were a mystery to him. He could tell what was in a book, recite endless facts, but in the absence of someone who had a particular personal knowledge, he was blind. He had been able to dictate Alastair Boyd's sermon, but only in the presence of Alastair Boyd. Languages were different. He had not experimented with how many languages he could speak, but he had no doubt that French was one of them.

And so it proved to be. Tied up at the Quai de Roche Maurice under the shadow of the Periphérique's uniquely steep climb over the Loire on the Pont de Chéviré, Finn thanked the skipper and made his way off onto the quay. Like its Irish counterpart, it was casual in the way of customs checking and Finn found it easy to bypass the block hut at the exit with its uniformed officials by simply finding a fence out of view and clambering over when traffic was not passing. In less than a mile he found himself at the Gare de Chantenay where he asked a ticket seller the times and prices to Nantes Central.
The railway official answered in rapid French, not looking up from his *Figaro*, clearly not detecting that Finn was anything other than a national. He also discovered where the nearest Crédit Agricole was and having determined it was two minutes from the station, thanked the man in perfectly accented Payes de la Loire French and set off on foot to acquire some Euros.
He had intended to get a local bus into the centre, but on leaving the bank and the day being so bright and warm, Finn decided to walk, a man at large, his only possessions on his back and pockets, the balmy French climate soothing some of the tension he carried like the accusing weight of an albatross carcass hung around his neck.

~~~~~~~~~~~~~~~~~

Jack McGregor arrived home and found his wife in the kitchen preparing dinner. He slipped behind her, wrapped his arms around her waist and kissed her neck.

"And how is my favourite wife today?" he joked.

"If you mean the only woman on this planet who could stick you for more than a week, then she's fine thank you!" she retorted, playfully tapping him on his head with a soupy spoon.

"That's called assault and battery in my day job," Jack grinned.

"Well then," Helen replied, turning around and poking him again with her spoon, "arrest me if you dare!"

As they sat at their tea, Jack set down his spoon, turned to his wife and looked serious. "I've been seconded to a case outside Glasgow," he explained. "I'm not sure how long for."

"Oh, where? Edinburgh?" It wasn't common, but her husband had been drafted in to larger investigations more than once before.

"Northern Ireland," he winced. "It's possibly got to do with a case I'd been trying to help Robert Jamieson with some time back."

Helen looked up from the table. "Oh, Northern Ireland?" She paused and then suddenly continued. "If it helps Doctor Jamieson we can't really refuse, can we dear?"

"Well, it's not the doctor who has seconded me obviously," explained Jack, "The Police Service of Northern Ireland is dealing with a missing persons case and it appears that it might be the man who awoke from the coma I mentioned a few months ago if you remember?"

"I do remember," she said. "Well if it's my Jack they need; I suppose I had better sign the permission forms then." She laughed and added, "Just as long as they don't need him too long!"

Jack McGregor had no idea how long it would take, but arrangements were soon set in place that he would fly each Sunday evening to Belfast's City airport and return to Glasgow on Thursday afternoons. Helen was accustomed to being the wife of a policeman with all the irregular hours that came along with that and was secretly happy that at least she would have him at home for three solid days a week. It was more than she usually saw of him.

The flight from Glasgow to Belfast was barely 35 minutes long. As pre-arranged, a plain clothes officer greeted him with a placard across which was written J.McG. Soon he was being whisked on a three-mile journey to PSNI Headquarters situated in a leafy suburb of East Belfast. The complex was heavily protected with high fences and electric gates. Although the guard at the gate was an unarmed civilian, he was wearing body armour, while through the thick glass of the sangar behind, a police officer watched carefully, the muzzle of a Heckler and Koch machine pistol visible and at the ready.

"Still a bit of trouble then?" he asked the officer in the front passenger seat. Jack was in the back.

"Not so much now thankfully," he replied. "Just the odd pipe bomb lobbed over the fences and that. There was a UVIED under a member's car less than a mile from here on Friday right enough. Bit of a Mickey Mouse contraption though – didn't function. Thankfully the dissidents aren't PIRA engineers."

"Prison officer got half a dozen shots rattled at his home in Armagh early this morning," added the driver.

"Intimidation probably," agreed the observer looking back at Jack. "Apart from that kind of thing, it's mostly normal policing now."

Inspector McGregor nodded and tried to look as if what he had just heard was not alarming. It was strange what was accepted as normal in Northern Ireland. Anywhere else in the U.K. and it would be front page news. He hadn't heard anything about an under vehicle I.E.D or shooting in the national news. Still, if the daily murders, atrocities and bombings of the past were no longer the norm, anything less was a huge improvement.

He was taken to the canteen where his minders left him with coffee and the assurance that a PSNI inspector would meet him soon.

"I'll just wait here then?"

"Aye, sorry we can't stay, we're needed at Hillsborough Castle in a couple of hours. We've a principal needs taken to the International. Take care." With that they shook Jack's hand with customary vigour and then were off with Jack left on his own at the round table in the pleasantly furnished police canteen. The tables were occupied by various individuals and Jack fell into his usual habit of labelling and classifying the occupants of the room. The uniform of the Northern Ireland police was strange to him, its dark bottle green so different from the generic blue of the mainland. It was however, incredibly smart and each uniform looked as if it had just been ironed and pressed that very morning. Shabby was a word that was nowhere to be seen and there was an almost militaristic sharpness to the uniformed officers in the room. Of those in plain clothes, he could tell that not all were police officers, some were clearly support staff. He smiled to himself. That was one thing was never changed. There was a bearing that betrayed a bobby no matter how much he or she tried to hide it – an authority, a stance, even a facial expression that said Police Officer Present.

He hadn't long to wait. It was probably less than six or seven minutes after arriving in the canteen that two plain clothes officers arrived, a man and a woman. They walked straight over to his table.

"Inspector McGregor?" said one, shooting out his hand and giving Jack a firm grip. "I'm Detective D.S. McKee - Kevin, this is DC Willis."

"Karen," interjected the second officer with a smile. "Glad to meet you."

"Jack," said the inspector, "You too. Sorry, I thought I was to wait for an Inspector Anderson?"

"He got called away to a shooting," explained the sergeant. "We'll get you sorted 'til he returns. Have you had a coffee?"

"Oh, yes, thanks, a shooting? Is that the prison officer?"

"Hmm? No, taxi driver in West Belfast. Probably dissidents."

As they led him out, Jack realised he had a few things to learn. He hoped he hadn't too much.

They took him to the local police training college where a three room apartment had been prepared for him. It was a simple enough accommodation, but since he imagined he would only be required for a week or two, it would suit him well. The tiny bedroom had room for a bed and nothing else, but the living area was large enough to have a study desk and computer along with an easy chair and settee. One end was the kitchen and the last room was the toilet and shower.

"The Common Terminal is on the PoliceNet," explained the sergeant. "If you ring the I.T. department on the number stuck on the monitor, they've been told to open a guest account for you. There's other information and so on in the green folder sitting on the study desk."

After a couple of minutes of chit chat, the two detectives excused themselves and left Jack to settle in and unpack. Seeing the opportunity, he took a quick shower and had just dressed when the door knocked. It was Inspector Anderson, his huge frame filling the doorway as Jack ushered him in.

"John, isn't it?" queried the Ulsterman.

"Jack will do just fine," replied his Scottish counterpart, shaking his hand. "Take a seat won't you."

"I'm Sam by the way," said the big man as he took the proffered chair next to the desk. He then quickly ran Jack through the details on his induction folder. That done, he leaned back and looked around.

"Sorry about the Spartan accommodation," he said. "Not quite the Europa, but with any luck you'll not need to spend too much time in here."

"I hope you don't imagine I'm here because I have any expertise lacking over here, I can assure you..." began Jack, who had been acutely aware of the sensitivities of being asked to assist another police service.

"Oh, none of that," dismissed the PSNI inspector, "I asked for you personally, I'm just pleased you could come." He looked at his watch. "But it's lunch time and there's a wee restaurant just five minutes from here. We can chat on the way."

Jack found the big man easy to get along with. He had a direct and straightforward manner, didn't cover his opinions in opaque language and clearly had a keen interest in detail. Like himself, he liked to get to the point and soon they were over the small talk and onto the case that had brought Jack from Glasgow.

They were sitting in a nook in the small restaurant, at the back beside the fire escape but with a clear view of the front door. Jack reckoned it was a table 9 out of 10 police officers would have chosen – out of sight, good for observation with a ready means of escape.

"So, you know our man Finn then?" asked the PSNI inspector.

"Finn?"

"The mystery man. I've arranged to meet someone he got quite close to." He looked at his watch. "In fact, we'll need to get on our way. You finished? I'll go and sort out the bill if you need the loo or anything."

They drove out of the city and as they went, Anderson explained what he so far knew.

"Scottish lad. Worked as a labourer for a local farmer for the last six months or so. A tragic fire in the farmhouse and he and the farmer and his wife all die. A week tomorrow. Then this minister..."

"Minister?"

"Aye, the Scots lad had made friends with the local church vicar. Anyway, he called two days ago with some new information. That's why I asked for you to come – we'll see what the vicar has to say."

Alastair Boyd was waiting for them as they drove up the drive. After introductions, they found themselves in a book-lined study with a tray of tea and scones. As they sipped their tea, Inspector Anderson opened the conversation.

"So Vicar, Reverend, ahm... you called us about some information you have on the fatal fire a few days ago?"

"Oh none of that *Reverend* business," smiled the Presbyterian. "Not Vicar either! That's C of I. Just Alastair will do fine."

"Yes, right, sorry. So, New information?"

Alastair explained about the night when he found the box. The two men opposite him nodded, both had their notebooks out.

"So you say this *Finn*, he mentioned my name?" asked Jack after a few minutes.

"Finn had lost his memory – said an Inspector McGregor in Glasgow had interviewed him in hospital. I took it from the way he told me that you were someone he trusted. He always had some idea that he had to be careful who he spoke with."

"Could be he had a criminal past to hide," interjected the big detective.

"I really don't think that was it," said Alastair, shaking his head.

"No," agreed Jack. "If Finn was the man I interviewed in Glasgow Royal, he had no idea of who he was or what past he had. Besides, he had lain in a hospital bed for eleven years."

Inspector Anderson's large eyebrows climbed up his forehead like two jumping caterpillars.

"Eleven years?"

"He awoke from a coma," explained Jack. "A friend of mine is a consultant there. "It could have been longer – they found him dumped at the hospital door one night – no injuries, no sign of having been in a fight, just a man without a past."

"You still have the box?" asked Sam. By way of reply Alastair reached under the study desk and brought out a stout wooden box.

"I have had it hidden in the attic until now," he explained.

Opening it demonstrated why.

"That's a lot of money," whistled the burley Irishman. "So, you think this was Finn's?"

"No, but I do think... well, see what *you* think." He lifted out some of the personal items and laid them on the table.

"These items obviously belonged to the McCracken's. They are all are connected with their son – he died of meningitis last year. He would have been around Finn's age."

Inspector McGregor took note. The minister probably did not know that Finn's age was an unknown entity.

"These other things, driving licence, school reports and so on. I'm guessing this is a repository the McCracken's had to store memorabilia that they couldn't part with. Everyone in the room knew that the explanation only partly fit. The large sum of money was hardly memorabilia.

Jack picked an item off the study table. He opened it idly and suddenly looked up at his host.

"This Bible is from Glasgow Royal!"

As Sam Anderson's caterpillars climbed back down into a puzzled furrow, Alastair Boyd simply nodded.

"I was coming to that. There's a piece of paper in it might interest you."

Jack found the folded sheet and read the first line of hand-written words.

'A.B. I can't put you in danger. Insp McGregor – Jack - I'm beginning to remember.

He tapped the paper lightly with his finger and looked up.

"Did he tell you he had awoken from a coma?"

"He had."

"Had he been anywhere else before he came to Donaghadee?"

"He had worked for Mrs McCracken's sister and her husband somewhere near Penrith in Cumbria. They'll be here for the funeral on Friday. We don't normally wait this long for committal in Northern Ireland, but the complications, you know."

"Aye," agreed Inspector Anderson. "Over here burials usually take place two or three days after death. I know it's longer in the mainland."

Jack nodded. A funeral three weeks after death in Scotland would not be unusual. Why the Irish were so quick to race to the graveyard was just another one of those idiosyncrasies that defined the differences that came with living in a land where history and tradition were current affairs.

"Mind you, it is not exactly proof of anything," pointed out Jack. "I'm taking a step here, but assuming that my missing patient and your Finn is one and the same person, are you inferring that he may still be alive?"

"Finn had a very peculiar ability Inspector," replied Alastair. "Part of that was what I can only conclude was an almost miraculous memory recall of things that did not pertain to his personal history. He was sitting in that very chair when he asked me to pick any page in a Bible, any line. It was a Bible he carried in his pocket, *that* Bible. The page that note is in is the page I turned to. The underlined verse is the one he recited when I asked him. It wasn't underlined then."

Jack opened the Bible again and showed the verse to his colleague.

"Finding the Bible in the box doesn't dictate that he is alive," considered Inspector Anderson. "That could have been put in there long before the fire."

"You said you heard a noise the night you found it?" asked Jack.

"It was the noise that took me outside. I had looked around the yard with a torch but saw nothing. The box was on the low wall when I came back up the drive. I'm almost certain it wasn't there on the way down. Someone put it there in the darkness while I was down at the road and slipped away, probably into the fields behind the house before I returned to the back door."

"What about these other words?" asked the big PSNI officer. "*I had to borrow some. He would have understood?*"

"He took some of the money?" suggested Alastair.

"Probably," agreed Jack. "The issue is; did he 'borrow' before or after the fire.

"We are forgetting one very inconvenient fact here," said his colleague. "Three bodies were recovered from the fire. The McCracken's and Finn whoever he is. Dead people generally don't go around leaving boxes on people's garden walls."

Chapter 20
The Hunted

Finn turned North and walked along the tree-lined Boulevard de la Liberté. The road was busy with innumerable Renaults, Peugeots and Citroens busily passing up and down the long boulevard. The French were avid supporters of their own car manufacturer's vehicles. Patriotism was a national pastime and among the countless little restaurants and cafés he saw no sign of American burger bars or fried chicken establishments. He walked for a couple of miles and feeling hungry, bought himself a pizza with frites in a takeaway café on the Boulevard de Anglais, continuing from there until he came to a leafy park away from the busy streets. Below an elegant poplar he found a bench and sat down to enjoy his food.

The simple basic act of eating allowed him to clear his mind and do nothing much more than observe the comings and goings of the people of Nantes. The park was green and the sun was warm on his face. Laughing children ran by, their happy chitter combining with the sound of the birds in the trees and the constant rumble of the city in the background.

He tried not to remember the night of the fire and the murders but there were so many demands for answers crying out in his mind that it was an impossible task. Then there were the dreams. Even had he been able to silence his internal disquiet, his dreams were outside of his control. There the events repeated themselves with a malevolence that had him often awaken in a cold sweat of anxiety and dread. He had had other dreams too. A dream of being taken to a cold and windy place. Laboratories, experiments and never-ending tests. Danger was the prime sensation of those dreams too. A constant sense that his very life hung on a thread whilst debates raged ceaselessly around him; debates which centred around his very existence. In those disputes, one name had managed to climb out of the fog of confusion and attach itself to his consciousness. *Nevotslov.* It was a name that had a hold on reality, uninvented, real and tangible. He had placed the name into a preserve in his mind that he had allotted to storing and processing information about his past. There it sat awaiting reinforcements. Painful though it was, he looked at his watch and resignedly committed himself to fifteen minutes of self interrogation. More facts were needed to add to the pathetically sparse few he had so far managed to capture.

A man had tried to kill him. A foreigner and a professional. Whatever he had done, whatever he knew, someone saw fit to have him killed. That much was fact. It explained his pathological reticence to telling anyone the little he knew. Of the few people he trusted two were dead because of him and had he not left immediately, possibly the Boyd family would have been next. The little he had shared with Alastair Boyd made him uneasy as it was and he almost wished he had just disappeared without leaving any clues at all. He slowly shook his head. No - that he had to leave the box in safe hands was a necessity. The money would probably go to The Kitchings and if that would be of any help to them it was one tiny piece of good he could have done in the sea of hurt in which he had left such a wake.

His would-be killer had carried a Russian pistol. Makarovs were plentifully available throughout Eastern Europe, but the commercially produced suppressor told him it originated from state, rather than criminal control. The language spoken in his dreams, the words of Nevotslov, if Nevotslov he was, were Russian and the connection seemed too much of a coincidence.

The gas tank that had been thrown into Tom and Anne's room couldn't have been done while they were alive. The noise would certainly have awoken them and given them the opportunity to escape. He thought again about the suppressor attached to the pistol in his rucksack. They had been shot in their sleep. It was probably the shots or the window breaking that had awoken him. The half minute between that and his exploration in the dark had saved his own life. Who would think to conduct an autopsy on three charred bodies, burned to death in a tragic accident? Only if the fire investigator determined that the deaths may have been the result of criminal activity would the post-mortem be undertaken by a forensic pathologist. Cause of death would be accepted as the blindingly obvious and it would be unlikely that the pathologist would even be informed. The gas cylinder was of a sort that was as commonly kept indoors as out and the complete conflagration of the house and its utter ruin would have avoided any suspicion in that area.

Finn's heart was heavy with the additional guilt of having taken the money that was not his. He needed to continually remind himself that he would return it once he had found some kind of financial means and that thought allayed his unease to some degree. The passport weighed less upon his conscience. It was worthless to anyone else and somehow it gave him a shared connection to two people who had so graciously opened their hearts to him.

One other thing bothered him and had stayed with him since its inception on the boat. Though he had left little enough of a trail, he was convinced that whoever wanted him dead was not finished yet. The sensation people sometimes have of being watched is almost always that, a mere sensation. Finn however had a sense of being followed that somehow stretched beyond mere imagination into an intuitive reality. He knew not how he knew, but if a man could feel hunted because there was indeed a hunter on his trail, then he was that man.

Finn finished his meal and walked over to a waste basket. Standing there he looked around. It was a beautiful park, Parc de Procé. He would walk along the banks of the Chézine river and think of other things. Enough pain for now. He would walk and do nothing other than observe a nation at work and play. The world would turn and life would go on. He could at least join it for a few hours.

The receptionist at the shipping company in Warrenpoint fumbled through her ledger. The men before here stood waiting doing nothing to calm her fluster.

"Do you not use computers in this place?" one of the men asked.

"Yes, but, we, you see, we only take a few passengers," she flushed. "Our licence allows for that you know." It was true, the company was quite old fashioned but having it pointed out by officialdom somehow put her off balance. She pushed her large round glasses back up her slender nose and continued flipping through the lined pages. The larger of the two uniformed Customs officers looked on, his face unreadable.

"The man we seek has a long history of smuggling," he said after a few awkward moments. "If you can provision a name, it will be helpful in assuring us that you have nothing to hide."

The receptionist turned the pages. He had an odd turn of phrase and an accent that spoke of foreign extraction. She was Polish herself; several of the staff employed by the company were, but she spoke English almost like a native and found his way of speaking unnatural. *The man we seek – provision.* It just seemed an odd way of saying they were looking for someone. Still, when Customs made inquiries it was always best to be as transparent as possible. Suddenly she found what she was looking for.

"Ah, here it is," she sighed. "*Niamh.*"

"That is his name?"

The receptionist looked up. "What? No, the ship was *The Niamh.* It was taking a cargo of road salt to Nantes and loading Hardwood and Nitrogen Fertiliser. I have the manifest and all the documentation here if you'd like to look over..."

"I am not interested in that," cut in the Customs man. "Did this ship carry any passengers?"

The receptionist gritted her teeth. There was officiousness and there was officiousness. This man was simply ignorant.

"I was just... yes, I have it here," she said, her voice sounding weak and small in her own ears. "One passenger. We checked his passport as regulations demand if the destination port is outside the Common Travel Area."

"Common Travel Area?"

"Yes, you know, The U.K or Southern Ireland. Anyway he was called Andrew McCracken."

The two officials glanced briefly at one another.

"You have a photocopy of this passport?"

"Well, no," the girl stammered, "I didn't think we..."

"No matter," dismissed the man abruptly. "Did you see him?"

She had. She had taken the payment for the passage personally and remembered a young handsome man with thick hair threatening curls but tamed by a short haircut. A man who looked as if he was used to being outdoors and who had been very polite with her. She felt almost as if she were betraying him by giving his details to these two brusque officials.

"Yes, he seemed pleasant enough. It is legal you know. We can take up to six passengers."

"Did he give you any idea where he was headed?"

"No," she replied simply. She had given enough information. She decided she wasn't about to go out of her way to help any more than she had to.

"You will give us the details of the disembarkation point and the name of the captain of this *Niamh*," demanded the officer. "That will be all." She scribbled out the requested information and handed over the note. Without another word the Customs men turned and left.

The interaction spoiled the rest of the receptionist's day. She wasn't used to men being so rude. The dockers and sailors were hardly gentlemen, but they didn't treat her like a dog. She narrowed her eyes and slammed shut her ledger. He was probably of German extraction. For a Pole that was reason enough to dislike him. One other thing bothered her about their conversation. How could a man working in Northern Ireland think Niamh was a man's name? Even odder, what Customs official could not know what The Common Travel Area was? Surely the long standing border arrangement between the U.K. and Ireland would be the fundamental, well understood fact defining their role?

Back in their car, the two men conversed in their native Russian. McCracken. It was too much of a coincidence. When the agent sent to eliminate the target had failed to return, the only plausible, however unlikely outcome, was that the third body found in the house belonged to the agent, rather than the subject. If so, and if he was as capable as they had been led to believe, then the subject now knew he was in danger. If he had been able to liquidate his assassin then this had just become a much more complicated assignment. Such a man would now redouble every effort to disappear. When that hypothesis had been recognised as the most likely, the checking of ports of exit had been the obvious next step. Airports, with their strict controls were dismissed. The busier ports at Larne and Belfast also would have been more difficult for him to leave by. The extrapolation was that a smaller, less monitored port would be sought and it seemed their hunch had proved correct.

"The *kulaks* had a son. If this is the man, he is probably using the passport of the dead son," said the taller man, stuffing the jacket and cap of HM Customs into a black bin bag.

"He will use it in France," agreed the other as he started the motor.

"So, we have a trail."

Finn had walked through the parks that joined one another through central Nantes. He had no particular destination, finding the ancient rhythm of simply putting one foot in front of another a therapy for his troubled thoughts. After some time he found himself facing the impressive walls of the Château des ducs de Bretagne. Standing with its imposing ramparts on what had once been the west bank of the Loire, it held its proud and haughty head above what was more or less the centre of the city. At this point the river ran under the roads and streets leaving the castle marooned from its underground course but surrounded by a brooding moat filled with cress-green water. He walked around the ancient fortifications, admiring the solid permanency of the ancient stonework when suddenly he stopped short before a banner hanging on the basalt walls. Within the fort was now housed a museum of the history of Nantes and the banner before him advertised a new historical attraction. A history of twentieth century naval warfare. It was the photograph that had suddenly arrested Finn. Below the text was a large black and white photograph of a German *Kriegsmarine* U-boat docked on the Loire during the Second World War. The picture suddenly threw open a hidden switch in Finn's mind with an almost visceral shock to his brain. He fell forward onto his knees on the grass and descended into a kind of semi-conscious trance, his head falling forward onto his chest.

His surroundings dimmed to almost black as he entered some kind of triggered hallucination. The darkness cleared as he saw the outline of a man appearing in his vision. Gradually the light increased until he could see his face looming over him. It was the man called Nevotslov – of that he was sure. He was speaking to him in Russian, but the Finn in the trance was surprised that he knew that and yet understood.

"*Gde ya?*" he heard his voice ask. He knew he had asked where he was, but the words he spoke were not English. Nevotslov turned and looked with surprise at another man in the room.

"You speak Russian?"

Finn had hardly been aware that he had. How, he did not know. He knew it was abnormal but neither could he explain it.

"*Da, nemnogo...* a little..." he replied, surprising himself. He reverted to English. "Do you speak English? I can understand you, but I cannot speak much."

The men looked at one another and slowly nodded.

"Da, we can speak English."

Finn continued. "Where am I? I was in a canoe, there was an explosion, or - the sea, it... where am I?"

"You are on board a Soviet *podnodvoy lodkoy*... a submarine," replied the first man in Russian. Finn understood every word. "My name is Boris Nevotslov, Senior Research Scientist and Medical Officer."

"A what? I'm on a *what*? How can I...? What? A *submarine*?"

"We found you in the water in somewhat... *unusual* circumstances, you might say," the man replied.

Finn in the trance looked around. He lay on a cot in a cabin, there was not much room and the two Russians took up much of what was left.

"I was tied up – in some kind of laboratory or something. There was arguing."

Again Nevotslov looked with uncomprehending surprise toward his companion.

"Yes, Igor and I..." again he looked at the man whose name had just be given, "Well, let us say we had some reluctance to other suggestions concerning your wellbeing."

"Or non-wellbeing," grinned the other man called Igor. He seemed to be more at ease than his colleague, his demeanour suggesting to Finn that some settlement had already been arrived at.

"The Soviet navy is very touchy about allowing westerners board a Lima class submarine. There were those who were of the firm persuasion that you be permitted to leave," explained Nevotslov carefully.

"Which might not have been your best option at 50 metres under the surface," added the still grinning Igor.

"Project 1840," said Finn, wondering why he said it even as he spoke.

"*Nifiga sebe!*" exclaimed Igor, the smile suddenly gone from his face. "Holy Cow! How does he know the project number of the boat?"

"Who *are* you?" asked Nevotslov incredulously. "And how are you even alive?"

Finn in the trance looked from one Russian face to the other.

"I am... I am..." He searched the faces vainly hoping to find some inspiration there. None came. Like a fading mist he could feel his memories slowly move out of his reach and disappear into the void.

"I was in a canoe – it capsized – the water, it was lit up, alive! I'm from Scotland... somewhere... my name, my name..." He struggled to get a grip of his vanishing memories. "Finlay. And my Christian name is... is, I'm from... my name, my name is..." He struggled as his voice petered to a halt. "I don't know anything, it's gone, it's all gone!" He could feel his throat tighten as a wave of terror swept across him. "Help me!" he cried out, gripping Boris Nevotslov's jacket. "I'm drowning!"

Finn could see himself shake and feverishly grasp out at the Russian. Nevotslov set his hands on Finn's shoulders and looked into his eyes.
"Have no fear my friend," he said calmly. He had switched to English, his words slower but reassuring for Finn.
"You are alive and well. How that is so we cannot tell, but you are in no current danger. The Captain has determined that no harm will come to you and you can rest now."
Finn ceased his sudden tremors and took in several deep breaths.
"Yes, I... I am sorry, I had a brief panic. I must have struck my head when I fell out of the canoe. I'm O.K. now, you can let go."
The doctor turned to a small table beside the cot. "These will help calm you. You should take two now," he said, putting two tablets into Finn's hand. "There is a glass of water beside you. They are little more than seasickness medication, but they will help nonetheless."
"Thanks," said Finn, following out the advice and swallowing the pills. He did not doubt the man and he knew he was safe in his hands. He turned and sat up on the bed, setting his feet onto the cabin floor. "I suppose I will have to stay in this cabin?" he asked. He also correctly assumed that the door would be locked when the two men left.
"Da," said Nevotslov simply.
"How did you see me?" asked Finn suddenly curious. "A Russian submarine was hardly sailing in full sight off the Scottish coast. I would have been a small enough object to see floating about on the waves. It was getting dark. I remember that."
Igor looked at Nevotslov with a shrug. Nevotslov nodded and turned to the patient.
"No one said you were afloat." He paused and ran his hand over his head. "We picked you up on the sea floor, lying there just as you are now, almost 250 metres down!"

Finn suddenly felt as if he were being drawn out of the dream by a huge hand. The images in the cabin, Igor, Nevotslov, began to diminish and disappear and he became aware of a blue sky and trees passing by.

He shook his head. He was lying on something. Faces were above him, there were blue flashing lights. Voices, this time speaking French. He looked around himself. He was being carried on a stretcher.

"Que ce passé-t-il? Que faites-vous?" he demanded. "Where are you taking me?"

He was slid into an ambulance and moments later the two tones sounded as the vehicle moved off.

"Tout va bien. Tu t'es effondré dans le parc," replied the paramedic. "All is well, you collapsed in the park, but do not worry. They'll check you over at the hospital."

Finn shook his head again. For a few moments he could not determine if he was still in the dreamlike trance or back to reality. The overpowering effect of the return of the memories was like an alcoholic daze. As the ambulance bumped over the cobblestones of central Nantes, its siren noisily pushing traffic out of the way, his head began to clear. No, he was back. The hallucination had been the most vivid so far and the only one he had had without first of all being asleep. But he was in Nantes and the recollections of the fire, the crossing to Nantes and falling at the walls of the castle flooded back, confirming the authenticity of his consciousness. He immediately began considering his position. Would he be required to prove his identity in the hospital? Probably. Andrew McCracken's passport, hastily shown to the shipping clerk might have got him a crossing, but a closer inspection was less likely to fool a keen eye. He lay back and tried to calm himself. There was no use in second guessing the next step. They would take him to hospital and he would go. Once there he would decide what to do next. Another thing meanwhile shook him. His *surname* was Finlay. The revelation, rather than encouraging him, somehow unsettled him. His Christian name, the most personal possession a person could own, remained as anonymous as ever.

Chapter 21
Threats

It was Chemeris and the man on his back was Yashkin. Rogov ran forward and the others in the room followed. There was blood running down Chemeris' shoulders and face, but it soon became apparent that it was Yashkin's and not his own. Yashkin's clothes were ripped apart and it was horribly apparent that he was in a bad way.

"I found him on a track," gasped Chemeris. "He's barely alive. Quick, get him to Medical!"

When one of the others tried to check up on Chemeris he dismissed them angrily.

"Forget me. Help Yashkin!"

They quickly laid him on a stainless steel trolley hostess and rushed him off to the clinic. Liminov ran off to find the Medical Officer at the base and by the time he had found him and brought him to the clinic, Yashkin had already been laid out on the theatre couch.

Dismissing all but his orderly, the doctor immediately began assessing the badly injured man while the rest returned to the recreation room.

Chemeris was sitting now, his head in his hands, collecting himself at one of the tables. The men gathered around and with a nod of understanding, Rogov sat beside him and put his arm on his shoulder.

"He's with the doctor now Chemeris. How are you?"

Chemeris dismissed his concern with a wave of his hand.

"I am only exhausted. I will be fine in a few minutes."

"What happened?" asked Rogov. The others looked on, keenly awaiting an answer.

"I don't know." He looked up and saw the others and he turned back to Rogov. "I was out checking up on something in the tractor shed." He hesitated as he carefully put his words together. He was exhausted, but he was not so tired as to betray the real reason he and Yashkin were outside.

"I heard a noise but thought little enough of it. You know how it is with the wind and the tin building out there."

Some of the others nodded. Being alone in the dark at Kola could be an eerie experience at times. Everything seemed to creak and groan with noises that could be interpreted a thousand ways, most of them malevolently so. It took a bit of getting used to.

"After twenty minutes or so I decided to investigate. I found Yashkin lying on one of the tracks that lead north from the complex. He was covered with blood but was still alive. I threw him over my shoulder and struggled in the wind to get him here. The snow had started again. I lost my bearings and began to wander in the darkness. I could no longer see the lights of the complex in the swirling snow. How I found my way back I'll never know. It was a miracle we weren't both lost."

"Did he say anything?" It was one of the other project workers.

"Something about being hit – by a truck I think."

"What would a truck be doing at this time of night?" asked Mikael Averin, one of the miners.

Rogov said nothing. It was a question he had asked himself many times before this night and one that had been the very reason for setting up their clandestine meeting. He had a theory about that very thing and nothing that had happened tonight had lessened its validity.

"How would I know?" spat Chemeris. "I only know that my friend Yashkin has been hit by something that has shattered him into a bleeding mess. It was like carrying a heavy sack of broken lumber.

He dropped his head again and the men fell silent. Rogov looked up and they understood. Quietly they drifted back to their tables or left altogether. Rogov continued silently in his vigil beside his friend, his arm still laid gently across his shoulder. After a few minutes he whispered into Chemeris' ear.

"Come old friend. I will help you back to your room. You need to rest and this is not the place."

Rogov helped Chemeris' off with his coat and placed it in one of the laundry bags that all the dormitories had at their doorways. It was covered in blood and material from Yashkin's clothing. The big man lay down on his bed and did not complain when Rogov removed his boots and pulled his blanket over him.

"Take these Chemeris," he said, offering him a tablet. "It's Temazepam. It will settle you."

"Rogov," said Chemeris suddenly, "I think this was no accident!"

Rogov slowly nodded. "Perhaps not. But you should rest." He leaned close to the big man and spoke softly. "We shall think about this later. Now is not the time for hasty action or thinking. With haste comes error and this place is not the place for careless mistakes. Especially not now."

Chemeris lay back and having taken the offered sleeping medication, turned in the bed and looked into Rogov's eyes. Rogov could see a change in the man and the change was fear.

"Not now," whispered Rogov into his ear. "Not now. Sleep now."

He left Chemeris on his bed and closed the door behind him. He had known that there was danger in this place. Inwardly he chastised himself that he had not comprehended just how immediate that danger was.

~~~~~~~

Lander opened the case and removed the large medium format Mamiya. He unclipped the film back and slid out the dark slide. He removed the piece of film that gave the appearance of normality which revealed items that had no place in a 120mm film camera. In place of where the roll of film and advancing mechanism ought to have been there were miniature electronic components and tiny switches. Taking off the back adapter from the camera body, he released a tiny catch and it unfolded into a long rod. Taking the rod, he plugged it onto the side of the film back. The covert aerial now in place, he flicked one of the miniature switches on one of the electronic components and a red L.E.D. display flicked into life. Pressing a small black button, he began to quietly recite a few short sentences into the apparatus. When he had finished, he pressed the button again, a red flash of the display confirming the recording had been successful. Another flick and the electronics compressed the ninety seconds of audible speech into a brief burst of encrypted data, less than a tenth of a second long. Taking the device to a window he double-checked his watch. Content he was correct in his timing and the requisite satellite being correctly positioned in its elliptic over the horizon, he flicked a small blue switch with the tip of his multi-tool. The display flickered, a series of numbers appeared and then changed to four zeros.

Lander looked up into the scudding grey that was Jan Mayen's sky and nodded to himself. His first report had been filed. He had been as succinct as he could to fit his findings into a ninety second recording and he wondered what Thames House would make of it. He wondered what he made of it himself. The data repository was something he had not expected but once Ari had told him what he knew, although a revelation, it was not really the stuff of assassinations and covert ops. There were many such backup servers and systems maintained by industry and commercial computing, what made this different was a matter of scale. That it should be undisclosed and run as a background operation made sense to him, particularly with the complications of the Doomsday scenarios envisaged in such a possible requirement. No, secret though it may have been, it was the findings of the volcanologists that rang oddest. Perhaps there was some rational explanation, and if so, MI5 would know.

Two well dressed men sat eating their lunch together on a bench at the embankment overlooking Victoria Tower and the Palace of Westminster. Beside them the bronze memorial to the S.O.E. reminded them of agents who had given their lives for freedom. Across the river the gothic limestone of the houses of parliament looked on, its unshakeable institution assuring stability in the daily turbulence of the world the two men inhabited.

"There must be some rational explanation," said Sir Simon Montague. "Mechanical noises? What about the LORAN-C? Possibly low frequency echoes?"

Jonas Smythe shook his head. "The Norwegian scientists had dismissed that. Lander reckons their interest in whatever it was, was enough to secure their murders."

Sir Simon wiped his lips with a tissue. "These Mango yoghurts are splendid." He looked into the empty tub with some regret. "The most eaten fruit in the world." He looked up at his junior colleague. "Did you know Jonas, that half of the world's mangoes are grown in India?"

Jonas Smythe shook his head. He did not.

"A wonderful source of export revenue," continued his boss, turning the plastic pot around as he looked idly at images of mangoes hanging on branches. "Or could be - they export less than one percent of them. Consume most of them themselves. Rough for the rest of us, eh?"

"Unless one doesn't like mangoes," added Jonas, watching the pigeons pick up the crusts he had thrown onto the grass beside the benches.

"Wouldn't bother me if they kept them all."

"So Lander knows about Operation Re-Start. Someone on Mayen must have told him," said Sir Simon setting down the empty tub. "Interesting."

"He seems to have dismissed the installation as a reason for the murders though," added Smythe. "You were right to allow him to find that out for himself. Makes his judgement all the more discerning."

Sir Simon looked out over the water and the constant passing of little boats on the Thames.

"Jonas," he said suddenly. "This 'Carrington Event'. How likely is it - I mean really?"

"Technically, it has already happened."

"How so?" Sir Simon oversaw a number of departments and operations run from Box 500. Jonas knew he couldn't possibly be fully informed on the details of all of them. Jonas had spent a considerable amount of time in researching classified files on the subject.

"It was an historic solar storm back in 1859," he began. "Two British astronomers recorded it, Carrington and Hodgson. A mass ejection from the sun hit the Earth's magnetosphere and played havoc with what electrical systems we had at that time. Apparently telegraph apparatuses were fried and the flashes of electromagnetic charges colouring the night sky convinced some people Armageddon had arrived. Some telegraphers were electrocuted - others threw the switches on their sets only to find them still live. It wasn't a one-off though, or even the most powerful."

"Other Carringtons?"

"Several. There have been others that have narrowly missed Earth or massive solar storms whose effects, if they had hit the planet, would have caused untold damage in the early 1900's. The flares are increasing in intensity and power. The last one, in 2012, only missed Earth's orbit by nine days. It is inevitable that the next one will be soon and bigger again. If a smallish one put out telegraph wires in 1859, the projected solar storms to come will destroy the world's I.T. networks and probably the hardware carrying it."

Sir Simon gave a low whistle. "And yet Lander has found something else," he said. "As if the threat of the sun bursting over our heads isn't enough." He looked down and picked up his empty yoghurt tub again.

"The East Asians gave us mangoes, the Aztecs gave us potatoes, and the ruddy Norwegians have presented us with a murder mystery. We need more information Jonas. When is Lander's next report due?"

"Next message is expected Friday," replied the younger man. "That's if he has anything more by then. If he has, he'll let us know."

"I'm of a mind to ask Reid to investigate all the probabilities," mused Sir Simon. "What do you think?"

Jonas nodded slowly. "You know, I asked him to assist me with the FARC thing last May."

"The Colombian connection?"

"Yes. He said if I wanted answers he needed a better question. Can be a bit too smart at times, but he's good at what he does."

"Well, speak to Reid. Give him what we know. See what he can come up with. Meantime, I'll hold off on contacting the NIS until we have a little more to go on." He paused and then added, "See if our man can get some sort of a recording. Reid will need hard data."

The two civil servants got up and began the short walk back along the embankment and over Lambeth Bridge to Thames House. As they went, Jonas Smythe glanced momentarily at the sun, high in the sky over Pimlico. Of course, he mused, if the Carrington Event were to occur, all of their investigations would hardly matter. They'd all be back to paper and pencil, chalk and blackboards.

Chapter 22
Questions

"I am going to the North Beach, in an hour from now," said Lars suddenly. Lander was filing barometric pressure readings when the Norwegian slapped him on the back with his statement. "There are the ruins of some four-hundred-year old whaling stations up there. Fascinating place it is. You are very welcome to join me. It should only take three hours or so."

Lander nodded. It would make an interesting diversion and see some more of the island.

"Aye, that would be fine," he said, "I should have these tidied away before that."

Lars drove the small two-seater quad-like vehicle known simply as the Mule over the gnarled trail. It had a fully enclosed cab and even boasted a heater which made the trip a lot more comfortable than Jon had expected. Unlike a quad, it had a steering wheel and side by side seating. A small area for stowage ran behind the seats. The trail was largely gravel and stone, though some parts had been eroded by rains and storms leaving much of it rutted and gullied. The small vehicle bucked over those parts, rolling and pitching as the two men held on inside the cabin.

"You know, this place is not so bad if you try to get to know her," said Lars, a grin spreading across his face. "Mayen is a frigid woman who has only known a stream of men who come and go. It has hardened her heart." He pointed through the front window to the Beerenburg while wrestling the jerking steering wheel with his other. "Up there is where she holds her haughty head, looking to the Arctic with her back to us as if she didn't care."

"Can't say she showed me much compassion," added Lander drily.

"Smashed my boat to matchwood and then tried to drown me as an afterthought."

Lars Guldberg gave a hearty laugh. "Ha! She was playing with you. Tossing her hair and swirling her skirts." His face suddenly straightened. "If she had wanted you dead you would not be here my friend."

Lander glanced at the meteorologist and tried to read his expression. From serious it was immediately back to jovial.

"Ha! But here you are!" Somewhat disconcertingly, he took both hands off the wheel and slapped them together. The vehicle veered wildly toward a deep gorge and he quickly took control again.

"A man could kill himself out here even without her help," he guffawed. "But I think her heart is warming. Look!" He pointed out the window again as a bright silvered finger of northern sunlight broke through the clouds over the mountain. "See, she is flirting with us now. Yes, Jan Mayen is not the wicked woman some say she is. She is just... *misunderstood?*" He winked at Lander and smiled. "Like most women heh?"

Lander laughed. The man was hard not to like with his infectious enthusiasm and unaffected gruffness.

The trail snaked along the western approaches, though Lars took a more inland route for part of the way, bypassing the beach where Jon had supposedly been ship-wrecked. He imagined Lars' intention was to thoughtfully avoid showing his passenger the spot where he had so nearly lost his life. Soon they were back hugging the coast and he pulled in to a grassy knoll and cut the engine.

"Down there," he pointed south to a huddle of huts on the coast, "is Puppebu, Jan Mayen's second largest city. Sometimes up to four people stay there!" He pulled up his collar and grabbed his mittens from the dashboard. "But, come, see something I found a while ago."

It was the tangled remains of an aircraft. All that was left were bits of aluminium fuselage and the engine block, a solid rusted lump of steel and iron half embedded into the gritty ground.

"Someone had it worse than me," said Lander. "It doesn't look like a landing someone walked away from. Any idea what the aircraft was?"

"Ya, I'm fairly sure it is the wreck of a German Focke-Wulf 200," replied Lars, his hand on a twisted strut.

"A Condor?" said the Englishman. "It's been here a while then."

"You are a constant surprise," said Lars shaking his head. "Yes, it is a Condor. How did you know that?"

"Oh, nothing surprising really," replied Lander. "I collected World War Two Airfix models when I was a boy. I knew all the Allied and Axis planes. The Condor was mainly a reconnaissance aircraft I seem to recall. I'm guessing it crashed out here on a mission during the war?"

Lars nodded enthusiastically. "On the 7th of August 1942 to be precise. We had a weather station out here to help the British North Atlantic Convoys. The Germans got wind of the radio traffic and sent it out here to kindly drop some bombs on it. Instead they crashed into the foot of Beerenburg and another nine young men never went home." He looked back at the wreckage. "War. Makes a good story unless you happen to feature in it eh?"

The sun had now broken out from the clouds and the whole bay to the west was lit up. Ahead a large lake glittered in the sunlight like a diamond in a pan of ashes.

"Is that Nordlaguna?" asked Lander. He knew that it was having memorised the topography to the extent he could name every bay and inlet.

"Good, ya, that is Nordlaguna, you English would say, the North Lagoon, heh? We are going that way; we will stop again before we head down to it."

As they rumbled off the stone path that had led from Olonkinbyen to Puppebu and onto the untracked tundra, it suddenly occurred to Lander that he had not corrected Guldberg's reference to him as an Englishman. It was almost certainly simply the Norwegian's ignorance, but Jon inwardly chided himself for his own lack of consistency. It was small slips like that that could, when added up, lead to suspicion. Lars' genial manner and easy company had allowed him to relax. He would need to take greater care.

Fifteen minutes of bumping over the uneven ground brought them to a series of square formations on the ground. This time Lars merely stopped the Mule and looked out the window.

"Vogelburg," he stated. "These are the remains of a fort built to protect the whaling stations that were here over three hundred years ago. Over two hundred men worked on the island then. They hunted Bowhead whales until they drove them to practical extinction. Thousands of them were cut up and boiled here. Oil for lamps and soap. The English and the Dutch came too, even Spaniards. All fighting over the oil."

"Oil. Nothing much changes," remarked Jon. "Just the geography. Oil and the lust for money."

"And power," added Lars. "Money buys power above all things and men will kill for that. Men will die for that."

"So why Beerenburg?" asked Jon. Lars did not immediately reply and instead looked back with a questioning expression on his face.

"Why would someone want to voluntarily come out to such a god-forsaken part of the world?" qualified Jon. "It certainly cannot be the weather!"

Lars laughed again. "It is precisely because of the weather that I am here! Jan Mayen is an open air laboratory for a meteorologist. Here we do not merely ruminate over maps, barometric charts and computer models. Here we measure and witness the skies, we feel the pulse of the planet, watch the forces that shape a world. Add to that living on the slopes of a living volcano and this place is a paradise for a man like me."

Jon shook his head. "Takes all sorts," he said with a smile.

"I might ask why a man would put himself on a few pieces of lumber nailed together, raise some canvas up a pole, call it a yacht and then throw himself out onto the northern seas," said Lars. "I think if one of us had to justify his position, yours would be the harder task!"

Lander laughed and made excuses about the longing for a solitary life that a man in the city ached for. After delivering a few words about finding the inner man and escaping the rat race, he looked back out through the windows. Talking about himself could be complicated, the required spontaneity in maintaining an invented persona easy to lead into personal historical inconsistency.

"So, what about this fort then?" he asked, pointing at the ruins, hoping the change of subject was not too jarring. Lars didn't seem to notice as by way of reply, he pulled up his hood and got out of the mule.

"Come, I will show you," he said.

As Lars guided Lander around the ancient lichen covered ruins, the agent could not help but marvel at the tenacity of the whalers who had built their forts and buildings so long ago. Not for them the aid of machinery or the modern conveniences such as electric heat, telecommunications or aircraft supply. Out here, they were as remote to the world as Neil Armstrong and Buzz Aldrin had been on taking their first steps on the moon. Whatever they did, they had to do with their own hands. There could be no help from outside. If it went wrong, it would be tragically, irrevocably wrong. Surviving the elements, the violent seas and the bitter arctic winds was a fight against the might of nature, man pitted against the uncaring relentlessness of a restless planet.

The wind whipped around his ears as Lars pointed out the areas of the industry. Places where the blubber would be boiled down to oil, pits where the pitiful remains of once proud sea creatures would be burned to ash. As Lars unfolded the clues to the ruins, Lander considered the clues to the more recent deaths. Men's lives had been taken and the clues were few and far between as to who had been responsible and for what reason murder had been resorted to. He had little hope of determining *who* when he was still so ignorant as to *why*.

Lars and he resumed their journey. As they rumbled over the trackless slopes of the mountain to their north, he pointed out the coast below them.

"Polar bears are sometimes seen out this way," he said. "In fact, last year Johannsen came back from the mountain as excited as a boy chased from an orchard. He had come across a bear as he was returning to the Metten in the quad, He said it had chased him for a hundred metres before it got bored and gave up. He always went out with a rifle after that!"

"Polar bears?" asked Lander. "How do they get here?"

"They swim," explained Lars simply. "They float on floes and swim between them. A polar bear can swim for hundreds of kilometres in open water."

Lander was about to comment when suddenly the Norwegian turned and looked directly at Lander.

"You have heard about Johannsen?" His voice was suddenly serious and his gaze intense.

Lander tried not to appear taken aback by the sudden change of tone and subject. He nodded.

Guldberg continued. "It is said he killed himself. I do not think so."

"Perhaps it was just an accident? I was told his car went off a cliff."

Lars gave a dismissive grunt. "Johannsen knew this place better than any other person on the base. He was careful in whatever he did. He was not a man to drive off a cliff. Not by accident and certainly not by design."

"So, what are you saying?" asked Lander hesitantly.

"Just what you know I am saying," said Guldburg, fixing Lander with his eye. "I think he was murdered!"

Just at that moment the radio in the cab sparked into life.

"Base to Guldberg, base to Guldberg!"

Lars pulled the mule up short and grabbed the mike.

"Guldberg here. Go ahead, over."

"The Commander wants all personnel out on the island to return to the station Lars," crackled the radio. "A huge front has just veered south. The glass is dropping rapidly. Jensen doesn't want anyone out there when it hits, over."

Lars pointed back over the quickly darkening head of the Beerenburg.

"She's called in the wolves," said Guldberg motioning toward the mountain. "Maybe she's got something against you coming to her island."

Wrenching the steering wheel, the Norwegian pulled the Mule around and started back along the way they had come.

"If Henrik is putting out an R.T.B, it must be bad," he explained as he drove. "He's a good man and wouldn't waste another man's time if he did not think it was necessary."

"Look out!" exclaimed Lander as suddenly a squall blew an old sheet of loose corrugated tin across their path. Guldberg braked hard as the tin slapped against the side of the vehicle before tumbling off onto the darkening landscape. Huge drops of rain suddenly came out of the greying skies and splashed off the windscreen.

"This could get interesting," grinned the meteorologist, glancing up at the rumbling sky. "Anti-cyclone. Could get rough my friend."

Jon could feel the rapid pressure drop as he watched the tussocky grasses outside suddenly begin to fight against the oncoming storm.

"Does a storm normally arrive so unexpectedly like this?" he asked.

"Asked the sailor!" laughed Lars. Suddenly his face turned grim. "If it has come in this fast, the pressure drop must be unparalleled. Olonkinbyen will suffer tonight."

As they made their way over the tortuous ground, it seemed that the storm increased in violence threefold with every mile they covered. Jon pulled the map out of the small pocket in front of him and did a quick calculation. He reckoned they had a good eight miles or more to cover and at their current pace, it would take them at least forty minutes to get back to the base. Already the lashing rain was beginning to run in streams across the gravelly trail. With the darkness of an Egyptian plague falling like an angry curtain, neither of them needed to mention that the journey back was going to get a lot worse before it got any better.

Back at Olonkinbyen, men were feverishly battening down windows while outside others were tying down anything that could not be moved indoors. Barrels of fuel and water were lashed together while wooden seats and tables were brought to the lee side of the building where it was hoped they would have a better chance of not being carried off down the island.

Henrik Jensen stood in the centre of a group of men who were watching the screen of a weather computer being operated by one of the scientists. He was pointing a stubby finger at the image on his monitor.

"Here sir," he was saying. "This is an unprecedented drop in pressure. The whole front is over sixty kilometres in width and is rapidly consolidating. From what I can see, it looks like we are precisely in the centre of its path."

The commander nodded grimly as he turned to his Oversersjant.

"Call the rest of the men in Ari," he said. "If this thing hits us with the speed and severity we expect, we can't risk men over property. Get them in."

Bjørnson turned and spoke quickly to some of his men. Soon they were out calling in the salvage teams. In five or six minutes they were all indoors.

"Lars and the Scotsman are still out," said Ari when all had been accounted for.

Jensen looked concerned. "I put out a Return to Base fifteen minutes ago," he argued, "Didn't they get the transmission?"

"Yes sir, they reported mobile to base as soon as they got the call, but they still could be a good bit out. Lars had plans to visit some of the sensors North East of the mountain."

Jensen shook his head. "Find out their E.T.A. This storm is only going to increase every minute they are out." He stared at Bjørnson. "I am not going to lose any more men on this island!"

Chapter 23
Nantes

The Coroner's report from the post mortem lay on Jack's desk. He slowly turned a pen through his fingers as he thought through what he had just read. He had asked for a copy before leaving Glasgow for Belfast and it had just arrived that morning. He had read through the pathologist's findings of the autopsies with considerable care and after a few more minute's rumination, he lifted the phone and dialled Glasgow Royal. He was in luck - Doctor Robert Jamieson was in his office and free to take his call.

"Jack!" he exclaimed down the line, "Good to hear from you. Is everything well with you?"

"Aye, it is, but I have a question. Do you remember the coma patient you called me in to see?"

When Jack finally finished the conversation, he made a few notes and immediately called the PSNI inspector on the internal line. Shortly after that they were both headed out toward the destroyed farm outside Donaghadee.

It was mid afternoon at the McCracken's farm and Jack was initially surprised to see activity around the yard. A tractor was lifting silage into a front loader and depositing the fermenting grass into the feeding racks of the cattle byres.

"Neighbours looking after the farm," explained Sam, "Strange. The farmer and his wife are dead and yet the farm lives on. Life goes on I suppose."

They made their way around to the back yard where Jack paused and looked around.

"The third body cannot have been Finn," he said suddenly.

Inspector Anderson spun around and looked at his colleague. Jack was down on one knee peering across the yard toward the blackened relic of the farmhouse.

"What's that?"

"I read the Coroner's report this morning. It has the full details of the pathologist's findings. Three bodies, too badly burned to identify. Two consistent with the bones of an elderly couple. Amazing how they can know that. They measure wear of the joints, spine curvature, bone densities. Anyway, the third - the body that should be Finn's – well it can't be his."

"How do you work that out?" asked Anderson. "It was barely distinguishable as a human being. I saw the photographs too Jack."

"The third body. The P.M. showed that the victim had a titanium plate on an old scaphoid fracture of the right wrist. Probably an old motorcycle accident."

"So, our man had an old motorcycle accident?"

"Except that we can be certain that he did not." Something on the ground had caught his attention as he spoke. He knelt down and poked at something in the mud of the yard as he continued. "I spoke to the senior consultant at Glasgow Royal this morning. It was he who had first brought the young man to my attention. He was able to assure me that his medical records showed no fractures of any kind – especially not ones clamped together with titanium plates." Suddenly he pulled a penknife out of his pocket and prodded the blade into the stone yard.

Anderson gave a low whistle. "That puts the cats among the pigeons. So if body three is not our man Finn, or whatever he's called, then who is he?"

"And where is Finn?" asked Jack standing up. He was holding something in between his index finger and thumb.

"What's that you've found?" asked Anderson somewhat quizzically. By way of reply, Jack took a paper tissue out of his pocket and wiped the object. A metallic sheen rewarded his effort. Sam leaned forward.

"The plot has just thickened," he said drily.

It was a bullet.

Finn lay on the bed in a ward of the Centre Hospitalier Universitaire de Nantes, better known as the CHU. He was on his back and as he began to push himself up, a nurse in her pale blue uniform quickly stepped over.

"Monsieur, soyez prudent. Tu as fait une chute!"

Finn waved his hand, "I'm fine," he said. *"Je viens d'avoir un sort vertigineux.* Really, it was just a dizzy spell, I'm okay."

"Still," she said, her French tinged with the particular *Marseillais* accent peculiar to the South of France around Marseilles, "Please just rest for now. The doctor will be round soon." She lifted his notes from the base of his bed and checked the patient monitor beside the bed.

"You're a long way from home," he said to her. "Marseilles?"

She smiled. "Yes, hard to get rid of the accent I'm sorry to say."

"No, no," he protested, "You have a lovely accent. I really like *Marseillais*. The rhythm is much more interesting than my old drone."

"You are from Paris, no?" she said easily as she made some notes on the pad.

"Here and there, I travel a bit," he replied vaguely. As he spoke he hoped she would see he had no particular need for close monitoring. It would give him an opportunity to leave quietly if she was relaxed enough to move on to other patients.

"You are French, but your name is English?" she said, pointing to the small whiteboard on the wall above his head.

"Oh, yes," he replied thinking quickly, "my father was British, hence the name."

"Ah," she said absently. "Well, I'll be back after the doctor is around Andrew, now please just rest for a while. You were unconscious and we have to be careful, you know?"

She moved off and Finn lay back. Someone had his passport. The nurse would only have been given his name, but someone had seen he had a passport issued by the U.K. He could not stay and would have left at that point had not the doctor suddenly appeared. He made his way over to Finn and peered over his glasses at his patient.

"How are you feeling Monsieur? You look a lot better I must say."

"I'm feeling well thank you. I'm sorry to have wasted your time. You must have more important cases than a man who tripped outside the Château des Ducs."

The doctor waved away Finn's dismissive comment with a hand. "No, no, you had some kind of an episode. I'm afraid I'm not quite able to say yet what happened to you, but it is certainly good to see you have your colour back." He lifted the same notes the nurse had replaced onto the bed end. "Have you ever suffered from epilepsy?"

Finn shook his head. "No, I've been fairly healthy thanks. It was hot, I haven't been drinking enough."

"Ah," said the doctor nodding. "Perhaps - but it would be best if we keep you in for a while yet. There are some tests we would like to run before we sign you off. Our first readings were obviously wrong so we are bringing in another monitor that is functioning correctly. Simple tests, you understand?"

Finn nodded as the doctor continued. "There are a couple of men outside, plain-clothes police, who have asked to speak to you. I told them to wait. Do you feel ready to talk to them? You don't have to while you are under my care."

Finn nodded. He knew that in France, the police did not have the same respect as at home. They were resented by the general population with a reputation of being over intrusive, arrogant and obstructive. Nonetheless, Finn could see no advantage in trying to avoid the inevitable questions.

"I'm fine. I'll talk to them if they want."

Once admitted, one man stood beside Finn's bed. The other remained outside guarding the door.

"I can only give you a few minutes with him," said the doctor as he left. He gave Finn a supportive look. "He is tired and needs rest."

Alone with the police officer, Finn look up amiably. "So, how can I help you *Monsieur*?"

"We are with the *Direction Centrale des Renseignements Généraux,*" he began, nodding toward his colleague outside the glass panelled door. "Just a few questions, that's all."

"If I can be of assistance to the RG, I will be glad to help, though I'm afraid you are going to have to tell me how?"

In reply, the intelligence officer pulled Finn's borrowed passport out of his inside pocket.

"It's about your passport." His eyes narrowed. Finn didn't bat an eyelid.

"That's not mine."

The officer looked surprised at Finn's assertion. He took a half step closer to the bed. "Yet it was in your bag."

"When I say that it is not mine, I mean, it is not my actual passport. That is a British passport."

"We know that," replied the officer curtly. "But why do you have it?"

"It belonged to a friend of mine. A student friend. He died a while ago and his parents sent it to me as a memory of him. We were close. I

190

stayed with him when I was in Ireland studying."

"So, where are you from then?"

"I live in Paris, Canal Saint-Martin, though I'm from Avranches, you know, near Le Mont St Michel? Country boy in the big city."

The officer was clearly put off balance by the false information. As he processed what he had been told, Finn carried on, further disorientating his thinking. He pointed at the passport.

"You can see it is obviously not me. Why else would I be carrying a foreign passport? Ah, you thought..." He nodded in an understanding kind of way. "I have the telephone number for his parents if you want to call them. Do you speak English?"

Finn quickly wrote down some numbers using the hospital provided notepad and pen on his desk. He handed it to the policeman before he could properly react. "Let me see Andrew's passport again please."

The officer dutifully handed over the passport without argument. Finn looked at it momentarily and casually set it on the table beside him. "Yes, that's him. Really, I mean it. Phone that number, it will clear everything up and save you wasting your time."

The man hesitated and then turned. "Wait here, I will give it to my colleague. He speaks English."

He stepped outside and Finn could see him talking to the other officer. Without a second's hesitation Finn slipped out of the bed, retrieved his backpack from the bedside cabinet and grabbed the passport along with his shoes. In one swift movement, he headed into the ward where he had seen a green medical gown hanging near the nurse's station. In a second he had it pulled on along with a theatre cap sitting on a trolley beside it. He threw his shoes and pack onto the bottom shelf. Pushing the trolley before him, he turned and confidently pushed out through the panelled door.

"Excusez moi s'il vous plait!" he said, his voice lowered and business-like. The policemen excused themselves and moved aside, not bothering to look up. Finn continued to a lift halfway down the corridor. The doors were open and he promptly stepped inside, bringing the trolley with him while pressing the button for the ground floor. As the doors closed he just caught a glimpse of the officer heading back to Finn's now empty bed.

His ward had been on the fifth floor. In the thirty seconds that it took for the lift to descend, Finn had thrown off the gown and pulled on his trousers and shoes. He had no time to put on his shirt and instead pulled on his coat just as the doors opened. A man and a woman entered – visitors, Finn determined as he strode across the foyer and out into the evening sunlight. The exit was straight ahead onto the Boulevard Jean Philippot, but instead of the obvious escape, he turned right along the wall of the hospital until he came to a staff car park. Still moving briskly, he crossed the park and spied a pedestrian exit leading out onto the Boulevard Jean Monet. He crossed that and soon found himself in a residential area. Taking various turns and streets, he soon left behind a route only a blood hound could have followed. Fifteen minutes later he found some trees and bushes running alongside the river near the Pont de Tblissi where he secured a bench facing the river but hidden from all other view. Here he dressed himself properly and began to make plans. He needed to get out of Nantes. The passport would be traced back to the McCrackens and that would immediately set off international alarm bells. Instinctively he knew he needed to head north. From there he had vague ideas already suggesting themselves, ideas that he suppressed for now. Time to deal with that would come soon enough. As he looked around his surroundings he saw a bicycle chained to a lamp post. The lamp post was gradually being overrun by raggedy undergrowth. The bicycle looked abandoned. Finn looked across the river, and spotted a Supermarché sign. An idea sprung in his mind and at once he got up and began to act on it.

"Forensics say it's a 9mm Makarov bullet. Fired from a 9mm Makarov pistol," said the big Ulsterman. He sat down at the desk opposite Jack and pushed a report across the mahogany.
"I talked to the Senior Scientist in charge of ballistic tracing. Apparently it's a straightforward gun to identify. The ammunition is pretty much made only for that particular pistol."
Jack lifted the sheet and read over the succinct summary of the ballistic report. He nodded thoughtfully and looked up at the PSNI inspector.
"East European?"
"Probably Russian," corrected Anderson. "It had no record of previous use in Northern Ireland."
"I see," said Jack, rubbing his lip with a finger. "They're sure?"
"Pretty much" replied Anderson, "We have a specialist department here that has recorded every bullet and cartridge ever fired and recovered in the last forty years in Northern Ireland. If this matched,

those people would know. Makarovs turn up here in the hands of Dissident Republicans and criminals fairly frequently. This particular gun however has never been encountered here. Normally they would now list this as a first use."

Jack looked up. "Normally?"

Sam Anderson gave a roguish smile. "They have a new machine."

"How do you mean?"

Apparently they have added a modern digital system to the old one. It's called IBIT. Linked into Forensic hubs all over the U.K, Europe and beyond, they can upload the imagery and digital information unique to each exhibit and the software cross-compares it to every other police service ballistic record held on their identical IBIT computer systems."

"Impressive," whistled Jack. "So, as long as other forces share the information, we can compare our ballistic records with theirs?"

Anderson nodded. "Exactly – and so find this." With a flourish he pushed another sheet across the table. This one had several lines of information with dates and locations.

"Our pistol may have made its first appearance over here, but it's been about a bit in Europe." He pointed at the sheet. "Look. Dresden, Milan, Zagreb. Each one a murder."

"Jack followed his finger. "The man who owned this gun knows how to use it."

"And there's another thing," added Anderson. "The ballistics recovered so far have almost all related to model PM Makarovs – this one is almost certainly a PB."

"What's the difference?"

"I said it was Russian? The ballistics expert told me that there are certain markings that are peculiar to each gun. Like I said, the model PM's turn up frequently, but a model PB leaves some additional, subtle, but unique marks on the bullet, marks left only by an integral suppressor."

"A silencer?"

"Yes. He said it was a pistol manufactured exclusively for Russian service, made for Spetsnatz troops and special KGB operatives."

"They can tell all this from a single damaged bullet?"

"We may be a wee country, but thirty years of shootings and murders have given us the most experienced ballistic experts in the world."

"So a silenced KGB pistol was fired at the McCracken farm at the night of the fire," said Jack with some amazement.

"Fired by a man who knows how to kill," added Anderson, pushing his hand back over his hair.

"Or did," added Jack purposefully. "I think we've just identified our third body."

Later on, in his room, Jack wrote out his thoughts and findings in his notebook. He was old school and liked to see in black and white the facts of a case excised from the tangle of his inner ruminations and laid out in the tangible world of paper and ink. He looked at the scribbles on the page before him. It was a mass of facts along with interconnected assumptions and conjectures. Words connected other words by lines and arrows, circles around some and others scored out. Overall, the result was to set out some of the building materials for an unconstructed building. All was still only circumstantial, only supposition, an edifice without the architectural drawing. Like a building site however, the materials observed in the yard might aid the curious in guessing what was going to be erected. And Jack was a very curious man. There was one line that sat above heavy underlines in sweeping strokes of his black biro. It was three words and it was one supposition of which he was certain.

Finn was alive.

Armed with two new tyres and tubes, some oil and a cheap set of pliers, spanners and assorted tools, Finn had returned from the super market and begun work on the abandoned bicycle. Within an hour he had it in reasonable working condition and half an hour after that he was cycling out of the centre of Nantes, heading north toward the suburbs and into the leafy countryside of the Pays de la Loire. He soon found himself on the quiet lanes and cycle-ways that wove around the banks of the Erdre river - herons and geese his only companions now that the city fell further and further behind.

The bicycle had given him the anonymity he had hoped it would. Twice, on cycling through the city, police cars had driven by, but the eyes within were on the footpaths, looking for a pedestrian as the man they sought cycled past in open view. Now in the country, Finn slowed his thoughts and took the time to appreciate his surroundings. The warmth of the air kissed his cheeks as he effortlessly pedalled the bicycle along the sandy tracks that followed the line of the river. On his back was the total sum of his life's belongings and the lack of them gave a lightness to his spirit that a man encumbered with more of life's possessions could scarcely appreciate. He breathed in the reedy scented air as the crunchy swish of his tyres ran a narrow line up the laneways. Occasionally he passed a fisherman, or another cyclist to whom he called a cheery *bonjour*, but the solitude of his journey was a draught of cool water to a man in a hot and sticky jungle. Overhead the sky was blue and the clouds linen white and as fluffy as clumps of loose cotton wool.

After having cycled two or three hours and some forty kilometres, he came to a small village called Joué-sur-Erdre where he pulled into a small grassy park by the river and found a stone seat facing the old buildings of the town. Leaving the bicycle there, he walked into the main street and found a small *Boulangerie* where he bought some food and a bottle of water. Back at the river, he ate the quiche he had purchased along with fresh French bread and, tired after the day's events, lay back in the late afternoon sun on the warm grass. A mother duck and her ducklings waddled close by in the hope for some crumbs from the drowsy visitor. Lying there, he had no doubt that his journey lay north. The once vague intent to make his way to Europe now became a distinct impulse. Almost as if he had a predetermined route laid out before him, he was conscious of a strong urge within him to make for a particular destination. It was an odd sensation, a compulsion almost. It was a certainty of direction and an assurance of a place he needed to be, but a place as yet unformed and unknown to his conscious self.

Jack flew home at the weekend. Before he went home however, he took the opportunity to call with his Head of Branch.

"KGB? Are you serious Jack?" The Chief Superintendent looked at his inspector with disbelief. "It could be just a stolen gun that has made its way though criminal hands to Ulster. They have AK47s and rocket launchers in the hands of terrorists over there Jack for goodness sake. The PSNI hardly need the KGB to explain a pistol."

"It's more than that," reasoned Jack. "This whole thing is just not ringing right at all. You know me, I don't do melodramatic, but I think there is more to this, much more."

The Chief Super acquiesced with a slow nod. Jack was right. He was not a detective who ran straight off to the end of his leash. If a case raised the alarm bells in Jack McGregor's head, then they were real bells.

"Look, this isn't our case and I really don't want to interfere in to another police force's investigation," said the Chief. "After all, you were only called over because of your link with this missing man. Have they talked to the Home Office, to Security Services? They tend to keep their cards close to their chest, but if there's any history of Russian involvement over there, I think they should know."

Helen was ready for him. She had made dinner and he relaxed as he enjoyed his wife's company and small-talk. She rarely asked him about his work, and tonight was no different. By the time they were ready for bed, he felt lighter and easier than he had for two weeks. As they lay in bed, he turned and looked into her smiling face.

"You know I love you, Helen McGregor," he said softly.

"And I love you too Jack McGregor," she smiled, her face shining with the truth of her words. He looked into the eyes of the woman he had always loved. The woman he once thought he had lost. He moved over and brought her into his arms, her head nestled onto his chest. No other words needed to be said. Later, as he drifted off to sleep, his thoughts wandered briefly across the Irish sea. There lay the charred remains of a farm, death and mystery.

But that was for another day. Tonight he would sleep.

Chapter 24
Deadly Questions

Yashkin was dead. Rogov stepped out of the medical centre and into the corridor outside. His mind was racing with a multitude of thoughts, some competing with others to take precedence over the drastic turn of events. Yashkin, the thoughtful and suspicious Mongolian was dead. He never resumed consciousness and despite the medical staff's best efforts, had died from the horrific internal injuries that the project surgery simply did not have the equipment or expertise to deal with.

Rogov moved into an alcove set off the corridor and stood looking out into the darkness through the Plexiglas window. A whirl of scenarios rushed past in his mind as he tried to tie down the simple facts. That Yashkin was dead was the starting point, after that it became a fog of assumptions. No driver had yet come forward to say he had run down a man in the darkness. Besides Chemeris' assumption, there was nothing yet to say that was the definite cause. He was admittedly found on one of the tracks – but why would he have wandered out into the dark bleakness, away from the place they had arranged to meet? Rogov tasted the bitterness of his own regret. He should not have been late. It hadn't helped that Gasparov had appeared and delayed him further.

Gasparov. Yashkin had threatened to complain to him but he himself had dissuaded him from going to the project head. He looked out into the swirl of the pitiless night. He should have been more forceful. If Yashkin had gone to Gasparov... He shook his head. It could just have been a horrible accident. Kola was unforgiving. A man could die out here just by simple carelessness to the safety protocols. The weather was vindictive, the machinery was dangerous and the cold was a killer in its own right.

But Yashkin's body was a broken, crushed and bloodied shell. It was no falling over a rock in the frozen dark. A truck then, just as Chemeris stated. He thought about the body he had glimpsed, the clothes cut away by the surgeon – a body with violent marks on every visible part of his anatomy and broken bones horribly apparent. If it had been a truck, he hadn't just been accidentally knocked down. He had been driven over by every wheel, leaving his shattered remains like a bag of rubble by the side of the road.

Chemeris took it badly. The big man pushed his fists into the cheeks of his bowed head. He slowly shook his head as his chest convulsed in unsuccessfully restrained sobs. Suddenly a low animal wail of grief escaped from between his clenched teeth. It was a sound like Rogov had not heard before and the anguish of it moved him to put his arms around the neck of the sorrowing engineer in heartfelt sympathy. There was nothing to be said and so he said just that. After some time Chemeris straightened up.

"Forgive me," he said, wiping his face with the back of his big hand. "I had hoped... I had not expected it so soon, though I knew he was badly hurt. And there is nothing they could have done?"

Rogov shook his head and sat back facing the other. "They used a defibrillator and even injected adrenaline directly into his heart, but his blood pressure was almost zero. His injuries were unsurvivable – especially out here."

Rogov let that sink in and after a few moments spoke again.

"You said a truck hit him?"

Chemeris shook his head. "No, I didn't see anything apart from Yashkin lying on the track. I heard a noise, but in the wind... I don't know."

"You said Yashkin spoke, said something?"

Chemeris slowly nodded. "I could barely hear him, he said he'd been hit, or hurt, or something. It was a broken mumble."

"Was that all he said?"

"It was all I could make out. He was trying to say something as I carried him back to the base, but it was nothing I could make out. It was all I could do to get him back, not that that counted for much."

Rogov shook his head. "You got him back Chemeris. You gave him his best chance."

"But not enough to stop him dying."

Rogov laid his hand on the big man's shoulder. "Some things are outside of our control. We can only do what we can. Sometimes that is not enough, but it is not our fault."

Chemeris slowly nodded. He turned and looked across the room at Yashkin's empty bunk. He sighed. "Then there is nothing more I could have done." He took in a long breath and exhaled slowly. "Mother Russia's demands always seem to be written in blood. This is our fate, the curse of our history."

He silently reached over and set two glasses on the small table beside them. "We can at least salute our comrade's passing," he sighed.

It was a tradition that somehow fitted the occasion and they both threw back the vodka, slamming the glasses on the table in unison.

"*Nashego druga!* To our friend!"

They sat for a while, staring into their empty glasses, neither feeling the need to refill them, but in studying the empty contents, to give reverence to the moment, to ponder a life closed, finished.

After some time, Rogov came out of his trance and looked up. He caught Chemeris looking at him.

"I think he spoke to Gasparov," Chemeris said simply.

Rogov did not reply, waiting to see if his colleague would elucidate. He did not want to put his own suspicions into a mind ready to seize any supposition as solid fact.

"You told us there was reason to be worried," Chemeris added after a while. He had straightened up and now looked intently at Rogov. He stretched his back. "What did you mean?"

Rogov hesitantly nodded his head. He made an inward decision. Things had gone too far now to leave Chemeris floundering about in his own guesswork and so possibly attracting attention from the wrong quarters.

"This place, this project," began Rogov, "Yashkin was right to have questions. There are many reasons why much of what we are being asked to do makes little apparent sense."

"That is what Yashkin said. He said it was a fiasco," exclaimed Chemeris. "He couldn't let it go. I told him to leave it to others to worry about it, but, well, you know... *knew* Yashkin," he corrected.

"Chemeris, whatever I say now, whatever you think, this must, this can *only* remain between the two of us. I told you before there was reason to be silent. I have not shared any of this with you. You both thought perhaps I was being unsociable. I was being cautious." He watched Chemeris' face, it was intently fixed on his own. "This death is a warning. We should suspect everyone and trust no one." He paused, ensuring from Chemeris' nod that the message had been understood. "This place is spending millions of roubles on drilling a hole, but it seems clear to me that it is not the real purpose of our being here. We are a distraction."

Chemeris looked uncomprehendingly at the mineralogist. "We are a what?"

"A distraction - a front for something else. Something bigger."

The petroleum expert shook his head. "Bigger than this? You are going to have to explain Rogov. You always were hard to understand, but now I have no idea at all what you mean."

"The Kola Superdeep project was halted years ago. It lay a vacant rusting experimental relic until suddenly it was reawakened three years ago. The drills were reinstated and a series of engineers and scientists co-opted in to operate it. In all of my conversations I have yet to meet anyone who has demonstrated any more knowledge as to what we are looking for than myself. One night I was in the machinery shed when I heard lorries heading to the slag heaps and something occurred to me, a suspicion that has only grown as the days have passed."

"So, the trucks dump the drill spoil, what is so odd about that?" asked Chemeris.

"This," replied Rogov. "The trucks carry the spoil from the drillings out and come back empty. But I have listened and heard trucks at night, trucks which did not leave the drilling rig, pass by and take their loads out to the dumping ground. That ground is five kilometres from here. No one here has ever been out there except our truck drivers. Have you ever spoken to a driver? Ever seen one?"

Chemeris shook his head. "I suppose they are based somewhere else."

"Somewhere where we never have opportunity to talk with them, nor they with us. I have measured the amount of spoil we take daily from the borehole. Six or seven loads at the most. I waited out one night at the rig. The road where you found Yashkin intersects with another coming inland from the north at that point. The wind that night carried the grunt of their engines so that I could just hear them as they passed outside in the darkness. I counted the engines of at least twenty vehicles before I could risk waiting out any longer. There is other work going on out here Chemeris, and we are only a fraction of it. We are the façade; behind us somewhere out there lies the real project. The project that we are a cover for. The project that Gasparov is *actually* complicit in."

Chemeris made no reply and instead brought his big hands together on the table before him. He looked again to Yashkin's bunk and then studied his own hands.

"So we are expendable. Serfs, slaves, subjects, sovetsky. Whatever we are called, always our lives do not matter. Always we lay them down like sheep. Nothing has changed has it?"

Rogov stood up and flattened his jacket. "Everything changes Chemeris. Finding out if it something we must accept, or something we must defy is the great challenge of life." He turned toward the door. "Say nothing of this conversation. Do not ask questions. Gasparov will want to speak with you. He will doubtless explain how Yashkin was the victim of an avoidable accident. Do not expect sympathy, but most importantly, do not ask him questions." He looked directly at Chemeris. "Do you understand this?"

Chemeris nodded. "Da. I understand."

Rogov left. He was not sure that Chemeris did understand, but he trusted him well enough to be sure he would do as he had been advised.

As he made his way to his lab, he pondered the fact that he had not mentioned Anya to Chemeris. Neither had he mentioned the strange results obtained from the mysterious samples. He was sure that the Kola Superdeep was indeed some kind of a front, but the Ringwoodite, if that was what is was, was a complication. If its discovery was total fluke or one of the aims of their presence here, he could not be sure. Somehow though, he felt that it had some kind of an importance which he had yet to determine. He sighed. What was he saying? He had yet to determine anything of any real substance. As he pulled his laboratory door behind himself he made an inward note. He must make sure to reinforce to Anya the need to remain silent on their discovery.

Gasparov called a meeting in the recreation hall first thing in the morning. Once everyone was gathered, he strode up to the raised stage and threw his gaze out into the assembled workers, soldiers and scientists.

"Due to last night's unfortunate accident, a man is dead." He paused but could tell from the mute response that his statement was no news. "This is not acceptable. You are here to work, not die because of your own ineptitude. I am disappointed that my leniency to your behaviour, rather than being treated as underserved benevolence, has been interpreted as a licence to play the fool. I should not be having to deal with a dead worker and all the inconvenience that flows from his idiocy."

Chemeris stirred in his seat and Rogov immediately placed a hand on his arm.

"Easy," he whispered under his breath. Chemeris sat back, but his eyes were a flame of loathing directed at the scarecrow figure on the stage.

"If proper protocol had been followed," continued Gasparov, seemingly unaware of the movement, "a man would not be wandering about outside on his own. From now on I will tolerate no deviation from the orders posted on every notice-board and on every dormitory wall."

He nodded towards the soldiers in the midst of the gathering. "Anyone travelling outside of the complex without accompaniment and outside hours of drilling operations will be treated as disobeying orders. I need not tell you again that this project functions under military rules. Any punishment will be treated as such." He pointed at a soldier in front of the stage.

"The assault rifles the guards carry are to protect us, to protect the project, but if that threat comes from within, then they have been ordered to treat it as they would an external threat."

Gasparov scanned the men and single woman before him. Anya shuddered as his gaze lingered a brief second on her before moving on. There was no noise from the room, no questions were asked.

"Now go back to your stations," spat Gasparov. "You!" he pointed at Chemeris. "You wait."

Rogov did not get an opportunity to speak to Chemeris until the end of his shift. Coming back from the rig and parting from his colleagues, he made his way to his room. After showering and getting changed into clean dry overalls, he made his way back to the recreation room.

As he had suspected, Chemeris was there, leaning against the bar. Unexpectedly, Anya sat beside him. She was chatting to him, her small girl's hand on his back.

"Look, she said to Chemeris, looking up as he approached. "It is Rogov come to join us!"

Chemeris peered hazily over his shoulder and returned to a drink he had on the bar before him.

"Rogov, Rogov," he mumbled. "The man who warns of... who warns..." He scratched his face with a stubby finger and yawned. "Sit here Rogov," he said, slapping an empty chair beside himself. "Sit here and... whatever." He threw the contents of his glass down his throat. Rogov leaned forward and took the now empty glass from his hand.

"You have had enough my friend. Come, we shall sit together in one of the cubicles and talk."

Surprisingly, Chemeris allowed himself to be guided to one of the soft chairs that sat around a table in one of the semi alcoves encircling the large room. Anya ordered coffee for three and as they settled themselves, Rogov nodded to Anya.

"I have not spoken to you in a while Anya Nevotslova, I hope all is well with you?"

"I am so sorry about Yashkin," she said. "It is so dreadful. I can still hardly believe it. Poor Yashkin!"

"Poor Yashkin," repeated Chemeris, his voice dull and low.

"It is tragic - this is an unforgiving place. Perhaps we had forgotten," said Rogov, looking toward Anya. He turned to the big man between them.

"Chemeris, Gasparov spoke with you?"

"Yes, yes, Gasparov spoke with me," agreed Chemeris. Rogov waited, anxious to know what had been said but too wary to ask with Anya present.

"I hate him you know," he said, raising a watery eye. "The man has poison for a heart and a mind more twisted than the remains of Stalingrad. He is not a man at all."

Anya placed his coffee into his hand and Chemeris took a sip.

"A bitter man, like this stinking coffee!" he said disgustedly.

"The coffee is fine," soothed Anya, "it will settle you. Here take more."

Obediently the big Russian did as he was told. Rogov touched his arm.

"So, what did he say?" he asked.

"Who?"

"Gasparov," replied Rogov. "He spoke with you this morning."

"I hate him you know," said Chemeris, his words slurred with the vodka.

"I know that," said Rogov, "but he must have said something?"

Chemeris raised a finger and waggled it in the air.

"Yes, but old Chemeris did as you told him. I listened and I did not speak. I told him nothing."

Rogov could see Anya dart him a sudden curious look.

"You had nothing to say old friend," said Rogov. "And that is good."

"He wanted to know why he was outside," said Chemeris suddenly. "Why he was outside on his own. He asked me who he was waiting for."

"What did you reply?"

"I said, 'I do not know comrade Gasparov.' That is what I said. 'I do not know.'"

"And he was satisfied with that?" queried Rogov. He could see that Anya was listening intently as her eyes darted from man to man.

"He called me a stupid *Kulak*. I would have killed him then but I did not have the courage." He looked up and thumped his chest. "I have the courage now - now I would kill him."

Rogov set his hand on his shoulder. "That is the vodka's boast. The man in there is wiser than that and that is good. You did well Chemeris. You did well."

Rogov was preparing to undress for bed when he heard a light knock on his door. Silently he crossed the room and opened the door a few inches to see who was outside. It was Anya. Quickly, he ushered her in.

"You should not be out of your room so late," he chided, his own words making him feel like a disapproving parent. "It is not..." he hesitated, but Anya finished his sentence.

"Safe?"

"I did not say that," he began, but Anya interrupted him.

"You have already warned me of being careful around Gasparov. Careful what I say - not to tell him about our discovery." She faced Rogov. "You think Yashkin's death was not an accident."

"I did not say that Anya, I am only saying we do not yet know how he died. It may well have been a terrible accident. The investigation is still ongoing." He had no idea if there was an investigation at all, but it would be very telling if there were not. Anya was undeterred.

"Are you suggesting Gasparov had something to do with his death?"

Rogov did not immediately reply. He looked at the girl and felt a weight of responsibility for her. She was young, and now he could see she was afraid. He was not sure that lying to her would help. He had already invested a trust in her, what was to gain from withholding another?

"I honestly don't know Anya," he admitted. "But there is danger here. Yes, Yashkin was probably driven over by a heavy truck, but was that was the cause of his death? The answer to that question determines just how safe any of us are here."

"Murder? You mean he might have been murdered? But why?" She nervously pushed her hair back from her face. Rogov felt another wave of vicarious parental care for Boris Nevoltslov's daughter.

"He spoke to Gasparov. He was suspicious of the project. He questioned Gasparov. Now he is dead. And there is another thing."

Anya's wide eyes looked expectantly for his disclosure.

"Chemeris and I were to meet Yashkin that night but we were both delayed. Had we been there, perhaps he would not have died."

"Or perhaps you all would have," added Anya slowly. Rogov merely gave a slight nod.

"Perhaps. So, we must be more careful than ever Anya. If Yashkin's impatient complaints were enough to have him murdered, then we are all under suspicion. It is not safe to act in any way that might attract particular attention."

Anya got up to go, but suddenly she turned and looked directly at Rogov.

"How well did you know my father?"

Rogov was caught off balance by the sudden and unexpected question. His slight hesitation was just long enough to encourage Anya to continue.

"You did know him, didn't you?"

Rogov looked back into the intensity of her small face. A face desperate to know more about a father so abruptly wrenched from her life. He could not tell her all he knew; he would not provide information that could only endanger her.

"Your father was my friend Anya."

Rogov could tell by the girl's expression that his reply was as unexpected as her question had been for him.

"Forgive me," he said, "but you must trust me if I do not say more. However, I can tell you that your father was a man of few equals. Boris Nevotslov was a father to be proud of."

Karmonov listened on the secure line as Gasparov related the recent events at the base. He let Gasparov continue without interruption, knowing that the silence on the other end of the phone would have caused him anxiety and fear of reprisal from the man who held such power over men's lives. Karmonov smirked as he heard the voice on the line rise in pitch and speed of delivery. Gasparov was nervous, his voice almost trembling as he related the circumstances.

"Yashkin was insistent, pushing me. He was no longer compliant in his obedience to orders. I could not have him spread his doubts like a virus among the others. I had to resort to direct action."

The phone remained silent and so he continued. "Do not worry about the means. I covered his killing by having him crushed below one of the heavy lorries. No one suspects anything other than he was involved in an accident of his own making."

Still Karmonov made no reply. Gasparov found himself speaking again. "I have cut off any dissenting sentiments before they had an opportunity to rise." He faltered. "Comrade Karmonov... can you hear me?"

"I hear you Gasparov," Karmonov's voice eventually growled down the line. "Are you finished?"

Gasparov tried to marshal his thoughts. He was used to being in control. Except when it came to Karmonov. Karmonov's power was as unassailable as winter in Siberia. Hard, indomitable, an irresistible will that subdued and controlled all others.

"Yes, that is my report."

Again, a moment of quiet before Karmonov's voice sliced the silence. "Are you capable, Gasparov?"

Gasparov nodded enthusiastically, it took him a second to realise he had not replied aloud.

"Yes, yes, be in no doubt of that. I have controlled this."

"The Nevotslova girl. Still nothing?"

Gasparov thought wildly. Did he mean her experiments or something else?

"She brought me some rock samples that she found intriguing. They were nothing, but her curiosity brought her to me. That is good."

"Make sure nothing is missed. Do you understand me *Grazhdanin* Gasparov?"

Gasparov did, and the pronoun made it clear where he stood. To be called citizen gave no sense of approbation.

"I will report when anything of note occurs. Have no doubt, I control these people. They have reason to fear me.

The silence on the phone lasted some seconds before Karmonov's voice finally replied.

"Good," he said, and the line went dead.

Gasparov replaced the receiver. His hands had a slight tremor and his throat was dry. Despite his anxiety, his awe of his superior was undiminished. A man worth emulating was a man who could radiate such authority down a telephone cable. He would not disappoint such a man.

It never occurred to Gasparov that even his personal determination was utterly influenced and directed by Karmonov.

In Arkhangelsk Viktor Karmonov sat looking out of his office window. The hand missing two fingers touched the scar above his eye. There were times when the old ache returned. A reminder of the ache for former days of glory. Days when the world trembled at the latent might of the Union of Soviet Socialist Republics. He recollected when the great Northern Fleet had had the British and Americans snapping like puppies at the heels of the Great Russian Bear. When the Americans grovelled as Khrushchev banged his shoe on their New York City tables. Days when the world bowed to the domination of the mighty USSR - a nuclear power unmatched in her ascendancy.

He called back his thoughts of the past and mused over the telephone conversation. One man did not dissent on his own. To be emboldened to broach authority a man needed some kind of subtle encouragement from other quarters. Yashkin had to have sympathisers at least.

For now however, he needed to trust Gasparov. He was probably capable of containing any deviation from the purpose of the drill project. The man was twisted enough, slavishly compliant. He had to hope his intellect was up to the requirement.

Chapter 25
Storm and Danger

Olonkinbyen shook, as the storm such as most of the men on the island had never experienced, came down with a mailed fist on the base. The wind was a living, violent animal, a wailing insane thing, howling with an ear-splitting scream at the doors and windows which shuddered and shook against the onslaught from outside. Now and then something loose outside would crash into a building, the noise causing its inhabitants to look nervously at one another for reassurance. A quarter of a mile out, a tiny vehicle swayed and pitched in the ferocious darkness.

"Almost there!" shouted Lars at the top of his voice. Lander nodded, holding on to the ceiling handle with as strong a grip as he could muster. The mule was bucking and lurching violently as Lars used all of his skill to maintain a forward motion. When they were 400 metres away, there was a sudden, blinding flash of light in the storm-filled darkness ahead. An explosion, dulled by the noise of the elements followed. Lander looked at the Norwegian.

"What was that?"

"Sounded like an explosion from the base. Look, we're just about here!"

They skidded into the base and headed straight for the main settlement building. Lars left the quad in the lee of one of the sheds and they both exited and struggled through the tearing wind to access the entrance porch. It was all either of them could do to wrench open the external doors, pushing them back against the wind and falling into the relative quiet of the porch.

When they made their way to the central lobby, all was a mass of activity. Men were running to and fro, some dressed in their full outdoor wear, others carrying tools and torches.

It was Ari Bjørnson who first noticed them staggering into the atrium. His agitated state was information enough that things were not good.

"Jon! Thank God! I thought we'd lost you both!"

Lander winced at Ari's elemental error. Lars was pulling his hood down and hadn't appeared to hear. He exaggerated his Scottish accent, hoping to remind the big man of his pseudonym.

"Aye, we'd thought we were done fer!" He caught the sudden light of comprehension on Ari's face and continued. "What was the noise? It sounded like an explosion?"

"It was. The main facility just erupted in a ball of flame!" He called a soldier over from the other side of the room. "Anders! Here!" He turned again and spoke quickly to Lander and Guldberg. "The storm must have caused some kind of catastrophic electrical malfunction. We need you both now. Lars, go with Anders here to the medical centre and bring as many bandages and Flamazine patches as you get carry. Sutherland, come with me, we have men who need our help!"

As Lander turned and ran behind Bjørnson, he could not help but notice that the Oversersjant seemed to have assumed a sudden mantle of authority. Briefly he wondered where Jensen was, but had no time to explore the thought as they climbed over rubble at a broken doorway and into a howling space of swirling snow that had once been the main command and control communications room.

It looked like a bomb had hit it. Pieces of equipment lay strewn about in tangled disarray. The stench of burning was still in the air and glass, tin sheeting and wooden beams lay in every shape on the floor. Most remarkable of all, one entire side of the room lay open and bare to the raging elements, elements which ripped and tore at anything loose and threatened to pull the entire building apart. The storm was a clawing animal, fighting the men over possession of the carcass between them. A group of men were desperately trying to tie down a ceiling and roof which creaked violently in the screaming wind. Others were frantically trying to shore up doorways and windows. It looked an almost impossible task. Ari led Lander to another side room off the half-destroyed C&C centre which, although damaged, still had its roof and walls intact. A soldier in his fatigues was bent over two or three men who looked like they had just been dropped from a war zone.

"We pulled them in here until we could get a way cleared through the mess behind us," shouted Ari. The wind whipped the words from his mouth as he spoke and Jon struggled to make out his words.

"We need to stop the bleeding before we can move them. Here, you help Pedersen while I treat Jensen."

Lander quickly moved over to the young soldier. He had his hands on the man's chest. A thick shard of wood protruded out from his ribs where it had been driven in by the force of the explosion. Blood was flowing from a deep slice across his forehead.

"Can you put pressure here?" shouted the young soldier. "I need to hold his head!"

As soon as he removed his hand and handed over, Jon realised that it was a sucking chest wound. The man was in a bad way. Just then Lars and Anders appeared, clambering over the wreckage. Lars went to aid Bjørnson while the other threw himself beside Lander and the other soldier, Pedersen. Without needing to be told, Lander grabbed the bandages and began stripping the patient's jacket and shirt off. He expertly began wrapping the rolls tightly around his chest, padding around the wooden spike as Pedersen immediately set about binding his head. Anders supported the wounded man to allow Lander to work. When it was done, he moved aside to allow the two soldiers space to lift the wounded man and rapidly proceed to remove him to the Medical Centre. Turning to Bjørnson, he saw that the other man was in no better state.

"It's Jensen!" shouted Ari. "Help me get him out of here!"

Lander took his legs while Ari supported his upper body. Leading the way, the Englishman clambered over the twisted panels of metal and out into the open violence of the destroyed part of the building. It was the only way to evacuate the man and he struggled over the debris, determined not to fall and negatively affect the commander's chances of survival.

It seemed as if the storm had only increased in intensity. The men trying to mitigate the damage were fighting a losing battle, strips of roofing ripped and tore off into the screeching darkness as Ari and he picked their way across the shards and ruins of the destruction below and all around them.

Once clear, they rapidly made their way to the Medical Centre. There were four or five there now altogether, but the two men most recently rescued were in the worst condition.

Ari had already performed a rapid triage and Lander assisted him and another orderly as they attempted to stabilise the two men.

Jensen had suffered a serious blow to the side of his head and that side of his body showed signs of having been close to a blast. Flesh all down that side was shredded and it looked like he had suffered fractures to ribs and possibly his right femur. His right hand seemed to have taken a huge impact, the bones clearly visible behind the torn and stripped skin. He was unconscious but breathing steadily.

Lander's casualty was less obviously injured. His head was bandaged and the blood seemed to have stopped flowing, but how deep the shard of wood had penetrated was difficult to ascertain. He was conscious but only just and he moaned in obvious pain.

"Bakke there needs x-rayed. I have a small scanner, but it is intended for small fractures, not body scans," said Ari, concern obvious in his voice. "I'm only medic trained – this is a job for the mainland."

"Have you any other way of contacting Oslo?" asked Jon. Ari shook his head.

"Not with the Communications Centre a smoking ruin. The only other radios we have are short distance FM sets.

Jon shook his head in thought. Contact with the outside world was no longer possible.

"We can't leave that in there," he said, nodding toward the wooden shaft. "Not if we can't evacuate."

"Won't Oslo react once they realise we are no longer sending our daily reports?" suggested the orderly.

"Even if they suspect a problem, no one is flying in this," replied Ari.

"We need to operate Ari," said Jon firmly. "And there is little to be gained by debating it."

Lars looked up and eyed Lander curiously from the other side of the room. Ari nodded.

"Yes, yes, you are right. You will have to assist me though."

"Well then, let's do it."

Leaving Jensen and the others in the hands of the orderly with help from Lars and the two soldiers, Ari and Jon wheeled the man into a side room containing a long flat elevated operating table and overhead lights. As a special forces veteran, Jon Lander, like his Norwegian counterpart, was trained in battlefield emergency aid. Ari bowed to his colleague's greater experience as Lander scrubbed up and went through a quick inventory of the surgical tools in the stainless steel cupboard.

"Cut off the stake to about an inch above his chest," said Lander. "I'm worried one of us will knock against it. It's probably already pressing against some vital organ."

The man, Bakke, had mercifully fallen into unconsciousness, which was a relief since there appeared to be no anaesthesia available.

Outside in the darkness, the raging storm continued to batter against the buildings. Lander wondered how long they could hold up against such relentless violence. Clearing his mind, he looked up at Bjørnson, his lower face already covered in a surgical mask, and began to work.

When they were finished and had tied off the final sutures, the two men left the still unconscious man on the theatre table and retreated to the main room. The orderly was cleaning away the shards of cloth from the many cuts and abrasions on Jensen's body. Lars was over with the others who seemed to have injuries mainly consisting of minor fractures, concussion and surface wounds. The casualties were all sitting up and conscious.

"I sent the others out to assist in storm damage control," said Lars, looking up briefly.

"Good," said Ari, then turning to the orderly, "How is the commander?"

"I think he needs proper secondary care," replied the orderly. Ari looked and agreed.

"I think we can stitch much of the wounds here once you get all the dirt cleaned away. His leg; well, it won't threaten his life, but I don't know about his head. It is a severe trauma."

Lander leaned over. "It looks like a compression fracture. It's not good Ari."

"He was right at the centre of whatever it was that blew up," replied Ari, "He must have tried to shield himself with his hand. What a mess."

"Probably lightning," said Lar's voice. "I saw some strikes in the storm when Donald and I were making our way back."

"How long do you think this will last?" asked Ari. "You're the senior meteorologist."

"This is a major front. It could last for days at these latitudes," replied Guldberg. "This won't blow over in an hour or two."

Two hours later Guldberg's professional opinion was still holding up. If anything, the storm had intensified. The ruined wing had been sealed off but judging by the crashing and banging, the wind seemed to be working away at the roof panels, leaving the whole building in danger of exposure and destruction.

"We could move to one of the other buildings," Ari explained to Lander, "but moving outside in this is probably too dangerous, and I don't think we can risk moving the seriously injured."

"Ari," said Lander, "the danger is perhaps greater than you think. The storm might possibly kill us, but I don't think it was the cause of the explosion."

Bjørnson's eyes narrowed as the import of Lander's suggestion sunk home.

"Johannsen's murderer?"

"Someone who wants to shut down this place, or silence something someone has discovered."

"You think it has something to do with the mountain," stated Ari. He was thinking, adding up the events and coincidences and coming into line with Jon's suspicions.

"Johannsen found something out and ended up dead. The two senior staff he reported to back in Norway disappeared off the face of the map. Henrik Jensen, in his confiding in you, showed he too had stumbled on something. He shut up the mountain because of it. I had said earlier that Henrik Jensen was either complicit in the murders, or in great danger. I was not wrong."

Ari clenched his fists together and his jaw muscles tightened.

"Then someone here is a murderer and he will stop at nothing. What do we do now?"

"We need to get word out somehow," suggested Lander. "Oslo might have some way of reaching us, there may even be Navy ships near at hand." He did not mention his covert satellite connection. It was useless in the current conditions in any case, unable to transmit in work in total overcast, let alone hurricane conditions. The frustration was that he knew for a fact that HMS Albion lay waiting somewhere out to the west. Apart from the safety it could provide, it also had a fully equipped medical bay and ship's surgeon. Without a radio though, there was no way of contacting its Captain.

Ari suddenly stopped and lifted his eyes. "The Beerenburg," he said. "There is a shortwave transmitter at the lab there."

Outside, in the maw of the incandescent gale, Jon Lander once again found himself alone as he struggled through the wind, making his way onto the eastern shore of the island. The hurricane, which was attacking from the north-west was robbed of its full power by the lee of the high hills to his left. Unable to rip the man off his feet, it did everything else it could, hurling gravel, detritus and stones through the air like volleys fired from the guns of madmen.

Ari had done all he could to dissuade him, but Lander forcefully insisted. There was no other choice. He had to make the attempt if Jensen and the other soldier were to have any hope. That Ari could not come was clear. There was a murderer somewhere at the base and Ari needed to be there to contain him. So he had donned protective foul-weather clothing and set out into the impossible conditions.

As he struggled against the tortuous winds, he knew he had made the only right choice on attempting the island crossing on foot. The high-sided mule was too susceptible to the raging wind. His plan was to head to Metten, where he had left the quad from his earlier foray. Lower to the ground, he estimated that it would be possible to use it, as he had done once already, to make the overland journey to the mountain.

He glanced back. Already the lights from the base were no longer visible, the faint glimmering rapidly dimming in the tumult behind and finally disappearing into the horizontal madness of storm, snow and hail. The noise was incredible. It was if all the demons of Danté had massed around him, screaming from their foul mouths threats of hopelessness and death to the man who dared venture into their lair.

But Jon Lander was no ordinary man. He had been places on active service unrecorded on official documents. He had climbed mountains in Afghanistan, crossed deserts in Yemen, cut through jungles in Guatemala and lain out for weeks in the sodden fields of County Armagh. Jon Lander had looked death in the face and developed an uneasy truce with the shadowy unknown.

Keeping low, he followed the dips of the ground, all the time buffeted by the heavy-weight blows that came from every unexpected direction. More than once he was thrown down by a sudden violent gust, but getting quickly up, he pressed on. The Metten now he knew was less than a mile distant.

Jon could run a six-minute mile pace, but the last stretch to the huts took him almost an hour. He was tiring and knew he would need the quad.

The quad was in its place where he had left it. Without wasting time, he got it started and closing the doors behind him, throttled out into the darkness. This time he did not worry about running without lights. As he wrestled the four-wheeler over the gravelled landscape, the beams foraged ahead, the light filled with streaks of storming snow and hail.

It was as he was approaching the shoulders of the Beerenburg that something to his left caught his eye. He did a quick second take - taking his eyes from the route ahead was dangerous and he could only take quick looks in short glances. He imagined he had seen a flash of light cresting a low hill on the central spine of the island. He shook his head and dismissed the idea quickly. He was the only lunatic out here. Most likely it was a reflection in his goggles from the headlights. He had to periodically pause to wipe obscuring snow off the shatterproof polyamide. The thick neck warmer pulled up over his lower face was crusted in icy frost from his breath and snow was constantly trying to force its way between his fur-lined hood and his head. Undeterred, he pressed on, the noise of the motor below him completely lost in the howl of the wind.

Eventually and to his immense relief, he rolled up to the steel entrance door of the tunnel into the mountain. The chain was as he had left it. He got off the quad, pulling a pair of bolt cutters from his backpack. No delicate lock picking this time.

Just as he approached the chain, he saw his own shadow appear on the door. He turned and saw a set of headlights crest the last rise on the track. He caught a brief glimpse of the bonnet as the lights lowered momentarily on a dip on the track. It was one of the base's Mercedes G-Wagens. Someone had taken their life in their hands and driven it up over the central track in the teeth of the storm – the madness of which could only be because of some new emergency that had occurred since he left. Had there been another explosion? A fire? And who was it? Was it Ari? If so, the situation could only have become drastically worse. He waited as the jeep approached. To his consternation it stopped thirty metres back, its headlights blinding him. He could just make out the driver's door open and a shape step out.

A sixth sense born by years of exposure to danger suddenly alerted Lander. Without hesitation he reacted immediately. Dropping to the ground, he reached into his coat even as he rolled out of the glare of the lights. There was a flash from the vehicle and the steel door behind him rang as if hit by a hammer. A loud crack from the vehicle followed almost instantaneously.

Most people, if under attack do the sensible thing - run away from the threat. Lander's life of military training sponsored an automatic response. Advance under fire. Raising the Glock he had wrenched from its inner holster, he fired three shots in quick succession at where he had last seen his assailant. As he did so, he darted forward, head lowered. Dropping behind a boulder, he rolled momentarily to his left and fired three more. He spun back as several high velocity shots came back, the supersonic cracks of the bullets passing over his head or ricocheting off stones around him. His would-be killer then was armed with a rifle, possibly a Kalashnikov. He was out-gunned. Nonetheless he was looking for another point to advance to when a noise alerted him to the vehicle moving. Raising his head above the boulder, another shot cracked over his head followed by the Mercedes rapidly reversing back down the track. Lander took aim and fired another three shots at the retreating vehicle. One at least found its aim as one of the headlights shattered into darkness, the copper jacketed bullet striking the lamp.

Not waiting for his attacker to stop and use his advantage of distance for his rifle, Lander wasted no time. Rushing to the gate, he picked up the bolt-cutters from the ground where he had dropped them and snapped the chain. Glancing backward only briefly, he leapt onto the quad which was still ticking over in front of the gate. Gunning its engine, he roared into the chamber and sped down the descending tunnel.

Ari had told him that there had been a short wave radio in the scientist's lab. His initial concern had been the journey through the storm to the mountain. His mouth tightened in a determined scowl. His concerns had just gone forth and multiplied.

Chapter 26
Paris

Jonas Smythe looked at the report on the desk before him. He lifted the sheets, rubbed the side of his nose, stood up and walked to the barred bulletproof window. He absently looked across the embankment and up toward Lambeth Bridge. People were passing by on the footpath beneath, people occupied with their own little worlds, ignorant of so much, and happier for it. He looked again at the report. A man with some kind of savant knowledge had appeared out of nowhere. He had been the apparent subject of an attempted murder and after leaving some evidence that he was still alive, had disappeared, turning up again in France with a passport not in his own name. His own name appeared to be Finn, but that was not certain. Finn.

Jonas watched a barge slowly pass by on the Thames. The large vessel passed with such elegant grace that he paused to watch the lazy ripples spread out behind the hull. Oily fingers caressing the water.

A gun traceable to possible KGB involvement had been used. Finn. He pondered the name. Eleven years in a coma the report had said. He tapped his fingers against the internal bars of the window. There was something, something he couldn't quite put his finger on. He looked again at the draft report. It wasn't even a case he was involved in. The PSNI in Northern Ireland had alerted the Security Services' office at their base in an army barracks outside Belfast. MI5 ran a counter-intelligence operation in support of the police's anti-terrorism efforts over there. They had sent their daily report over and he had only happened to come across it in Thames House's daily briefing. What were the KGB doing in Ulster? They had no interests there. He set the report onto his desk. He had a contact at the Russian embassy at Kensington Gardens. He would make a quick telephone call.

Leaving Joué-sur-Erdre, Finn set out again on his bicycle. A few hours ahead lay the town of Châteaubriant. From there he could get a train to Vitré and from there a direct line to Paris. The cycling was a pleasure to him, a joy almost, but he knew he did not have the time to cycle through France. He was headed north, much farther north. He cycled until darkness fell and he found himself on the outskirts of the town. There was a small wood off the cycleway and walking in fifty metres or so, he came to an old fallen oak, its trunk covered in moss. Dry brown leaves filled a dell alongside it. The night was warm and he formed a bed out of leaves alongside the tree. Lying on the soft ground, he pulled his coat over himself and turned over onto on his back. Looking up through the gaps in the forest canopy he watched the stars pass by in their eternal circuits. Tiredness bid him enter its realm of sleep and soon Finn was oblivious to the sounds of the wood at night and awake to the dreams that awaited him.

There was a girl. Golden haired and deep blue eyes; eyes that a man could get lost in. She was smiling, a smile that radiated from the depth of her soul and filled his own as a pitcher from a flowing stream.

"Father says we must be careful," she said. She was speaking Russian, her accent softer than normally allowed by its Slavic cadences. "He says not to talk to anyone while we're out." She laughed and looked at him over her graceful shoulders.

Following her, Finn looked around. The long thin branches of the birch trees reached into the pale blue sky, hands raised in praise, silent songs rising from silvery limbs. Vibrant mosses tumbled around their slender trunks as sun speckled birds flittered across their path. Beside them, a stream babbled its way to the river beyond.

Reaching the broad river, grass-lined shores bordered the lazy waters while across the other side, Finn saw the forest stretch for as far as the eye could see.

"This is a beautiful place," he said. He wanted to add that it was so because of the light that was the girl beside him, but he didn't quite find the courage.

"In winter it becomes a snow globe here," she said. "Snow covers the branches and flurries scatter across the river, sparkling in the light. It is a magical place. I'm glad you like it."

"Is that Lake Onega?" he asked, pointing through the trees to where the river seemed to widen into a silvery strip."

"Yes," she smiled. "As big as a sea. I think it is almost the largest lake in Europe, even though this is Russia."

" I think... yes, Lagoda is bigger, but Onega has one thousand six hundred and fifty two islands," he added, immediately regretting issuing such a pointless statement.

She turned to him, a slightly curious look on her face. "Father told me you would do things like that," she said.

"Like what?" he asked, kicking himself for his awkwardness.

"Say things, just know things," she replied. "He said not to be surprised if you seemed to, well, just know things."

"Sorry," he said with a mock grimace, "I just spout off sometimes – ignore me and hopefully I'll just go away."

"Oh!" she said suddenly, "I hope not!" She immediately flushed while Finn felt something like a wave of electricity suddenly rush across his chest. They both laughed and began walking along the soft pine needles of the track along the river.

"Your father is a remarkable man. I owe him my life," he said.

"He says *you* are remarkable. He says you have a capacity to learn that is unlike anything he has ever seen. You are not Russian and yet you speak just as if you are. Where did you ever learn our language?"

He shook his head. "I did not learn it, I concentrate and I know. I know this makes no sense, but it has something to do with something that happened to me in the sea." He shook his head quickly. "But no more about me. I am boring. I want to know more about you, I want to know about your life, your dreams, what you like, what you hate. Tell me about your studies, about metallurgy, about Arkhangelsk, tell me about you."

She laughed again and playfully punched him on the shoulder. He cried out in mock pain and grasped her hand. She looked up, her eyes a magnet for his own. After a moment, she smiled, turned and continued walking slowly along the river bank. He walked beside her. He still held her small and slender one in his own. His clasp was light but she made no effort to recover it and so they walked silently under the green sun spangled branches, hand in hand, hearts beginning to beat with a nascent excitement of anticipation only those who have known it would understand.

It was the birds that woke Finn. The dawn chorus was a harmony of calls, song and chirpings that seemed designed to re-awaken a person into a world of lightness and hope.

"Anya," he said aloud, his voice an interruption to the sounds of the stirring wood. He lay on his back, the lightening sky visibly taking on colour above him. He had dreamed of a girl – a girl who lived, a girl who was the first person he felt he knew- and did not know. Anya, the daughter of Boris Nevotslov. His name had come as a fact, hers as a revelation. The dream he knew was not a fabrication of the unconscious mind in sleep. Just as a person can tell on waking what was memory or the invention of dream, Finn knew that he had remembered a person of flesh and blood. The want to know more, specifically, to know more about her was an ache he knew would not easily fade.

Around him the forest was chittering and singing. In the distance he could hear the background of the waking world of men, distant lorries, the sound of roads and the arousal of the local French town.

Clearing his mind as well as he could, he got up and collected his cycle. Brushing the leaves off his trousers, he retraced his steps out to the track. There would be a place to wash in Châteaubriant. Then he would find a café. After breakfast he would head for Vitré and the connection to Paris. He needed to pass through Paris - he was not sure yet exactly why, but he also knew that he would.

Anya. He could see her face, recall the touch of her hand, the warmth of her eyes, the brightness of her laugh. For the first time he felt an assurance, a purpose that had eluded him since his awakening in Glasgow Royal Infirmary. He needed to find the girl, if nothing else made sense, one thing alone did - finding the girl with the golden hair and vibrant laugh that suddenly give birth to something in his being that he had forgotten. Until now.

"So, we've given over the lead to Security Services," explained the PSNI inspector to Jack. "We'll continue in the investigation of crime surrounding the cause of the fire, but the hunt for your missing Scot is being taken up by them."

Sam Anderson sat on the edge of Jack's desk, a cup of coffee steaming in his hand. Jack was back in his office in the Northern Ireland Police headquarters outside Belfast and Sam Anderson's statement was not one he had expected.

"But we don't even know where he is," exclaimed Jack. "He could be still here, possibly injured for all we know!" He motioned his question with open hands. "Security Services? So how will that work anyway?" Privately he wondered if his mentioning the possible KGB connection to his Chief back in Glasgow had initiated the MI5 involvement. Having a case taken from under his feet was humiliating enough, to have it annexed by MI5 stank of deference to a supposed superior agency.

"Look Jack, this aspect of the case is not really our specialism. Since power was devolved to the Northern Ireland Assembly, intelligence primacy has been given to MI5. We don't like it much, to be honest. We were running rings around the Provos all day long and they knew it. Why do you think they called a ceasefire? Out of the goodness of their hearts?"

"Hardly," acquiesced Jack.

"So now the powers that be tell us that it's a grand idea to put the murderous perpetrators of our troubles into positions of power and give them free reign to govern the population they spent thirty years terrorising with bombs and bullets. That's the cross we have to bear for no longer being shot in our doorways or blown up in our cars, taking the kids to school." The big Ulsterman gave a sigh and was quiet for second before continuing.

"Anyway," he said, "the way around preventing the terrorists, ex-Provos, dissidents and loyalist factions – who we now have to call *politicians* - having access to the intelligence gathered against them was to hand it to Security Services. So don't feel bad about not feeling trusted. I know exactly how it feels."

"I understand," admitted Jack, "but still, we were getting somewhere with this. There's more to a man with a missing memory here, I'm sure of it."

"Maybe," admitted Sam, "and maybe you'll find you're still involved in some way. All I know is, the case of Finn the mystery man is no longer our business. On the plus side, you get to go home."

Jack nodded. Not that coming to Belfast had been onerous. He had enjoyed the big man's easy manner and company. Whatever the future might hold for his country, Jack was sure that as long as men like him existed, it would be in good honest hands.

As Sam went to leave the office he suddenly stopped and turned back to face Jack.

"Oh, I forgot in the middle of my complaining, we do know where your man isn't."

"What, what do you mean?"

"He's isn't in Northern Ireland. He left Warrenpoint by boat to Nantes on Friday apparently. Using the McCracken's son's passport. So, sounds like he's a problem for the French now in any case."

Finn had bought some bread and cheese in Châteaubriant for the journey onwards. It was a little over thirty miles to Vitré and in the end he decided to cycle the distance. Much of the way was on dedicated cycle-ways and he reckoned he could cover the distance in less than three hours.

Continuing by bicycle also avoided public transport and places where he might come across police. He was also reluctant to leave the quiet peace of the French countryside, its green pastures and lazy rivers a salve to his ever active mind.

At Vitré he was able to buy a single ticket to Paris. He was pleased when he discovered there was a bicycle storage area on the train. Settling down for the journey, he watched the Loire countryside pass by the windows, the rhythmic trum-de-trum-de-trum of the train a metronomic cadence, bringing discipline to the riot of his thoughts.

A few hours later he stepped out of Gare Saint-Michel Notre-Dame and into the late afternoon light of central Paris. The first thing that hit him was the noise and bustle of the city, its disinterested busyness a contrast to the pastoral ease of the Central Loire.

He walked out, pushing his bicycle and made his way to the Pont Saint Michel. Standing over the Seine he could see Notre Dame's twin spires to the east while across the river the Gothic windows of the Sainte Chapelle loomed over the Ile de la Cité. Still pushing his cycle, he made his way to Pont Neuf. Crossing it he turned left and after a few minutes arrived in the Jardin de Tuileries. Behind him the glass pyramid of the Louvre sparkled in the warm sunlight while down the avenue of the park, the Champs-Élysées stretched all the way out to the Arc de Triomphe. Finding a park café along one of the dusty paths, he bought a coffee and croissants. Nantes seemed a long way away. Leaning back and closing his eyes, he began to consider his next steps.

Jonas Smythe thought over what he knew. His contact at Kensington gardens had been helpful. Without directly saying it, the Russian official had let him know that they were aware of the transit of a person of interest who had travelled to Ireland. A person closely monitored by state security. He was suspected of having information concerning a series of murders in Europe and Russia, but evidence was thin. He had apparently met others likeminded somewhere in Ireland but now he had disappeared off the radar. Any information Jonas might have would be greatly appreciated.

Jonas mentioned the missing Scot – the man with particular abilities, but suffering some kind of long term memory loss. The official's unknowing response convinced Jonas that Finn was not someone he had heard of. He left it at that, unwilling to alert his equivalent in the embassy to any particular interest Thames House might have. Then there was Lebedev. Sergei Lebedev. An agent who was hard to define. He had worked for the SVR, the Russian Foreign Intelligence Service. There was a suggestion that he had moved over to the FSB, the Federal Security Service. Either way, he was a man whom Jonas had had dealings with in a case where shared national interests had made it imperative that sensitive information be disclosed. The fact that it had remained secure had persuaded him that Lebedev was that rare thing, a foreign agent who could be trusted. He wondered if he was still attached to the SVR headquarters at the Yasenevo District in Moscow.

Jonas dismissed the idea of any communication on that front, at least for now. Nonetheless, he decided it was possibly time to mention what he had garnered from the embassy to Sir Simon. The man had an encyclopaedic brain, an ability to put together tiny bits of information and make a greater sense of them.

"You say it is already being investigated by the police in Glasgow?" asked Sir Simon when Jonas mentioned the circumstances of the case to him. They were having lunch together in the Thames House cafeteria - often a place where business was discussed in a less formal way.

"Yes, an inspector John McGregor," said Jonas, setting his coffee back onto the table before him. "He was brought into a team investigating deaths in a fire in Northern Ireland. Apparently he had some previous knowledge of the Scot and had already been conducting some kind of enquiries into his background."

"Hmmm… *Finn*, you say?" In response to the younger man's nod, he continued, "See if you can't set up a meeting sometime in the next week. Not over the 'phone. Let's have a talk with this inspector face to face eh?"

Jonas tried not to show the surprise he felt. He had only expected a listening ear and possibly a reassurance that he was only shooting at shadows, not the birth of an investigation.

"Will do sir. Here in London then?"

"Oh yes, I should think so," responded his boss, "and Jonas?"

"Sir?"

"Invite Commodore Legge to the same meeting."

Finn found himself outside the vast train station at Montparnasse. Famed for having a steam locomotive crash out through its walls and onto the street below in the early 1900's, it was now a huge building on several levels with trains arriving and departing day and night.

As if he did it every day, he made his way to an offshoot under the station. As if following some invisible line in the ground, he followed a subliminal urging to where there was an underground plaza featuring dozens of secure lockup boxes lined along two walls. Each cabinet was marked with a letter and a number and Finn moved along until he came to one stencilled J23. No key was required as there was a keypad with letters and numbers on each door. Without thinking about it, Finn reached forward and keyed in two letters followed by a six-digit number. Turning the knob, the door opened easily. Inside the cabinet was a thick brown envelope. Marked on the outside in Russian was written, Ob'yasneniye - "An Explanation."

Suddenly Finn became aware that he was no longer another anonymous visitor to a French train station. He was the single subject of attention to someone near at hand. That someone was watching him – had eyes on him at that very moment. Without looking around, he shut the cabinet door. Clutching the envelope in his hand, he left his bicycle lying against the station wall, and turned and walked straight to the nearest stairs. He knew the expectation was for him to leave the station. Instead he took the downward steps where he came to an escalator. He didn't look back but he could sense that he had a follower. The escalator was two-deep with people on their way to various platforms. It was too much of a press to push past but as soon as his feet hit the tiles at the bottom, he dashed forward and took an immediate left. A short transit corridor split into two offshoots leading to platforms heading different directions. He took the left and skidded out onto the platform heading south and country-bound. Careering down the platform, he took a connecting corridor at the end and ran back up a flight of stairs, three steps at a time. As he ran, the envelope in his hand caught a handrail and was knocked to the ground, papers spreading out across the tiled floor. He turned back to pick them up but immediately heard running footsteps on the floor below. Ahead was another escalator. Only able to recover a couple of sheets, he was forced to leave what was still scattered and bolted up the escalator, arriving onto a circular court. From there several exits led away. He rushed forward and took the one with another set of upward leading stairs. As he reached the top, he chanced a quick glance over his shoulder. Two grim looking men were sprinting and had just reached the bottom of the stairs. The hard eyes of one closest caught Finn's look and as he did so, in a single fluid motion, he pulled a pistol from an inside pocket, took aim and fired. The bullet slammed into a step above Finn's head, a dull suppressed crack from the weapon following immediately. Finn broke into a mad run as above his head other shots followed. The intent was obvious. They wanted him dead. No matter that they were in a very public place, they would shoot him dead like a dog in the street.

Suddenly Finn erupted out of the station into the sunlight. Right in front of him, not ten metres away a police officer was directing traffic. Finn ran toward him.

"Deux kamikazes! Just derrière moi!" he shouted. "They have guns!"

The policeman stared at Finn, processing the information he had just received about two suicide bombers. Half a second later the two heavy-set men suddenly appeared as they careered out of the exit Finn had just used. In one glance, the officer gauged the situation. He immediately unclipped his holster and drew his issue Sig-Sauer. As he did so, Finn's leading pursuer fired a wild shot toward them. Finn heard the bullet ricochet off the pavement between himself and the police officer.

"Se mettre à couvert!" the officer shouted to Finn as he dropped down and fired three rapid shots at the gunman. Finn hardly needed the advice; he took cover behind a parked Renault but was able to see that his assailants had managed to get back into the station. The officer had his pistol in one hand aimed at the exit while calling for assistance on

his radio with the other. In what seemed less than a minute, Finn heard the odd French *hee-haw* of an approaching police car. He would have left the scene at that point except that, seeing an opportunity to take cover himself, the officer ran over and crouched down beside him.

"How do you know they are suicide bombers?" he asked Finn breathlessly, his face fixed toward the station, his gun still aimed at the exit. Other sirens could now be heard approaching and people were running out of the doorway, scattering into the street in wild panic.

"I overheard them say they were going to detonate at the stairs – I just ran for my life and saw you!"

The policeman did not turn his head as he kept his vigilance on the train station exit across the road.

"Why were they chasing you?"

"I don't know... do you think they were chasing me?"

The officer did not reply, instead he was responding to his radio, directing the backup as it arrived. Within minutes the street was alive with armed police, some with carbines and sub-machine guns. Gradually the police took control and Finn's companion was joined by several others. He waited for an opportunity to slip away unnoticed, but none came. As the scene escalated into one of securing the area, an armed response team entered the station in full protective body armour, gas masks and ballistic helmets. Unable to get away, he found himself now the interest of the police. Led away from the scene, Finn was processed through a couple of police officers until he found himself in the back of an unmarked Police Nationale saloon and being driven by two officers to the *Hotel de Police du XIV Arrondissement*. It was less than half a mile from the train station and Finn was no sooner in the car than he was out of it and in a room inside the large multi-storey police station.

He was left for fifteen minutes on his own until at last an officer in plain clothes entered, a coffee in one hand and a *gauloises* cigarette in the other. He pulled up a seat and sat opposite Finn.

"So," he said, his voice gravelly and low. "You are O.K?" Finn detected from his accent that he was not a Parisian. Almost certainly from Marseilles.

"I'm fine. A bit shook up," he replied, changing his accent to the same Marseilles twang of his interviewer.

"You up on holiday, or a student?"

"Just visiting," replied Finn, "It's my first time in Paris."

The detective smiled. "I don't suppose you expected to come all the way from Marseilles to be shot at eh?"

"No, though things can get rough enough there too."

"Don't I know it," said the officer, his face smiling again. "My name is Pierre Martin. I'm a detective here. We just want to ask you a few questions if you don't mind. Hopefully it'll not take too long. How do you feel? Can I get you a coffee?"

Finn shook his head. "No, I'm fine. Just so glad the police were there. No, I'm good."

When the officer asked his name, Finn gave *Guillaume Bisset*. It was a combination of names he had seen on a French movie poster on the train. The detective asked several questions about what had happened. Finn stuck to his story. He had overheard them agreeing to blow themselves up. He had run to get help. They had tried to stop him.

"Yes," nodded the officer quietly. "Unusual though, Guillaume. If they were going to blow themselves up there and then, why chase after you? I mean, it's not like it would have changed anything. Why try to stop you?"

Finn shrugged. "I've no idea; I don't know what they were thinking. I just ran like mad."

The officer eyed Finn carefully. "Have you been in Nantes recently?"

"No, Nantes? Well, yes, the train to Paris came through Nantes. I didn't get off though."

"Do you have you I.D?"

"Yes, I should have it here." He rummaged inside his backpack. As he did so, he directed his mind into deep concentration. "Let's see..." he pulled out his borrowed passport but kept it face side down, hiding the nationality. He was thinking rapidly.

"You know what," he said suddenly. "I've just now realised how I know you. You're Pierre Martin from La Valentine!"

The officer had taken the passport but Finn's unexpected exclamation made him suddenly look up in surprise. "What?"

"*Monsieur* Martin. You live out near the cemetery at Vaudran. Your son Michel and I went to school together."

"You know Michel?"

"We used to race together at the velodrome. We were in the same team. I remember he was so pleased when you came to his events. I haven't seen Michel in years! I thought I recognised you. Ha! What a small world!"

"I don't think I recall Michel mention a Guillaume Bisset," said the detective thoughtfully. Suddenly he was interrupted by the door opening and a middle-aged woman went to enter. She halted when she saw the room was not empty.

"Oh, sorry sir," she said, "I hadn't realised the room was in use."

"No problem Agnès," he glanced at the passport, still face down in his hand. "Actually, you could do me a favour. Photocopy this please, and bring it straight back?"

He handed her the passport, and apologising again, she left with it in her hand.

"*Bisset*, you say? So where do you live in Marseilles then?"

"Just down the road from you," said Finn with a grin. "You know the Traverse du Grand Valla? I live at the bottom. Michel and I built a hut in the pine woods there right beside where the stream runs into a pond at the bottom. I'm sure you know it?"

The detective lifted his coffee mug again and set it down after putting it to his lips.

"Yes, I know it very well. I used to walk there often... ugh!" he grimaced abruptly. "This coffee is cold. Are you sure you won't have a coffee? I could do with a hot one."

"Actually, I think I would, thanks."

The detective got up, headed to the door but looked back curiously at Finn.

"He competes at national level now you know," he said, rubbing his cheek.

"Oh, Michel does? That's amazing! I thought after the accident and all... you know. That's great! Cycling again? Tell him I am so pleased for him when you see him!"

Both Pierre Martin and Finn knew that Michel Martin's car accident two years earlier led to him having to give up cycling altogether. The detective had been testing him. He could not know however that Finn was aware of the subterfuge.

As soon as the man left the room, Finn was up. His passport was gone now, but there was nothing he could do about that. What he could do was to act quickly and he needed to if he were to get out and away.

He was in the corridor even as the officer's back turned a corner ten feet away. Without hesitation, Finn went the other way and after pushing through a set of double doors, quickly descended several flights of utilitarian concrete stairs. They were an emergency exit and at the bottom Finn emerged into an underground garage. A police van had just driven in and Finn waved him down.

"Quickly, follow me! There's an incident upstairs! Have you your gun? Pierre Martin has been shot!"

The single uniformed officer hesitated but Finn opened the door of the van.

"Hurry Bastien!" he urged, using the man's name. "We can get behind them on the fire stairs! Quickly, quickly! *Se dépêcher!*"

Finn turned and ran to the doors that led to the stairs he had just come down. To his relief he heard the confused officer hard on his heels. As they began to ascend the stairs, Finn suddenly halted.

"My pistol magazine, I've left it in the car!" he began to return to the garage. "Fourth floor, just beside the shredder! Wait for me at the top!"

Finn retraced his steps to the underground garage and darted to the van. As he suspected, the policeman had left the keys in the ignition with the confusion Finn's unexpected intervention had caused. Leaping in, he gunned the engine and sped up the exit ramp. As he thought would happen, the exit gate opened via a pressure switch under the roadway, a switch he could not have activated without a vehicle.

Exiting onto the road, he pulled hard on the wheel and turned right, heading toward the Seine. As he passed the tomb of Napoleon, he turned on the lights and sirens and raced across le Pont de Invalides. Now on the North bank of the river, he kept the two-tones on and skidded into a narrow street not far from the American embassy. Jumping out he left the police vehicle jammed in the street where it would cause an obvious obstruction, then turning back on himself he began walking briskly back toward the Seine. A street vendor was selling cheap souvenirs at the side of the river. Finn bought a pair of sunglasses and a baseball cap in the colours of the national flag. His appearance suitably altered, he went to the nearest Metro and bought a ticket at a booth. He didn't have long to wait and soon he was headed back south but underground, passing back toward the 15th Arrondissement not far from Montparnasse. He guessed that above him the police would be focusing their attention in the direction of the stolen police van and the north side of the Seine. Emerging out of the station, he made his way back to the train station at Montparnasse. He entered by another route and after a few twists and turns, found himself back at the plaza where he had opened the safe box. As he had guessed, his bicycle lay where he had left it only a couple of hours previously. Police were moving through the station, in some numbers, moving people along, eyes out for the two gunmen who were almost certainly far away by now.

Finn made a decision. It was risky staying longer in the station, but he returned to the stairs where he had dropped the envelope. Quickly looking around, it was clear that the pages had been scattered and blown all over the concourse. He found one jammed under a ticket barrier, another in a waste bin. Seeing no others, he sighed, shook his head and left. The risk was too great. There were CCTV cameras everywhere and the police were still scouring the station. He could only hope that what pages were left would be cleared away be the cleaners. The information on them was lost to him now and he could not help that. He put the envelope in his rucksack and taking the bicycle, Finn matter-of-factly strolled to a set of stairs leading out on the way he had entered. Carrying the cycle over his shoulder, he left the station on the opposite side to where he had first been chased out earlier. Calmly mounting his bike, he was spotted by police at a barrier. One shouted at him, ordering him to get away. He waved in compliance and cycled carelessly past the barrier as the officers impatiently gesticulated for him to hurry up. He passed a series of police cars and response vehicles, did not look back and headed west.

A couple of hours later he was passing the Palace of Versailles and into the countryside of a myriad of little French villages and towns.

As he cycled, Finn appraised his position. Unfortunately, he was now a wanted man. The CCTV at the police station would have reasonable images of him and with their possession of the McCracken passport, would undoubtedly commence an investigation which would lead back to Ireland. He had been as careful as he could but he had not foreseen the gunmen at the station. Who they were and how they had known to wait at the plaza was a blank to him. One thing he knew for sure. The days ahead were going to be a lot more dangerous than just avoiding arrest and delay to the vague but urgent compulsion to head north. He was finished at Paris; of that he was certain. The thought suddenly reminded him of the envelope in his backpack. At last he could find time to see what it contained, but not right now. Now he needed to find a place to stay for the night.

Chapter 27
London

Inspector John McGregor had never been in the MI5 headquarters before. He had no reason to imagine that he ever would. Nonetheless, here he was, sitting around a leather-topped board table in the heart of Thames House. Five other men sat around the table, only one of whom he had so far met.

Jonas Smythe had arranged it all, including the flights and the hotel. No one had yet mentioned the reason for his presence, though Jack guessed it could only have something to do with the suggestion of KGB involvement in the Northern Irish case.

"So, gentlemen," said the dapper Jonas Smythe, "best if we are all introduced." He smiled a smile possessed by a man used to being at ease with himself and his grasp of events. "This is Detective Inspector Jack McGregor, CID at Glasgow."

Jack nodded. The man had done his homework. Jack, not John.

"The rest of us know one another, but let me introduce to you Sir Simon Montague, head of MI5."

Sir Simon folded his hands together and nodded benignly toward the police officer.

"Good of you to come old man," sir Simon acknowledged with a smile toward Jack.

"And this is Commodore Legge whose naval expertise has been invaluable to us of late."

Jack dipped his head toward the commodore. He looked the least comfortable of present, but he nonetheless put his hand across and shook Jack's.

"Nice to meet you Inspector."

"Alex Harker-Bell here has probably more experience than the rest of put together," said Jonas, introducing the oldest man in the room. "Am illustrious career in the Navy, Alex then worked in Vauxhall House for some time before we managed to get our hands on him. Part of the furniture now, eh Alex?"

"Vauxhall House - *MI6*?" queried Jack as the older man took his hand in a firm grip. He winked at Jack's question.

"Spying on the spies," he said, a smile creasing his face.

"Our own Desmond Reid is here as our technical advisor this morning," continued Jonas, "Thanks for coming Desmond."

"Well," said Sir Simon, when Jonas had finished. "I can only echo what Jonas has already said. Thank you all for coming at such short notice. I think it best if we just get straight to the point. Inspector, Commodore, you will both no doubt have questions. I will try to answer them as much as I can, but in the meantime I've asked Jonas to give a short outline for the reason we requested your attendance. Jonas?"

Taking his cue, the MI5 man opened a presentation on the laptop in front of him and pointed to the projected slide on a screen at the bottom wall. It was a map of Europe.

"Detective Inspector McGregor was asked some time ago to look into the case of a man who had awakened from a coma in a hospital in Glasgow." A red circle appeared over Glasgow on the map.

"Jack will do just fine," protested the inspector.

Jonas nodded in appreciation. "Thank you Jack." He carried on.

"The next time he appears is at Stranraer in Galloway where he evidently boards a ferry to Larne or Belfast." Another red circle appeared on the town at Loch Ryan.

"He had worked for some time in farm near Penrith near Carlisle before that," pointed out Jack, interested in how they determined he had been at Stranraer.

"Ah, yes, the relative of the McCrackens?"

Jack simply nodded and Jonas continued.

"He works for several months at a farm not many miles from Belfast, and after the circumstances there that we are hoping Jack can elucidate upon, he leaves Ulster via a tramp steamer from Warrenpoint, bound for Nantes in France."

He advanced the slides and more circles appeared on the places he had mentioned.

"We then get intelligence that he arrives via train in Paris, where he becomes embroiled in some kind of terrorist attack at a railway station in Montparnasse. It seems someone attempted to shoot him in full public view. He is then detained by police and taken in for questioning. Somehow he eludes the police, steals one of their vehicles and disappears in central Paris."

Jack tried not to look visibly shocked. Finn was a constant surprise, never ceasing to produce some new turn in events that mocked any prediction.

"The National Police," Jonas was saying, "are going on the premise that he is intending to, or has possibly already left the city."

A further set of circles faded into the map where they were joined together by a dashed line, showing his presumed route.

Commodore Legge fidgeted slightly in his chair. He pointed at the map.

"I'm not sure how this involves me," he said pointedly. "The Royal Navy does not run ferry companies nor run a missing persons bureau, last I checked."

"I know it is of little interest to you at present," put in Sir Simon, "but there is more to this story. I think you will come to be interested as we proceed Commodore."

Legge grumbled an acceptance and returned to his quiet observation. Jonas Smythe continued.

"There are several issues with this particular case that have raised questions in intelligence circles. It appears this man has no knowledge of his past, is that correct Inspector?"

"I was asked, as a favour, to investigate his circumstances over a year ago," replied Jack. "He had lain in Glasgow Royal for some years in a deep coma."

"*Years?*" queried Legge.

"Extraordinary, but yes, years," answered Jack. "On awakening, his consultant was alarmed enough at his medical condition, to ask me to help in his identification."

"His medical condition?" inquired Sir Simon.

"Aye. Apparently the apparatus used to measure brain activity was damaged by the degree of electrical discharge that came out of his head. Doctor Jamieson, his consultant, told me it was impossible for him to be alive."

"And yet he very much is," added Jonas. "Alive and able to find ways of evading police on four occasions."

"Four?" queried Jack.

"Apart from Paris, he managed to dodge two detectives in a hospital in Nantes. Dressed up as a surgeon and walked right past them."

"That's twice," prompted Jack. "You said four times."

"Well, ahem," said Jonas, scratching the bridge of his nose, "I'm including avoiding interview by the PSNI and, well, yourselves in Glasgow?"

Jack grunted. "I'm not sure I like your adding much. That said; if he's been shot at in Paris and then more or less arrested by the police as a reward, perhaps he has reason to avoid our attentions?"

"Amongst those present here today, you alone met and spoke with him. Perhaps you could colour in some of the detail for the rest of us?"

Jack looked around the room. He still had not put together the pieces that formed any kind of a picture as to why he had been so urgently called down to London. Nonetheless, he was able to describe his meetings with Finn.

"He can remember nothing. He had been left at the door of the hospital by persons unknown in an unconscious state. No physical injuries obvious, but completely comatose. For eleven years he remained that way; unresponsive and kept alive by tube feeding."

"*Eleven* years you say?" interrupted Alex Harker-Bell, shooting Sir Simon a quick look. "In a vegetative state?"

"No, not vegetative. He was far from brain dead. I saw his readings. He was an enigma to one of the best neurologists in the country. Unresponsive yes, but a brain that was generating enough electricity to light an electric lamp, and I'm not exaggerating for effect."

"But he became conscious and you were called in?" asked Sir Simon.

"Like I said, as a favour. Mr Jamieson has become a personal friend. He saved my wife's life when others gave no hope. Doctor Jamieson is an extraordinary man." He paused for a moment before continuing. "Anyway, when the patient awoke he had no knowledge of anything to do with his own personal history. I conducted a series of interrogating strategies. He appeared to have no memories whatsoever. I don't believe he was hiding anything. His mind was just a blank."

"Though he could speak, have a conversation?" The voice was Desmond Reid's the technician. He was taking notes as Jack spoke. "Did he have normal spatial, current awareness? For example, he knew there was a place called Scotland?"

"When I say he his mind was a blank, I mean anything to do with normal self-awareness that we all have. Yes, he knew where Scotland was, knew what was the food on his plate, could tell me who the name of our Queen. It was anything that related to himself or his personal history. For example, He could tell me about the Second World War as an historical event. He had no idea how he knew, where he learned the facts, what school he attended. He did not know if he had family, where he came from, what age he was – which was another issue – or even his own name."

"What age of a man would you say he was… is," asked Jonas.

"He looked to be in his early twenties. But that may not help much. Apparently his physical appearance had not altered in any way in the years he spent comatose. It was another enigma to the medical team looking after him. He could be in his thirties possibly, though looking much younger."

"But there were other abnormalities I believe," said Sir Simon, his fingers pressed against one another on the table before him. "Certain… issues around his ability to possess *information*?"

Jack looked around the room. "He demonstrated several abilities. Some with possible explanations, others, less so." Somehow he almost felt that he was somehow betraying Finn with his candour, but knowing it was an unreasonable emotion given the location of his disclosure, he continued.

"He seemed to possess an uncanny knowledge of anything he was questioned about. I spoke to a clergyman who had befriended him back in Northern Ireland. Apparently he took part in some kind of a club quiz, where no matter the subject, he answered every question correctly."

"He may just have been adept as pub quizzes?" asked Desmond Reid again.

"Perhaps, except that when a local councillor jokingly said he would know his age, Finn gave it immediately.

"I could probably guess most people's age in this room," dismissed Harker-Bell.

"No, you don't understand. He gave the hospital of his birth, the ward, the day, date and exact hour and minute of the man's birth," Jack responded.

"Some kind of a savant?" asked Sir Simon.

"Possibly. There was a nurse at the hospital. She told me that one day she was reminding herself of something she had to do when she was in

Finn's room. She happened to be muttering it aloud and he overheard her. She told me he spoke to her in perfect Tagalog – she was a Philippino – in fact, in her local accent. They had a brief conversation before she was called away. He was gone the next day, but she told me he was absolutely fluent."

"That's a lead then," interjected Commodore Legge, who despite himself was becoming interested. "Possibly brought up in the Philippines."

"Our information from Paris is that he was able to pass as a Frenchman, so good was his French also," added Jonas, "so possibly not much of a lead."

"I agree," continued Jack. "There were too many odd things like that. Let me tell you another. I introduced myself to him as Jack. When I was leaving he called me Inspector McGregor. No one told him my rank or surname. I purposely didn't, and yet he knew."

"Tell us again how he arrived at the hospital," asked Sir Simon. "You say he had been left there unconscious?"

"By two men, who then ran off."

"And some eleven years later he is attacked on a farm by someone carrying a Russian pistol? Jonas, you have a slide there?"

"Oh, yes," said Jonas, quickly clicking his laptop. A photograph of a fired bullet alongside a close up of a cartridge headstamp was projected onto the screen.

"The PSNI have a world-leading ballistics department. Thirty years of terrorist related shootings and murders helped of course. This is one of the cartridge cases that Jack here submitted to their lab. As Jack is aware, the gun that fired these has had quite a history. It has been responsible for a series of murders in Europe and Russia. As it happens, we have been made aware of a particular connection between those murders. None of them were approved by the Russians. It was not a KGB operation. It seems someone is trying to shut down some loose ends. That is part of another operation which we are not sanctioned to discuss here, you understand, but it does raise a question."

It was Jack who spoke next, finishing off Jonas Smythe's sentence.

"Why would a rogue Russian operation turn its attention to a young man who is working on a farm in Ulster?"

"Precisely," agreed Jonas. "And quite determinedly so. He was followed to the port at Warrenpoint by two men posing as Customs officers. They just missed him by an hour. Two others, possibly the same two, but not necessarily so, tried to shoot him at a train station in Paris. We haven't seen the ballistics report yet – the Frenchies aren't quite as expert as our Northern Irish friends – but I would bet my pension that they were using silenced Makarovs."

"He knows something," said Jack quietly. Sir Simon glanced briefly at Jonas Smythe. He turned to the room, a pen held like a pointer toward Jack.

"So, our questions are these," he posed. "Who is this man who goes by the name of Finn? Why does a certain Russian grouping want him dead? And what is the *something He knows*?" He let the question hang in the room for a moment before turning to the Commodore.

"Commodore, I must point out before I ask this question, that the Inspector has not been Develop Vetted." He turned to Jonas. "Though I think we need to start the ball rolling on that one." He turned back, alternating his look between the Commodore and the detective. He addressed Jack. "I believe however you are STRAP inducted?"

Jack nodded.

There had been an occasion when shared intelligence between the U.K. and the U.S. had had reason to cross his desk. Known as the 'Five Eyes' it was an international agreement for intelligence-sharing between five nations, including Australia, Canada and New Zealand. Jack had been signed off by internal security some years earlier. The Developed Vetting procedure however was higher again. It was the highest level of security vetting in the U.K. Even the incumbent Prime Minister had yet to have his completed. That Sir Simon was prepared to action the process for Jack was evidence that he was prepared to share intelligence that very few would have access to. But not yet.

"So, Commodore, with that understood, I would like to ask you to divulge something of *Operation Neptune*."

The Commodore blanched. He had not heard the words in twenty years. More, he corrected himself. Immediately his mind flashed up images of a night so long ago when he had been given a task that had involved sailing silently and without beacons or lights up the Irish Channel. He remembered. There had been MI5 involvement. He hadn't liked it.

"I'm not sure I can... It was highly classified."

"Yes, I know Commodore, and it shall stay that way. Let me put it like this. There was a package. The rules were very, very unambiguous. It was to be lowered and set with extreme caution on the seabed at a certain point. A very precise operation suffering no deviation from its planning. There was a winch specially placed on the afterdeck?"

He studied the Commodore's face, his eyes not blinking. "I suppose I might be just looking for confirmation that this indeed was the reality of the recorded narrative. You see, well... there was a rumour?"

Legge was flabbergasted. He knew the Security Services had, by their very nature, to be possessors of information vast in its breadth and depth, but still, to hear command of such detail staggered him. Nonetheless, what Sir Simon had just described as a sequence of action had a flaw in its accuracy. It was almost a relief to be able to put voice to that, to relate the facts he had witnessed with his own eyes

"I, ahm, I can confirm that the requirements as you have just detailed them, well... they were not entirely the history of events as I remember them."

"Would I be getting near the events as you remember them, if I was to surmise that the control of the, em, process of discharge, was in fact carried out by someone who was not trained so to do?"

"I couldn't say," replied the Commodore and then added, "If he was trained, he acted like he had forgotten everything he was told. It was a very slipshod affair and none too tidy. There was no 'setting down with extreme caution' that I can say."

Jack looked from the Commodore to the head of MI5. He had almost no idea of what they were discussing. It was clear they were relating to some past clandestine act, but none of it made sense to him, nor did it seem to relate to anything they had previously been discussing in the room. Even Jonas Smythe looked somewhat blank.

"Let me ask you this Commodore, continued Sir Simon, "could it have been possible that - and let us say the contents were extremely fragile - could it have been possible that there was sufficient mismanagement to permit damage to such contents?"

Commodore Legge grunted. The box had been lowered like a bundle of old spanners. Not only had it collided with the side of his ship, it had crashed into the water like a beaching whale.

"More than possible; almost certain."

Sir Simon, apparently satisfied that his line of questioning had yielded decisive results, sat back in his chair and folded his fingers together. He looked at the man at the other end of the table.

"So, Desmond. You know better than all of us what might the results of such handling might have led to. What if someone was somehow in the water when sufficient leakage took place. It might have been months, years, later. What might be the effects?"

Desmond Reid looked around the table and hesitated.

"Like the Commodore said sir, this is highly classified."

"I know that Desmond, but it takes six weeks to have a man vetted to D.V. standard. We do not have that time. I think we are going to have to work on the premise that Jack here will have his security clearance. He is strapped after all. You can be as vague as you feel comfortable with, but I think we can stretch the letter of the law a little, eh?"

Reid nodded. "Yes sir, well, we had some pretty horrendous outcomes in Porton Down with the stuff. Lost three good scientists. In the end it was that that led us to get rid of it. We also needed to have deniability when we were getting ministerial questions; you'll remember how we got hold of the material. The Beaufort Dyke seemed a good solution. If we no longer had it, then we could honestly hold our hands up and say we didn't have it. As to your question; I suppose salt water might have diluted its effects, but then again, with sea water being an electrolyte, I don't know how it might have altered its properties."

Sir Simon sat forward.

"Yes. In other words, you have no idea."

"It reacted like nothing seen before. It was utterly unpredictable. Getting rid of it was the best option sir."

Jack looked at Jonas and then the Commodore. At least he was not the only one who looked bewildered.

"There was an event," Sir Simon Montague began, picking his words carefully. "It happened eleven years and six months before your man appeared in Glasgow Royal. Near Kircudbright. Fish died in the tens of thousands. Devil of a job explaining it. Luckily for us it coincided with outflow issues from Sellafield. The story got lost in the surrounding haze. Another event took place at the same time. A young man disappeared from Ardrossan on the West Coast. His name was Allen. He had a brother and a mother. The brother died in a car accident a year later and the mother six months after that. Her husband had been a captain in Two Para. He died on active service some years earlier. She never remarried. With the loss of her boys, she just lost the will to live. No other relatives that we know of. The family name was Finlay. Now we have this man who appears out of nowhere and adopts the name Finn. Coincidence?"

"It still doesn't answer why some Russian terrorist grouping, or whatever, so ardently want him dead," said Jack. "Unless there's much more to this than the facts so far related."

Sir Simon made no comment and calmly observed the detective with an expression that said nothing whatsoever.

Jonas rubbed his chin and advanced the slide. Several lines on the European map spread out from Paris – most in a northward direction.

"Analysis indicates our man is headed somewhere. We don't think he is moving in a random fashion. It is a possibility that France has just been a thoroughfare to somewhere else. The question is; where is that somewhere?"

"We would like you to stay on the case Inspector," said Sir Simon suddenly. "No one else outside of this room is to know that however unless I indicate otherwise. It seems to me that you have a head start. You alone have met him, and that might prove useful in the days ahead. That is, if you are willing to assist?"

"Does a police officer refuse the head of MI5?" shrugged Jack. "What do I tell my Super?"

"Leave that to us," smiled the MI5 man. "It is our operation so Jonas here will be in charge. Desmond will assist in whatever technical requirements are needed. Your remit will be to assist and advise and provide what help you can. We have fingers in a lot of pies Jack, but sometimes it takes an experienced nose to tell which pie we should be putting in the oven first."

Commodore Legge cleared his throat. "I take it my services are no longer required?"

"Actually Commodore," Sir Simon replied, "as well as the critical information you were able to supply today. There is another matter which concerns your attendance today." He nodded to his subordinate. "Perhaps Jonas, if the Commodore is in agreement?" he gave a nod of deference toward the naval man. "You and he could find a quiet spot to discuss that very thing eh? You never know," he winked at the Commodore, "he might even be stretched into getting you a bit of lunch!"

He shook Legge's hand enthusiastically as he and Jonas left. Alex Harker Bell got up and followed immediately with a nod to the room. Desmond Reid was next to exit.

"Thank you Desmond. As ever, your advice is invaluable."

As Desmond took his cue, Sir Simon quietly closed the door, leaving Jack alone with the knight of the realm.

"My apologies for the cloak and dagger," said Sir Simon apologetically.

"Not at all," said Jack with a dismissive wave of his hand. "I understand 'need to know' very well."

"I would like to share something with you," the older man said, beckoning him back to his seat. He sat next to him and turned his chair to face the detective.

"This whole thing has a lot more involved in it than we at first believed. An added complication is one of a personal nature."

Jack's eyebrows raised.

"I understand the sense of immense debt you have had toward your doctor friend," began Sir Simon, "I have a debt of my own, one of similar weight. You see, Captain Robert Finlay was a close friend. More than that. We served together in Ulster when it was bad, very bad. We were part of a stick doing a satellite patrol around a manned crossing point on the South Armagh border. We were careful, but the IRA had time on their side. They took their time, watched our patterns and worked out where we were likely to pass while on patrol. There was a bank of gorse we had used to brew up in a couple of times. It was on high ground and gave us a good view of the outlying countryside. Whatever else they were, the IRA weren't stupid. They managed to hide a 500kg bomb filled with ball-bearings and shards of steel in the earthen bank. Then they waited. We were always being watched. Daylight hours were the worst. Cross a field and the local active service unit knew about it before we had reached the far side. At some point they were going to get lucky. You just hoped you weren't there when it happened."

Sir Simon set his pen onto the table and stared at it for a moment before carrying on.

"None of us were lucky that day. Some less than others. I never heard the explosion, just a massive hand lifting me off the ground and throwing me to the ground like a handful of dirt. Two of the men were picked up in pieces no bigger than a fist. The rest of us were scattered about, cut to ribbons, utterly stunned by the force of the explosion. Then the IRA moved in to finish the job. I remember seeing the grin on the thin lips behind the balaclava of the terrorist as he raised his Kalashnikov into my face. At that moment I knew I was a dead man. I remember the pathetic littleness of it – lying on my back in a wet hole in a field. It seemed so pointless. A life so insignificantly ended. A bullet from the thin faceless grinning man. Just as he went to pull the trigger, he suddenly stopped and fell forward onto his face as if he had just been switched off. The noise came an age later. A gunshot, but not from his gun. It was Bob Finlay. He was lying on his side, his Browning Hi-Power in his bloody hand, the pistol shaking with the effort to lift it. He turned to me, and long as I live I will never forget the look in his eyes."

Sir Simon stopped and looked out the window. There was silence and Jack quietly waited while the man hung in the long gone mist of another time. After a few moments, he gave an almost imperceptible shake and suddenly turned.

"I passed out. I came to in the Musgrave hospital in Belfast. Bob Finlay was dead. I was alive - just. There had been a brief fire-fight, enough to force their withdrawal until help came. He had emptied his magazine. He died from his wounds in the Wessex. So, I have had a life and he gave his that I might have it." He paused again and faced Jack.

"I don't talk about this Jack. You are probably the first human being I have ever told. I think I want you to understand. If there is any chance, any chance at all that this man Finn has anything to do with Captain Robert Finlay, then, I want him to live."

Chapter 28
Pursuit

Descending inside the mountain, Jon Lander made a quick appraisal of his situation. He had managed to buy some time, but only by trapping himself. Whoever was trying to kill him had the best hand. There was no other entrance or exit; he had no food or water and only one spare magazine for the Glock. His killer was better armed, and if he chose, could simply barricade the exit and leave him to die.

He rode on, thinking as he did. No, Ari would come looking for him, or Lars, or Jensen. No, not Jensen, what was he thinking, the commander was barely alive. Ari or Lars then. But if they did come looking, what was to stop the killer getting them first? Who was it anyway? He began thinking through the personnel. He quickly realised that was a waste of time. It could be anyone. A double-agent for all he knew. He thought of the big sergeant and the laughing Guldberg. No, he was achieving nothing. If he could find the shortwave radio that would be something.

The lab was nor far down. It would have been better had it been deeper, the greater the distance from the entrance, the more time he would have. For all he knew the killer was already silently making his way on foot down the descending tunnel. He turned the quad and left the lights on, the beams lighting back up the way he had come. He killed the engine. The lights would drain the battery, but he needed to hear any approaching noises. He hoped the battery was a good one. He would need the quad again.

The lab consisted of a couple of portable huts set into a small hollowed-out cavern on the side of the descent tunnel. Not the large project he had discovered far deeper down. This was a staging post. It had PPE hung on pegs, dosimeters, some assays, balances and other measuring apparatus. It also had communication equipment and it was amongst this that he began to quickly search for the short wave radio. When he found it, he gave a silent sigh and shook his head. If he had hoped to find some modern miniaturised set, what he was looking at was pretty much the opposite. It was a huge green box. *Telefunken S236* was printed on its ancient casing. It was studded with a host of black knobs and dials and Jon studied its complexity with some concern before finding faded instructions typed onto a sheet of yellowed paper stuck onto its side. It was not however altogether unfamiliar to him. He had come across similar looking sets as a young soldier in field exercises with NATO in Germany. Beside it was its control stage and power pack allowing for it to be transportable. Quickly looking outside and listening, he returned and turned on the power. To his relief the radio lit up. Following the instructions, he was able to tune to the 31 metre band where he knew most radio traffic would be. He plugged in a pair of vintage headphones and fiddled with the fine tuning dial. Nothing, only a crackle from the speakers in the headset. He tuned further up the metre band. Amateur radio hams would usually frequent higher up the band. The noise in his ears altered with added squeals and crackles, but there was nothing resembling intelligent noise. He twisted the connection on the antenna. More crackles. He thought hard and as he did so, the sudden realisation struck him. Shortwave was an almost untraceable frequency, capable of being directed at such an angle into the sky that could allow it to skip off the ionosphere and cross continents. It was unlimited by the visual horizon and could travel unimpeded for many hundreds, if not thousands of miles. But not here. Shortwave could not penetrate rock. The unbroken crackling was because he was neither receiving nor transmitting. The mountain was strangling it. He had no hope of getting any kind of transmission out from inside the Beerenburg.

He thought of the men back at the station, Bakke, dying from his chest wound, Jensen in urgent need of critical care, men whose only hope for outside help was placed in his hands.

But his hands were tied. Tied by a killer lurking outside the mountain. Outside to where he needed to take the radio set. Outside where death awaited in the muzzle of an assault rifle.

The set may have been transportable, but not man transportable. It weighed over 150 kilos. Lander was a strong man, but 23 stone was not something to throw over a shoulder. Nonetheless, with a considerable expenditure of his energy, he managed to get it out into the tunnel and onto the back of the quad. The power pack was showing about 25 per cent power and he tied it on beside the radio. Looking up the tunnel, he weighed the risks. There was nothing to be gained and much to be lost by simply hiding in the volcano. Equally, there was much to be lost by attempting to escape, but that was balanced by what could be gained. The trouble was; the attempt was like the charge of the Light Brigade at Balaclava. Outside, the maw of the cave awaited like the Russians on the Fedyukhin Heights. The mountain of death behind him and the valley of death before him. He was trapped into doing one or the other and only the latter offered any hope at all. And not much of a hope at that.

But Jon Lander was a man whose life consisted of taking risks. He turned out the lights of the quad and looked into the darkness.

"Qui audet adipiscitur," he breathed to himself. Who dares wins. He had spent a life daring and getting away with it. There was little point hesitating now.

He gunned the engine and began up the passageway. He kept the lights off and travelled about a hundred metres where he stopped, turned off the engine and listened. Hearing nothing, he started the engine again and repeated the process. He wished he had pulled the gates shut behind him on his escape down the tunnel, but the 7.62x39mm calibre bullets kicking around his feet had been a strong dissuader at the time.

After a few minutes of this sporadic climbing up the incline, a blue-black arch of darkness ahead, slightly lighter than the pitch black of the surrounding rock signified the opening. He was possibly less than a hundred metres from the exit now and even from here he could hear the noise of the still raging storm.

Suddenly it dawned on him. His hunter would not hear the approaching engine. Outside, the squall would be a thunderous clamour. He had discovered a single advantage. Not a big one, but at least a percentage point removed from the statistics of failure.

At thirty metres from the exit he stopped and slipped around to the rear of the quad. He turned on the set and waited for it to heat up. With some dismay he noticed that the action had lowered the power reserve. Again he tried the bands. He worked down from 20 MHz. At around 10 MHz at 31 metres, he thought he caught an indistinct voice, but lost it and was unable to catch it again.

"I'm still too deep in," he muttered under his breath. Remounting the quad, he kept the revs at almost tick-over and began crawling up the slope. There was no point in wasting what power there was left, so he advanced to almost 5 metres from the exit and again killed the engine. Now the noise of the storm drowned out even the sound of his boots on the gravel as he once again returned to the radio.

The radio suddenly became alive with the sound of humanity. Voices from commercial radio stations and indistinct chatter filled his headphones. He found an area where he heard what appeared to be radio transmission and keyed the microphone.

"Mayday, Mayday Mayday. This is a distress call from Jon Lander on Jan Mayen island. 70 degrees 59' North, 8 degrees 32' West. Mayday, Mayday, Mayday. Urgent request for assistance. Major disaster at Norwegian base. Request urgent medical aid and rescue. Mayday, Mayday, Mayday!"

He repeated the message two or three times. Just as he paused to listen for a response, the set died as the power needle dropped to zero.

Had he time, he would have been frustrated with disappointment, but time for such luxury was suddenly snatched from him as a loud retort split the darkness with an orange flash from the exit. At the same time, the remaining light from what could only be the G-Wagen flicked on, the light banishing the darkness of the passageway.

The bullets thudded into the back of the quad and pieces of the radio splintered above Jon's head.

He quickly got behind one of the rear tyres and fired a return shot from his Glock. His bullet was replied to with a burst of automatic fire from the outside.

He was pinned down behind the quad. He could not get to the seat of the machine, there he would be a sitting duck, neither could he make a break for the passageway behind where he would surely be gunned down before he had got more than a few metres. How much ammunition his assailant had was probably evidenced by the profligacy of the bursts directed at him. His own situation was that he had less than a full magazine. Seventeen rounds in a full magazine, he guessed he now had some fourteen or less.

As if to underline his conclusions, another burst rattled into the quad and he was nakedly aware of what little protection it was affording him. Sooner or later the bullets would find a home in his body. He rolled out and fired two more shots at the right of the vehicle before rolling back, but taking cover now behind the other back wheel. Almost immediately another burst of fire ripped the ground up where he had just been a second earlier. It was no amateur he was up against. He quietly reached up, untied the power pack and, hidden as it was from the entrance by the larger case of the radio itself, placed it as an added protection between himself and the rear wheel. Another series of bullets tore into the quad and Jon felt the impact as a bullet crashed into the power pack he had just recovered.

"This can only go one way!" a harsh voice suddenly shouted from the outside. "You may as well come out now and we'll see what we can work out!"

The voice was distorted by the wind and the shouting, but something about it was vaguely familiar.

"What do you want from me?" Lander called back. To underline that he was not without cards in his hand, he fired two more shots back, this time to the other side of the Mercedes. The reply was quick in coming and he hunkered in behind his meagre protection as high velocity bullets crashed into the superstructure inches above his head.

"You tell me what you know, and I might just let you go back into the mountain. There is food in the lower Electronic Data Store. You might last a month or so. Long enough for what you know not to matter."

"What if I don't feel like baring my soul?" he shouted back.

"So, you die where you are. I have no lack of ammunition, *Sutherland*," he said with a sarcastic mockery in his voice, "and you have what, six or seven rounds left?"

"I have as much ammunition as I need," lied Lander, firing two more precious bullets back, this time, bracketing the vehicle.

"You lie badly," replied the darkness. It was less of a shout and suddenly Jon recognised the voice.

"So, you killed Johannsen and the others," replied Jon. "You had me fooled *Guldberg*."

A laugh echoed back. "*Guldberg* now is it, not Lars?"

"I suddenly don't feel just so chummy now funnily enough," Jon retorted.

"And you don't sound so Scottish," said the voice who was evidently Lars Gulderg. "Or so innocently *civilian* come to that."

"Seems we all have our secrets."

"So, what do you know, Sutherland, or whoever you really are?" asked Guldberg. "I mean it. Tell me and I'll turn out the lights to let you run for it."

Lander fingered the Glock in his hand. It was true. He had almost no hope in his current position. The only reason he was still alive was that Guldberg really did want to know what he knew. It was little enough, but perhaps it would be enough of a lever to find out more.

"I tell you what, I talk if you talk. I've a few questions of my own."

There was silence for a few moments. Then the voice spoke again.

"O.K. You go first. What do you know about The Program?"

Lander thought quickly. *The Program?* Did he mean the study of the volcano, or the semi-secret computer backup systems buried in the mountain? It sounded like something else. He remembered some of the information Henrik had passed on.

"It was the noises that first alerted us. Noises that shouldn't have been possible. When Johannsen discovered their true origin, at first we didn't believe him."

"We? Who is *we?*"

"The *Etterretningstjenesten.* They knew there was a mole on the island. I have to admit you were not one of their prime suspects."

"I will take that at a compliment. So why is a non-national working for the Intelligence Service? No matter, don't answer that. You said at first you didn't believe him? Now you do?"

"It's like Sherlock Holmes said, 'When you have eliminated the impossible, whatever remains, however improbable, must be the truth.'

"And is it known why our craft are operating down there? What is known about the aims of The Program?"

There was that term again. And what craft? Jon thought quickly.

"You said you would answer some questions too. I will give more when you play the game. It wasn't an accident at the base, was it?"

There was a pause, and Jon tensed, expecting another burst of fire. Instead, Guldberg had evidently made some mental concession with Jon's demand.

"No, I was simply awaiting the opportunity. The oncoming weather front was perfect. I actually am a trained meteorologist. I simply withheld the information and arranged to be outside the base when the timer set off the charges. I took you with me as additional alibi. That was my first suspicion that you were not quite the bona fide lost sailor you claimed to be. What sailor could possibly be surprised at the suddenness of a weather change?"

"So why the sabotage?"

"Isn't it obvious?" chided Guldberg. "We need the Norwegians to give up on this base, or at least concentrate on something other than noises which are a nation's destiny to greatness being reborn beneath their feet!"

Guldberg suddenly laughed. "The so-called Cuba missile crisis will seem like a child's game when our resources are in place. The oh so mighty United States, how those degenerates will plead like beggars. The E.U. will surrender without so much as a whimper and the British? Have-beens who will finally see the ridiculous pomposity of their pretended authority crumble like the sandcastles they are so fond of building on their beaches."

"The Chinese won't be so easy," tried Lander, plucking hopeful sentences out of the ether.

"And what will they do? We will wipe half of them out before they know what hit them. No Sutherland, we are almost complete and we will not be stopped at this stage of the game."

There was another pause and Jon Lander knew in that moment Guldberg had no intention of risking anything. There would be no escape down a dark tunnel. No chance whatsoever that *The Program*, whatever it was, would be compromised by his being allowed to live.

It was pure animal reaction. Without planned thought, working on a gut intuition honed from years of sensing the moment, Jon leapt from behind the quad and raced forward the five metres to where he estimated Guldberg had been standing during his tirade. As he ran, sprinting with all of the muscle spring he could possibly put into his legs, he simultaneously fired the last few remaining bullets from his pistol ahead of his accelerating mass.

Bursting out into the open, the shape of Lars Guldberg was outlined against the lightening sky as the Englishman hurled himself like a missile at the surprised form of the Norwegian traitor, his shape leaning back against the Mercedes. He threw his empty pistol with the violence of a madman before him whilst leaping forward with all of his might. As he did so, the AKM in Guldberg's hand sputtered its final spit of death at the Dervish that was Jon Lander.

Then, like the flicking of a switch, all was darkness.

Chapter 29
Comprehension

Anya first noticed the phenomena as she sensed, or was incomprehensibly certain that Gasparov was about to enter her room. Not a feeling - a knowledge, the kind of knowledge normal in regard to a recent event, except this was one yet to occur.

Even as she cross-examined the feeling, the door handle turned and Gasparov entered. He had not knocked.

"You are wasting time," he rasped, making no introduction to his meaning.

"I... I'm sorry, wasting time?" She was genuinely confused and realised the feeling was probably the planned result.

"You send me samples of nothing of importance. How can the daughter of the so-called expert, Dr *Nauk* Nevotslov be so incompetent as to fail to find anything of interest 12 kilometres below the earth?"

Anya felt her face redden. She knew enough of Gasparov by now however to be aware of his technique. Unbalance, frighten and overpower. Seize from the victim any time to think. Force his opponents into unintentional confessions.

"I have submitted various reports Comrade Gasparov. The presence of ferrous metals in Ophiolite was entirely unexpected for example. That iron could be found encased in..."

"Who cares about that!" shouted Gasparov and Anya shrunk back. She had seen him angry, but something had really antagonised him now. What is might be, she could hardly think... unless...

"You think this is some kind of recreational research venture, is that what you think?" His face was livid and for a moment Anya began to wonder if the man was mentally unhinged.

"No, why I..."

"You have no idea!" he screamed, banging the table in front of him with a closed fist. "There is something to find, something your father..." he suddenly stopped and began again. "You have three days. If by that time you have nothing other than a few bits of tin and iron, then I will have no use for you on this base." He shoved his fists into the pockets of his jacket and returned to the door. "No use at all!" As the door slammed, Anya fell back on her chair. She pushed a strand of hair from her face and was surprised at how quickly her calm returned. The man was hysterical, and yet, even as he vilified her in his angry outburst, she was strangely witnessing something of which she had somehow a prescience.

Riding out the storm in the Southern reaches of the Arctic Ocean, HMS Albion received an encrypted signal from Devonport. Captain Currie read the plain decryption in the heaving bridge as twenty metre waves crashed over the fore-deck of the LPD. It was not a ship intended for such seas and had not his brief been made very explicit by the Commodore, the young captain might well have made for calmer waters. As it was, the ship creaked and complained in metallic shrieks at the beating she was taking from the violent anti-cyclone.
He read the message and turned to bridge team.
"The distress call. We're to respond," he explained. "We're heading back to Jan Mayen."
They had already been aware of a local distress. No one needed told that sailing across the wind in such a storm was going to require every bit of seamanship they possessed.

Jon Lander's distress call had been picked up by an Irish Pelagic trawler out of Killybegs, fishing for cod in the Norwegian Sea. Unable to respond to such a far off call for help, she had relayed the mayday back to Donegal where it was passed on to the Irish Coast Guard. They in turn contacted the Norwegian Coast Guard, the *Kystvakten*, at Sortland Naval Base. Dispatching one of their *Nordkapp*-class offshore patrol vessels, and their P-3 Orion patrol aircraft, they also put out an all ships alert for the area. It did not take long before Thames House was made aware of the shortwave distress call.
"How sure are you that it was Lander?" Sir Simon asked Desmond Reid. Reid stood beside Jonas Smythe who had brought him to relay the information to the MI5 head.

251

"The transmission was poor quality and seemed to break off suddenly," Reid explained, "but I ran it against the voice prints we have for Lander – I'd say 90 per cent certain."

"He has his own covert transmitter," said Jonas. "Why he didn't use that I can't understand."

"It needs at least a partial clear sky to work," explained Reid. "If this storm is as bad as we are being told, he may have had no option."

"Why shortwave? Why not use the base communication systems?" conjectured Jonas.

"He is telling us something," mused Sir Simon. "Why give his name? He would not have broken cover unless something has gone seriously wrong."

"I think we have to assume this is no natural disaster at the base," added Jonas. "He is asking for our help."

"Call the Commodore," said Sir Simon suddenly. "This is a job for the Royal navy!"

Legge knew already. He had been immediately informed of the distress call as soon as the *Kystvakten* had. He had sent the signal to HMS Albion some minutes before the All Ships from the Norwegians. Captain Currie was aware that their mission was highly covert and involved lying out until further orders were received. The secret signal from the Commodore was clear and to the point. Make full speed to Jan Mayen and render assistance.

The men in their black berets arrived at the Beerenburg a few hours after the fire-fight. Two men lay at the entrance where there ought to have been one. The Spetsnatz leader knelt down beside one. He was dead. The other was slumped against the vehicle, the barrel of a Kalashnikov clenched in his hands.

"*On zhiv* - He's alive," he said. "Take him and go – leave the other."

The Special Operations team took the bloodied man, lifted the weapons and quickly retraced their steps down toward the coast. On the beach the rib was waiting. The storm was beginning to abate at last and the journey out to the waiting submarine was only marginally less treacherous than the journey in had been.

With an expertise born of ceaseless training, the six men plus their recovered asset were soon back inside the dark hull of the silently throbbing Russian vessel. Five minutes later the sea swallowed the metal intruder as the K-329 *Severodvinsk* slipped back below the heaving waves and began the long underwater trek back from whence she had come.

Even as the Yasen Class sub had been dipping her hull into the frigid depths, the Norwegian P-3 Orion overflew the base. The weather was still too rough to attempt a landing, but all indications were that the storm was in the process of more or less blowing itself out, the diminishing squalls moving off toward Greenland. It was decided to go into a holding pattern for an hour, after which time conditions might allow a possible landing at the Olonkinbyen airstrip.

HMS Albion was making hard going into the violence of the anticyclone. A Landing Platform Deck vessel was wide and not designed for heavy seas. Tacking across the massive swell made for the most uncomfortable sailing anyone on board had ever experienced. They were fifty nautical miles west of Jan Mayen and at the current rate would take at least four hours to make landfall. It was however an ETA ahead of the Norwegian Coast Guard's NoCGV *Andenes*. Normally operating within the Barents Sea, the patrol vessel had been on exercise 200 miles west of Sortland in Northern Norway when the Mayday had been received. That still left it still having 400 miles sailing to get to Jan Mayen - still a full day away.

Captain Currie was thinking. He looked out into the wild waters through the bridge windows. The foul weather wipers were barely able to keep up with the lashing rain and seawater. The ship was heaving and tossing like a drunken man in a fit, but that wasn't what was preoccupying his thoughts. It would be one thing getting to Jan Mayen, quite another trying to land a boat there in these conditions. He kept his bridge officers busy. Checking and re-checking weather reports, navigation, comms and lookouts posted at the windows. He studied the coastline map of the western approaches. There seemed to be nowhere any better or worse than the spit of beach where he had deposited the agent Lander. It had been a feat back then; to repeat the performance was going to take a miracle.

Leaving the Officer of the Watch in charge of the bridge, he made his way back to his cabin. Shutting and locking the door, he once again opened the small safe bolted behind his cabin work desk. Reaching in, he withdrew a small manila envelope. He opened it and re-read the words that had been addressed for his eyes alone. They were written in the graceful script of Commodore Legge.

The instructions you have been given have doubtless left you with a number of questions. These questions will include professional misgivings about the nature and danger of the task you have been given. As captain of your ship and with the weight of responsibility that comes with that, I am fully aware that the feeling of having information withheld from you will not sit easily. Making choices that may have a direct impact on the safety and perhaps, the lives of your crew are choices you would want to make armed with whatever intelligence is available to hand. I understand this, probably more than you know. What I can assure you of however is this: The man you are landing on Jan Mayen has a responsibility on his shoulders that may well be greater than any man has had in our generation. Whatever it takes, he must be facilitated in his mission. I can tell you this: I myself am only partly briefed on the full details, but I know enough to assure you that you will never again command a ship whose mission success will have such critical necessity. It is not an exaggeration to say that the outcome of this venture may well determine the history of the next one hundred years. I tell you these things because I want you to know that if it comes to having to make very difficult decisions, make them in the certain knowledge that no matter how high a price that decision demands, it will not be too much.
Good luck James, and God speed.

Currie looked at the letter and contemplated again the words. It was a letter unlike any he had ever read. He sensed the Commodore was trusting him with far more information that possibly he was supposed to share. At the same time, it was pregnant with unanswered questions. The mission and its purpose was just as opaque to him as it had been in Devonport. The agent he had landed, Jon Lander – what could be so important that one man was to be valued above a ship and its crew? What could possibly be so critical that its failure could impact the world to such a degree implied by his commanding officer? He closed his eyes as he considered his own questions. Opening them again he looked at the last line. Commodore Legge had used his Christian name, and that was almost the most startling thing of all.

In Arkhangelsk, Viktor Karmonov was deep in thought. He had seen the pathetic demise of the greatest military might the world had seen. Once mighty and proud, striking fear into all who would oppose her. It had been Yeltsin, the greatest traitor to the motherland. Raised to power, brought to a place where he could have reversed the travesty that Gorbachov had instituted. Instead he had pandered to the voices of defeat and collapsed the Supreme Soviet, replacing it with the prostitute that was the Duma.

The Duma, The *Gosudárstvennaya dúma*, a westernised mongrel democracy. Parading itself so self-importantly in central Moscow - those impotent flabby-chested deputies playing their politics as they whimpered like submissive puppies to the witless masses. He grunted with the ignominy of it all. Mother Russia ruled by her own spoiled children; children with eyes hungry for the sickening consumerism of the decadent West. A people dying for the want of the iron fist of authority. A lost purity, a proletariat devoid of true leadership. Their only redemption a supreme leader to reawaken the greatness of their past sacrifices.

Karmonov closed his eyes and dreamed the dream he had so long cherished. A dream that that soon would cross from seeds of long imagined hope to glorious reality. It had taken years, many years. It had meant sacrifices. Sacrifices that only old order Stalinists could comprehend or have the courage to deliver. People had had to die for this. Many of them former comrades, friends even.

But the sacrifices, the careful pruning and emplacements over the years had at last reached the synchronisation that The Program required. The main directorate of the General Staff of the armed forces did not answer to the Duma or its Speaker. With the GRU, the power had moved, as planned, to an organisation outside the control of Federal Assembly. Even the Prime Minister was an office neutered by careful orchestration of the secret committee at Arkhangelsk. The once merely ceremonial role of President now held the reins of power and to that man reported the heads of the various intelligence agencies, the SVR, the FSB and the FSO. That the current incumbent of the office of President was the type of man who would surely agree to the aims of The Program was no accident. He was no Yeltsin. With his credentials and KGB background he would understand and acquiesce to their aims. But even were he not to submit to the demands when they arrived on his desk, those intelligence services of which he was chief were dwarfed by the reach and power of the GRU. The GRU was utterly subordinate to the Russian military command. The GRU was controlled by the Minister of Defence and the Chief of the General

Staff and they were men both under the control of Karmonov. Given an almost free hand, the Arkhangelsk committee could command the Russian Navy to its bidding as well as 26,000 special forces and all its allied resources. With the GRU controlling the military intelligence service, when The Program was ready to initiate, it would be unstoppable.

Anya turned the Ringwoodite variant over in her hands. The obvious answer suddenly occurred to her like the sudden opening of a door into a room before unseen. This was what Gasparov was after! Somehow he was aware of its existence. Not only that, but he had some unknown anxiety that made him impatient for it to be found and identified. But what? What was it about this strange green, fluorescing material that had a man like Gasparov driven to distraction?

The door suddenly opened and Rogov entered.

"Forgive me Anya Nevotslova," he said breathlessly, "The Ringwoodite, has Gasparov guessed yet?"

"Gasparov? Why, I..."

"He was here, Da? Does he know?"

Anya shook her head vigorously, "No, though he suspects something I think."

"When he discovers we have it; we shall become expendable."

"Like Yashkin?"

Rogov nodded. He did not need to go into details. Anya held out the mineral in her hand.

"Gasparov screamed at me like a madman. I thought he was going to strike me. I am sure this is what he wants, but why Rogov, why would he act in such a way?"

"Do you remember the radiance?"

"How it reacted to Ultra-Violet?"

"Have you noticed any... any personal symptoms since then?"

Anya shook her head. "You think it is dangerous? It did not register on the Geiger counter."

"Yes, I think it is dangerous, but not the way you think. I have been experiencing some... *odd* effects - effects of the mind."

Anya remembered the pre-cognisance she had had just before Gasparov had entered her room.

"I thought it was only coincidence, but I feel I *know* before I should. Does that make sense?"

"And I know how Yashkin was killed," replied Rogov. "I don't mean I think I know; I mean I *know* I know. He was beaten to death with metal bars then his body was crushed to make it look like an accident. I have no doubt about this Anya, none at all. I do not believe in lucky hunches, but like you, I *know* that I know. This mindset is alien to me and it only happened after the exposure to the reaction."

"You think something about the strange irradiance has something to do with it?" asked Anya with a questioning frown.

Rogov nodded slowly, as if admitting to his belief that it was so was an admission of some kind of heresy.

"I have had a metallic taste in my mouth since that day. It is mild, but I also sense things in sharper detail. It is as if... as if my thinking has been accelerated."

Anya watched Rogov cautiously. He seemed the same old Rogov. The same, but...

"How would Gasparov know anything about this? We have told no one, and what would he want that would make his possession of it so critical? I tell you Rogov, he was maniacal!"

Rogov shook his head. "I do not know little sister. He knows something of which we know nothing. I suspect your discovery was not the first time this strange compound mineral was found. I think he has lost the first discovery and for reasons that we do not know, he is desperate for its re-discovery. Possibly it has some use. If Gasparov is so hysterical to possess it, I think we can assume it is not any benevolent purpose."

"Then we must make sure he never gets his hands on it," said Anya determinedly.

"Maintaining that will in itself be a dangerous undertaking."

"I think I knew before I was brought here," said Anya slowly, "that I was on a one-way road. First my father, now me."

Rogov looked at the small figure before him and saw the face of his old friend. He recalled a long given promise, a promise he had made with all the earnestness he possessed.

Not if I can help it, thought Rogov. *I owe him that.*

"There is one thing I forgot to tell you," said Anya suddenly interrupting his thoughts. "Gasparov told me I had three days to bring him what he wanted."

"Three days?" repeated Rogov. "If he is making ultimatums then something must be imminent."

"If it really is this," said Anya, looking at the greenish rock in her hand, "maybe we just should just give it to him. It must be valuable – perhaps the chance to be a wealthy man is driving him mad."

Rogov slowly shook his head. "If it were only Gasparov wanting to be rich, I would not be so worried Anya. I am convinced what relative freedom we have is only because he has not yet got possession. There is something, someone perhaps, driving him and I think it is more demanding on him than just a wish for wealth."

"So what do we do? If we give it to him, or withhold the discovery, time is still against us," said Anya desperately. "I wish my father were still alive. He would tell us what to do!"

Rogov looked up and fixed his eyes upon Anya's.

"Perhaps he already has," he said.

Anya's spine tingled with his words, but did not ask Rogov to explain them. She sensed it was something she did not want to hear.

The *Severodvinsk* crossed the invisible underwater line between the North Norwegian Sea and east into the Barent's Sea. Her pressurized water reactor propulsion was capable of pushing the submarine for short periods at speeds in excess of 35 knots. Her orders were such that the submarine's commander was maintaining a speed close to that since they had slipped away from Jan Mayen. As the nuclear powered vessel silently lanced her 450 feet long hull through the depths of the icy waters, the tension began to ease as the mission progressed into its final stages.

The surgeon reported as requested to the Spetsnatz captain. He knocked the cabin door and was brought in by the burly Russian. Several more soldiers were in the cabin.

"*Skazhi mne, kak on?*" he asked, "How is he?"

"I removed a bullet in his thigh. Another cracked his skull," replied the submarine's surgeon. "I am keeping him sedated, but he will recover, albeit with the mother of all headaches. He is a very lucky man."

"Good," nodded the special forces captain, "So he hasn't spoken yet?"

"*Niet*, only incomprehensible mutterings," confirmed the surgeon.

"I need to know as soon as he wakes," insisted the officer. "Withdraw the sedation if needs be, but it is important that I speak to him as soon as possible. Let me know the moment that becomes possible."

After the doctor left, one of the captain's lieutenants spoke.

"The dead man had an American Glock by his side. Our man was holding a Kalashnikov. I really think we have the right man."

"I hope you are right Ivan," mused his superior. "Arkhangelsk puts a high value on him. He has been in deep cover for years. He has some information critical to their timing. I was told this man is one of the greatest assets in the field. It would not be appreciated if we had rescued the wrong man."

"We have the right man," assured his junior officer. "I am sure of it. He was at the appointed position just as planned."

The rest of the soldiers in the room grunted in approval. The mission had gone perfectly. As Spetsnatz specialists, they knew one thing was certain. They were unequalled in what they did.

Chapter 30
Further North

It was late to be turning up at accommodation. Finn weighed the risks. The Gîtes de France sign and its familiar French cockerel at the end of the lane had another beneath it: *"Chambres D'Hotes."*

The thought of a bed and shower persuaded him, and two minutes later he found himself standing at the farmhouse door as the lady of the house opened it.

"Bonsoir, comment puis-je vous aider?" she asked politely.

"Bonsoir madam," he replied. "I am sorry for arriving so late. I had a puncture and it has ruined my plans. I had booked a room at Ableiges in Val-d'Oise, but I will never make it now. Would you possibly have a room free for tonight?"

"Certainly," smiled the older lady, her face an immediate picture of sympathy. She looked over his shoulder. "Are you are on your own?"

He informed her he was and five minutes later he found himself in a cosy upstairs room, his bicycle safely stored in an outside barn. His hostess insisted on making him some hot chocolate and toast for supper and he was brought down to sit with her husband and dog before a wood fire in a large wooden ceilinged kitchen. The dog eyed him suspiciously for a few seconds, but finding nothing out of the ordinary, resumed its business of lying sleepily before the fire like it had been dropped there from a great height.

The husband was evidently used to visitors and after a few pleasantries, followed the example of the dog and returned to inspecting the inside of his eyelids.

His wife was more socially interested. She asked Finn a hundred questions, especially when he told her he was from Marseilles. She had always wanted to go to the south of France. Was it hot? Did all the houses have orange tiled roofs? What about the food? She had heard it was very different, very Mediterranean. They had siestas didn't they? She had heard people just sat about for half of the day, was that true? She had read somewhere that southerners thought those in the north were rude, did he think that?

Finn tried to answer as many as he could and he especially assured her that he thought people in the north were every bit as friendly as those in the south, maybe more so. "After all," he told her, "where else would someone invite in such a late arrival to her home and then make such a supper as this."

She smiled with obvious pleasure at his last comment and with the pause in her questions, he took the opportunity to rise and make for bed.

"Oh, if you are leaving in the morning," she said as if suddenly remembering something, "be careful on your bicycle. The news was full of an escaped gunman in Paris. He shot at a police officer and then stole a police car. He could be anywhere. They say he is dangerous!"

"Oh, I'll be fine," he said, "he'll hardly be after my bicycle - I expect I'll be left well enough alone."

In his bedroom he considered the information. Perhaps she had garbled it, or maybe the police or media has reported it as she had described. Either way, he was going to have to be careful.

Remembering the sheets of paper he had recovered from the train station at Montparnasse, Finn opened his bag and drew out the marked and crumpled pages. They were numbered at the bottom, the highest page number was twelve and it did not finish in a full sentence. He possessed five sheets, so he was missing at least eight, possibly more. The lowest number was page three, so he settled himself down on the bed and began to read there.

"...so you will understand now why I have withheld this from your conditioning," it began. Finn shook his head. "Withheld what? What conditioning?" he asked the empty room.

"He does not yet know what I have done," Finn continued reading, *"though I think he suspects something and also that it involves you in some way. If you have managed to secure these documents, then at least part of the plan will have been achieved. That in itself is probably more than I could have hoped for. The cues that may only seemed like dreams to you were actually a map in your presynaptic neural membrane. That there existed such an astounding capacity for the mental abilities we have studied together in the gap between the plasma membranes of the signal and target cells is a revelation of such astounding human knowledge, that I cannot let my research or discoveries fall into Arkhangelsk's hands."*

The rest of that page went into some length of describing potential functions of pre-synaptic and post-synaptic membrane research. It was clear that there was a presumption from the author that these were details of which Finn was fully conversant. It was highly technical, and as he read it, oddly none of it did indeed seem outside of his knowledge. Nonetheless, he moved to the next page to discover what was being expected of him. That information was blank to him. Page four was missing, so he read from page five.

"... can be no doubt then. That plan already threatens peace and possibly even life on Earth. Armed with the higher function capabilities of which we are possibly only beginning to unravel, like the fallen angel, they would pervert them to the worst purposes imaginable. It would drive them to a lust for power and with that unchallenged power, become heartless, cruel world dominators – dictators unlike any history has ever seen. Stalin and Hitler were at least limited by the human limitations we all share. Freed from those, the director and his co-conspirators would be utterly impossible to stop."

Finn suddenly found his mind a maelstrom of thoughts. Reading the account in the pages he gripped in his hands had pushed open some kind of a doorway into his mind. Like removing a final barrier, the door so temptingly part open was now flung wide. Rushing into his consciousness, great crashing waves of images and memories flashed in such uncontrollable surges that his capacity to hold on to reality was rapidly loosing from his grasp. Floundering in the morass of the tumult, it was only with the greatest concentration of pure willpower that he managed to somehow stem the tumbling torrent of random information cascading like a mighty floodwater through his brain. For the longest time he lay on his back and tried to moderate the flow of imagery, memory, data and emotion into a manageable stream. Eventually, it all seemed to assimilate and become absorbed into his consciousness. An hour or two later, the waters calmed, he could feel his heart rate return to normal and his ability to present a rational thought in an ordered way, resumed.

He knew his mind was in possession of newly released information, if he were to delve into his deep memory he knew that what lay there now was of a magnitude many times multiplied. However, he was impatient to finish what he did not yet know, and he picked up the pages where he had dropped them on the bed at his side.

"So I secreted this portfolio to the safe box in Paris. Had you already been apprehended, or worse, then nothing you have done will lead his operators to these documents. The chain of information is only in your deep subconscious. Should you be interrogated, even tortured, there is nothing you could reveal, no matter how enthusiastically you were persuaded. What you are now reading, if you are, was not imprinted. I wish I could witness the success or failure of this desperate attempt to thwart such wickedness, but I doubt if I shall be permitted what little freedom I still possess for much longer. I think I have resigned myself to losing more than that, probably my life. This is not an easy thing to write, there is so much to learn, so much to know, to discover, research to reveal to a wondering world. Not being able to realise that is possibly one of my greatest regrets.

I digress. You are the only way I can think of stopping him. Nations move too slowly; the weakness of western democracy is that it cannot act with the critical haste required. The endless discussions to reach the only inevitable decision has first to pander to the pointless appeasement to decorum and petty national niceties. If VK as much as catches a scent of a preventative action, by Russian or foreign government, he has already enough resources in place to launch his plan – his Program. On the following page I have a map and plan of how you can access the peninsula without detection. Later I will describe what must be done when you get to the Superdeep."

Finn turned to the next page. He sighed. That page too was absent. As was the next. He turned to page eight.

"...that I saw it happening. My daughter has an intellect far above those of her own age. Other fifteen year olds have barely left their dolls behind while she is already conducting research of an order more fitting to a second year pre-grad."

"Anya!" said Finn aloud. He knew it could only mean one thing: the author of the letter was Dr Boris Nevotslov! Nevotslov had engineered this all so that he would somehow be directed to Paris. No, not to Paris. He crossed his hands across his chest and closed his eyes. He was going north, much, much further north.

Suddenly he paused and challenged his own conclusion. Was it really inevitable? Was he bound to follow a path that led to nothing but personal danger and risk to his life? So far he had stumbled along a route almost preordained. He was acting like some kind of programmed robot. What about his own choices, his own free will?

Already he had survived at least two murder attempts, why did he feel he had to proceed at all? He instinctively knew he could set up a life for himself wherever he choose. He could speak multiple languages, had skills and abilities that seemed almost boundless and a prescient well of knowledge far beyond that of one man; of many men. Knowledge he had only scratched the surface of. He could disappear into the culture of his choice, settle down, enjoy life, be happy.

He shook his head and smiled as he opened his eyes. Of course he couldn't. He was imbued with a purpose far above the whim of personal satisfaction. Woven into his very self he knew that he carried a responsibility singular to himself but affecting all else. Whatever his past had been, he could not return there. It was his past and a man could not live there. A man could only live in the moment given to him and alive in that present, invest for the future. His eyes narrowed with a new determination. Boris Nevotslov had been a good man. It had been he who had saved his life in the submarine. Somehow he had been rescued from some kind of sinking, an incident following some occurrence that had something to do with the coma and the phenomenon of what was happening in his head. He observed he was thinking of the doctor in the past tense. With a heaviness of heart normally reserved for the loss of a friend, he innately knew that Boris Nevotslov was dead. It abruptly made him feel again the naked loneliness he had last experienced when awakening in the Glasgow hospital.

Suddenly he thought about Anya. What about her? He thought of her gentle form and saw her in the clearest waking vision so far. The sun glinting off her straw-golden hair and her face lit with her smile as she turned at looked at him from beneath the high birch trees so long ago. How long ago? He imagined it to be ten or twelve years. She would be in later twenties now. A woman. An odd ache throbbed in his heart. So much was lost. Not just the past, but the years the locust had eaten included what hopes he may have had, what desires a young man might entertain for a future.

It was a future lost to him now. His only future was to follow his instincts and the plan the doctor and he had somehow imprinted into his subconscious.

He held no bitterness about being used. Inherently he knew whatever plans or mission had been secreted into his mind, it was not an aim contrary to his will. He wanted to do this. He needed to, and that was fine with him.

The peace of that conclusion lingered with him as tiredness eventually overtook him and he fell into the first dreamless sleep he had had in months.

The following morning, after breakfast and a long goodbye - Madam Auberge was a very talkative host - Finn finally set out on his cycle. The dog idly followed him to the end of the lane, and, having done its duty in delivering the visitor to the accepted limits of its property, returned to the front porch and lay down in another similitude of a dog fallen to Earth.

Finn knew that the bicycle was quickly becoming redundant. He had enjoyed the peace he had enjoyed cycling through the byways of rural France, but now he needed to accelerate his actions. Time was not on his side.

The phone on the desk of an office in Boulevard Lannes in Paris rang and was picked up by the personal assistant of the rezident, whose office it was. The secretary, a sober looking man dressed in a black suit topped by a balding head nodded to the *rezident* – the embassy station chief who was watching from his desk. The resident picked up his receiver when the call was transferred and listened for a few moments, nodding solemnly.

"*Vy uvereny?* - are you sure?"

After the call, he replaced the receiver and thought for a moment.

"Do we have an operation on that I should know about?" he asked the other man. "Or even one that I should not know about?"

The balding man shook his head. His boss was the official resident, the legal spy of the Russian Federation in the Parisian embassy, but even for him, there were certain things that took place below his radar. In previous days these things were undertaken by the *nelegal'nye rezidenty*. It was a role of illegal resident spy, a position required if the legal resident was to be able to claim deniability on certain sensitive actions considered necessary for the USSR.

But these were different days. Days sculpted by Glasnost and Perestroika. The Russian Federation was now a democracy and operated under different rules. Even so, there were occasional requirements that came around and the resident simply looked the other way when those actions were essential but critically, not acknowledgeable by him.

"Niet," replied his assistant. "We have no one in the field currently. You are fully conversant with all the embassy business."

The older man turned a pen between his fingers.

"That was London on the phone," he said. "Apparently they have it on very good grounds that a team is hunting. So far their prey has eluded them, but they have followed him here, to Paris."

"A team from London? Operating here, in Paris?" exclaimed his confidante. "But how could that be?"

"No," mused his superior. "Not a team from London. They assure me it is not one of theirs. Did you hear about the shooting in Montparnasse yesterday?"

The assistant nodded. It had been front page news.

"That was part of the hunt. They missed again."

"If not London, and certainly not ours, then..."

"Whose?" interrupted the resident, completing the sentence for him. "Now that is the question. Make a few calls. Find out whom we should be considering. Rogue Russians is exactly what we do not need, but we do need to know who is behind this. Get me Moscow."

Chapter 31
Intelligence

When Lander awoke it was with a headache so painful that he was unable to hold any kind of a fully coherent thought. If he had been struck with a sledgehammer it could not have felt any worse. His head was bound in bandages, as was his leg, and he could not at first think what had happened to have had him awaken into such pain.

As he struggled with the thudding in his head, a man appeared beside him.

"*Vot, voz'mi eto,*" he said, holding out a glass and two large capsules. Lander's Russian was rudimentary, but he could understand painkillers being offered when he saw them.

"*Spasibo,*" he groaned, He might have said thank you, though it could have been *please*, or *good day* for all he knew, so dysfunctional were his thoughts. He hardly cared, the pain was excruciating. He did not even have the mental acuity to ask what had happened to him. He threw the pills down his throat, not bothering with the water and lay back with exhaustion. The man watched him for a moment as Lander closed his eyes. When they flickered open momentarily a few seconds later, the man was gone.

"Well?" asked the Spetsnatz commander. "Is he awake? Did he say anything?"

The medic nodded. "He awoke momentarily. The rush of pain almost immediately rendered him unconscious again, but not before he managed to take some painkillers I gave him. They should help."

"But did he speak?"

"Da," replied the doctor, "but not much. He just thanked me for the pills."

"In what language?" pressed the agitated officer, "Russian?"

"Yes, of course Russian," shrugged the doctor. "What else? I thought you said he was one of ours?"

"You can go now," dismissed the special operations captain abruptly, "but as soon as I can speak to him, you must come and get me, understand?"

The doctor nodded and left the room. There was far too much testosterone in the cabin and he was glad enough to have been dismissed from it.

"That is good," said the officer to his team. "If he wakes and speaks Russian, that is very good."

His men slapped one another on their backs. It was a good enough piece of news to merit opening a bottle of vodka. Their destination was less than 12 hours away and already they could feel the imminent approbation of a job well done. Yes, the doctor had delivered exactly the news they had hoped to hear.

Jack had an appointment with Jonas Smythe. Jonas suggested the embankment where he often sat on a sunny lunch hour.

"So, how are you getting on now Inspector? I believe you and the Commodore have already had a private tête-à-tête?"

It was true. Sir Simon had insisted on Jack being given unfettered access to investigate as he saw fit. He had already talked privately to Desmond Reid, in the case of the Commodore, he had actually contacted him.

"Yes, Sir Simon has given me quite a free hand. I didn't expect it."

"Us being spies and all that, eh?" smiled the dapper MI5 man beside him on the bench. Jack shrugged and made a triangle with his index fingers upon his lower lip.

"Initially Finn could remember nothing about his past, but in conversation with the Irish Presbyterian minister – they had become good friends – he confided in some dreams he had."

"Dreams?" frowned Jonas suspiciously.

"I know, but Mr Boyd, the minister, told me that Finn thought they were memories. A clever man, that reverend. He would know when to ask the right kind of questions and how to draw out of Finn details he would have missed himself."

"Sounds more like a detective than a church minister," smiled Jonas.

"They go through quite an extensive training. Sometimes we lay people imagine that the incumbents of church office come from those who would not qualify for other professions. The opposite I have found to be the case. Alastair Boyd for example. He had a first class honours degree in mechanical engineering before he decided to go for Theology. He completed a Masters in that and did a subsidiary in Psychology. Add learning Latin, Greek and Hebrew as well as Classical History and Comparative Religion and you have a man who knows how to use his head."

"I have no quibbles with that at all," said Jonas, a smile wrinkling the corners of his mouth. "Studied Theology myself at Oxford."

"Theology?" replied Jack in some surprise. "Unusual career path then, into the Security Services."

"Not as unusual as you might think. Not too many tertiary level qualifications for our kind of work. Usually we are sought out with regard to experience, adaptability and a wide breadth of diverse knowledge. Anyway, you were saying about dreams?"

"Finn related some images that may have been memories. Drowning in a chemical sea. A rescue, some kind of ship. I put the times together and along with the details revealed at the last meeting across the way," he nodded with his head across the water to Thames House, "a few things flagged up. The operation in the Irish Sea, the cover up of whatever it had been that had been dumped and leaked and a certain Russian scientist – Boris Nevotlov?"

Jonas looked genuinely surprised. "My, you have been busy. How did you get that name?"

"By being a detective," replied Jack without expression. "Desmond Reid mentioned the name briefly when I was asking him about Operation Neptune. I don't think he intended to and he quickly moved on to other aspects of my questions. That in itself was noteworthy. I looked him up. There were records in scientific reports at the time. Nevotlov was a well respected and internationally regarded scientist and it wasn't too hard to find some archive material that mentioned him. From that I'm surmising he had been involved in some research that had connections with your own - probably clandestine?"

Jonas's eyebrows lifted slightly. Jack continued.

"Then he disappeared suddenly, not long after Finn's arrival in Glasgow interestingly enough. Would I be correct in saying that Thames House had some kind of avenue of communication with the doctor?"

Jonas straightened the handkerchief in his jacket pocket. "I think we could assume that," he said.

Jack nodded quietly. "Finn was an ordinary young man who disappeared from Ardrossan almost twelve years ago. So, sequence of possible events: At that time Captain Legge is in charge of a ship which has been given a covert operation to dump some possibly secret chemicals into the U.K's deep munitions disposal site off Scotland. Allen Finlay – Finn, as we know him, is dumped by persons unknown a considerable time later at Glasgow Royal. Boris Nevotslov, who has been communicating some kind of information with MI5 is uncovered by his own side and disappears – probably killed."

Jonas nodded slowly. "Go on Jack."

"Come forward. Jon Lander is sent on a mission. It may in itself have a Russian connection. Whether that is true or not, he has not reported back in some time. You are concerned, especially since a Russian sub was tracked leaving the island he was operating on just two days ago."

"Now you are intriguing me. How could you know about the movements of Russian submarines?" asked Jonas.

"Alex Harker-Bell. Don't forget, you gave me a free rein. Mr Harker-Bell was fairly forthcoming. He seemed pleased to be able to assist. He complained that he thinks Thames House moves too slow."

"That's MI6 for you. Vauxhall House are a bit ram-stam and bulldoze. We tend to be a bit more, ahm... *discreet*?"

Jack sat back in his chair. "I wouldn't know, but in any case I'm informed that the sub is heading to the Kola Peninsula. Boris Nevotslov, according to your own accounts, was last known alive on Kola. He was working on something, something so sensitive that the Security Services have spent more on this than possibly any other operation, including Northern Ireland, in the last ten years. Meanwhile Finn is being hunted by possibly KGB or some other Russian service. Whatever has happened to him, they want him dead. Add it all together and something big, very big is happening."

He put his hands flat on the bench either side of himself. "Look, I am only a Detective Inspector in the Strathclyde Police. Something is bothering me and I may as well let you know. Why bring me in?"

"Because of Finn," replied Jonas simply. "Sir Simon took a risk and now I see he was entirely correct. We needed another angle, another perspective, one outside the department, one unalloyed by the mindset difficult to avoid when working in the prism that is our line of work."

He paused, turned and looked directly at Jack.

"But now we would like you to go further. You see, there is another reason we brought you in. MI5 is a house of mirrors. Mirrors that distort and obfuscate. We deal in secrets, but secrets are lucrative things. Secrets attract alien interests. If those secrets are lucrative enough, even the most trustworthy of men can be corrupted." His voice grew quiet. "We think we have a mole. If we dig around we might find who it is, but the digging will be messy. It will have other effects and it is imperative, especially at this time, that no digging be detected."

"What do you mean? Are you asking me...?"

"To be our silent spade. Yes. Unearth him. But from the outside. Trust no one. Not me, not even Sir Simon if needs be. But do it as you have done this. Silently."

Ten minutes later, he and Jonas Smythe separated. Jonas, back across the river, Jack, back to the hotel room he had been given by MI5 on this side of the Thames. He needed to make a phone call. His wife would need to know he would not be home for a while yet.

"How did that go?" asked Sir Simon.

Jonas folded his long legs where he sat on the chair opposite his boss.

"You were right Sir Simon. The man is sharp, very sharp indeed. From scraps of information and digging around, he has put together a quite reasonable intelligence. He doesn't know anything about the Neptune material, what it is, how we got it, why we needed rid of it – though I wouldn't put it past him to get there eventually given enough time. I told him about our suspicions. I also told him to be discreet. Hopefully he will not be anticipated by whomever it is that is responsible for the leak."

"Good," said Sir Simon thoughtfully. "It was I who informed him of Lander's silence. Legge has a ship landing some marines there shortly. Hopefully the Jan Mayen situation will become clearer as they go inland. Have you informed the NIS?"

Jonas nodded. "I hope we were right in taking that risk. Since they have long suspected a mole in their own ranks it will be kept tight. I only hope tight enough."

The captain of the *Severodvinsk* brought his boat to the surface on the approaches to Kola Bay. Low grey stratus clouds hung like formless sheets overhead while a damp mist clung onto every surface, the wet drapes adding to the silence except for the flat waters breaking over the bow and spilling off the thirteen metres of beam. The four hundred and fifty feet of charcoal coloured hull was barely visible, only the sail and deck of the boat rising above the languid waters of the bay. The submarine was brought around a couple of degrees to the south-west as the helmsman responded to orders. The vessel was making for Polyarny, twenty miles north of Severomorsk. The town was a closed administrative-territorial section in Murmansk Oblast. Situated on the western approaches of Kola Bay, it had facilities dedicated to the docking and repair of the Northern Fleet's nuclear powered submarines. The sub's commander had originally intended to return to Severomorsk, the submarine's home port, but the Spetsnatz captain had pressed for a quieter disembarkation. He saw the rationale. Severomorsk, although open for Russians required a special pass for anyone else. Few were given. It was also a place of great interest for the intelligence agencies of foreign governments. American satellites were known to log the comings and goings of the fleet. Polyarny would be less watched. The agent who had been recovered from Jan Mayen had not yet recovered consciousness and Polyarny had a fine Naval hospital that serviced the entire town. Doubtless they would want to take him there first.

Jon had awoken again, but this time with a headache that was manageable. When the doctor had returned, he kept his eyes closed and feigned sleep. He sensed the man approach and stand by his cot. He felt him lean forward and check the monitor above his head. Apparently satisfied, his footsteps receded to the door and he was once again left to himself.

He lay on his back and thought hard. He was on board a ship, that much was obvious from his surroundings. There were no windows and the ceiling was low. The vessel was obviously moving, but there was no swell – possibly even a submarine. The doctor had spoken Russian. What had happened to him? The last thing he recalled was looking for a radio inside the mountain at Jan Mayen. No, there was more. He had taken it back to the outside and...

Lars! Lars Guldberg had been waiting for him. There had been a fire-fight, he remembered it as if in a half-forgotten dream. The effort in trying to recall made his head pound and he winced with the stabs of pain. He put his head involuntarily to his head and felt the bandages. Yes, he was wounded. Another bandage was wrapped around his right thigh. He tested his leg. It was painful, but he could move it. Why had Guldberg let him live? Despite what the films depicted, there was no such thing as shoot to wound. The only purpose of shooting was to kill. If he wasn't dead, then why not? Wait, his Glock, had he used it? He had a faint idea he did, but nothing clearer would come to mind. Whatever the answer to all these questions, one overarching one overshadowed them all. What about the men at Olonkinbyen? Had he been able to radio for help? He could not remember but had the dread suspicion that he had not. Those men had depended on him. He set his jaw as he imagined the position they were in. Was he in any position to help? That was the one question that needed answered first of all.

HMS Albion struggled to hold her position as the ribs exited her stern. Captain Currie watched as the little dots on the churning waters made their precarious way to the shore a quarter of a mile away. Twelve marines sat in those violently pitching rubber craft and Currie did not envy them. They were good men - every one of them focused on what they needed to do and prepared to risk their lives to save others. It was times like this that made James Currie proud of his nation. There was much about it that appalled him, much that had been lost to the inverted psyche of modern social mores, but that British soil could still raise men like those marines crashing onto the surf of one of the most hostile places on earth was something that lifted a man's heart.

Had there been a camera to record the soldiers as they tramped across the tussocks on Jan Mayen, the similarity to The Falklands campaign would have struck the older observer. British soldiers moving with purpose across a landscape like that of the Scottish moors. Men of the British Isles who followed their predecessors with the same grit and dogged determination.

Two hours later the marines of 3 Commando arrived at the smoke and ruin at Olonkinbyen. The Norwegian Orion had been unable to land and had had to return to the mainland. There were many seriously wounded at the base and the marines wasted no time. The relief of help unexpectedly appearing, dressed in friendly uniforms was something to see on the faces of the survivors. The marines had two field-trained medics along with their supplies. They wasted no time in triaging and getting to work. A comms link was established with the ship and with the anticipation of the storm rapidly beating itself out, the ship's Chinook was put on standby for bringing the wounded back to HMS Albion's medical facilities.

Once Henrik Jensen was in the hands of the marine medic, Ari Bjørnson sought out the officer commanding. Explaining the situation of Jon Lander and the caution he now had of Lars Guldberg since he had mysteriously disappeared, he expressed his anxiety for his friend.

The Major nodded and thanked him. He put the information back to the ship and requested another patrol from the ship be despatched to the Beerenburg. Back on board, the marines who had not been selected for the initial mission clenched their fists with pleased anticipation. Two more ribs were prepared and already the conditions had improved so much that their trip to the shore was considerably less perilous than the first.

An hour later, the scudding clouds began to clear and the general improvement allowed the helicopter to recover the more critical cases from the base. Once in the care of the ship's surgeon, the outlook for those men was vastly improved.

"But no word of Lander?" asked Sir Simon.

Jonas Smythe shook his head. "None yet. Marines from Albion got to the Beerenburg and found a body outside. Seems it is likely that of one of the Norwegian meteorologists on the island.

"How did he die?"

"There was a gunshot to his head. There were a number of ejected empty casings around the tunnel exit. Interestingly, from two different firearms. Some were 7.62 short and others 9mm.

"But no weapons?"

"Seems that whoever won the fire-fight took the guns."

"If his nemesis was Lander, then why disappear? 7.62 Short? One of them had an AK47 or something like it then. Did they search inside the volcano complex?"

"As much as possible. It goes for miles apparently. The NIS agent on Mayen – the Norwegian sergeant Lander had contacted, said Jon had gone to the volcano for a short wave radio, the communications at the base had been destroyed in the explosion. The marines found an ancient military radio at the entrance. It must have been the one he got the distress call out on, but there is no sign of him. It seems he has just vanished."

Sir Simon shook his head. "Something is wrong here Jonas. If Lander could contact us, he would. I hope he has not bled out on that god-forsaken rock somewhere. Make sure they carry out a search of the area. He could be bleeding to death under some rock, unaware that 3 Commando have arrived."

"There's another thing," added Jonas. "The Norwegian sergeant wants to pass on a message on a secure net. I've asked Desmond to arrange something. Perhaps that will shed some light."

"Perhaps," agreed Sir Simon. "I would hate to think a man has lost his life for nothing."

The vessel had slowed and eventually came to a halt. A few minutes later the doctor returned to Jon Lander's cabin and began putting straps across his chest. A few seconds after that he saw through partially opened eyes two more men in dark uniforms enter. Someone spoke in Russian. It was directed to him. Jon decided he could not feign total unconsciousness indefinitely, so he uttered a low moan. The gruff Russian voice spoke again. Jon rolled his eyes and groaned incoherently. Apparently satisfied that that was much as he was going to get out of the wounded man, the Russian motioned to the others toward the bed. He felt his cot being detached from its legs and he was carried out of the cabin and through the steel passageways. As he emerged from the hull of the vessel he caught a glimpse of the tall sail of a nuclear powered submarine. The small red star on the side confirmed its nationality.

The air was bitingly cold and in the grey distance he could see snow spattered roofs of the low buildings around a dockside. The soldier with the gruff voice - a uniform consistent with Special Forces and with a deportment that betrayed seniority - called over two sentries who were lounging at a barrier. He barked some orders at them. They came over and slinging their weapons over their backs, helped carry Lander across some rail lines and into a squat ambulance. Once inside, one of the commandeered soldiers muttered something to his colleague and unenthusiastically stepped up into the vehicle. He took the seat beside the injured patient. Jon reasoned that he was probably being taken to a hospital; the soldier ordered to accompany him. His guard set his rifle upright on the bed, its muzzle pointed toward the ceiling as he fumbled for a cigarette in his top pocket. The last thing he saw before the double doors were closed, was three of the dark uniformed forces mount a UAZ utility jeep and move off ahead of the ambulance. Lander guessed they were escorting him to the hospital.

Lander was, if nothing else, a man who knew success lay in acting before the moment passed. As soon as the vehicle moved off, he whipped out an arm, grasped the Kalashnikov and swung it round into his hands. Pointing it at the shocked soldier, he turned in the bed and sat upright. His head pounded for a moment with the rush of blood, but he kept an even face as he chambered the weapon. A round of ammunition ejected with a clatter onto the ambulance floor. He thought it might have been loaded, but he needed to be sure. Nonetheless, the action had the effect of making the Russian sit back and take very serious notice.

"Do you speak English?" asked Lander. The Russian looked back wide-eyed.

"*Englis?*" he repeated, his hand still ridiculously dipped into his top pocket where it had frozen in time.

"Da, *English*, as in, do you speak any? *Govorizh' po-angliyski?*" he added, remembering a snatch of very poor Russian.

The soldier nodded, his eyes fixed on the weapon pointed at his chest.

"A little," he said. Recovering somewhat, he drew his hand back out of his pocket and pointed at the rifle "*Vkho?* Why... this?"

"Change of plan," said Jon, indicating with the muzzle of the rifle. "Take off your uniform."

Ari looked at the body the marines had brought in to the ship. All of the personnel from the base had now been transferred to HMS Albion where the wounded were being given first class care in the ship's surgery. The body from the mountain was the last to be brought on board.

"Lars Guldberg!" gasped the *Oversersjant*. "What happened?"

"Lead poisoning," said the major sardonically. Ari Bjørnson did not need to be told what he meant.

"Did you find Jon, I mean, Sutherland?" he queried.

The major shook his head. "We checked several square kilometres around the exit. Got the Chinook to fly past with the thermal imaging.

If he was out there, we would have found him. Sorry, I believe he was a friend of yours."

Ari nodded and as he did so, a navy lieutenant beckoned to him.

"We have a comms link available for you now if you'd follow me?"

An emergency meeting was set up in Thames House. It was a select group made up of Sir Simon, Jonas Smythe, Desmond Reid, Alex Harker-Bell and Commodore Legge.

The five men sat around the table in the same room they had met in before. Sir Simon cleared his throat and began.

"We have just received this morning a secure burst from HMS Albion. It appears that the fire at the base was not an accident. It was the result of an explosion. Desmond, you have some information?"

"Traces of RDX and PETN were found at the site," replied Reid without further introduction. "That would be concurrent with the use of plastic explosive, probably Semtex. Being hard to detect, it could be easily hidden and utilised. Pan Am Flight 103 was brought down with it. It wasn't detected on their monitors."

"Thank you Desmond," said Sir Simon. "Two men lost their lives, several others were seriously injured. The base is, for all practical purposes, destroyed."

"Espionage?" queried Harker-Bell.

"So it would appear," nodded the head of MI5. "The Norwegian Intelligence Service had a man in cover there. Sergeant Ari Bjørnson. He had made contact with Jon Lander and was assisting him. After the explosion Lander went to the mountain facility to try to get help using a radio based there. After getting a transmission out, he appears to have been in a fire-fight with the base's chief meteorologist. Bjørnson believes this man to have been a spy, probably Russian."

"And you think he blew up the base?" asked Harker-Bell. "What the devil is going on?"

"Good question," agreed Sir Simon. "Meanwhile Jon Lander has disappeared."

"Disappeared?" said Commodore Legge with some concern in his voice. "How could he disappear?"

"Jonas?" said Sir Simon looking towards Smythe.

"We have had intelligence that a *Yashkin* class Russian submarine was in the area at the time. They are a very quiet ship, occasionally used for covert ops. We are considering the possibility that Lander may have been intercepted by forces from the submarine. He was onto something. It was probably why the agent acted when he did. Whatever Lander had discovered, they wanted it silenced. I'm afraid that Lander has probably been killed."

"Seems like a lot of conjecture there," contested Harker-Bell. "It might have been better if we'd kept Vauxhall House in the loop. They have more of a military mind on this kind of thing."

"Possibly," acknowledged Sir Simon, "but not as much conjecture as you might think. Bjørnson was able to tell us more. Jonas?"

"In the secure burst from HMS Albion," Jonas said, taking his cue, "the Norwegian Sergeant told us that Lander had discovered something about the noises emanating from below the mountain. Apparently notes were found and they suggested that there was human activity going on, deep below, possibly miles below the volcano."

Desmond Reid was the first to react. "Human activity? Mining? You are saying the Norwegians are mining below an active volcano?"

"Not mining, and not Norwegians," answered Jonas. "Russians."

Chapter 32
Risks

Finn eventually found himself in Amiens. It was a big enough town to get lost in, but more importantly had a rail link that did not have to return to Paris to secure an internationally bound train.

At Gare d'Amiens, he found an area out of bounds to the public. There he walked confidently into a staff rest room with changing rooms and toilets attached. A couple of staff looked up from their coffees as he passed through, but seeing nothing out of the ordinary – it was too big a station to know everyone – returned to their small chat. Finn found an open locker where he found the overalls of a maintenance worker, complete with yellow hat, hi-vis jacket and even an I.D. card tucked into the helmet.

Dressed now as an employee of the SNCF, he left the staff room and made his way to the ticket office. A quick flash of his pass got him past the barrier and a few minutes later he was on the train destined for Cologne. All the countries he planned to pass through were members of the Schengen agreement. As far as lack of a passport went, he would have nothing to worry about all the way to Finland. His SNCF pass would get him free rail travel as far as Germany – Belgium respected agreements with the French railway employees – but after that he was going to have to dip into his fund of Euros.

In the meantime, Germany was over twelve hours distant. He was tired after his long cycle to Amiens. He had had to ditch his bicycle, which he regretted, but that loss was tempered by the note he had left on it when he had set it over the hedge of a house in Amiens. The house had children, he could tell by several toys lying around in the garden. A dilapidated old bicycle lay propped up against a wooden shed. He left his bicycle there with a note in French. *I hope you can find use for my bicycle. I have no more need of it. It is a fine cycle. I hope you enjoy it.*

The tiredness made his eyes heavy. Placing his bag on his knees, he tipped his yellow hat over his eyes and promptly fell asleep to the rhythmic chatter of the wheels clattering over the *chemin de fer* below him.

Lander, now dressed in the uniform of the soldier, peered through a tiny window at the front of the patient cabin. There was one driver in the front. Ahead he could see the military jeep leading about twenty metres in front. He looked out the back through a small round window in the rear door. There did not appear to be a following escort.

On the cot, the Russian soldier was strapped down where Lander had tied him, a blanket covering his bonds, a bandage across his mouth. Ahead, a junction suddenly caused the driver of the ambulance to slow to a walking pace. Jon turned to the soldier, put a finger to his lips, promptly opened the rear door and jumped out.

He did not manage to stay upright. Landing on his two feet, the pain in his leg caused him to roll over as the vehicle sped up and drove off. Lander knew he could only buy a little time before he was discovered missing. The hospital was probably not far off and as soon as his absence was discovered, the whole town would be on alert. Getting awkwardly to his feet, he tried to hide his limp and made his way to the footpath. Fortunately, there were very few people about, and he did not wait to see if anyone had witnessed his strange exit from the back of the ambulance. As quickly as he could, he headed into the streets and began looking for a building that would have what he needed.

He had no expectation of remaining at large for long, but he only needed fifteen minutes of freedom to achieve his aim. As he had hoped, his uniform made him more or less invisible to the few people he passed as he searched for what he wanted. Most of the nondescript dull concrete buildings appeared to be accommodation, not what he was looking for. Turning a corner, he saw overhead lines converge on an official looking building. A large sign above the entrance doorway appeared to suggest a shipping company or something like it. It did not matter, the lines were not power, they were telephone lines and that was what he needed.

He marched in, followed a corridor, saw light from the upper glass door of an office, pushed it open where he saw a man at a desk, typing on a keyboard. A woman was opposite him, near a wall with a large pile of box files on shelves. She had more on her side of the same desk and was obviously sorting through them. She had just got up from her seat when Lander entered. Hearing the door fling open both she and the man looked up. Lander marched over and unslung his rifle. He cradled it in his arms, but did not point it at either. He pointed at the two phones on the desk.

"Telephone!" he said, "Moscow!"

Neither moved. Lander repeated his words, but now with the gun pointed at the man.

"Telephone – Moscow!" He said with some force. He had no intention of making a call to the Russian capital, but he had to have a phone capable of making an outside line.

The woman seemed to comprehend first and nervously pointed at the one nearest her. Lander moved over and indicated for the two of them to stand against the wall with the box folders. As they complied, he stretched out and grabbed the receiver. He punched in a series of numbers, numbers that had the ability to route through any public line to a phone in an office in London. He knew any outside line in the place he was in would be monitored. He would probably only have seconds before it would be shut down.

A series of clicks and tones followed. The sequence of numbers he needed to respond with were details Lander had had to commit to memory for just such situations as this. A public phone line anywhere in the world is part of a vast global network. Despite its limitations as to government control and security, it is still an invaluable asset to an agent denied any other form of more secure communication.

As certain tones sounded, he punched the requisite number. Relays clicked in exchanges across continents as they were initiated, bypassed or coerced into forwarding the connection. As they did so, Lander kept his eyes on the two in front of him, his weapon still directed toward them. In the background he was aware of the distant sound of sirens. The phone continued through a series of silences, punctuated by distant electronic noises. He needed just a few more seconds.

Suddenly a voice crackled in the receiver.

"Hotel lobby. Is this an outside call?" said a woman's voice.

"No, this is internal, staff only," responded Lander with his unique coded reply. He did not wait to be forwarded, he knew the call was being recorded.

"Recovered consciousness in a non-NATO submarine. Am in a

Russian naval port. L.G. is high order threat. Immediate evacuation required Jan Mayen – explosion, many wounded. Subversive operations detected beneath the mountain. Not related to resilience programme. Foreign involvement, major, I repeat, major hostile intentions. A.B. or H.J. trustworthy sources," he hesitated as he heard the sirens grow louder, suddenly another voice came on the line. It was a demanding woman's voice speaking Russian. Lander ignored it and continued.

"Find radio – further information stored and..." The voice interrupted again. There was a click and the line went immediately dead. Jon closed his eyes for a second, opened them and dropped the muzzle of his rifle. He pulled out the magazine and showed it to the two office workers. It was empty. The rounds lay scattered below the stretcher in the ambulance. He set the rifle on the desk and took a step back. He found a chair and sat down.

"Apologies," he said with a wan smile. "I hope I didn't frighten you too much. Needs must and all that?"

The two uncomprehending Russians looked at one another wide-eyed but had no opportunity to speak as just then the doors crashed open and several armed Spetsnatz soldiers burst into the room.

Three train journeys, several buses and three hitch-hikes later, Finn stood in Helsinki. He had crossed through France, Belgium, Germany and Denmark by train. From Copenhagen he had managed to hitch-hike a lift on a lorry transporting solar panels across Øresund Bridge and undersea tunnel from Denmark to Sweden. It had taken him three days to get to Sweden, but Schengen, the world's largest visa-free travel area had allowed him to get this far without border checks. By abolishing internal borders, twenty-six European countries had created a zone with free and unrestricted movement. For Finn this had allowed fairly uncomplicated travel. His next stage however would be less straightforward. A ferry could have got him across into Finland over the Gulf of Bothnia but the checks at the terminal north of Stockholm made that route less tenable. Eventually he decided that the answer was to make his way up the eastern coast of Sweden to the northern border between the two countries. It was over six hundred miles and without proper I.D. he knew that renting a car would be next to impossible.

He began looking for second hand car dealers in and around Stockholm. A shop with Telefonshoppen printed in bold letters above its large windows seemed a good bet and after parting with a few Euros he had a budget Smartphone with a loaded pay as you go sim-card. Logging in to a Swedish online car market he was able to take note of some inexpensive cars and the addresses at which they were for sale.

The day was beginning to lose its light when he found a cheap room at a city centre hotel. He was able to book online and on arrival paid with cash. A few minutes later he found himself in a small single bedroom with a tiny en-suite. The window looked out onto a wall not three feet from the window. The Hilton it was not, but it was discreet and anonymous and those were qualities at the top of his current list.

In his office in Archangelsk, Karmonov was listening to the voice on the other end of the phone. As he listened, his grip on the receiver became so tight that the plastic actually began to crack.

"Find him," he said, struggling to maintain an even voice. From Karmonov, it was a tone that had the absolute assurance of consequences for failure. "Find him and kill him," he repeated. "I do not want to hear of anything less than this. You understand."

The last part of his sentence was not a question. It was a simple statement. Many men had understood before. Failure was not an option. As far as Viktor Karmonov was concerned, those who failed were those who were not fully committed. Only the fully committed deserved power. To be fully committed a man had to make choices that others would not. To even countenance failure as an outcome deemed a man unfit for service. Karmonov could no more tolerate the idea than to imagine a future without decisive leadership. That the world could exist without that was simply unthinkable.

Back in Stockholm the trail had gone cold. He had always been a step ahead of them but in Paris only the intervention of the police had narrowly prevented their success. Their contact in the SNCF had provided information that led them to Cologne and as the trail became warm again, they at last had definite proof when the CCTV at the Øresund Bridge had picked him out as a passenger on a commercial truck. Since the roads out of Stockholm were under their surveillance and no further sightings had been reported, they were confident he was in the capital. They had awakened all the sleepers. It had now become a massive manhunt with resources almost unimaginable to western agencies. Stockholm was practically home ground to them but all they needed now was a piece of luck. As the Irish Republican Army had once said; they only had to be lucky once – their enemy had to lucky every time. Sooner or later, for him, that luck would run out.

Karmonov called the committee to an emergency meeting. To convene it, he flew to Saint Petersburg. The meeting place was in a large, luxurious private apartment secreted within St Petersburg's Russian Ballet Theatre near Liteyniy Avenue.

The city of some five million souls had undergone several name changes in a hundred years. St Petersburg, Petrograd, Leningrad and finally back to St Petersburg. Situated at the head of the Gulf of Finland on the Baltic Sea, it was Russia's second-largest city, but for the committee, it would be something far greater than that.

Their meeting place was on the southern bank of the Neva River; it was not far from the Winter Palace. The events that took place there in 1917 were not lost on the secret group. An old order had been overthrown and a new one resurrected from the ashes. In 1927, Sergei Eisenstein re-enacted the storming of the Winter Palace in his iconic film. The dramatic black and white images of *October: Ten Days that Shook the World,* were embedded into the mass consciousness of an entire people. In Soviet artwork, the definitive symbol of the Russian Revolution was the heroic proletariat assaulting the palace below a single red flag. It was the moment of birth.

Critical to their plans following the implementation of The Program, the city was home to many federal government bodies. The Constitutional Court of Russia presided in the city and plans were in an advanced stage for the relocation of the Supreme Court of the Russian Federation. The consulates of many of the world's nations were located in the city along with international banks, global corporations and dozens of cross-national business headquarters.

When Karmonov called the committee to convene in the place they had selected as the seat of the newly restored United Soviet, every man in that committee knew that decisive events were imminent.

Each made his own separate and surreptitious way to the meeting. Experts all in counter-espionage, every effort had been made to ensure their presence in the city was unknown. Different routes and modes of transport were employed and their arrival times were staggered. On the avenue, trusted eyes hid in shadows, watching for external surveillance. There was none.

When at last all had arrived and were seated at the large Cherry-wood table in the luxurious setting of a Romanov era wood panelled and chandeliered room, Karmonov began.

"You will have guessed that your being here intimates more than just another meeting," he said, looking at each man and holding the gaze of every eye. "Within a few short months from now we would have commenced but matters outside our control have dictated that we must act immediately and delay no longer."

"What matters?" asked a voice. It belonged to a man of significant political influence. His place within the Federation government had garnered inside information that had been invaluable in their plans.

"We are all aware of the Norwegian interest on Jan Mayen," explained Karmonov. "This has come to a head. We had a man infiltrated into the operations there. He was able to uncover the possible presence of foreign intervention. He was ordered to eliminate that threat. We have not heard from him since. It appears he may not have been successful."

"You mean he was killed?" asked another man, his thick set frame filling the chair in which he sat.

"Probably, Igor Gurevich," admitted Karmonov. "We had an exfiltration in place for him. It had appeared successful. They brought back an unconscious man, but it turned out not to be him."

The room stirred. Karmonov held up a hand to silence the room.

"He was brought via the nuclear submarine *Severodvinsk* to Polyarny at Kola Bay. As you know, the Northern Fleet is to all intents and purposes entirely under our control. At this point there was still some confusion as to his identity. On the way to the local hospital he managed to escape but was quickly recaptured. During his time at large however, he attempted to make contact with persons unknown via a public telephone line."

"So, we know who he contacted?" asked Geim.

"No," replied Karmonov, shaking his head. "The line was externally scrambled in such a way as to be untraceable. He was overheard by two office workers in the naval pay section, but neither spoke English."

"An American?" asked a man to the left of Karmonov.

"We do not know. He has not spoken as yet – though I am sure he will soon enough."

"Then if he is a foreign agent, we must go ahead with The Program immediately," said another from across the table."

"We could be overreacting," interrupted Gurevich. "We do not know for sure that this imposter knows anything yet."

"I have not told you of another issue," added the head of The Program. "Nevotslov has somehow managed to create a threat of unknown capability. This alone necessitates we commence operations."

"But Nevotslov is dead!" exclaimed Gurevich, who spoke for the room. His statement was accompanied by several nods of assent.

"In war, ships have been sunk by torpedoes arriving after the submarine that released them was already destroyed," explained Karmonov.

"Nevotslov was working on a subject he was fascinated with. A man who had been somehow altered by chemicals or minerals infused within his body. By withholding this information, Nevotslov paid with his life. This subject is at large. He has been moving through Europe and our last information placed him in Cologne. We do not know his intentions, but he has eluded our agents several times already. He managed to kill one of our best agents sent to silence him in Ireland. I am sure he will be eliminated, but we cannot take that risk. The Program is far too important. He may have been given information by Nevotslov - information that endangers all we have meticulously accomplished up to this point." He brought his fist down heavy upon the polished table. "This cannot happen. We have come too far, there is too much at stake. For us there can be no return in any case. We are fully committed, are we not?"

His last statement was greeted with strong assurances. It was Geim who spoke for them all.

"Then we must initiate The Program. We cannot delay. We must take our positions and prepare for the final stages. *Za Rodinu* – For the Motherland!"

"And what of the *Uralmash* – what of the decoy at the Superdeep?" asked someone quietly.

Karmonov shrugged. "It has served its purpose. I will have it closed down."

Of all the dreams Finn had experienced so far, this latest was the clearest of all. He knew he was dreaming. It was less like a dream than as if he were witnessing his unconscious from a conscious perspective yet all the while being itself unconscious.

Not only was it a dream of images and words, he was aware of knowledge in his mind as the observer of the dream that lay outside the dream but which informed and narrated the events he observed.

Images came in short streams of events. He was in a kayak. Below him, the sea heaved and surged as if it were boiling. The waters were effervescent and luminous green, increasing in violence until his struggle to remain upright suddenly ended and he was thrown over, screaming as he sank in the aerated, lighted waters. Dispassionately watching the images of the dream, Finn knew that he would not drown. Neither would he rise to the surface. He would sink and yet remain alive.

The scene changed and another stream played out before him. Boris Nevotslov was in the room with him. He had no fear of this man. He was to be trusted. They spoke of science, of phenomena that had kept him alive, the same phenomena that had altered his mental state into something beyond anything the doctor could accept could possibly be true.

And yet it was.

It came from the vials disposed of by the British. Vials containing material surreptitiously sequestered from cores drilled deep under the Earth's crust at the Kola peninsula. Material so secret and so dangerously unstable that to bury it 300 metres below the Irish Sea was undertaken as the most veiled and covert naval operation in peacetime.

But not covert enough. He listened as the Nevotslov in his dream explained how he had been selected to provide expert advice to the ultra-silent Lima Class Experimental submarine following the C Class British destroyer.

The planned disposal of the vials had been leaked from a mole deep within British intelligence, this had led to the silent unseen trailing of the surface ship.

The British scientists had discovered something about the materials the Russians had not, and now they wanted it back. They would steal back that which had been stolen, the irony being that the man who had facilitated the theft was in fact the man sent to identify and affirm its return.

The images changed again and now Finn was hooked up voluntarily to dozens of electrodes on his head. He slept within his dream as electrical impulses were constantly communicated to the membrane surrounding his neural pathways. Impulses that digitised information into synaptic signals. Information formed to resonate with the brainwaves of the recipient.

Boris Nevotslov was engaged as a mineralogist at Arkhangelsk, but as a true polymath, metallurgy was only one of his specialisms. Though He was a brilliant metallurgist, unknown to most of his peers, his work in understanding just how to decode the electrical impulses of the brain was something he had probed and experimented with over a lifetime of personal investigation.

Now he marvelled at the capacity of Finn's presynaptic neural membrane to absorb and contain such huge amounts of synaptic target code. The hard drives of the super-computer whirred. Nevotslov was inputting beyond Pettabytes. A Zettabyte was information comparable with all the grains of sand on all the beaches of the world. The young man's mind seemed capable of even absorbing that.

This and more Finn was able to watch unfold in his dream. He was able even to comprehend the thoughts flowing through the mind of the dream Nevotslov.

The stream stopped and a new one started.

It was Anya. She smiled at him nervously from the foot of his bed. He sat up as he saw her.

"How do you feel?" she asked in her careful but competent English. "Father promised me you would not be hurt in the experiment."

"I'm fine," he replied. "My head is buzzing less, in fact, I feel really well."

Anya's mouth fell open in shock. Unseen by her, her father entered the room.

"You spoke Karelian!" she exclaimed.

"What?" asked the doctor behind her.

"Finn," she said, turning to her father and then back again to Finn. This time she spoke in her native tongue. "He... you speak *Karelian?*"

Finn shrugged. "Yes, I suppose I do, didn't I always?" He paused. "No, I don't suppose I did."

Boris Nevotslov almost fell onto the floor as his legs weakened beneath him.

"It worked Allen. I included a local Finnish dialect – Anya and I both can converse in it. You weren't able to speak Karelian before. It has worked!"

Everything began to retreat and diminish, but the more Finn tried to hold onto the dream, the faster it faded. Finally he awoke and found himself lying on his back in a tiny bedroom.

He was back in Stockholm and he knew two distinct facts.

One, that what he had dreamed was memory of real events.

And two - his name was Allen.

Chapter 33
Flight

He was beaten. Beaten, kicked and struck with rifle butts. The two soldiers were constant in their violence, taking it turn about to punch and kick the already wounded man. It was not torture as yet; not yet the coldly calculated methods that would make a man cry out for the mercy of death, but he was no fool, that would follow if he persisted in refusing to speak.

Lander wondered how long he could hold out. In the Service there had been R2I – Resistance to Interrogation training. At the time he had thought it realistic, but it was a poor cousin to the treatment he had experienced in the last two hours. He put a hand tentatively to his nose. Almost certainly broken. He could barely see out of his left eye and his arms throbbed with the cuts and gashes received from defending his face from the blows of the rifle butts. They had ripped off the jacket he had taken from the soldier in the ambulance, and his white shirt was torn and shredded, saturated in the crimson of his own blood. They had wrenched off the bandages on his head and thigh and then proceeded to beat the wounds with rubber batons.

It was, of course, entirely contrary to all international law. He did not appeal to any such agency. He replied to all questions with his assumed name, the name of his wrecked yacht and the circumstances of his rescue. It was a pattern intentionally mirroring the information permissible to be surrendered when under arms: name, rank and serial number.

Suddenly the beating stopped and the soldiers left, only to be replaced by the officer he had seen on the dock and another in civilian attire.

The first pulled up an upended chair from the floor and invited Lander to sit facing the low table in the room. Lander did not resist. The civilian stretched outside the room and fetched another. He set it in the corner and sat on it, watching impassively.

"I must apologise for my men," said the officer in English. His voice was a deep baritone. The words were heavily accented but Lander recognised a voice which was acquainted with command and authority.

"We were told you were prepared to kill two innocent office workers. I have since learned you had unloaded the weapon. I find that interesting."

He waited for Lander to respond. When all that returned was silence, he continued.

"Since you are familiar with firearms, I think you have had military training? Tell me again, why were you on Jan Mayen? Why did you try to escape? Who are you working for?"

"I've told you several times. My boat was wrecked in a storm. I was rescued by the Norwegians."

"Strange storm that left you with bullet wounds," replied the Spetsnatz captain. "Who are you, really?"

Jon looked up at the hard face of the uniformed man at the other side of the table.

"I have told you, what do you want me to say?"

The officer suddenly slammed a hard fist onto the table. "Do you think this is a game? Whether you live or die is completely in my control. Continue this foolishness and I will hand you back to my men!"

He was suddenly interrupted by the man in the suit. He said something quietly in Russian and after a short to and fro between the two, the captain glared at Jon, turned on his heel and marched out of the room. Something in the conversation suggested that some kind of seniority had been brought into play. If so, the Spetsnatz officer had clearly not appreciated the overruling that robbed him of his immediate command of the moment.

After the soldier had left, the other man loosened his tie and pulled his chair over to the table. Facing Lander, he pulled out a packet of cigarettes.

"Smoke?" he asked, his voice smooth and somewhat quiet. Jon shook his head. The man shrugged and tapped a cigarette out of its box. He lit it and took a long draw. The smoke he exhaled hung around him like a veil as he rubbed the bridge of his nose and looked up.

"Special Forces," he sighed. "Because they are so sure of their own superiority, they think they are masters of every field." He regarded Jon through the haze for a moment or two, seemingly considering something.

"But then, you would know that wouldn't you? I mean an ex-SAS officer would know that, hmm?"

Jon looked over the table through swollen eyes and effected no reaction.

The man facing him sighed again. "Now you are thinking, 'Was that a lucky guess or does he know more?'"

He drew another lungful of smoke and blew it out in a steady stream from the side of his mouth. He dropped the only partly smoked cigarette onto the concrete floor and extinguished it with his foot.

"I know, a waste. They say it is the last two thirds of a cigarette that kills you. You can survive if you don't go to the end." He paused and looked meaningfully at his captive. "Let's try not go to the end Jon Lander."

Jon failed to hide a glimmer of shock at his name being so easily brought to play.

"They have no idea of course," he said, indicating toward the door with his head. "Probably imagine you are an American or maybe even *agent provocateur*? I think we'll just keep it between ourselves that you are British MI5 eh?"

Jon's head was reeling. How could this man possibly know? Before he had time to wonder any more, the door opened and another man in civilian clothes looked in. He nodded and stood at the door, looking back along the corridor as if watching for someone. Lander's interviewer arose quickly and came around to his side of the table. He took Lander's arm.

"Time to go," he said. "Please do not struggle. I promise you, it would not be an intelligent action at this time."

He supported Jon to the door and at a signal from the other; the three of them stepped out into the corridor, the latest arrival scanning left and right as they moved toward a door at the end. A set of stairs led down to another door. Going through they were immediately outside. A car was waiting. Still holding his arm, Lander's captor guided him into the back seat and got in beside him. The other man quickly got into the driver's seat and they promptly drove off. An arm pushed Jon's head down as they drove through a simple checkpoint. A card was flashed: they were not stopped. The driver accelerated into the wide concrete-building-lined streets. Ten minutes later they found themselves at a dirt airfield west of the town. A small drab grey helicopter was waiting, its rotors already turning.

As they rose from the airfield and skirted the town, Lander looked out and saw several Russian naval ships as well as submarines in the docks. He had at least got part of his information correct.

The flight was no more than fifteen minutes and during the journey he was not spoken to. As they came in to land, Jon could see that they had arrived at a sizeable airport, larger commercial aircraft were parked up at the terminal buildings. The helicopter however made for a remote part of the airfield and landed next to a small twin turboprop. He was led out of the helicopter and directly into the fixed-wing craft. Once seated and belted, the man who now sat beside him, leaned over.

"Sergei Lebedev," he said. "Since I know your name, you may as well know mine." He looked around himself. "I like this little plane," he said. "It's a *Technoavia Rysachok*. Russian aircraft with American engines." He shrugged. "Would you believe that? Less than a dozen made, but made to go fast and far. You'll be doing both today."

The plane taxied and accelerated up the runway, seconds later they were climbing into the dull grey skies, banking as it did into a southerly bearing.

Once at cruising altitude a man unbuckled from a back seat, came forward and nodded at Lebedev.

"This man is a medic, he will fix you up a little," he said to Jon.

The medic led Jon to the rear of the fourteen seater and sat him an a seat with wide access front and side. For the next fifteen minutes his wounds were tended and carefully bandaged. After examining his nose, the man put his own hands either side of his own nose and rehearsed what he evidently intended to do to him. The pain did not last long, but it was as if he had been hit by a sledgehammer. Having reset the break, he gave an apologetic look and commenced taping over the bridge of his nose.

Led by to his seat beside Lebedev, Jon was buckled back in.

Once he had settled again, he thought about his current position. He was at a total loss to comprehend just was unfolding. He knew he was compromised. How, he did not know, nor by whom. He simply could not believe that Ari or Henrik Jensen could have been responsible. He realised then that he had no idea of the chain of events that had followed his leaving the base for help. Possibly they had been captured by the Russians. He shook his head. Russians? It made no sense. He wondered at the subterfuge he had seen in getting him out of his imprisonment. Lebedev had abducted him from the Spetsnatz's grip, clearly there was a second agenda. Something was going on. Some kind of rogue agency within the state? Russia had no lack of internal problems – Chechens, Neo Nazis and others.

His thoughts were interrupted by Lebedev.

"I hope you are a little more comfortable?" Jon nodded. The man continued.

"Once the Spetsnatz captain had convinced himself you were a spy, I think he would have had you shot. We were lucky." He turned in his seat to face Lander. "We live in the same world, you and I," he said, looking across Lander to the land passing below the oddly square windows.

The ground far beneath was as much water as solid ground. Lakes and rivers shone silver below them, silver flowing through snow sprinkled grey. The man who called himself Sergei Lebedev returned to face the Englishman.

"An in-between world of lies and semi-truths, where no one can be really sure of who can really be trusted. A life without being able to trust another human being is a poor enough existence. You must think so too?"

Lander did not reply. His head hurt when he tried to concentrate. In fact, he hurt all over, there was barely a part of his body that had escaped the beating he had been given. He was glad of the medical attention he had just received, but was careful not to be lulled into incautious speech. He regarded the Russian beside him and realised nonetheless the truth of what he had been told. Trust was pure gold in a world abounding in brass.

"I think you do," replied Lebedev for him. "Look at us, here we are, both carrying out our orders for the greater good. Strange that the greater good can be an elusive idea, often hard to define. It always seems to depend on who is doing the defining. It makes us into cynics, unwillingly so perhaps, but cynics all the same. Never acting because we believe, but because we don't. Mistrusting our closest friends, sceptical of any action of good intent, even suspicious of the love of our own wives. A life lived in suspicion breeds nothing of value. Are you married Jon Lander?"

Jon thought of the one woman in his life, a woman whose loss Jon could never think of replacing with another human being. Involuntarily he found himself slowly shaking his head. The Russian detected the pathos. He nodded quietly.

"When it comes down to it, there are only a very few realities that truly matter, and they are the simplest of things. We tell ourselves that what we do is one of those things, but we fool ourselves. Nations, Empires, all of their Kings and Queens eventually fall, but these few, precious fundamental truths remain. Look at you. Your blood lies dried on your ripped clothes. Is this the price we pay for being the only ones who know that?"

He looked upwards as if trying to recall something.

"Your Milton, he wrote a poem, about a traveller in an ancient land coming across a broken statue in a desert. Below it there were words engraved, how do they go? *Look on my works and despair.*"

"Shelley," Jon heard himself reply. "Not Milton. *My name is Ozymandias, king of kings: Look on my works, ye Mighty, and despair!*"

"Ah, yes, and then...?"

Jon obediently complied. *"Nothing beside remains. Round the decay of that colossal wreck, boundless and bare, the lone and level sands stretch far away.'"*

Lebedev gave a soft laugh. "Yes, yes, that is it. All greatness becomes wreckage in a wilderness eventually. Every act deemed so important, every irreplaceable actor on the stage. So why do we do what we do? I will tell you Jon Lander: because we are the men who shot the albatross. We are the ancient mariners, the wandering Jew, the travellers in an antique land. Cursed to serve those who say they have the truth yet being the ones, alone among them all, who truly know it. We serve those, who, even if the truth stood before them, would not recognise Him."

Lander turned and looked at the agent beside him, intrigued as to whether or not he was being drawn into a psychological trick, or if the man was actually sincere. His reference to Pilate before Christ was unexpected. Was he a man to trust, or a man simply playing his part? Lebedev seemed to read his thoughts.

"You see it, don't you Jon Lander? That is the paradox. We two and our trade? We are the only ones who can trust one another while we doubt all else. Men who do not recognise the truth claim that they do, while we who know the truth pretend we do not. It is funny, yes?"

He reclined his seat and closed his eyes, a strange smile fixed on his face. The conversation seemed to have come to a conclusion. Jon watched him for a few minutes and resigned himself to accepting he was where he was and he was not about to be able to do anything about it. He might as well follow suit. He lay back in his seat and hoped for rest. He was not spoken to again and when he was, he surprised to hear he had slept for over an hour.

"Welcome to Arkhangelsk Jon Lander," said Lebedev. "We are descending and shall shortly land. You are to be collected and taken to people who want to speak with you here. The Russian Federation has many enemies who wish us no well. The men who await you are people committed to preventing harm to our great and ancient nation. This does not mean you will be greeted as a particular friend. The Duma has concerns and your appearance has given an unexpected opportunity. I will give you some advice, as a fellow inhabitant of the shadows. Do not continue to pretend you are someone else. These men need to know what you know." He looked out of the window and was silent for a moment before continuing.

"Neither should you trust everyone, for many are wearing masks. I have brought you this far, but this is where we part. You must judge for yourself who is in masquerade and who is not. Whatever, do not become careless again Englishman. There are men who would simply kill you to get rid of the evidence."

His face grew almost considerate as he studied Lander. "I have snatched you from danger today Jon Lander. What happens next? You will have to make your own judgements. I wish I could offer you more, but I repeat my advice. Be very careful."

Chapter 34
Parting

Anya sensed something different about the complex. There was a tension, or maybe a change in tension. Something had changed, some kind of invisible line had been crossed and a different set of rules put in place.

As she moved from her lab to the recreation area, men went about their business as before. She passed Sergei Liminov, but his head was down and he did not speak. Gasparov's announcement had been like a declaration of martial law. It had sobered everyone almost as much as Yashkin's death had shocked them.

Anya did not often go outside, but the explicit order not to do so made living at the drill site even more onerous than it had already become.

There was an empty room upstairs in a largely unused part of the base that she would sometimes go to when she wanted to spend some quiet time on her own. A place where she could pretend she was somewhere else, some other place, some other time.

It was a large open room but had a wide landscape window that looked south into the vast empty landscape. Protruding out of the modular base, it had nothing visible of the base, the drillings or anything else man-made. Probably intended originally as a control room to oversee future operations in that area, its prospect made that an unsuitable choice as the project developed to the west and north, and so it fell into disuse.

She lay on a couch she had drawn up to the window and gazed out, her imagination transforming the frozen winter tundra into the green and yellow of summer in the taiga. Involuntarily, memories she had long suppressed began drawing themselves onto the scene before her. Like children unsure of the safety of coming out of hiding, daring to look, but ready to dart back into the shadows, they slowly emerged with increasing confidence.

She had been much younger then. A girl of barely sixteen, years that had carried the long sadness of her mother's death had suddenly been infused with a joy she had never known before in her young life.

He was only two or three years older than her and as soon as she had been introduced something within her danced.

Why that should be, she could hardly describe. He lay on a bed, mostly dipping in and out of consciousness, barely aware she was there at all, as she helped her father tend him and bring him back from a state hovering on the balance between life and death.

His arrival was a mystery. All her father would say was that he was under his protection, that she must tell no one of his existence, but that her care might help.

She watched him recover, saw the daily changes that brought colour to his face, strength to his body and at last, the occasional indistinct words from his lips.

Every minute she had free, she sat with him. She dabbed the perspiration from his face and calmed him with a cool gentle hand upon his forehead when delirium caused him to him shake and toss.

Looking back, she wondered if it had only been a simple girlish fascination with the enigma of his survival, with the mystique of his English words and unknown origins. Perhaps - but something about him drew her to him, thrilled her at seeing him respond to her care. He was different, not just because he came from another nation and language, but because he had made her grow from a girl to a young woman just by coming into her life.

As he began to utter sentences, she was able to communicate in the broken English she had learned at school. Her father warned her not to tire him with her endless questions, but soon left his care into her hands alone.

Then there were the experiments of which her father would say nothing. Something brooding and malevolent was darkening their lives, but he would not speak of its source, nor say why it troubled him. The more she questioned him, the more silent he became.

Eventually he began the experiments with the young man she had come to care about more and more. Her father had waited until he was convinced in his own mind that he was well enough and that he himself was sure he wanted to assist. The nature of the tests was not revealed to her but her father had promised no harm could be done.

And then the awakening.

Speaking in Russian, in Finnish, French and a dozen other tongues. His mind was a vast repository of human knowledge, almost limitless in its capacity to learn. Every superlative was reached in every field and the enormity of it was impossible to conceal forever.

If she thought he would change, she was elated to discover that he was the same young man in every other way that mattered to her most.

The weeks passed into months. As they grew to know one another – all the more with the barrier of language removed - his empathy and warmth drew her to him as a wanderer drawn to a flickering light in a darkness once without hope.

He brought light into her life. She knew she was bookish, enthralled with ideas and the boundaries explored in the science she loved. She did not know many girls of her own age, but those she did were preoccupied with self-image and talk of nonsense things that were too silly to spend a moment of life upon. She therefore had spent most of her time on her own, reading and soaking up all her father could teach in the short snatches of time she could steal with him.

Finn listened to her as she explained the things that captivated her thoughts. He listened, asked questions, suggested others, discussed proposals, conjectured along with her and explored her ideas as a traveller on a journey where once she thought herself alone.

And he made her laugh. He made her heart a light thing and filled her dreams at night. She loved his smile, his kindly face, the breadth of his hands, the colour of his eyes. She was in love and desperately wished that perhaps one day he could love her too.

Anya gazed out of the window into the summer taiga that was not there and remembered. A summer romance, and yet years later, like a well-loved book rediscovered, she allowed herself the luxury of the thoughts of her heart in those teenage years.

His name had sounded like the name of a fish in Russian and when he discovered why she laughed, he told her to call him Finlay. She changed it to Finn, never realising she had gone from a fish in her language to a part of one in his.

He liked it nonetheless and she and the stranger called Finn became inseparable in those days when each day was only better than the day before when it was a day together.

One afternoon he held her hands and looked into her eyes. The river played its tinkling songs in the background and the birdsong in the larch and silver birch echoed in the air above as he made a promise she would never forget.

He said there would be no one else. No matter what, no matter life or death, she alone had captured his heart.

Anya opened her eyes. She was a fool. A fool to sink into such escapism. The past had lived and now it was gone. He was gone.

She shook herself, angry with herself and annoyed with pandering to her own weakness. She was stiff from lying on her side on the couch. Those memories were of days years ago. She looked out of the window as the green trees grew silver grey again and the imagined yellow sun faded to a dull light that barely filtered through the sodden skies.

Her father had taken him away one secretive night. He had vowed to her that he would return. Promised her.

But her father was dead. Murdered by men who wielded a power latent in its malevolent secrecy. The months spent in the forest hideaway had been the best days of her life and now the two men who had made it so were gone.

She sat upright on the couch and looked into the endless grey and colourless whiteness outside the window. She had drowned her despair in study. Determined to honour the name, Anya Nevotslova achieved far beyond those in her university. Now twenty-seven, she was renowned in the discipline she had followed in her father's footsteps.

But what was her life? From despair to hope, then years buried in the isolation of education, she now found herself back in the familiar ground of despair. Wasting her time thinking about a boy of her youthful ignorance. She wondered what became of him, he who once possessed her heart. Lying cold beneath the soil of an undiscovered grave, or lost forever to her in a future where she was only some girl whose name he could scarcely remember?

She wrenched herself from her melancholic reminiscences. Gasparov had promised consequences if she could not provide him with the findings he sought. If she failed, she was sure the consequences would be of the worst kind. But then Rogov had insinuated if they were to present what they now called the Novel Kola Ringwoodite, then their usefulness would be completed and their future equally insecure.

It was then that she slowly became conscious of a muted noise in the background. It was a thudding, or sporadic metallic banging. It was coming from the complex and so she rose from her position and made her way out of the room.

In the main corridor, the noises were louder, but still far off and indistinct. Her interest piqued, she followed the sounds to find out what had broken down or was awry in the project. Perhaps the drill had collapsed, a generator broken from its mounting? Something was not right.

Suddenly, as she turned the corridor that led to the library, she met Rogov. He was running toward her and he was carrying a pistol.

"Anya! Thank God, you're alive!"

"Yes, well, I...alive? Why have you a gun?"

"Quick, follow me!" he shouted, ignoring her question. He turned and she cautiously followed him as he tore down a flight of stairs.

"Hurry Anya! We have to get outside!"

"But Gasparov said..."

"He either did not hear or chose not to reply. Either way, he took her arm and forced her to run. The thudding she had heard earlier was now a distinct sound and it was the sound of automatic gunfire. Rogov took some doors that led into a corridor she had never been in before. They ran through a kitchen area then burst through a set of double doors behind the bar in the recreation room.

As they did, they suddenly came upon a soldier. He was standing over the bloodied bodies of two men lying on the ground below the muzzle of his carbine. He spun at the sound of Anya and Rogov, immediately raised his rifle at the same time and swung it toward the two who had just careered into the large room.

He was fast, but Rogov was faster. Three rapid shots rang out from the Tokarev pistol in his right hand. The soldier managed to loose a short burst as he fell but the bullets went wide as the man went down. He made no further move.

Anya was shocked beyond thinking. She opened her mouth but no scream came out. No noise at all, only a gasp of horror as she saw a man die before her eyes. She stared, still open-mouthed in terror at the man she thought she knew, the man who was suddenly a killer and who would surely kill her next.

"You – you – you killed him!" she finally screamed when her voice returned. Rogov turned, grasped her shoulders and held her, staring into her eyes.

"They are killing us all!" he said in a steady, strong voice. "Do you understand Anya? Look, Siminov and Baranov. They have just been murdered in cold blood!"

He indicated the two bodies lying behind the soldier. Anya stared, her eyes seeing but not yet comprehending.

"I need you to focus Anya, shake yourself. We need to escape and we need to do it now!" He let her go and stepped over to the soldier. He retrieved the carbine and ripped off the extra magazine pouches from his utility belt.

"It's an AKS-74U," he said, the words a haze to the girl. "These aren't normal guards. Only special troops carry these. They are systematically eliminating the base. They intend to leave no one alive. Now come, and quickly!"

He led her to the furs and outside winter clothing. They rapidly dressed. As they were still pulling on the jackets, the sound of boots could be heard rushing down the far corridor. Rogov grabbed Anya and dashed out through the external airlock doors.

The cold ripped the air from their lungs as they ran through the skittering snow in the semi-light and across to the machine shed. He led her through the tin walled buildings until they came to an open yard with a light cargo truck sitting at the far side.

"Get in!" he shouted. As he did there was a burst of fire and the metal walls of the building beside them rang as bullets strafed through the thin sheets. Two soldiers followed, running as they fired. Anya ran around and wrenched back the passenger door. Rogov dropped to one knee and returned two short bursts back at their pursuers.

Suddenly aware that their targets had teeth, the two men dived for cover behind a shed. Rogov ran to the truck, gave another series of aimed shots and jumped up behind the wheel.

The vehicle roared into life after a few long seconds and as the truck lurched out of the yard, the soldiers reappeared, firing their weapons on fully automatic.

But Rogov had turned hard to the left as he left the yard, causing one of the outside buildings to obscure their escape as he pushed hard on the throttle and rapidly made his way up through the gears.

"Listen Anya," exclaimed Rogov in a strong voice over the noise of the racing engine, "I am FSB – Federation Security Service. I was sent here on behalf of concerned parties within the state Duma. I had to shoot that man, they have already killed half the base. Averin, Chemeris – I saw them shot down as they sat."

"You're FSB?" exclaimed Anya. "But when...? You mean you were undercover all this time?"

The lorry heaved and lurched as she spoke and she grabbed a handrail.

"Yes, I agreed to be seconded into it some years ago, but I am principally a mineralogist. I worked with your father. He was one of the best men I have ever known"

"I hadn't known you knew him so well!"

Rogov nodded as he looked in the side mirrors. "Dr Nevotslov was a giant in his field; a genius." He braked hard into a tight corner on the gravel road. "But he was more than that. He was a man of such moral strength and integrity that the rest of us were midgets beside him. His intellect was matched by an almost spiritual authority. Somehow he could move men, even the basest of men, to come to the truth despite themselves."

"I wish you had told me this before. I knew he was a great man, but I longed to hear of how others knew him."

"Did he tell you about his work?"

"Only that he was doing important work for the government," said Anya.

"Boris – your father, had uncovered something, but he was murdered before he could pass it on. You being brought to Kola had something to do with it. The discovery of the novel Ringwoodite was part of that, but not why he was murdered."

Suddenly he interrupted himself with a shout. "Hold on!"

The lorry leapt as it went airborne over an unseen crest. It landed heavily with an ominous crack. Almost immediately there was a loud metallic screeching sound from below. The vehicle slowed. Rogov brought it to a halt and jumped out. Thirty seconds later he was back.

"It was probably in the yard for repairs," he said. "It has a broken lower swing arm. That last bump has split it in two."

"Can it still drive?"

"Just about, but they are bound to be following by now. We'll never outrun them in this."

As if to illustrate his point a light in the distance behind them flickered and disappeared.

"They're about two kilometres behind us," said Rogov, gunning the engine. The truck was clearly very sick. Any speed at all and the screech returned and the vehicle became difficult to control.

"The suspension separates when I go any faster and rubs against the drive shaft," he said. He checked his mirrors and then looked at the assault rifle sitting beside him. He glanced across at the girl beside him and gripped the wheel, determination written across his face. Anya caught his expression. He looked as if he was coming to some kind of decision.

"Listen Anya. Listen to every word. Sergei Lebedev can be trusted. He is a colleague. Try to contact the Duma in Moscow, ask to be put through to the FSB desk. Tell them it is a code 511. Got that? Give your name, identify whose daughter you are and ask for Lebedev. Make sure you speak to him. Tell him what has happened. Tell him that the Superdeep is a feint. The real danger is several miles north-west. I don't know what it is, but it is big. Tell him Gasparov is a small cog. He answers to Arkhangelsk – almost certainly V.K. Tell him about the Ringwoodite. It has some kind of mind-altering or even enhancing effect. Gasparov was using you to find it, but that is secondary to the primary danger. Tell him I said we must act immediately. Can you remember that Anya?"

"Any nodded in confusion. "Yes, but, why me?" she begged, "Why can't you call yourself?"

Rogov sighed and returned a sad smile.

"Boris made me swear to protect you. I would never break a promise with that man." He looked in the mirrors again.

"They are getting closer. Looks like two vehicles. Probably a squad."

They came to a junction. To Anya's shock he pulled over and climbed into the back. A second later he was back with a five-gallon metal fuel can. Opening the cap, he threw it out and let it empty onto the ground. There was a part used a box of matches on the untidy shelf in front of the wheel. He lit one, threw it into the box and as it erupted into flame, cast it out the window. He Immediately drove off as the sky behind burst into an orange ball of flame.

"That might delay them a few seconds, at least cause some confusion as to which way we went," he explained, his eyes half fixed on the rear view mirrors.

They limped on another kilometre when suddenly he stopped again. He opened the door and jumped out, leaving the engine running. Reaching up, he recovered the assault carbine and motioned to the driver's seat.

"Drive," he said rapidly. "In about two kilometres you will come to a junction. Take the right. Proceed for ten kilometres then take the first right again. That road will take you back the way we have come, but on a parallel route before veering west. I don't think they will expect that. Keep going, I don't know how far, but you should come to the Finnish border within an hour or two. Use your intelligence. Try to find an unmanned crossing. There are villages along the coast. Get to a phone. And Anya?"

He paused and looked up at the girl he had come to care for as a daughter.

"*Da blagoslovit tebya Bog moy dorogoy.* God bless you my dear."

Suddenly she realised the import of Rogov's intentions.

"What? Aren't you coming?"

He looked back along the road. "I have a promise to keep Anya Nevotslova, and I can't keep it standing here talking." He pulled the Tokarev from his belt and slid it onto the shelf below her knees. "Take this, it only has two or three rounds left. I hope you do not need it. Now go!"

His last words were said with such a command that Anya immediately pushed the gearstick into first. As she released the clutch she looked down at the man who had been her friend, who had guided her as a father. There were no more words. What words were there to say?

As the vehicle limped away, she saw in the fading light Rogov take up a firing position behind a boulder.

It was the last time she would ever see him.

Chapter 35
Interview

Arkhangelsk, a city of over a third of a million was built on the western banks of the Northern Dvina River. It stretched along the river some twenty-five miles and was sundered where the river separated into several other outlets that made their own independent journeys via the delta that led to the White Sea thirty miles to the north.

The *Rysachok* landed at Talagi Airport outside the city. A car was waiting and Lander found himself being taken through the flat green landscape, increasingly urban as they approached the metropolis. Lebedev sat in the front with the driver, but made no move to continue conversation with the MI5 agent.

Eventually the car stopped outside a large building near the waterfront. Two men were waiting. Lebedev opened the door and let him out. The men stepped over and escorted Jon to the building. Lebedev nodded as he left and returned to the car.

So, let's see what happens now, thought Lander to himself as he was led by several classrooms and at last to an office at the rear. One of the men opened the door and nodded to him. They remained outside as he entered.

The room was evidently the office of an official within what appeared to be some kind of university college building. A man was sitting behind a desk, his back to Lander. When the door was shut, he turned and faced him. He was a heavy set, dark man with a grim look as he surveyed the man at the other side of the desk. He indicated for Jon to sit opposite him.

"So, our British friend," he said, his face betraying nothing of friendship. Jon waited.

"I see you have received some medical attention, that is good."

Jon nodded. "Thank you, yes."

"I will get straight to the point," he began. "My name is Igor Gurevich. I am a member of the Duma, but also work for the SVR, you know this agency?"

Jon nodded again. "Yes, I know of the SVR."

"Good. I am part of a unit who have infiltrated a terrorist organisation whose aim is the overthrow of the state. Our intelligence indicates that you have come across members of this group in the Norwegian island of Jan Mayen; that the wounds you have received are as a result of this. This is correct?"

"I was shot by a man purporting to be Norwegian. I believe now he was a foreign agent," replied Lander, carefully choosing his words.

"He was a member of the group of which I speak," said Gurevich. "Why were you on Jan Mayen?"

Lander studied the face across the table. Lebedev not only knew his name, but also his former military past and his current role within MI5. It seemed possible that this man would know what his mission had been on the island.

"There was reason to suspect foul play. I was sent to investigate."

"Don't the Norwegians have their own means of investigation?"

"It seemed pertinent to employ outside assistance."

The large Russian nodded as he digested this. "They thought they had a leak?"

"Something like that."

"Hmm. Do you know what was really happening on that island?" asked Gurevich.

Something about the man troubled Lander. He could not pinpoint it, but if he was a colleague of Lebedev's, then he was probably bon fide. But on the other hand, was Lebedev a trustworthy source? Who was Lebedev, really? He remembered his conversation on the plane. If he was playing him, why then warn him to be careful?

"It was heard deep underneath the Beerenburg," replied Lander, choosing to be as vague as possible, yet trying to appear explicit.

Gurevich looked steadily across the table.

"Have you been able to report back to London?"

"I awoke on a submarine. I have not spoken to anyone."

"You made a call from Polyarny."

"I was cut off," he said truthfully.

"I will take you to Moscow. From there we will make arrangements for your return to England. In the meantime, it would be of great mutual assistance if you could provide descriptions of those you feel are involved in the terrorist group."

"I only saw faces; I don't speak Russian."

"But you were taken by rogue Spetsnatz forces. This is a worrying development. This grouping has managed to gather significant military sympathies. I will be honest with you. They are looking for a highly classified mineral that may hold the key to Nuclear Fusion."

"Odd," said Lander curiously. "A terrorist group whose aim is to introduce clean energy?"

"If they secure it," explained Gurevich, "they hope to overthrow the legitimate government and use this breakthrough to make Russia the world's leading superpower."

It still didn't seem to quite add up to the MI5 man. A terrorist grouping wanting to enhance the nation they terrorised by supplying electricity? He listened as the Russian continued.

"We have very friendly relations with the UK," he said, "The sharing of sensitive information is much more than you know. The noises you heard deep in the volcano were the covert digging operations of this terrorist organisation to extract the secret mineral. Our friends in MI5 and the CIA need to know what we are dealing with. It is time to call on them for assistance."

Jon wondered what kind of assistance the Russian Federation might require. Hardly military.

"There is a phone on my desk. It has access to international dialling. You may use it while I organise our transport to Moscow."

He pointed at the phone and got up from his seat, indicating for Jon to take his place. He himself made his way toward the door. He opened it and said something to one of the men outside. He heard the door close behind him.

Lander moved round and lifted the receiver with his back to the exit. Once again he used the coded numbers that short-circuited national exchanges. Once again the woman's voice recited the standard message.

"Hotel lobby. Is this an outside call?"

Lander gave the recognised reply and was promptly put through to Thames House. He asked for Jonas by name. A few seconds later he heard the familiar voice of the well dressed Englishman.

"Lander? Is that you? Where are you man? We thought you were dead!"

Jon gave a quick précis of his recent experiences including Lars Guldberg and his capture by the Russian submarine.

"I'm in Arkhangelsk with Igor Gurevich," he continued. "The SVR are trying to suppress some kind of a coup. I'm told to tell you that the noises below the volcano are Russian terrorists digging for..."

Suddenly he heard a noise he had heard thousands of times in his life. It was done so silently and surreptitiously that almost no one else would have noticed. But Jon Lander was not no one else. His instincts were tuned to constant threat and the flicking of a safety catch on a pistol was one that rode high in that list of hazards.

Without a second's hesitation, he threw himself down and below the table as behind him the unmistakeable clack of a suppressed pistol spat subsonic 9x18mm Makarov bullets into the oak table top. Without pausing, he careered out the side and rolled at the feet of the man holding the gun. Gurevich went down, shock frozen like a mask on his face as the planned execution suddenly became something different.

Lander managed to get a grip on the suppressor and point it away from himself as Gurevich fired off another shot. Now Lander was on top of him, although weakened by his injuries, still a muscled ball of fighting violence as he put all he had into shutting down his pre-empted killer.

It was a few short seconds of a brutal, animalistic man-on-man wrestle, but it ended suddenly as two shots into the chest of Gurevich ended that man's life on earth.

Jon fell gasping over onto his back. Miraculously he was unharmed. The third time in as many days he had cheated death and his head pounded with the sudden vicious exertion.

A warning rushed into his head. Outside were two henchmen. He grabbed the pistol, rolled over and pointed it at the door. Seconds passed and nothing happened. The door was solid oak and the pistol was silenced. The fight had been brief and neither man had spoken during it. It was likely no noise had been heard outside.

Getting up he went to the phone. Gurevich's shots had missed Lander, but they hadn't missed the phone. It sat, shattered and useless on the table.

At the other side of the room was another door. Quietly he made his way over and opened it. It was a bathroom. He halted suddenly. A body lay on the floor. Checking the man, Jon confirmed he was dead, though still warm. He went through his pockets and found several official documents. In his wallet was an ID card which stated that the owner was an official member of the State Duma. The name was in Cyrillic which made it hard to read, but it was obvious what had happened. Gurevich, if that was his name, had murdered Lander's intended interviewer and taken his place.

Lander would have liked to have had time to work out the implications, but time was not something he had much of. He dragged Gurevich's body onto the chair behind the table, propping him up with his back to the entrance door. He tried his pockets and found some papers. He stuffed them into his jacket pocket. He would look at them later. He opened a window behind the desk and saw that it was a short drop to a grass courtyard. Taking the murdered man's wallet and the pistol, he slid to the ground and silently made his way unseen into streets beyond the college. Any future plans were secondary to disappearing before the two men outside the office became suspicious and investigated.

Chapter 36
Chase

Finn awoke, a thought in his head entrenched as a certainty. He needed to cross Finland. He had a simple breakfast in the hotel's tiny restaurant, paid his bill and left. Stockholm's Central Station on Norrmalm was some distance away, but it was a clear bright morning and he decided to go on foot. The sun was not warm, but its light lent a crispness of detail to the cobblestones and made vibrant the colours of the ancient streets. Spring was lurking in the air, already threatening to wrestle away winter's grip on the city. The air was clean and fresh as was the uniquely Scandinavian architecture standing like multi-coloured guards along the many inlets and bays of the Venice of the North. Built on over a dozen different islands, bridges criss-crossed the streets and parks of the city spread across the Baltic Sea archipelago.

Finn made his way through the old town of *Gamla Stan* where several of the ochre-coloured buildings had stood for over six hundred years.

Suddenly he was aware that he was not alone. Without turning to check, he knew that eyes were watching him, eyes that held no benevolent intention. It was not entirely unexpected. He had known that there was a strong likelihood considerable efforts were being made to track him down. He was now convinced that the dreams and visions he had been experiencing were not haphazard psychological events, but a planned release of information, placed there almost certainly by Boris Nevotslov. Those revelations had led him in his journey so far and had also aroused within him the certainty that he would be hunted.

Still acting as if he was ignorant of any surveillance, he continued through the old town, weighing his options and deciding his next move. Ahead of him the huge spire of the 13th century Storkyrkan Cathedral rose out of its ancient foundations. There was a short queue of tourists moving forward through the front entrance, a tour guide leading them into its closeted darkness. Quickly moving forward, he attached himself to the dozen or so visitors as he lifted a glossy guide from a wooden table in the vestibule. No one seemed to notice the addition of an extra person to their entourage, but when the guide stopped and pointed at some feature for the party to see, Finn slipped away and rapidly made his way to the rear of the church. He quickly found what he was looking for, an exit marked with the regulatory green running man. He burst out into the sunlight and was in a back avenue. He jogged along it until he came to a wider street and turned left. Constantly moving, but always headed north, he crossed several bridges and city islands until at last he arrived at his destination. He sensed the confusion behind, but did not wait to see if his watchers had managed to follow his chaotic trail.

Ten minutes later he sat on an intercity train bound for Umeå on the western shores of the Gulf of Bothnia, some six hours' train time up Sweden's east coast.

The Russians got to the station too late. The train had just pulled away. Discovering its destination, they made a quick series of calls. Making their way quickly back to their vehicle their initial sense of alarm abated. He may have eluded them in Stockholm, but hunting was all about funnelling the quarry into a smaller and smaller kill zone. They were the beaters and soon Umeå would have the backstop in place. In between, the hunted would be run to ground. A city was a big place to hide, on board a train, their target had merely fled into a cage.

Karmonov was less positive. He slammed the phone onto his desk with such violence that his secretary dared to open the door to see if her boss had had an accident.

"Get out of here!" he shouted at her. She quickly retreated. He picked up the abused receiver and made another call. Gasparov's voice was on the other end in seconds.

"Is it done?" spat Karmonov without elucidation.

"Yes," replied the voice down the crackling line. "All your orders have been carried out. It is finished here."

Karmonov let out a slow breath. At least something was going right.

"Good. And the Nevotslova girl, did she discover the substance beforehand?" He assumed Gasparov had carried out all the protocol. The details were clear enough. No survivors to tell the tale.

"No, she found nothing. She was incompetent comrade." He had made a dangerous decision in not mentioning her escape, but since Rogov had been dealt with on the road to Murmansk, he knew for a fact that her killing was imminent. The radio sat on his desk. He expected a report from the field within minutes.

"Perhaps," rasped the voice of Karmonov, no less threatening on a poor line than a good one. "Certainly someone was," he added ominously. "Make your way to The Program's location. I will speak with you there. We commence immediately I arrive."

Gasparov grinned as he replaced the receiver. Karmonov had said *we*. He wanted him there, part of the greatest moment in Russian history, and he, Gasparov had been personally invited by Karmonov himself. He sat back in his chair, flushed with a sense of personal significance. The pursuit of Nevotslov's secret was clearly over. The failure to get the daughter to uncover the father's discovery had only been a hindrance to his personal advancement. Now that that was forgotten he felt his tensions subside. It was he who had alone been selected to head up the decoy operation, he alone who had been trusted with the necessary neutralisation of the civilians. His thin grin spread wider over his thin, wiry face as he pushed a hand back over his thick close-cropped black hair.

Yes, the future was bright for Ilyich Gasparov, successful administrator over the final closure of the Kolskaya Superdeep Project.

Back in St Petersburg, Viktor Karmonov's conclusions differed significantly from the ones being fantasised over in Kolskaya. For now, however, other things were taking priority. For the third time in the last couple of hours he tried Igor Gurevich's number. There was still no reply. The man had so infiltrated the security apparatus of the Duma, that he had known about the Jan Mayen infiltrator's planned release from their captivity on Polyarny right from its inception in Moscow. Gurevich could be hard to control, but he had a mind like a razor. He had immediately left the meeting in St Petersburg and flown directly Arkhangelsk with the aim of intercepting the handover. That the man would succeed he had little doubt, but it was unsettling that he had not yet reported back.

Of equal concern over the identity of the Jan Mayen stranger was the news that had him slam the phone down in frustration. The team tasked with finding the Nevotslov betrayal and bringing him to bay had still not managed to bring their assignment to a successful end. Their confidence on the phone betrayed the fact that success still eluded them. How a hapless, witless nobody could still be at large and therefore a nascent threat was beyond comprehension. Several times now he had eluded them and now a distinct pattern was showing itself. He was slowly but steadily heading north – back toward Arkhangelsk from where Nevotslov had managed to slip him out from beneath their noses.

He slammed the desk again with his fist. Perhaps it would not matter. In two or three days they would have started the final phase. Once commenced it would be unstoppable. Once initiated, his qualms would come to nothing. They would have no substance.

But why did he still feel as if they did?

Sir Simon presided over the briefing. He turned again to Jonas Smythe.

"We are absolutely certain that the calls were made by Lander?"

Jonas nodded towards Desmond Reid. "Desmond?"

At the cue, the technical officer opened a folder and quickly scanned the contents.

"Ninety per cent," he said. "Not only did he use the correct codewords, the voice analyser's results point to an almost perfect match. I have the recording here if you'd be happy for me to play it?"

The briefing once again consisted of Sir Simon and Jonas, Desmond Reid, Alex Harker-Bell and Commander Legge. Two other men were present, The Minister of Defence and the other the Colonel in charge of the Marine force. Sir Simon nodded and Reid played the recording from the first call, followed immediately by the second.

"Was he under duress?" asked Harker-Bell. "He sounds tense."

"The first recording matches his normal voice levels," said the scientist, "though as you can hear, he is speaking in some haste. The second is not so straightforward."

"Let's consider the first to begin with," interrupted Sir Simon. "Break down the intelligence Jonas."

"He is spirited away by the crew of a Yashkin class submarine detected in the area," began his colleague. "He is taken to a Northern Fleet port, Severomorsk possibly. He identifies Lars Gulberg as a possible Russian agent, probably the bomber. Whatever is deep below the mountain is so significant that its danger surpasses the importance of the pre-emptive anti-Carrington Event programme."

"The what?" asked the minister.

"A resilience programme in the event of a solar electrical storm wiping out the digital data of the UK. Basically a huge underground backup on Jan Mayen. Highly secret you understand sir."

The minister nodded. Jonas continued.

"He indicates the integrity of Ari Bjørnson and the base's commander, Henrik Jensen. Bjørnson has been very helpful. Before Lander was cut off he seemed to indicate he had further information for us on his burst-encrypted radio. Unfortunately, that has yet to turn up."

"I have some of my men retracing the route your man took from Olonkinbyen to the Beerenburg," interjected the Colonel. "Others are in the mountain itself. As you say, nothing yet."

Thank you Colonel," nodded Sir Simon, "if that is found it might prove a critical piece of information. So, the second call Jonas?"

"As Desmond has already pointed out, it was less straightforward."

"In what way?" asked Alex Harker-Bell.

"Again, he mentions a Russian submarine, and again he gives a warning about Guldberg. Interestingly he appears to be unaware that he is dead. A Glock's polygonal rifling makes matching fired bullets notoriously difficult. Nonetheless the bullets recovered from Guldberg's body match those of Lander's gun."

"We have Jon's pistol?" asked Legge.

"No, all firearms held under a firearm's licence in the UK are test-fired before being issued. Those bullets and cases are then stored so that they can be compared and eliminated as suspects in any criminal shooting."

Legge nodded. He had found it strange that Jon Lander would have a gun and yet leave the island without it. Smythe's explanation made sense.

"So it can't have been your man who shot the Norwegian," conjectured the cabinet minister.

"It would seem not sir," agreed Sir Simon, "but it does leave us in a bit of a hiatus as to who did. Carry on Jonas."

"If he is in Arkhangelsk, then the sub would need to have been travelling at its maximum speed for the entire sailing," he said. "Unless he is in fact at Severomorsk and has been misled. In any event, he mentions an Igor Gurevich. This is where it becomes somewhat complicated. The embassy has indicated to me that Gurevich, a senior member of the Duma, is ostensibly in Moscow, almost one thousand miles away from Severomorsk. He then indicates that the Russian Foreign Intelligence Service is involved in attempting to prevent a coup? Again, the embassy was emphatic. No coup is threatening the Federation."

"What else would you expect them to say?" dismissed Harker-Bell. "Lander could be describing the actual conditions, conditions unlikely to be reported to us by the SVR."

"True," admitted Jonas, "but then Lander said *I'm told to tell you...* Why would he frame a statement like that?"

"Unless he were making a point that it was not what he believed, but what he was told to say?" It was Legge's voice again. He could see Lander in his mind's eye and could imagine him finding some way of passing information hidden within information.

"Precisely!" exclaimed Sir Simon. "Lander was not informing us as to what was happening, but what was *not* happening!"

"In other words, this second call was made under duress," added Smythe, "and he was trying to tell us that what he was being told to pass on was intended to lead us down a blind alley."

"Or perhaps he was just simply telling us the facts," sighed Harker-Bell, some frustration in his voice. "Sometimes the simplest explanation is the correct one gentlemen."

"Again, that is an entirely valid conclusion," agreed Jonas, "but for another aspect of the conversation."

"Which is?"

"Just before the sudden end of the call a loud report consistent with a gunshot was recorded."

The cabinet minister looked up with some concern. "Are you saying this Jon Lander has been shot?"

Jonas looked to Desmond Reid, who took his cue.

"That is a distinct, possibly even likely conclusion, however, if that were the case we might expect to have heard something immediately following the report. In the recording the data from the line died immediately the report was heard."

"You mean; the line was possibly severed by the bullet?" asked the Colonel.

"That is the possibility," nodded Reid.

"And the point is," put in Jonas, "hypothetically, someone in the room stopped Lander because he had gone off script."

"So," said Sir Simon, making a bridge with the tips of his fingers,, "the question we need to ask ourselves and one which we hope our political masters can give us direction on," he gave a nod of deference to the Minister of Defence, "is this. What, if anything, is our next move?"

The intercity to Umeå had no scheduled stops after Västeraspby. From there the final one hundred kilometres of the six hundred kilometre journey continued to its destination though several tunnels and bridges in the increasingly wild landscape.

When the train suddenly slowed and then came to a halt twenty kilometres short of the growing city, Finn immediately knew there was a problem and that it was not mechanical. An attendant was passing out fruit and drinks and Finn spoke to him in Swedish.

"Excuse me. Why have we stopped?"

The man smiled as he replied. "Nothing to worry about sir, apparently a maintenance team failed to clear the track on schedule. The sensors on the line pick it up and alert the driver. I'm sure we'll be on our way in a minute or two." He gave a laugh. "Someone will lose their bonus today!"

On board the train, two men in the SJ train company uniform made their way through the carriages. A critical electrical fault had been detected by maintenance in Stockholm they said. Somehow it had failed to be reported. Due to very real risk of fire, the train had been brought to an emergency halt to allow immediate inspection. They would not be long.

Finn thanked the attendant, and as the man moved down the train, Finn grabbed his bag and made his way smartly to the nearest inter-carriage section. Without hesitation he pressed the emergency door button. An alarm sounded as the door opened and he quickly climbed down onto the track. Ducking below the windows and staying close to the body of the train, he began to run toward the back, some seven or eight carriages. On the train, the two men dressed in company uniform heard the door alarm and rushed to the still open door. Jumping out, they spotted Finn running down the track and immediately broke into a run while pulling out suppressed pistols.

The first shots screamed over Finn's head just as he reached the end of the train. Diving left, he leapt across the rails and vaulted a low fence in front of the shrubby cutting. Bullets cracked into the thicket as he struggled up through the thick undergrowth. Ahead he could see the bushes thin out and seconds later he fell out onto the top of the cutting. Behind him he could hear his pursuers as they pressed close behind. Fifty metres of open ground lay ahead. Without hesitating, he sprinted for a road he saw at the other side. Behind him he sensed as much as heard one of the killers take aim.

Finn could *feel* the man's thoughts. It was as if he was able to be a hidden presence within his head. Without taking the time to wonder at the experience, he instead focused on two things he now immediately knew. One, he was Russian and two, his right index finger was squeezing his automatic's trigger. In a wild dive, Finn straightaway threw himself to the right and rolled over onto the road. The fired bullet tore through his jacket, missing its target and only grazing his abdomen. Finn felt the heat and sudden pain, as his heart pounded in his chest.

"Come on Finn!" he shouted aloud to himself, "No time to panic, *think*!" He immediately picked himself up and dashed across and into woodland on the other side.

In taking time to aim and fire, the men had allowed Finn a couple of seconds to open the gap. Unable to see him when he had rolled up onto the higher road, they crossed the open ground and saw a single-lane road with no sign of the man they were ordered to kill. On the other side two lanes split off in different directions into the woods and after a quick discussion, they split up, each man taking a trail each.

Meanwhile Finn had taken the right lane. A hundred metres down was a wooden house with a large garden and paddock to the front and side. A Nissan Patrol sat parked on the lane. Finn ran straight up to the vehicle and found the door open. The keys were still in the ignition. A man was walking back from the house, distracted by a large dog running around his feet. Jumping into the jeep, Finn started the motor and put it into reverse. As the man opened his mouth to shout a useless protest, suddenly in the rear-view mirror Finn caught sight of one of the Russians. He was raising his pistol to shoot as Finn quickly ducked and lay across the seats, his foot still hard on the accelerator. Five bullets crashed through the rear windscreen as he kept down, aware not only that the shooter had leapt out of the way of the Nissan speeding in reverse, but conscious of the track's route despite being unable to see it.

Skidding out onto the road, he slammed the gearbox into first and sat up as he moved rapidly up through the gears. Behind him, the second

Russian had got to the road, but his shots were wild and inaccurate as Finn roared around a corner and out of sight.

As he sped off north along the road which ran parallel to the train track below him to his left, Finn caught a glimpse of the carriages still stationary down through the trees. A little further along, a black saloon was parked in a lay-by and he knew that it belonged to the men chasing him. Thinking quickly, he pulled in and reversed the Patrol into the car, pushing if off the road and over onto its side. It was all he had time to do. Doubtless they would be able to right it and continue the chase, but he reckoned he had given himself fifteen minutes of a head start. It would be enough to lose them.

In the brief exposure to the man's consciousness, Finn was shocked at the cold emotionless attitude of the assassin. Killing was nothing to him. Life was nothing to him, a cheap thing of little concern. Finn gave an involuntary shiver as he expunged the tainted touch of that mind. Life was a gift and no one had a right to rob another of it. Especially not a gift so precious. Finn knew now that he needed to be even more careful of his. He drove on, his chest tight with tension and slowly following relief. Looking down at his hands on the wheel he saw that they were shaking. But he was alive.

On the train, passengers thought it odd that the hunt for the electrical problem was immediately suspended as the men left as quickly as they had arrived. In doing so they left confusion on behalf of the train driver who contacted the company by phone. The response that no fault had been reported and no maintenance crew had been dispatched was further confusion. Some had seen activity outside their windows but it was passed before they had time to work out what it was. Additionally, the passengers on the train were to be almost unique in experiencing a Swedish train over an hour late on their eventual arrival at Umeå.

Finn headed for the coast. Holmsund was an old sawmill town, and at ten miles from the modern town, was Umeå's port. He did not head for there however. Instead he took several turn-offs into smaller roads that wound their way some miles to the south of the port.

He knew his pursuers would be expecting him to head for Umeå by some other means now he had eluded them. Finn had other plans. He needed a boat. There were regular ferries from Holmsund, but the coast had countless little inlets and private harbours.

Less than half an hour later he was pulling up at a small gravel car park fifty metres from a private marina. Over the low barrier he could see several variously sized boats in their moorings. The light was beginning to fail and he parked the Nissan, leaving the keys in the glove compartment. It would be found and returned undamaged to its owner. Slipping through the fading Nordic light, he bypassed the barrier and quietly made his way through the thin trees. From the cover of some low scrub he watched to make sure the marina was deserted before making his way onto the wooden pier. Moving along the pleasure craft, he began looking for the vessel that would be capable of making the trip he had in mind. It would need to be one with sufficient fuel to complete over forty miles.

In Arkhangelsk, another pursuit was on. Jon Lander moved as quickly as his injuries would allow. He slipped surreptitiously through the buildings around him until he came across a narrow river. A cycle lane ran alongside it with industrial buildings either side of its banks. His first priority was getting away. His next was to avoid recapture. Suddenly he heard behind him the sound of running feet. Quickly he crossed a small footbridge and ran along a narrow alleyway. Skidding out the end, he found himself in a commercial part of town. Behind him he could hear men running over the metal bridge. He ran through the sparsely populated footpath and spied a newly built shopping centre running along the other side of the road. Trying to appear as unobtrusive as possible, he quickly unclipped a shopping trolley and entered alongside a couple of other shoppers. A quick glance back the way he had come caught sight of two men in suits. They were running down the road in his direction, but shooting brief scans into the open doors of the small shops on the other side of the street as they ran. Lander walked as fast as he could without drawing attention to himself into the centre. Unexpectedly, the first shop on his left was a shiny new Burger King. He passed it and made his way further in until he found some public toilets. Unusually, they were free to use and Lander immediately made his way in, finding it a large and well appointed facility. Several new looking metal chairs sat at one end. The room was largely empty. Making his way briskly to the bottom, he chose a receptacle furthest in, entered and locked the door. Sitting down, he let out a long controlled breath. As his heartbeat began to return to normal he was at last able to gather his thoughts and think of his next move.

He was fairly sure the men had not seen him enter the shopping centre. He clenched his teeth in frustration. He had been foolish in taking such an obvious route. The men would clearly assume their prey would have entered the centre. Doubtless they were already in, checking the units, hot on his trail.

He thought quickly. He was cornered in the toilets, but couldn't risk leaving them yet. He had noticed a door just outside his receptacle, but for all he knew it was merely a cleaner's store. There was no sound of pursuit outside. If he could wait a few minutes, slip out and double back the way he had come, the agents would not expect that. Arkhangelsk was a sizeable Russian city, but where would he seek help? He doubted whether it had a British consulate. He needed to contact London but how? How many were involved in his capture? How wide was their net? Were the local police likely to be involved? Dressed as he was he would be easily spotted. He still wore the blood stained military jacket and trousers. Ripped and torn with his abuse at the hands of his interrogators, he could hardly blend in with the local population.

It was as he rapidly processed his situation that it suddenly got worse. He heard men's feet enter the far entrance. Something about the way they entered and stopped inside the doorway told Lander they were not passing customers.

Gurevich was still not answering his phone. Karmonov had expected to have news by now. He was a man who got things done and without wasting time about it. The aircraft that had flown the enemy agent had landed some time ago in Arkhangelsk. Gurevich would have him now. Why had he not called?

Karmonov made another call. Time to call the faithful. He had a flight ready to take him directly to Murmansk. From there they would all converge at The Program's entrance in the Hind helicopters which were waiting on a secluded part of the airport. The excitement at Kola would be palpable by now. The news that they were about to initiate at last the greatest ever shift in world politics would have been announced there by now. The base would await his arrival and then it would begin. The beginning of the end of Russia's years of humiliation and national ignominy. The beginning of the New World Order when those truly qualified, *destined* to lead would ruthlessly unseat the pathetic demagogues whose only appeal to influence was the wealth born of inequality and perverse capitalism.

Karmonov almost experienced an epiphany of visceral joy at the vision of the future that lay imminent before him. Enraptured by the virtual realisation of a dream planted in his mind so long ago from the man who had rescued him from the ruins of Stalingrad, he closed his eyes and allowed his dreams the weight of reality.

So distracted, his concerns about Igor Gurevich were silenced.

Chapter 37
Borders

The lights from the west coast of Finland flickered in the still darkness. The diesel onboard engine of the twenty-foot fishing boat drummed oily beats into the black darkness below its hull as Finn cautiously approached the land. Some forty miles of Finnish water had been crossed in a boat intended for close coastal cruising. The Gulf had been like a millpond and Finn had simply pointed the prow on a bearing of one hundred and thirty-four degrees SSE and maintained a steady eight knots into the darkness of the Nordic night.

It had not been difficult to cross-circuit the wiring and start the Perkins diesel. It was an old clinker-built with a single cabin for the wheelhouse and rudimentary galley. A small bunk was in a hatch below his feet but he had no use for that, except to check for what fuel reserves were on board.

He was alone on the surface of the cold, deep waters. At one point the lights of a ferry bound for Holmsund had passed, but some five or six miles south and of little concern to him.

He found himself reliving a journey across a sea in not such different conditions so very, very long ago.

It had been a dare of sorts. A young foolish man treating his life with the carelessness that only the young dare to do. Another night over dark still waters in an even smaller vessel. He remembered making for shore, a rising panic, too late crying out the warnings he nevertheless would not have heeded had he heard them.

There had been an eruption of light and air below his keel. The canoe had turned and dropped into the hole that once had been water but now turned to green, fluorescent gas.

It had been a lifetime ago, but now, reaching into rooms of recall so long barred, he heard himself scream as the sea below became the sea above. He had managed to wrench his body from the fibreglass cockpit, but still he sank, holding his breath until at last, his lungs on fire and bursting for the oxygen denied them, he gulped the cold green water that would finish his life.

Except that the water was gone and replaced by a swirling mix of effervescent emerald coloured and strangely radiant air-filled solution. The last fading visions he remembered was incomprehensibly sitting on sand and shale, deep in the grave of the Irish Sea, aware that he could only be dead but knowing he was not. As the pictures escaping from a closed memory began to dissipate, he saw a long black shape, outlined by the light within the phenomena, hovering nearby and two shapes come and draw him into the creature of Jonah's nightmare.

And just as for Jonah, the vision had shape and form, taking him into its belly, so he knew he had entered another realm. A realm of iron and steel.

A diesel electric submarine.

~~~~~~~~~~

Jonas and Jack met again alongside London's river. Autumn's cool colours painted the skyline in weak watercolours of muted blues and hints of pink. This time they walked along the embankment as cyclists and joggers passed by in sporadic interruptions to their conversation.

"This *operation Neptune*," said Jack, watching the other man's reaction. Jonas merely nodded and waited.

"Something happened to Finn. Something that brought about his particular abilities. Desmond Reid talked about experiments at Portdown Down?"

Jonas hesitated before replying. "That part is all very highly classified Jack," he said. "I'm not sure of the wisdom of..." He was interrupted by the police inspector.

"I know Jonas, I know, so let me save you the accusation of breaking the Official Secrets Act. It seems apparent to me that the U.K. got hold of some highly secret material from, and I'm only guessing, an agent sympathetic to our country within Russian intelligence - your Boris Nevoslov to be precise."

Jonas said nothing in reply as he cocked an expectant eye at the policeman.

"It was so volatile a material - Reid said some British scientists died in experimentation, that it had to be got rid of – *deniability* I think you call it?"

Jonas shrugged noncommittally and nodded for Jack to continue.

"There is some kind of a connection in operation Neptune, the material, the Russians and Finn. I will give you a hypothesis."

"Please do," said Jonas.

"Finn, like we considered last time we met, is the Allen Finlay who went missing around the same time. With what Sir Simon shared, I returned to my investigation and have interviewed some retired colleagues who worked the west coast. A contact in Ardrossan told me Allen Finlay was a bit of an outdoors lad. Had a mountain bicycle, ran a bit, had a canoe, did a bit of rock climbing. He remembered him as a reckless kind of a lad, bit of a daredevil, but well liked. Anyway," he said continuing his premise, "I'm going to suggest the lad was out on or near the water that day. Somehow, the material intended for the Beaufort Dyke and which leaked, killing the fish, had some psychological effect on him."

Jack didn't add that he had asked the doctor, Robert Jamieson on possible causes of neural abnormalities. He may not have understood much of the consultant's reply, but it was enough to know that the brain was a hugely complex electrical system and highly sensitive to external stimuli.

"Sir Simon's account of the timing and the known length of Finn's coma correlate enough to allow the suggestion of association of the known facts," he concluded.

"Interesting supposition Jack," replied Jonas. "Possibly stretching it bit in parts? As you stated yourself in one of the briefings, it doesn't explain why some Russian terrorist grouping want him dead."

"Because he knows something," replied Jack. "I surmised before that there is something about Finn that has had this unknown group go to extraordinary lengths to kill him. There is a time gap between Allen Finlay's disappearance and Finn being left on the steps of the hospital. That gap is the critical piece of information. Where he was in that time, who he was with and why he was left at Glasgow Royal are the pieces of the jigsaw that will make sense of the picture."

"But do those pieces exist Jack?"

"I think they must," replied the detective, "and I think they are pieces that indicate time outside these islands, possibly even Russia. If so, then his arrival back in Scotland was a benign act inconsistent with the aims of those now chasing him down. They want him silenced before he speaks what he knows, but does not know he knows."

"What could he know that has a manhunt after him stretching across half of Europe?"

"He has power to affect something. I think Finn is headed to attempt that. They want to stop him, but because of this unique ability of his, he keeps one step ahead."

Jonas involuntarily moved closer to the policeman. "Ahead to where Jack?"

"Nevotslov was last reported alive in the Kola Peninsula near the arctic circle - where do you think?"

Jonas stopped and looked across with increasing regard for the man beside him.

"Some say men's lives are random events decided by what chance circumstances they stumble across. Others argue that some men are born with predetermined gifts that lead them to their vocations, vocations destined for them. Are you one of those men John McGregor? I think perhaps you are."

Through a countless maze of inlets and islands, Finn piloted the little boat another thirty miles. He had motored through to daybreak and as the aspirin sun rose over the hazy mountains in the distance, he finally brought his commandeered boat into harbour some ten miles north of Vaasa on the Finnish coast.

Leaving the boat with a note indicating its origin in the wheelhouse, he walked confidently across the small public marina and out onto the road. After a short walk, he found a bus stop where a regular service passed between Vaasa and the coastal villages.

An hour later he was in the large town and looking for a particular type of car dealership. A few inquiries at the bus station helped and soon he was in a dealer's forecourt which specialised in off-road vehicles.

When he explained the requirements of the vehicle he wanted, the salesman took him to a military green jeep sitting with other utility vehicles in the back yard.

"Ex-Russian military, but you couldn't kill it," explained the Finnish dealer. "A UAZ-469. Russians built them to go anywhere a man can walk, climb or wade, and some places he can't."

The price seemed steep to Finn for what is was - it had to be twenty years old, but was assured that their solid build and rugged go-anywhere abilities made them a much sought after vehicle.

"I'll have this sold in a week," explained the man. "Like hen's teeth now. The enthusiasts buy them up and customise them for forest trailing. This one already has a front winch and raised suspension."

Purchasing it left little enough of the money he had borrowed from the McCracken's hidden box but given his next steps, he would have little use for money after the couple of days ahead. Beyond that, he had not planned.

"If you're going deep off-roading, let me give you some advice," said the dealer when the paperwork had been done. He was pleased to have been paid in cash. Finland may have been the most law-abiding country in the world, but it was also very heavily taxed. The odd vehicle sold without bank transfer gave the man a bit of financial latitude. Finn had told him he was planning the trip of a lifetime. When his two friends flew in from Helsinki in a couple of days, they were going to join up with another group and spend two weeks exploring in the eastern wildernesses.

"Listen to experience," he said. "Keep well back from the Russian border. Don't you young men be tempted to tick some kind of adventurer's box by an unauthorised crossing. The area within about two or three kilometres of the border is out of bounds. If you come across yellow warning signs, turn and go the other way. Regular patrols of the *Rajavartiolaitos* will not be easily fobbed off by excuses of Helsinki ignorance."

Finn thanked him for the advice and lied in promising him he would keep well back. He was certain that the armed Finnish Border Guard took their job very seriously. The Russians on the other side however would be the greater threat.

The rest of the day Finn spent in securing the necessities his plan would require. A tent, sleeping bags, various camping equipment. He also bought a supply of tinned food and a medical kit. Passing a mobile phone shop, he bought a used pre-loaded pay as you go phone. It was an older model but came with an accessory clip-on back that permitted the mobile to act as a satellite phone. The shop owner had what Finn thought was a high price on it but on impulse, he paid the money and left with it in his bag.

The journey north-east took him the whole of the day. He pulled in after three hundred miles at a small town and easily found a farmhouse offering Bed and Breakfast.

Kicking off his boots and pulling off his clothes, he fell into the soft sprung bed in the ground floor bedroom. Totally exhausted and spent, he fell immediately asleep.

In Moscow certain deputies of the State Duma considered likely to be sympathetic to the coming revelations were being taken aside and their loyalties established. As the lower house of the federal government, deputies had much more power than members of the upper house, the Council of the Federation. The Council was a talking shop; it could be discounted.

The Prime Minister was a powerful man, but not the most powerful. That position belonged to the *Prezident Rossiyskoy Federatsii*. The President was not only head of state, but the Commander in Chief of the Russian Armed Forces. Karmonov had good reason to believe that this particular president - once the ultimatum was made and the proofs enacted, would back it as his own. The Russian Federation's fourth president had a proven track record of always backing the winning horse and Viktor Karmonov was about to unleash a thoroughbred onto a course occupied by indolent donkeys.

The Secret Committee had not only spent years and untold millions of Roubles in the covert operations at northern Kola, it had carefully nurtured the careers of men whose compliance could be assured when the moment came.

For those who demurred once the declaration was made, it already be would be a fait accompli. Whatever protestations were dared would be mere noise. Noise that would be silenced.

Had he time, Karmonov would liked to have flown first to Arkhangelsk. Gurevich's silence could have been due to half a dozen authentic reasons, but it was irritating to Karmonov that he had still not heard anything.

The flight landed in time at Murmansk and he was picked by two members of his hand-picked Spetsnatz troops. The helicopter was waiting and a few minutes later he was on board. Two others were already seated. One, Iosef Geim, peered over his spectacles. Karmonov sat beside him.

"We are making history comrade," he said to the thinner man. Geim looked concerned.

"You have not heard about Gurevich?" he asked, pulling down his glasses and scanning Karmonov's face with dark, inquiring eyes.

"I have not heard *what* exactly?" demanded Karmonov. He did not like the question or what it suggested.

"Gurevich will not be coming," shouted Geim over the increased noise of the rotors. "He was shot dead yesterday."

Lander listened as he heard the footsteps make their way down the row of toilet receptacles. If it was the men who were chasing him, they were seconds from finding him. He looked up but saw nothing but the ceiling. He could think of nothing except to fight when the moment arrived.

Suddenly the door was kicked open and a gun was pointed at his head. "*Ubiraysya!*" came a coarse and urgent command. Lander put his hands slowly up into the air, stood up and took a step out of the toilet. He watched as the thick-set man's thumb flicked off the pistol's safety catch. He was just about to make a last ditch desperate lurch forward when he was interrupted by a loud shout from the other end of the lavatory. The man, still pointing his weapon at Lander, glanced left toward the voice. Jon looked right. The accomplice to the man holding a gun to Lander was standing with his hands behind his head. Behind him stood a third man whose particular stance and what he held, explained why. He was holding a pistol to the accomplice's head.

Lander looked in surprise as he recognised Sergei Lebedev.

"*Polozhi oruzhiye, seychas zhe!*" he said in an ominous, demanding voice.

Obediently, the gunman facing Lander did as ordered and set his pistol on the ground. Its owner took a step back. Lander quickly moved forward and lifted it, half expecting to be shot by Lebedev for the effort. Instead, Lebedev spoke again in Russian and the two men slowly made their way to the door to Lander's left – the one he had noticed at the bottom. It was a cleaner's store after all. Lebedev ordered the two men in and pushed shut the door behind them. Quickly grabbing one of the metal chairs beside the door, he jammed it against the handle.

"Quickly Jon Lander, that will not hold them for long!"

Whisking him outside, Lebedev bundled him into a car which was parked on the footpath, and running around to the driver's side, leapt in and immediately drove off.

"I am sure I had told you to be careful," said Lebedev as he sped through the light traffic. "Perhaps you misheard me and thought I told you to get yourself killed?"

"No, I heard you well enough," replied Lander. "But it's not easy when everyone in this country of yours seems hell-bent on putting a bullet in me."

"Ah, that is something of a tradition here. I did advise you against it though, did I not?"

"You didn't add that you were going to deliver me to my executioner," replied Lander, glancing at his door, conscious that he could not escape the car at their current speed.

Lebedev was silent for a second before replying.

"We will talk, you and I. First we must get out of Arkhangelsk, it is no longer safe here. You will have to trust me Jon Lander. Meanwhile we have a flight to catch; we can talk on the plane."

Finn slept late. The breakfast was typically Finnish, yoghurt rather than milk for his cereal and an open sandwich with meat and cheese. There was plenty of it and Finn left the hostess in no doubt that she had fed a hungry man that morning.

The roads were smaller now, and as he headed east the forest became the only backdrop, opening into hidden lakes and rivers more and more often. After a while it seemed there was as much water as land and he had to take several long circuitous tracks around the many obstacles of dark and silent water.

He had several jerry cans of fuel on board along with a camping and hiking equipment. The UAZ was as sure-footed as the salesman had promised and as the roads turned to gravel and the gravel to narrow tracks, the four-wheel drive churned and bit into the increasingly common sloughs of mud and rutted trail.

This far north, the electronic surveillance measures which were prevalent in the south were absent. With almost nine hundred miles of border and most of that through uninhabited taiga forests, the only way he would know he was at the border would be the yellow signs in the controlled zones warning not to enter and the reindeer fences on the Finnish side.

Not quite the only way. There was still a risk of stumbling across Finnish or Russian patrols. He had already seen his first sign warning of armed army patrols in the area.

Suddenly he came across a clearing in the trees. There was no reindeer fence and instead a wide slash of open ground lay ahead of him, running like a huge unending firebreak in a north-south line. One hundred metres away lay the five-hundred-year old border with Russia.

Finn stopped the motor and got out. He stepped out into the no man's land and stood quietly listening. He was more than using his sense of hearing. He had found some time ago that he was able to perceive the unseen presence of other human beings. It was a sense beyond the six. He could detect a kind of ambient sentient existence as an unexplainable signal deep within his conscious. Like a drop in barometric pressure can be felt or when the sense of being watched raises the hairs on the back of the neck, so this awareness was hard to explain, but real and tangible nonetheless. It was as if electrical stimuli were tickling the nerves below his scalp – a disturbance in the ether – a movement on still water.

He stood for three or four minutes. The only sound he could hear was the soft waft of air through the pine and birch – the call of rooks and a far off plaintive high-pitched *pee-yow* of a buzzard wheeling high in the rising air above the forest.

He returned to the jeep, started it and ventured out into the clearing. He was committed now. There would be no going back. How far he could take the UAZ he was not sure, but if had to end up walking, he would. He knew now where he was going. No longer a vague longing to go north, an urge to follow a faint scent that led a barely distinguishable trail. Finn could almost see a route and it led to a place high on the Kola Peninsula – a place where the earth opened to an entrance. To a Hades of human nightmares.

Chapter 38
Converging

"So, who exactly was Igor Gurevich?" asked Lander.

Lebedev had taken Lander to the Talagi airport where he had used his authority to secure two business class seats on a Smartavia Boeing 737-800 bound for Moscow. The four-hour flight was at cruising height before Lander had spoken. Lebedev unbuckled his belt as the seatbelt light extinguished on the ceiling above him.

"So it was you who killed him?"

"I didn't have much choice," replied the MI5 man. He was about to shoot me in the back of the head.

"He must have told you something before you spoiled his plans?"

"He told me many things. What was true and what was false determines how you and I are going to get along, Sergei Lebedev."

Lebedev looked over and studied his fellow passenger.

"After I left you off," he said, "it struck me as strange that Deputy Gorsakov's men did not come over to the car. I know his men, yet they kept well back."

"I take it Gorsakov was the body I found in the bathroom?"

"It was he who was supposed to debrief you. It seems he was compromised. The two men I saw at a distance were either not Gorsakov's men at all, or else under Gurevich's control. Either way, it was well for you I came back to investigate."

"So, where exactly are we headed now?"

"Lubyanka Square, Central Moscow."

"KGB headquarters?"

"No, I am FSB my friend. Federal Security Service. Same building, new occupants," smiled Lebedev enigmatically.

"Gurevich said he was SVR."

"Gurevich, it seems, was many things. SVR is our foreign intelligence. I was attached to them at one time. FSB deals with internal matters. We have people within the State Duma you need to talk to, or should I say, who need to talk with you."

"My information is that the SVR work practically synonymously with GRU - the Main Intelligence Directorate," said Jon, watching Lebedev's reaction.

"Very good Jon Lander," replied Lebedev drily, "but because Gurevich said he was SVR does not mean that he was."

"Nonetheless, and correct me if I'm wrong, but I thought that the GRU reported pretty much directly to the president?"

Lebedev looked across Lander to the clouds below. He was quiet for a moment and then turned to face the bruised face beside him.

"We are flying thirty thousand feet above the Great European Plain. Below us lies a landscape neither of us can see, obscured as it is by the clouds." He nodded toward the glass. "Just by looking out of the window, neither of us could prove that it is Russia down there. The pilot could be taking us to Estonia, or Finland, and we neither of us would know until we landed. There are many clouds in my country Jon Lander. Certainties are often obscured."

"It seems to me you have problems greater than simple geography."

"Perhaps," admitted Lebedev, "or it could be that geography is the greatest problem of all."

~~~~~~~~~~~~~~~~~~~~~~~~~

Anya drove, the tears running down her face making the road ahead hard to see. The horrors of the last hours were surreal. Soldiers executing human beings like animals. People she knew, scientists and civilians lay dead where they had been shot in cold blood. Chemeris, Yashkin were gone. Rogov, the quiet man for who had become her trusted friend had sacrificed himself that she might live. He had become a father to her and now, like her father...

Suddenly she realised she should have come across the first road Rogov had told her to take. He had said it was only two kilometres down the road. Had she missed it in her distress? She did not think so, but neither was she sure. She could not possibly go back. She drove on, the vehicle limping along with ominous creaks and thuds. It can't have been going at any more than thirty kilometres per hour. How long since Rogov had got out? It felt long, though it was probably shorter.

Still, it had to be fifteen minutes, maybe twenty. How many kilometres would that get her? Five, six? There was no sign of following vehicles, though that would surely be only a matter of time at this rate. She had to get off this road. Just then the road ahead forked. The main road kept on in a gentle left and mainly south, the smaller track took a gradual right. Was that the road Rogov had meant? Could she have passed one already? She pulled hard on the wheel and took the track. Pulling up, she ran back and obscured the vehicle's tracks with her foot. She glanced back up the road – still nothing. She darted back and leapt back into the cab. The vehicle rattled and complained, but she managed to get it moving again and she nursed the wounded truck along the trail. Keeping alert, she checked her watch. Rogov had said ten kilometres to the next junction. She prayed she had taken the correct road; she would not miss the second.

An hour later the truck was still churning along the gritty track. Everything around her was isolation. Only occasional sparse, strangled clumps of stunted spruce and low shrubs punctuated the wild vista of tundra and watery flatness. The light was almost gone but she was afraid to turn on the lights in the huge landscape, afraid that it would make her visible for miles. Above in the midnight blue sky, streaks of green, magenta and turquoise flashed in iridescent displays as the aurora borealis gave an otherworldly sense to the surroundings.

Another hour later and she was forced to either stop or turn on the lights. Still worried, she turned them on and was rewarded with the sight of the gravel track slowly becoming less distinct and gradually merging with the low grasses. Now she realised she had probably covered almost thirty to forty kilometres from the fork and no junction had appeared right or left. A cold dread that had been haunting her now gripped her with an increasing strength. She was not on the road Rogov had indicated.

She now had another choice; keep going, in all likelihood into a trackless wilderness, or turn back with the risk of running into her pursuers.

It was when she had chosen, and attempted to turn the truck that both choices were snatched from her. As the wheels turned and the vehicle strained around on the uneven tundra, there was a loud snap as the front suspension finally broke in two and the driver's wheel buckled in below the cab.

Anya looked out into the cold dark wilderness, eyes wide, her knuckles white on the wheel as she realised she was now lost in every meaning of the word.

~~~~~~~~~~~~~~~~~~~

When the storm had subsided, the Norwegian P-3 Orion was able to return and airlift the injured, including the still unconscious Henrik Jensen back to Norway where a hospital was on standby. The remainder of the Norwegians were taken by HMS Albion to Bodø on Norway's coast. The British LPD was escorted on the last leg of the journey by NoCGV *Andenes* out of the maritime city.

Lander's radio was found by one of the marines on a final check of his ruined room at the base at Olonkinbyen.

The encrypted message was relayed to Thames House where Sir Simon and Jonas listened privately to the revelations Lander had pre-recorded for transmission. The information included details Jensen had secretly passed on to Lander, which Lander had already partly verified and *Oversersjant* Ari Bjørnson had confirmed.

Jonas looked out of the window and sitting on the sill, looked toward his boss.

"The inspector offered a very persuasive argument to me the other day," he said. "With what limited information we gave him and along with his own digging, he presented to a proposition that connects the whole Jan Mayen thing with our missing amnesiac."

"Finn?" queried Sir Simon, his eyebrows raised. "How so?"

Jonas explained how Jack has laid out his supposition and then backed it up with the circumstantial evidences.

"He connected Nevotslov to Operation Neptune and Finn to that. He posited that Finn has been in contact with the Russian and that his mental abilities are somehow directing him toward north-west Russia – specifically the Kola Peninsula."

"Finn headed for Kola?" exclaimed Sir Simon incredulously. "Did McGregor know about Lander's calls?"

Jonas shook his head. "No. But you have to admit, his conclusions are somewhat significant if true?"

Sir Simon slowly nodded and walked across the room. He looked out the window beside where Jonas sat and was quiet for a moment.

"We need to inform the P.M," he said at last.

No.10 wasted little time when the outline of the intelligence was explained. A COBRA meeting was swiftly scheduled for that afternoon. Sir Simon was to brief the ministers himself.

"I want you there with me," he said to Jonas, "and call Legge," he added. "See if we can't get him an invite. If naval questions are going to be discussed, we'll need to know how to reply."

He watched the world passing by outside the window. A world content in the ignorance it was Thames House's job to supply.

"Time is no longer on our side Jonas. Decisions will be made today that may well be the greatest this nation has had to make in sixty years."

~~~~~~~~~~~~~~~~~~~

Lander was taken, as promised to Lubyanka Square. He was given fresh clothing and an opportunity to freshen up. As Lebedev escorted him along a long, wood panelled corridor he suddenly stopped, looked around and spoke quietly to him.

"I have saved your life twice. The first time because it was an order; the second, because you and I have more in common than most. Tell these people what you know. It is in both our interests that these men, above all others see the ground beneath the clouds."

Turning, he led Lander to a large conference room, the walls decorated in oil paintings of unknown patriots. He was directed to stand before a large mahogany desk with several grim looking Russians all looking in his direction. Lebedev sat on a chair next the wall, an observer now rather than a participant.

A large man, his face creased in a lifetime of heavy responsibility, asked most of the questions. Others posed theirs in Russian, which he then relayed to Jon. After each reply, the men would take several minutes to discuss the replies, during which time Lander was ignored until the next question.

"Why did MI5 send you to Jan Mayen?" asked the Russian. Lander guessed he was a state deputy rather than FSB. Jon had not admitted to his being British Intelligence, but it was obvious by now they had no doubt that he was and would pose all questions with that certain knowledge. He decided there was nothing to gain by pretending otherwise.

"We have strategic interests on Jan Mayen which we share with our ally, Norway."

"Naturally the LORAN-C is no secret, if that is what you mean," replied the Russian. "If you are referring to your joint I.T. Data Resilience Programme, we are not unaware of that. We would be fools not to have our own. We all exist beneath the same sun and Russian astrophysicists are no less expert than your own. I could ask the question again, but please, save me the trouble."

Jon glanced back at Lebedev. He was leaning back in his chair, disguising his presence with disinterest. He caught Lander's eye and gave a barely perceptible nod.

The first rule of intelligence Jon was perfectly aware, was to trust no one, but he had seen something in the Russian who had twice saved his life. Some part of him had the ring of truth, a sacrosanct kernel within him that had the reliability of authenticity. He turned and faced his questioner.

"The Norwegians heard noises deep below the Beerenburg volcano. Very deep - miles deep. There were suspicious deaths, I was sent to investigate."

"What kind of noises," asked his interrogator, looking not at him, but at his compatriots, his eyes narrowing with some kind of shared knowledge.

"Man made. A scientist on the base determined them as rhythmic hydrostatic interruptions – machinery in or below water."

The reply initiated a furious and sudden chorus of voices, all fervently making their points. Lander's questioner took a few seconds to restore order. When he had, the discussions deepened and lengthened. After twenty minutes he felt a touch on his arm. It was Lebedev. He motioned for him to follow. Leading him out of the room, he took him back to where he had been given fresh clothes. Lebedev invited him to relax.

"I'll see if I can't get a room for you somewhere," he said. "I'm sorry I can't give you a phone just yet. They may want to speak to you again, though I think they heard what they needed to hear."

"I might have just sunk my career, if not my freedom in there," complained Lander. "An MI5 agent spilling what he knows to Russian intelligence generally doesn't go down too well back home."

Lebedev paused and smiled. "Thank you Jon Lander. I asked you to take a huge gamble. I hope I would be as courageous were the situations reversed."

"Who knows, you may get your chance," replied Lander, his face still grim with the knowledge of the risk he had taken.

Anya heard the vehicle coming before she saw it. She had been lying with her face propped against the wheel, her shoulders covered with canvas sheets that she had found in the back. Too cold to sleep, but too tired not to, she looked up and saw the lights approach. They were probably a kilometre away and coming in roughly her direction. Suddenly fully awake, she looked quickly around. Hide? Where? In the truck, under it? She shook her head, no, that was no answer. She still had time to flee into the darkness outside, maybe lie low until the danger had passed. Suddenly it occurred to her that the lights were approaching from the south. She had come from the north. They had circled around and had caught her unawares. As she pondered the hopelessness of her situation and the incongruity of being found in such a vast wilderness, she realised that her tiredness had slowed her thinking and her reactions. The vehicle was a hundred metres away, its lights sure to pick out all the detail of her position. Feeling uselessly helpless, she chided herself for her foolishness and looked around for a weapon. She had forgotten the pistol Rogov had left, but as she searched for a spanner or a wrench, her hand swept across the Tokarev in the lower front shelf. Pulling it out, she gripped it in her hand and ducked down onto the passenger floor.

Peering briefly over the dashboard, she watched the military vehicle pull up, its lights illuminating the back of the cab in a harsh white light. She slowly dipped her head back down and listened. The engine was cut and she heard a door open. The crunch of feet on the dusting of snow on the stony ground came closer and then paused. She held the pistol in both hands and pointed it across the driver's seat at the door. All was quiet. Her heart beat in rapid thumps that she imagined in her terror could be heard outside the truck. Still no noise since the footsteps had halted. Suddenly they moved again. Two steps, then a halt. One more. The soldier was standing just outside the driver's door. She watched the handle. It did not move. The window was high off the ground, his head could not be seen, but he was waiting in stillness, just feet away.

For a full minute the standoff persisted. Anya's chest was burning, she had forgotten to breath and when she did, it was all she could do not to gasp at the frigid air like a fish out of water.

Outside she heard the sound of a man clearing his voice. He seemed hesitant, unsure. Anya pointed the gun. How many bullets? Did Rogov say two, or was it three? What if she fired them all now and missed? If she fired one, would she live to fire another? How many others were with him? Outside a soldier undoubtedly stood, his automatic assault rifle trained on the door. What if he fired first? Was she about to be shot? Was she going to die like this, curled up in the dirty floor of a broken truck a hundred miles from another human being? Her finger tightened on the trigger as she raised the pistol to where she imagined his head to be.

"A..Anya?"

The shock of hearing her name from a voice out of the silence made her whole body tremble in confusion. It was not a loud voice. Just a simple question in a name. It was repeated with added words.

"Anya... is that... is that *you*?"

Anya's utter bewilderment almost rendered her completely immobile. She could neither move nor think. It was not Rogov's voice, no matter how she wished it to be so. It was a younger man's and something in the unreachable recesses of her mind tried and failed to retrieve its origin.

"Please don't be afraid. I'm not armed," said the voice. "If I open the door, don't pull the trigger. I'll do it slowly, very slowly."

The handle began its downward track until it clicked. The noise suddenly awakened Anya out of her frozen stupor. The door slowly began to pull out. She backed against the passenger door and took aim.

He stood there, the light from his jeep lighting his face. He held his two hands out to show them empty. From his hands, she raised her eyes to his face. She looked but could not comprehend. The disconnect between what she saw and what was impossible to see was too great.

"Finn?" she heard her broken voice exclaim as if from the mouth of someone else. He smiled and Anya could take no more. The blood drained from her head as darkness descended like a curtain and Anya Nevotslova fainted.

~~~~~~~~~~

Karmonov sat with sixty or so of his peers. Each had made their way to The Program's location at different times and by various means. The sheer remoteness of the vast underground base had dictated that the final legs of their journeys be funnelled through the frigid city of Murmansk. This was the riskiest part of the final assembling of the full committee, but unavoidable given the circumstances.

Now in place, none of the conspirators would leave the huge complex until their demands had been communicated and were fully met. They would live in specially constructed personal habitations built deep below the tundra, awaiting the inevitable reports when that new reality would be accepted; not only in Russia but also by all the major governments of the world.

From above, The Program's site looked like a small quarry, one of many in the vicinity. Nothing about it suggested anything out of the ordinary. Situated some twenty kilometres from the Kolskaya Superdeep Borehole, it would be at most regarded as a spoil area for the significant scientific interest at the drill site.

The Superdeep was now closed down and all its scientists disposed of. It had only ever been a distraction, reopened to hide the real excavations near the Finnish border. Deep underground, billions of roubles intended for the dismantling of the Soviet Nuclear Programme had been diverted into the practically complete engineering miracle that would change the world.

As Karmonov and the committee had planned, hiding the real operation in full view under the shadow of the drilling project had been a complete success. They had managed to so infiltrate the ranks of the state Duma that nascent questions were expediently silenced before they had time to form into effective challenges. Such had been the collapse of the USSR that the complete mismanagement and total lack of fiscal controls allowed for the movement and concealment of the vast sums of money had swallowed up.

The USSR's loss of control of the nuclear arsenals brought about by the secession of the Ukraine had been what had turned The Program from a theory into a possibility.

It had been Karmonov who had seen the vision as a reality. From the beginning he had committed his life to it. He also committed any other life whose extermination was of benefit to the outcome. Along the years many lay buried in the cold earth whose continued existence could have posed a threat to final success.

Now Karmonov surveyed the assembled men. Men who had proved by various sacrifices and actions that they were qualified to serve the new dispensation.

Across the large horseshoe-shaped conference table, the huge purpose-built command room was the hub of screens, controls and satellite communications that were central to controlling the final phase. Operators sat at their stations, monitoring their responsibilities, running tests and awaiting the countdown.

So deep were they now that no nation in the world had anything in their arsenals that could so much as cause a ripple in a cup of water. They were untouchable – impervious to all that the world above could do.

But not detached. The hand that stretched out from deep below the freezing treeless earth above reached out to every continent in the world. Reached out and grasped it in a grip that none would be able to escape.

As the delegates took turns to confirm the successes of the specific parts they had set in motion before leaving for Kola, Karmonov sat, barely conscious of their accounts. He looked and saw before him, like Adam's first steps into the Garden, a sight never seen by human eyes. His realisation was that before him was the creation of a new world and he was witnessing the moment of its birth.

No, not like Adam, he corrected himself. Adam had created nothing. Like God. He was seeing through the eyes of God. And it was very good.

~~~~~~~~~~

When Anya opened her eyes she was dreaming. She knew she was because of the simple fact that she could not be awake.

And she could not be awake if the man looking down at her was who he was.

She was covered in a warm rug with the man beside her. She was in a vehicle, spread across the front seats with her head set across his lap. It was not the truck. She pushed herself up and felt dizziness threaten to blanket out her surroundings.

"Easy," said Finn, supporting her as she managed to rise to a seated position. Outside was darkness, inside was incomprehensible.

He put a gentle arm around her shoulders. "Anya," he said, "It is me, it's Finn, I've found you!"

Anya was almost overcome with seeing the man she had loved and lost so long ago sitting beside her, his arm supporting her and his smile, heart-lifting and real, the one she had dreamed of in diminishing detail over the years. She raised her hand and set it, unbelieving on his cheek. This could not be real. It simply could not be. Was she in a vision, hallucinating? She suddenly chilled. Could she be... *dead*?

"Finn," she heard herself say, "Is it really you? How can you be here? How can I be seeing you?"

Finn pushed back a strand of hair from her face and softly touched her cheek. They both looked at one another; hands caressing each other's faces as outside the cab the eternal stars followed their infinite courses across the sky, accompanied by fleeting glimmering from the northern lights.

They sat like that for some time, each reaching across the bridge of time that the years had flowed beneath. Careers, lives, deaths, threats, fears, hopes, disappointments. The shimmering birch forests of Arkhangelsk and the present met together but the water under the bridge was the past and could not return. Now in each other's embrace, the present seemed impossible to immediately comprehend. In an almost sacred moment, both were still and quietened in the suspension of the flow of time. The world seemed to come to a halt, pause and slowly restart before the reality could be believed.

When at last one of them spoke, it was Finn's voice that broke the silence.

"When did you last eat?" he asked.

The simple practicality of the words somehow broke the spell and Anya burst out laughing. Finn grinned and joined in. Laughing together, laughing and crying, tears ran down their faces and they threw their arms around one another, hugging each other with joy. It was real after all. Impossible, unbelievable, beyond any comprehension, but there he was. Finn. He was beside her. Her Finn.

Chapter 39
Ultimatums

The largest country in the world, stretching across eleven time zones and more than four thousand miles wide, was still not so big as to not notice the sudden disappearance of dozens of its state officials. Over thirty of the State Duma deputies and Federation Council senators were no longer answering their phones and several members of the Executive and Judiciary had likewise seemingly just vanished.

As investigations began to get underway, the reports that came back increased the sense of alarm in the seats of power throughout the Russian Federation.

Had it been the days pre-Glasnost, when the state was prepared to make its subjects prisoners in all but name, the orchestrated desertion of so many senior positions would have alerted the authorities to a mass defection, unprecedented in scale though it might have been. With Russia more or less a functioning democracy, it was difficult to come to such simple conclusions. While not yet in a state of panic, nonetheless the Duma in particular was alarmed enough to call an immediate recall of all its deputies to an extraordinary session at Manege Square in Moscow. The Prime Minister and President were both informed but with the Constitutional Court judge among the missing, only the Supreme Court judge was able to respond on behalf of the legislature. Several of the lower court judges were also absent.

When it convened the following day, several theories were proposed by various deputies. Some involved sickness, technical problems with communications or outside interference; others were wild suppositions, including one of alien abduction by a deputy from an oblast in the far east. None of the theories explained the situation fully and at the end of the session, although much noise had been generated, there was very little light shed on the perplexing and inexplicable phenomena.

It was only afterwards that the smaller and select committee of deputies and FSB securocrats began to ponder possible connections with their interview of the MI5 agent a couple of days previously. A small group of influential deputies met at Lubyanka Square again late that evening and armed with that day's information at the State Duma headquarters, tried to put parts of the jigsaw together. The pieces were still very vague in outline and conjecture played as much a part as fact. It was to be a late night.

As Jonas Smythe sat in his office preparing his part of the report for that afternoon's hastily arranged COBRA meeting, his phone suddenly rang. He picked it up. It was his contact in Kensington Gardens. He hurriedly picked up a pencil.

"You inquired about Igor Gurevich some days ago," stated the voice on the phone. "Was there some particular reason?"

Jonas turned in his chair and thought carefully. Intelligence was like a game of Scrabble. To score, two needed to play, but each was careful not to open a disadvantageous lead for the other.

"His name crossed my table in connection with interests we had in Norway," he replied noncommittally. "Probably nothing, just a name among many." He decided to set down a letter beside a double point box. "No interest now really... I don't suppose he's of much concern to either of us now."

There was a pause at the other end. A response was being formed.

"His concern to anyone has been somewhat overtaken by circumstances my friend. Gurevich was found dead yesterday."

Jonas' mind worked furiously. Gurevich – dead? What did that mean for Lander?

"Oh, so sorry old man. In Moscow?" Again there was a slight hesitation in his Russian equivalent's reply.

"No, not Moscow. He was in Arkhangelsk at the time of his... death."

Jonas decided it was his turn to play another move.

"We had heard something, but we were not sure that it was him. We thought he might have had company at the time. In fact, it was the company he kept that we had interest in. We have a particular concern there. Intelligence our end seems to indicate some kind of emergency had been taking place, but then you had assured me earlier that we were mistaken?"

"Things change," replied the Russian immediately. "Emergencies suddenly appear where none before existed."

Suddenly his voice lost its careful cadences. "I will be open with you Smythe. Over sixty highly sensitive members of our government have disappeared. Gurevich is the only one we have recovered and him dead. We are shutting down our borders and initiating a nationwide emergency. Suspicions are not confined to Russia, and I must emphasise that neither shall our government's reaction be if outside interference is confirmed. Do you understand me Jonas? This will escalate quickly if we do not find it possible to suspend the play with words. This is beyond a game now."

It was now Jonas's turn to hesitate. The information he just been given, if true, was unprecedented in its frankness. How much he could justify in releasing to the agent in the Russian embassy was a huge gamble. A man's life could depend on it – or the lives of many.

"We had an agent on Jan Mayen," he said. "We believe he was abducted and taken via a Yashkin class submarine to somewhere in north west Russia – possibly Severomorsk or Murmansk, maybe even Arkhangelsk. He called us and claimed he was being interviewed by Gurevich. The line was cut. We've heard nothing since."

Jonas let out a long breath. He was unaccustomed to passing on so much sensitive intelligence to an agent of a foreign power, particularly one with which the United Kingdom had such a wary relationship.

"Was he sent to assassinate Gurevich?"

"No, absolutely no! He was conducting an investigation with Norwegian intelligence. It was your navy that illegally apprehended him."

"He told us there were anomalies in Jan Mayen. Is this true?"

"He told you? You mean, you have him? I must demand..."

"Please," interrupted the Russian. "We have known one another too long. Do not demand. Your information is of significant help at this time. I am taking enough of a risk by sharing more than I am authorised to release; but I will add this: We sanctioned no mission to Jan Mayen. This fact is our most critical concern. It may well prove to be yours also. Let us both hope not."

When Jonas set down the phone, the tension had caused beads of perspiration to form in his brow. He sat for a second, gathering his thoughts, before quickly leaving his office to seek out Sir Simon.

"You mean to say a Russian nuclear submarine is used to perform a covert mission in foreign waters and Russia denies any involvement? Tell me you don't believe him Jonas."

Sir Simon's incredulity at Jonas' account shook his conviction, but he quickly recovered.

"I do believe him. Why would he lie about that and then tell me that they have Lander? If it is true that they have had some kind of a mass abduction or even killing of dozens of members of government, then they are facing a massive terrorist attack unlike anything even the Chechens could manage." He looked steadily into the face of the head of MI5. "The only deputy they have found was seemingly in the company, or had been in the company of a British agent. What are they to think?"

"They hardly think the United Kingdom has assassinated a fifth of their government. Even the Russians can't be that paranoid!"

"What was it Churchill said? 'I cannot forecast to you the action of Russia. It is a riddle wrapped in a mystery inside an enigma.'"

"The Russia of 1939 is not the Russia of today," replied Sir Simon. "Still..." He studied the face of his most trusted officer, "...if they have lost control of a Yashkin class, there's no knowing what else," he said, his voice serious and low.

~~~~~~~~~~~~~~

The first tranche of communications was uploaded and sent via complex series of untraceable satellite links to nine national governments. Each country was selected on the qualification that it had a nuclear capability. The communication was succinct and its demands direct. Each country was to secede to the three demands and as proof of capability, the New United World Soviet would demonstrate their willingness to carry out their threats by destroying a target verifiable by all. It was timed for 1600hrs G.M.T. precisely.

The message was received in London as Cabinet Office Briefing, Room 'A' was taking place. The Prime Minister was presiding over the gathering of chosen cabinet members and including Sir Simon and Jonas, Commodore Legge, the Chief of Defence Staff as well as the heads of MI6, the Office for Security and Counter-Terrorism, GCHQ and the Joint Intelligence Organisation. The COBRA room was full and questions were in full flow after the shock of Sir Simon's briefing when an aide handed a note to the head of GCHQ. He scanned it quickly and passed it immediately to the Prime Minister. The room gradually quietened as the face of the Head of the United Kingdom's government visibly blanched.

He looked up, the note limp in his hand.

"It's an ultimatum," he said, his voice noticeably tense. "An organisation calling itself the New United World Soviet is claiming it is going to destroy an American and Chinese target in less than an hour from now."

There was complete silence and then suddenly pandemonium broke out.

At the same time, the communication was being handed to the President of the United States. The Secretary of Defence's face was grim as he strode through the West Wing and was ushered into the Oval Office. The Chairman of the Joint Chiefs of Staff was already present, among several others, including the chief of the National Guard Bureau and the secretaries of the Army, Navy and Air Force.

"You have it with you?" demanded the president brusquely. Calling such a meeting in so short a notice had seriously upset his schedule for the day. The chairman nodded.

"Yes sir, I have it here." He handed over a note to the president who read the contents. He looked up, his face devoid of comprehension and read it again, this time aloud.

"What is the *New United World Soviet?*"

"We do not know yet sir. Moscow claims to have received the same ultimatum."

"They would, wouldn't they?" interrupted the secretary for the Army.

"This is a direct threat against the national security of the United States," exclaimed the head of the National Security Council - how credible is it?"

"Some kind of elaborate hoax? Beijing?" queried the president.

"We believe China also received the communication, along with Israel, France, the United Kingdom, India, Pakistan and possibly several others."

"The countries you have just listed all possess nuclear armaments," pointed out the chairman of the Joint Chiefs of Staff.

"The NSA was unable to trace its origin," added the Secretary of

Defence. "It has been routed in encrypted packets through several satellite systems before being auto-decrypted on address verification. Whoever is behind this has access to resources on a national level."

"This mandates DEFCON level three," suggested the Secretary of the Air Force. The president looked to the Secretary of Defence, who nodded in agreement.

"Let it be so," he said, hearing the words from his own lips and shocked by what he had just initiated. The Cuba Crisis had been DEFCON three. The Secretary of Defence left the room to begin the sequence of events necessitated by the alert level.

There was a shocked silence in the room, broken by several voices at once who immediately understood the consequences of the heightened alert and the part each was now expected to play.

Similar emergency sessions were held in Paris, Tel Aviv, New Delhi and several other capitals. Direct communications were established in secret channels preserved for just such emergencies as a picture began to emerge that was as confusing as it was lacking in detail.

At 1600hrs G.M.T. two enormous destructive events took place within seconds of one another.

On the Chinese island of Hainan two square miles of the centre of the island lifted like a huge carpet being shaken and collapsed in a turmoil of unbelievable destruction. Centred as it was near the massive Songtao reservoir, the dams were shattered and some three trillion cubic metres of water flowed north, overwhelming the city of Danzhou and killing almost a third of its one million souls. The death toll was beyond anything experienced since the massacres by the Japanese in the second world war. A tidal wave hit the southern shores of Guangxi province a half hour later resulting in further thousands of deaths and massive devastation to homes and infrastructure.

The second was a brutal earthquake of biblical proportions near Indian Springs in California. Again, a large body of water, Millerton Lake, escaped its enclosure when the dam ruptured and billions of gallons of water rushed down the San Joaquin River to inundate the north of Fresno, again with huge loss of life along with accompanying colossal damage to roads and washing away of whole sections of the city.

Where the attacks had come from, no one could say. No ballistic missiles were tracked and neither site appeared to have a ground zero.

Even as fingers began to be pointed between belligerent nations, a further communication was received via the same encrypted satellite routing as before. It simply claimed responsibility and warned that further attacks would follow and be centred on capital cities. The deaths would move to millions and governments would collapse. The time of the next event would follow in due course. The alternative was again offered.

Total capitulation to all demands.

Jon Lander was awakened and told to dress. Still rubbing sleep from his eyes, he was found ten minutes later, standing with Lebedev at his side before some of the men who had interviewed him previously.

"Why did you kill Igor Gurevich?" demanded the same time worn face he had stood before earlier. He looked tired and troubled. Something had changed.

"He had a gun to my head," answered Lander. He had nothing to gain by saying anything other than the truth. Whether or not he was believed was not something he could control.

"How many others?"

"Others?"

"Igor Gurevich was a deputy of the State Duma. We have reason to believe you are responsible for the disappearance of others."

Lander pondered the question. Government ministers missing? Something was very wrong.

"I have no knowledge of any other Russian deputy except the one who tried to murder me in a small college in Arkhangelsk. He had already murdered another man. I still have his identity that I took from his jacket." He fished about in his pocket and produced the two cards - Gurevich's and the man in the bathroom.

"That man – Gorsakov, was also a deputy," said the heavy man, his face full of accusation.

Suddenly Lebedev's voice spoke.

"Forgive me for interrupting, but I have reason to believe this account," he said. "I had been taking Jon Lander to our deputy after having released him from the rebels. Gurevich murdered Gorsakov and assumed his place. I managed to rescue Lander from them."

"Nonetheless, it would be in the British interest to assist our enemies," suggested the Russian.

Jon looked around the room. What he saw in the faces of those studying him was not the usual superiority of the interrogator. There was disquiet in the room. Disquiet that smelled a lot like fear.

"The United Kingdom is no enemy of the Russian Federation," he said carefully. "I do not know what is happening, but it can only be serious. If the submarine that brought me to Russia, or the sailors and special troops were outside your government's control, then my government has every reason to offer your country whatever assistance we can. Particularly if it proves we have a common enemy."

Again the Russians returned to debating the words and information Jon had given them. They asked further questions, but Lebedev's intervention seemed to have changed the tone and affected their assessment of him. After a while he was dismissed and Lebedev returned him to his room.

"They are aware you cannot know what has happened a few hours ago," said Lebedev, remaining with Lander in his room and taking a seat opposite the bed. Lander's expression of confusion encouraged Lebedev to continue.

"A city in China and another in the United States was destroyed by some kind of geo-located nuclear detonation. A grouping claiming to originate here has claimed responsibility and is threatening further strikes. You were taken to Polyarny. The committee is recommending a major force be directed there immediately. I fear we are on the edge of a disaster that will make Nagasaki and Hiroshima look like a firework display." He undid a button on his jacket. "We are too late Jon Lander. The wheels of Armageddon are rolling and I fear they cannot be stopped."

Jon stepped over toward the man he had come to respect.

"I need that phone call Sergei. Can you give me that?"

Lebedev sighed. He looked at the ground for a moment before standing up. "Follow me," he said. "It would be interesting to hear what an MI5 agent would say on a phone from the old KGB headquarters."

Lebedev sat in the room as Lander made the call. It was pointless to ask him to leave – the fact that he was being given access to a phone was a gift he could not dismiss.

"My ears are the least of your worries," said Lebedev as Lander lifted the receiver, "not everyone in London is as loyal as you undoubtedly are."

He went through the usual verification process. It was slightly altered from previous calls as the code words were affected by the date of the call. A listener would barely notice the difference in the pauses between the sentences and the pitch of the first three words.

He was unable to contact Sir Simon, he was at a meeting, but he left a message which included his location and what he had determined from his questioning.

"From my perspective we can be confident that the attacks of which I have just been informed are not sanctioned at this end," he finally added. "It appears a highly secretive terrorist organisation including dissident Duma officials is behind this and the events at Jan Mayen."

When he had finished, Lebedev gave a wry smile.

"Wheels within wheels," he said. "Sometimes I wish I was back on my father's farm on the Steppes. Life was so much simpler then." He sighed and pushed himself up from the seat he had been sitting on.

"Come my friend. Let us take a walk down to the Moskva River. I will show you St Basil's."

Chapter 40
Weapons of Apocalypse

Karmonov was jubilant. The Program up to this point had always been a project. Like a man who has gambled all he has to watch his horse stride first across the finishing line, his wildest dreams had become real. All the theories and conjectures were justified in two acts of mass murder and he was ecstatic with joy.

The weight of what they had unleashed was a shock to others, particularly recent defectors from the civilian Duma for whom the concept of total war was simply that, a concept detached from the harsh reality of experience. As Karmonov celebrated with Geim and several others of the Committee, there were those who glanced at one another, the chilling realisation of what they had done striking feelings other than rejoicing in their otherwise traitorous hearts.

"Our ultimatums will surely be acceded too with such a demonstration," vocalised the Supreme Court Judge for them all. "Further destruction of this scale will not be tolerated by any rational government."

Karmonov actually frowned. "The unassailable force of our will must be beyond debate comrade," he replied as the room quietened. "We have given a demonstration, but we must finish what we have started. When we have ruined their capitals, when smoke rises from the wreckage of their prideful, glittering Babylons, then they shall cower at our feet like beaten dogs. We must drive the anger from them, kill any hope of retaliation, leave them beggars grasping at our ankles for mercy."

"But if they accept our terms?" asked a deputy from Yamalia.

"A man will say anything, agree to any condition if you agree to withhold the violence you are inflicting on him. As soon as you stop, he begins to think of escape, and as soon as he has escaped, how to return with schemes of vengeance to visit upon your head. No, we shall leave him without hope of escape, let alone imagine revenge. In fact, we will make it that we are his only salvation since none other shall exist. He will plead for us to stop, then plead for us to rule him. The United World Soviet will be the first successful system that shall eradicate all the inequalities that have caused humanity's woes since he first crawled, gasping out of the mud."

Geim was grinning as Karmonov spoke. He began to clap and was quickly followed by obedient applause that echoed around the huge table. Karmonov basked in the adulation and no one doubted who would lead that system.

~~~~~~~~~~~

Anya had so much to ask, so much to tell. As Finn cooked a meal for them both on his gas stove in the rear of the UAZ, Anya would involuntarily touch his arm, or his head as if physical proof had to be continually reasserted.

"Where did you go? Where have you been? What have you been doing all these years - did you think of me often Finn? Did you know father is dead? How did you find me and how did you even know where I was...?"

Finn smiled at the sound of her voice. It was the voice he had dreamed of, the face that had been his companion in visions of the night. He took her hair in his hand and let it fall from his fingers and then caressed her cheek with the back of his hand. She was as beautiful as he had envisaged. More beautiful. Her small ears, her slender neck, the colour or her eyes, she was altogether loveliness in all of its forms. He placed an arm around her shoulders and drew her to him. She came, her eyes never leaving his.

"So many questions," he said softly, "but first I must tell you this." There were no words in what exchanged then between them, but when they parted, she lay her head upon his shoulder and held onto the only man she had ever loved like this.

Finn was complete. As the dawning of the sun, he knew that no longer were there closed corridors within his mind. As love for the girl nestled below his arm filled his heart, his mind was suddenly clear without shadows or semi-memories. The questions she would ask would be as much a revelation to him as he heard his own voice explain circumstances so long shrouded even to himself.

"I awoke in a hospital bed in Scotland," he began. "I had been in a coma for eleven years."

Anya's eyes opened wide at the revelation. Much more was to come as he recounted and put together the years that had passed.

He explained his sinking in the Irish Sea and the phenomenon that had kept him alive, but had somehow altered something within the neural structure of his brain. The British had been disposing of a dirty secret and the scientist who saved his life was the very double-agent who had supplied the reactive mineral drilled from the upper layers of the Mohorovicic Discontinuity on the Kola Peninsula. Boris Nevotslov had been ordered to sail on board the Lima Class Experimental submarine whose mission was to recover the stolen material from the Beaufort Dyke. A spy within MI6 had provided the intelligence, but fortunately for Anya's father, had not known of his complicity.

Karmonov had managed to use his influence as the senior head at Arkhangelsk University to authorise the use of the submarine since he was convinced that the material had the capacity to produce a weapon beyond anything in the current nuclear arsenals. The British covert mission to bury it confirmed it to him, not knowing in doing so they were in fact protecting their source – the very man following in the Lima Class behind the British destroyer.

Finn explained how, in trying to restore his memory, Boris had discovered the uniqueness of new neural pathways and synapses capable of almost infinite learning and retention. With Finn's agreement, he had experimented with a method of imprinting information that had proven spectacularly successful.

It was around this time that the doctor had uncovered the Committee and Karmonov's intentions behind the Superdeep decoy and The Program. By now a virtual prisoner at Kola and kept under continual surveillance, he had found a way of implanting within Finn's mind all the information that was critical for uncovering the conspiracy.

"Somehow your father found a way of spiriting me away on a Russian trawler from a small fishing port in Kola which landed in Ullapool on the west coast of Scotland," explained Finn. "One night a thunder storm struck. The lightning followed and seemed to centre around the boat. It was as if I were some kind of earthing point. A bolt choose me as its connection to earth and I immediately collapsed into unconsciousness. The sailors panicked and drove me to Glasgow where they left me on the steps of the hospital. I was in that coma for the eleven years and on awakening, had no knowledge of anything, not even my name."

"What about your family?" asked Anya, "Weren't you missed right from the capsize in the sea off Ireland?"

"My father was dead already. By the time I awakened from the coma, my mother had followed him. My brother had died shortly before in a tragic accident. The missing persons file was more or less forgotten about or lost."

"But you know everything now, what happened?"

Finn explained about his leaving the hospital, his work in Penrith and subsequent arrival in Northern Ireland. He talked about the kindness of friends he had met there and the happiness at the farm. His face hardened as he recounted how death had stalked him and found his friends instead. From there he sketched his journey through Europe and the gradual revelations in visions and fits that gradually drew him north.

"I found that I would think and just know," he explained carefully, watching Anya's face for an expression of disbelief. She was listening intently and so Finn continued.

"Your father imprinted huge amounts of information. This information became learned knowledge as it was imprinted. I am fluent in over twenty languages and have an encyclopaedic knowledge in virtually any subject."

"What is Ringwoodite?" asked Anya suddenly.

Finn was set back, but replied immediately. "It's a form of magnesium silicate, usually found in high pressure and extreme temperature environments. It's created deep below the Earth's mantle, about four hundred miles below the surface but has never been recovered." He studied Anya as he spoke.

"Any Ringwoodite seen has been from meteorites. I can tell you a lot more Anya, but if you're asking me this, you should know I realise it is a test. You should also know that Polymorphous Ringwoodite was part of the substance supplied by your father to the United Kingdom and also the material that was responsible for altering the plasma membrane structure between my synaptic neural pathways."

Anya gasped. "How do you know this?"

"Exactly how I'm telling you my dearest. Another thing your father did not discover but I have since proved; if I am close enough, I can harmonise with the weak electrical signals of another person. Mind reading is a primitive way of explaining it, but the term gives the idea of the outcome."

"You can read my mind?"

"I can sympathise with the pattern of your synaptic signals – it's not quite reading your mind."

"But you would know what I'm thinking?" asked Anya incredulously.

"In a way, if I concentrate."

"What am I thinking now?" she asked.

Finn half closed his eyes and was silent for a few seconds. Suddenly he smiled.

Finn smiled. "And I still do, Anya Nevotslova," he said. "You're remembering the last walk we had together in the forest outside Arkhangelsk – the day I told you I loved you."

Anya broke into a wide smile and her face slightly blushed. Then she shook her head in disbelief.

"But... how...? You can just..." she blinked and exclaimed in wonder, "...enter my mind?"

Finn shook his head. "No, it's not like that. I need to correlate your electrical stimuli with my own. I can't go around constantly reading and aware of the thoughts of others. I have to make an effort. It's actually not that comfortable and it's also unpleasantly tiring."

"You said father had imprinted vast amounts of knowledge. Is that how you knew about Ringwoodite, or were you reading, or correlating or whatever, my thoughts?"

Finn paused and thought for a moment. "No, I didn't get if from you. If I think hard, I can find the details and facts on an incredible range of human knowledge. Your father called it The Total Sum. I don't think it's quite that encompassing, but it is significant." Again he paused, thinking about how she had replied. "You know something about Ringwoodite?"

"I came across it in a bore sample. We were studying it, Rogov and I. It had unusual properties..." She tailed off and her shoulders heaved. "I'm sorry," she sighed, wiping a tear from her eye, "Rogov was a good friend to me."

She told Finn all about Rogov and how she was alive because of his sacrifice. She told him about all three, Rogov, Yashkin and Chemeris. She drew him a picture in his mind of the workings at the Superdeep, about Gasparov, the secrecy, the fear and the loneliness. After a while she returned to the Ringwoodite and to Rogov.

"He was a great man. Greater than we knew. He was always pushing me, encouraging me in my work. He and I both experimented on the sample. Anyway, it reacted with Ultra Violet in a way that was beyond any reaction I have witnessed. A huge burst of light in colours that more than dazzled – almost hypnotised."

"Did you feel different afterwards?"

"Different?"

"Stretched. As if you had been pulled wider and room left for...how can I say it... *thinking*, if you know what I mean?"

Anya thought for a moment. "I do know what you mean. Rogov and I never discussed it, but things seemed, sharper, less vague maybe? I never really thought about that before."

Finn simply nodded and was quiet. Suddenly he pointed to the pot he was stirring.

"The food is ready. I hope you like pasta!"

Anya laughed. She was so hungry she doubted that there was anything she wouldn't like. The pasta would be a banquet.

When they had finished the meal he had made, Finn realised that the urge to head north was as strong as ever. He also knew why. Hiding it from the person he now knew he treasured above all however was not an option.

"Anya," he began, "I must tell you something."

She was lying beside him, her head in his lap as she rested after the meal and the hours of talking. It was three in the morning, but Finn could not sleep. He was aware that Anya was only dozing.

"You have something to do?" she pre-empted.

"Karmonov must be stopped," he said, "and your father has given me the... ability to do something about it."

She sat up and kissed him. "Then I'm coming too Allen Finlay. You have not found me after all this time to leave me again. I will never let you leave me ever again."

And Finn said no more. He kissed her back and ten minutes later they were both asleep in the cab.

The birdsong in the morning was a chorus of astounding variety and beauty. Trills and whistles, songs of the purest notes along with chirrups and plaintive cries filled the air. It was so joyous and heart-lifting that after a while Anya and Finn looked at one another and simply laughed. Not the laugh of humour or a joke well received, but the laugh of a rejoicing heart, cleared of all care and abandoned to simple joy.

"Isn't it strange," said Anya, as she listened while helping Finn to tidy their camp, "to think that when we move on, the dawn chorus of the birds in the taiga will still sing tomorrow as wonderfully and not an ear to hear it?"

Finn stopped and looked around as the birds, invisible in the sparse trees around them continued in their song.

"I have a friend back home - in Northern Ireland," he corrected himself. "He's a Christian minister. He told me once that we are only eavesdroppers. He said God is always praised, even when human hearts grow dull, bitter and sceptical, the creation itself can never forget its Maker."

Anya listened and like Finn, looked around at the endless land around them, framed in the calls of birds and coloured in their songs.

"Yes... I think I see..." She had been raised in a culture largely devoid of the knowledge of God and hearing Finn was a kind of a revelation. "I suppose it would seem such a waste otherwise. It's nice to think it has a purpose."

"We all have," replied Finn. "Life without it is cold and hard." His thoughts went back to the days after his awakening, days when he had only an empty canvas for memory and a void instead of a past. They were distressing days of empty pointless existence.

His life in Penrith had been the catalyst, but the McCracken's and the days spent chatting with Alastair Boyd at the manse were the beginning of hope.

"A man cannot live without hope," he found himself saying. Anya stopped and looked at him. He was far away in a place beyond the taiga.

"Hope gives a purpose; an aim. A man once told me, 'If you aim for nothing, you're sure to hit it.' It took me a while to understand what he meant."

"But you do now?" asked Anya, who had moved over to stand beside him.

Finn nodded. "Yes, I think I do. Without purpose, life is only a jumble of meaningless accidents. If that were true, then each person's life would be meaningless too. Futile little existences, little pulses of insignificant being, a brief flash then nothing. A man could just lie down and die because of such thoughts."

"You think we have a higher purpose?"

"Is it even conceivable that we don't?"

She was quiet for a minute and then slowly slipped her hand into his.

"You give me a purpose Finn, and I want to be a part of yours."

He took her other hand. "Today we must drive north. We should arrive late tonight. I hardly know what we shall do when we arrive, but I do know there is no other option. Not now."

Anya lay her head on his chest and Finn wrapped his arms around her slender shape. It seemed so cruel to head to danger. The temptation to get in the jeep and drive west to a life of freedom with this girl was almost overpowering. They could live such a live that would be a daily awakening into happiness.

Except he knew without a single doubt that that world would not exist if they turned and ran. Not for them, not for anyone.

From London to Paris, Washington to Tel Aviv and in every centre of government, the shock of the attacks left administrations practically paralysed. Without a clear enemy, the bewilderment was as terrifying as it was baffling. Emergency meetings fell into disorganised chaos as officials were confounded in forming a reaction. Above all was the unspoken dread, the horror of anticipating where would be next. If such murderous destruction that had claimed so many lives was claimed as only a demonstration, the threatened following attacks would be apocalyptic beyond the imaginable. In some countries, leaders were evacuated from their capitals with those left behind staring into the maw of threatened oblivion.

Back in Thames house after COBRA had been adjourned, Sir Simon was silent as he stood at his window looking out across Millbank and the familiar arches of Lambeth Bridge. Each department had been ordered to make preparations for possible outbreak of war, but without a visible enemy, it was difficult to negotiate any course of action.

The door knocked and Jonas entered the office. He moved over to stand beside his colleague at the window.

"You do know London will be almost certainly be hit next Jonas?" said Sir Simon quietly. Jonas gave a slow nod but could think of nothing to add.

"The P.M. is being airlifted as we speak," added Sir Simon. "He's being taken to a secret location in Scotland."

"Not Corsham?"

"It was decommissioned a couple of years back. After the end of the Cold War we knew underground facilities like the bunker for Central Government War Headquarters would never be needed." He laughed a humourless laugh. He turned to his junior. "How did we miss this Jonas? We had all the signs."

"Hindsight never prevented anything sir," said Jonas, "and we can't read minds."

"Nevotslov tried to warn us and we just hid the evidence. The effort to silence Finlay, whom we should have taken greater care of; the missing warheads from the Ukraine, the disquiet among the old communist regimists in Russia. A Russian nuclear sub was commandeered by some grouping and we did not join the dots. We knew all this Jonas and we did nothing"

"HMS Vanguard and Victorious have been deployed. Vengeance is being readied. That'll be three of four boats at sea," Jonas said. He did not need to add that the UK only ever had one of the Vanguard Class of Trident missile deploying submarines at sea at one time. Three was utterly unprecedented.

Sir Simon was thinking. "Jan Mayen. How does that island fit in Jonas? What was it that they thought Lander had uncovered?"

"Their secret base?"

"Then why take him to Russia? Why not deal with him on Jan Mayen?"

It was a question neither could answer and its mystery was the door that they had never found a key to unlock.

Suddenly Sir Simon's phone rang. He answered it and listened to the call. After a couple of questions, he set it back in its cradle. He looked pensive.

"Lander called when we were in COBRA," he said. "He is in Moscow and is certain that they are as frightened as we are. Gurevich tried to kill him in Arkhangelsk. He was a senior member of a secret group, probably the group responsible for the attacks."

"Everything points north," pointed out Jonas. "It must be centred there, Arkhangelsk probably."

"He added something else," said Sir Simon. "The leak we've been trying to plug? I think he knows who it is."

"Who, who is it?"

"He didn't say..." suddenly he let out a sigh. "Does it matter now Jonas? London will have to capitulate. Washington, Paris, the rest of the world. It's too late to stop anything. We lost, Jonas. A new world tyranny has won."

Jonas struggled to find a response and failed. After a few minutes he excused himself and left the office.

As he made his way down the corridor, his mobile rang. It was Inspector McGregor.

"Jonas, are you able to talk?"

"Yes, go ahead."

"I'm on my way over. I've just had a call from Finn. You are not going to believe this, but he called from The Kola Peninsula near the northern Finnish border. He's in Russia."

"Russia?" exclaimed Jonas, coming to a halt.

"That's not it all," said the voice on the phone. "He's not alone. He's with Boris Nevotslov's daughter!"

The satellite phone Finn had bought had not had any practical use in his mind up to the point where Anya suddenly remembered Rogov's last words. They had come to a settlement built around a Nickel mine at a place called Prirechny. It was a pitifully poor looking place with a few wooden huts erected near the dirt road. Finn had risked driving on the road, weighing the risks of the advantage of speed versus the chances of being stopped at a roadblock. Telegraph and electric wires hung carelessly from wind-blown poles along the road.

"Can we get to a phone somehow?" said Anya suddenly. "I must make a call!"

Remembering the mobile he had bought, they passed through and pulled in to a clearing just outside the Sami village.

Finn had to erect a small satellite dish, but after a few minutes, the screen on the handset showed a symbol signifying a successful satellite capture.

After a few calls, Anya eventually got through to the State Duma. She said who she was and asked for Sergei Lebedev by name. It took another ten to fifteen minutes, but to her amazement she found herself talking to the man whom Rogov had told her to contact. At first he seemed hesitant, suspicious, but she continued nonetheless and explained all that had happened at the Kola Superdeep. She told him about the extermination of the staff and the involvement of Gasparov.

"But Rogov told me to tell you he is only a pawn. Viktor Karmonov, head of Arkhangelsk State Technical University is the central leader. He plans to do something terrible. He must be stopped! Oh, and he said to tell you a code. He said to tell you 511."

A minute later she handed the phone back to Finn. The satellite fix was fading. He stepped out of the vehicle to try to get a better signal. The battery was running down rapidly. He made one call. It was to Jack McGregor.

When he got back in the jeep, Anya related what Lebedev had told her about the horrific loss of life in two coordinated attacks.

"We need to hurry," she said, without asking him whom he had called. She did not know what exactly they could do. She had a growing sense however that Finn knew more than he had told her so far. Strangely, she felt no resentment toward him for that.

The Russian president, as Supreme Commander in Chief authorised immediate deployment to Severomorsk of the 2nd Spetsnatz Brigade. The Duma did not trust the military currently stationed in Severomorsk, suspecting that it had already been taken over by the rebels.

The special troops being activated were based in Promezhitsa near the Estonian border but were currently on a training operation some two hundred miles north of their base. It made them the closest troops available. Being under the command of *Kombrig* Kormiltsev, they were therefore led by a Brigadier whose loyalty was unquestioned. Several Antonov An-22 aircraft were quickly fuelled and despatched to transport the soldiers and their equipment the five-hundred-mile trip north. Throughout Russia, other battalions once raised to fight a war against the West were mobilised, ostensibly as a huge training event. Almost inevitably, the ICBM launch sites throughout the nation were put on alert. Programmed with pre-planned coordinates throughout western Europe and the United States, no one had the initiative to suggest alternative targets. Since none were identified, the old ones remained.

Back in Moscow, Lebedev was troubled. Rogov had been a personal friend. A good man whose integrity and cool courage set him apart in a world where lies and subterfuge was the daily diet.

Anya Nevotslov? It seemed incredible that the daughter of the scientist and double-agent should be centre to the current crisis. She had mentioned a man with her - British. He thought it over. He needed to talk again with Lander.

Jon Lander shook his head. "Never heard the name – *Finn* you say? Are you sure he's British?"

Lebedev simply nodded. "I need you to find out, Jon Lander. It is time for you to cash in some of what you are due I think. This time I will leave you alone. I can give you five minutes, no more."

Once again Lander found himself on a call to London. Once again he went through the vocally coded logins. This time he was put through to Jonas Smythe.

"It's Lander. Listen Jonas. I don't have much time," he said, giving the MI5 officer no time to reply. "Things are moving fast over here. A Russian Brigade is being rushed to Kola. They think the rebels may be operating from there. I need to know something. Boris Nevotslov's daughter is being aided by a British national. The only name we have is Finn. *Finn*, did you get that? It this someone I should know about?"

Jonas literally gasped down the line. "Good grief! Did you say *Finn*?"

There were only two minutes left, but in those two minutes Lander learned details that were as unlikely as they were bizarre.

Lebedev made a decision. If Nevotslov's daughter was right, Rogov had issued the code that confirmed the worst of their fears. He knew that to immediately pass that on to the Duma would almost certainly initiate a series of events that would be as lumbering and ill-judged as they would be catastrophic. The government ran the country, but it was the small unseen company of men like Lebedev who supplied the intelligence that informed their decisions. There was a time when that information was best withheld –at least for a few hours.

As a senior FSB agent, he had considerable licence. West of Moscow was the Kubinka Aerodrome. Within an hour he and Lander were in a car making their way west to the airport. When they arrived, a Yakovlev Yak-40 triple engined jet was waiting for them. Five minutes later they were climbing into the Russian skies, headed north-east, skipping over the troops below who were still arranging and preparing for deployment.

"Our army is going in with an iron fist," explained Lebedev as the aircraft levelled off. "Before they scorch the earth, someone needs to know what is actually happening. I fear the fist may only stir the hornet's nest and bring the end of all things upon our heads. Perhaps you and I can do something before the air becomes thick with the smoke of Armageddon."

Chapter 41
Convergence

Finn and Anya drove north as fast as the gravel tracks allowed. Now and then they would thunder by simple houses of birch wood, chickens and dogs scattering as the jeep roared past. A trail of dust followed them, but Finn was past trying to be invisible – he had a gut feeling, a knowledge that now his greatest enemy was not hidden assassins, but time.

Deep underground some thirty kilometres ahead of them, the committee who would rebuild the world were conscious of the mile of rock above their heads. For years the fissures that led inexorably down had been a secret known to a select group of human beings. Apart from the committee, there were the labourers and machine operators. Men who were the builders of The Program. Given promises of land and undreamed of wealth after the new order took over, they were nonetheless guarded night and day and kept as virtual slaves within The Program's boundary.

Karmonov was secure in not only eventual success, but also the impregnability of their underground fortress. No weapon devised by man could reach them in the depths of the massive caverns that had been discovered less than twenty miles from the Russo-Finnish border. Now engineered into the vast complex that could sustain life for at least five years without seeing the light of day, the natural phenomenon, when first discovered, had made utterly redundant the drilling project that lay a few miles to the east. The Kolskaya Superdeep drilling project had fulfilled its purpose in drawing eyes away from the activity further west. It also gave cover for the spoils of rock that had been excavated from the caverns in order to create the roads and the ability to descend into the bowels of the earth.

The Nuclear Powers of Britain, France and the United States had conferred in a state of confusion. No launch sites had been identified. The Russian strategic ICBM launcher sites, reduced to less than eight hundred under the bilateral non-proliferation START treaty, were all under satellite surveillance and none had launched their missiles. The idea of nuclear warheads being smuggled into Hainan and Indian Springs to detonate remotely was considered completely unfeasible by NATO scientists. The Americans and British in particular were paralysed, having the ability to strike back, but no target at which to do so.

Six hours after the attacks in China and America, the same pattern of encrypted and untraceable routed communications were received by the same nations as before. This time as the second set of attacks were announced, chills of genuine cold fear shook the seats of governments.

The targets were London, Washington and Beijing. The United Nations was given the ultimatum this time: In four hours each of the targets would be destroyed unless there was total surrender to all demands.

Washington immediately made a decision. The VC-25B that was Air Force One took off with the president and his team aboard. Once at cruising altitude, the nuclear football, the case that held the launch codes was brought into the conference room. The president looked up and addressed his staff.

"There are four items in this case," he said, his single voice sombre and deliberate. "Among the retaliatory options and site locations is 'the biscuit'. If I break this and read the Gold Codes, I am beginning a chain of events that will unleash a nuclear apocalypse on our enemies. Before I do that I need to know that we have no other option. We have no definite proof that Russia is behind this, but also we have no other suspects."

"What other options do we have sir," put in the Secretary of Defence. "It is simply impossible for the United States to idly stand by and await destruction. Even if the smoking gun has not been identified, we know where the gun cabinet is."

"But we don't know, we don't *know*," interrupted the Chairman of the Joint Chiefs of Staff. "Moscow could be as blind as they say they are and we just visit Doomsday on them?"

For two or three minutes the same arguments they had had in Washington were thrown around the conference room. The president was looking out onto the pure blue outside the windows at thirty-seven thousand feet. Suddenly he turned.

"Not to decide is still a decision," he said, his voice silencing the large cabin. "And above all, the constitution, the nation requires that someone make it. I am that someone."

"We should pray," suddenly interrupted a quiet voice. It was the president's personal secretary, a young immaculately dressed black woman. A lump caught in the president's throat. She was totally out of order and had no right to open her mouth, but she did and he was glad that she did.

As one man, everyone bowed their heads.

~~~~~~~~~

Jonas met Jack McGregor in Victoria Tower gardens. Jack had suggested the venue. He could get there more quickly than Thames House. There was some kind of emergency taking place; police were closing down roads all around central London. Jonas made his way on foot, wondering what news he had garnered from the Scot.

Jack arrived at almost the same time. He looked uncharacteristically out of breath.

"Sorry, every minute counts and I was already on my way," he began. Jonas nodded and sat on the bench beside him.

"You say Finn called you from Finland?"

"Russia," corrected Jack. "His memory has returned – almost all of it. What he told me is almost too fantastic to believe!"

Jonas wondered if Jack would believe the catastrophe that was on its way. Although every police officer in London was currently involved in a massive hunt, only a few people in the upper echelons of Whitehall had any idea of its true nature. They were not, as described by Security Services, trying to trap an Islamist terrorist cell, they were trying to discover the nuclear warhead that must surely be parked up in a van or hidden in a lock-up. With only three hours to go, it was decided that an attempted evacuation was simply impossible and the panic that would ensue would only create massive log jams of people and traffic. That way no one would escape. Currently people identified as strategically critical to the future running of the country were being driven out of London. Jonas and Sir Simon were not on that list.

Listening to the police inspector, Jonas was intrigued as to what Finn was doing, but also resigned to the fact that it could make no difference to his own fate, or the millions of civilians within London.

"He is headed to a secret underground complex. He says it leads down, over thirty miles down and ends in something so utterly unexpected that it sounds more like science fiction than fact," said Jack, his words bursting out in a staccato far faster than his normal rate. "He says there is an interruption in the strata below the Earth, a vast, globe encircling sea."

Jonas's expression said more than a spoken disbelief. Jack took a hold of Jonas's arm.

"I know, I know, but listen to me Jonas. He says a secret group operating within, but unknown to the Russian government has been years preparing some kind of fleet of automated nuclear warheads – mounted on submarines, or torpedoes or something capable of sailing through this vast underground body of water. Nevotslov had programmed Finn to tell it to the world, but he was uncovered and before he was caught and executed, he managed to spirit his protégé away to the U.K. Something went wrong and Finn lost his memory in some kind of accident. Whoever he was with, they panicked and left him outside Glasgow Royal."

"So why has he returned to Russia?" asked Jonas, a thousand questions in his head, but knowing he had not the time to ask or to listen to the reply.

"The two disasters in China and California? They were attacks by this group. Finn is on his way to try and stop any more!"

Jonas' head was wheeling. "We need to get to Thames House. Sir Simon needs to know, come on!" he got up and began to make for the MI5 building only five hundred metres away.

Jack shook his head. "No, I met you here Jonas because Finn told me something else. The spy you asked me to find? He's not in MI6. He's in Thames House. He has been passing on everything. The mission to Jan Mayen, the information about Finn. I have no idea who it is, he didn't give a name, but it could be anyone."

"Why trust me then?"

"I had to trust someone. I took a gamble. Was I wrong?"

Jonas shook his head. "No Jack. You weren't wrong. It's isn't me, but neither is it Sir Simon Montague. I would lay my life on it."

Sir Simon was on the phone even before Jack had repeated his incredible story. He spoke to Commodore Legge and gave him instructions that he was not authorised to give. His next call was to the P.M. who was now in Scotland. Jack and Jonas looked at one another in alarm.

"Extraordinary events require extraordinary measures," said Sir Simon simply, seeing their expressions. "At this stage there is nothing to lose. Did you tell him about London Jonas?"

Jonas shook his head. "Orders sir."

"We are moving too fast to await orders Jonas." He turned to Jack. "London, Washington and Beijing are the next targets Inspector. You have a wife in Glasgow. If you leave now you may get to see her again."

"What will we do when we get there?" asked Anya. "Rogov told me to contact Lebedev, and I've done that."

Finn looked at the girl who had inhabited his dreams. He had loved her for so many lost years and now he knew they would never be recovered. His chest hurt with the pain he felt and yet he could see no other way.

"I'm sorry Anya. I am so sorry." His voice cracked as he spoke and he hesitated. Anya put her arm on his.

"I know," she said. "I didn't think I would live this long anyway." She looked up at him as his hands tightened on the wheel. "But we found one another in the end, didn't we?"

Finn could not speak. This throat was tight and dry, and his eyes welled so that he could barely see the road ahead. He struggled to compose his words.

"I have to stop Karmonov," he said. "I can't see how to do that without... I don't think we can... we cannot live through this Anya. I... I'm so sorry. I don't know any further ahead. This is as far as your father saw." His jaw muscles hardened as he tried to maintain self-control. Tears formed on his eyes and Anya pulled herself across to lie up against him.

"It's alright Finn. It's like you said. Life has a purpose. Maybe this is ours. I accept that."

They drove wordlessly for ten minutes until Finn's voice broke the silence.

"Karmonov had discovered a subterranean feature," he began. "It was hidden by a volcanic plug. Originally looking for a drill site, he quickly realised the possibilities and moved the Superdeep to the south as a distraction. The real project – it's called *The Program* - leads down to a subterranean sea. A sea that contains maybe ten times as much water as all the oceans of the world. It explains the Mohorovičić Discontinuity. He quickly realized that this vast single underground ocean allowed unfettered access to every continent of the world – or at least, twenty miles below them. He and a select group of committed former soviets have assembled a fleet of small nuclear vessels that can be directed beneath any spot on the surface. The impact on the ground above when detonated is utterly hellish. Nowhere is safe. Nowhere can be protected. If they want, they could bring down civilization. That may well be their plan. They don't like this one and are set on building another out of the ashes."

Anya listened and found the pieces filling the missing gaps in the jigsaw. The high concentrations of hydrogen impregnated water they had hit in the boreholes, the presence of Ringwoodite, the American journal and the hypothesis of the water below the earth.

Suddenly they came across a huge fence, its shining steel and concrete an incongruity in the bleak sameness of the scrubby landscape.

"We're here," said Finn. As if to illustrate his words two military trucks appeared from behind a rise in the ground behind them. They had nowhere to go, blocked by the fence before and the soldiers behind.

Anya and Finn looked at one another and simply nodded. Carefully they got out of the jeep and stood beside one another facing the oncoming vehicles.

The first came to a halt twenty feet away. A figure got out of the passenger side. Two soldiers appeared from the back. The first figure advanced, flanked by the soldiers, weapons drawn. Anya quaked when she saw who it was.

"Anya Nevotslova!" demanded the ugly voice of Ilyich Gasparov. "Why are you still alive?"

~~~~~~~~~~~~~

Less than two hours after leaving Moscow and nine hundred miles across the watery forests west of the White Sea, Lander and Lebedev landed at Murmansk. There they quickly transferred to a waiting Hind helicopter. Within minutes of arriving, they were once again airborne and crossing Kola Bay.

A large grab bag lay at Lebedev's feet. He unzipped it and pulled out fur-lined parkas and lined trousers.

"Here, put these on," he shouted across the noise of the rotors to Lander. He brought out boots and gloves and handed them over to the Englishman. "No need to die of the cold out here," he shouted. "Plenty enough other ways."

It was a one hundred kilometre flight to the Superdeep. The Hind came in on a steep bank and dropped suddenly about a kilometre back from the buildings. Lebedev thumped Lander's shoulder and pointed to the cabin door. The crewman who had been strapped at the doorway during the flight pulled back the door and Lebedev jumped out. As Lander followed, the helicopter immediately pulled up and rotated back the direction they had come.

As the thudding of the aircraft faded into the background, Lebedev pointed to the complex ahead. Wisps of smoke were rising from the structure.

"Come on," he said, pulling a squat AKSU from his pack. "They'll only have seen us if they were looking for us. Hopefully they weren't!"

The two men trudged through the spindrift snow. It wasn't deep, but it was hard ice under the light snow and the opportunity to slip and break something was real enough.

They reached the first building without event. Lebedev led the way around the metal fabrications, keeping them in cover from the main building until they found an entrance on the west side. The door was unlocked and as soon as they entered, the first thing they noticed was the smell of smoke.

"There's been a fire here," said Lebedev. Through the airlock doors was a large canteen. On the floor lay three or four bodies. One was a soldier. It looked like all had been shot. There was no sound at all and their footsteps sounded all the more obvious in the eerie silence.

"Here," said Lebedev, tossing a Makarov to Jon. "You hardly need me to tell you how to use that," he added. He pointed up a long corridor running north from the far end of the room. "You take that end; I'll check the other way."

"What are we looking for again?" asked Lander.

"Survivors," replied the Russian. "Hopefully the right sort."

As Jon made his way to the corridor he pondered the unspoken expectation of what to do with the wrong sort. He checked the pistol. The magazine was full with a round already chambered. He flicked off the safety and made his way as silently as he could. For a moment, the bizarre situation he found himself in occurred to him. In Russia, in a top secret facility, aiding a Russian agent and armed in case of ambush from other Russians. His life had never been ordinary, but it had never been this far from it before.

There was nothing. Bodies were strewn throughout the building. Apart from the soldier at the entrance, they all appeared to be civilians. Several of the rooms were badly burned. A rudimentary attempt had been made to destroy the complex but the airtight nature of the compartmentalised rooms and passageways had prevented the escalation of the fire.

"It is empty," announced Lebedev. "This has been a mass execution." His face was hard. "This should never have happened. These people are animals."

Except that animals usually only killed for food, and that one at a time. It went without saying that the people of whom Lebedev spoke had already killed many thousands. Millions would just be a larger canvas.

"We need to find a vehicle," said Lebedev. "We have nothing to do here."

In one of the outside buildings they found a military green maintenance van. It was four-wheel drive and fitted with large all-terrain tyres. After a search, Jon found the keys in an open key safe in a small office to the side. After several attempts, the diesel finally started.

"You drive," said Lebedev. He laid the assault carbine on his knees and pulled a map from an inner pocket along with a compass. He pointed a finger north west. "Take that trail Jon Lander," he said. "Rogov said it was twenty or thirty miles. If we see anyone I will do the talking."

"Just as well," shrugged Lander, "since I doubt if they meet many Brits out here."

"You do know you haven't really explained much of our objectives," said Lander after they had been driving over the rutted tracks for five minutes or so. "Might help if I had some sort of an idea."

Lebedev had unclipped the magazine from the AKSU. He checked its contents and pushed it back into the receiver with a click.

"A properly built fortress can withstand the attack of an army. It prepares for that, is designed for all an army can do. That same fortress is entered by mice, because mice are not a threat."

"So, we are the mice?"

"Perhaps," said Lebedev, his eyes saying more than his voice.

"And do these mice have a plan?" asked Lander.

"Once we see the cheese I am hoping that between us we will make one. Until then we go carefully and try not to die."

"Great plan Sergei," sighed Lander, "the last part I like, the rest of it needs a bit of work."

"Which is why you are here my friend. Two minds are better than one, yes?" He grinned and looked out the window.

"My plan involves not being here in the first place," said Lander. "But since I am, do you know what this fortress we are looking for looks like?"

"We will know Jon Lander. I think we will know."

Finn eyed the Russian before them. He was a thin wiry man and nothing about him was in any way attractive. Taking a slow, controlled breath, he spoke in as confident tone as he could muster.

"So," he said in clear Russian. "The famous Ilyich Gasparov."

Gasparov was giving an order to the soldiers either side of him. He suddenly stopped and faced the speaker.

"Who are you?" he spat.

Finn feigned an attitude of casual disinterest. "What I don't understand is why Ilyich Gasparov, one of Russia's lead scientists and noted specialist in his field, is out doing guard duty on a perimeter wall. I must be missing something."

Gasparov went to say something, but seemed to change his mind. "How do you know who I am?"

"Well, you are hardly unheard of. I have read articles in the western press extolling your work. I just find it hard to understand why you should be doing such a duty as..." Finn spread out his hands in the direction of the trucks, "...this kind of thing."

"I asked you who you were!" demanded Gasparov, his face showing the signs of his inner confusion. Finn replied carefully. How he delivered his next statement would determine Gasparov's response.

"My name is Allen Finlay," he said. Anya's eyes widened and she looked at Finn uncomprehendingly.

"I worked with Viktor Karmonov and Boris Nevotslov some years ago. I am a U.K. national. I think Viktor would be interested in meeting Anya and myself. In fact, I imagine he would be very highly interested indeed."

Gasparov's unfinished order to the soldiers to execute them where they stood was suddenly forgotten. Finn felt his tension ease. Instead of being shot there and then, they were bundled into the nearest truck while two other soldiers were detailed to bring the UAZ-469 jeep.

The trucks headed to a gate in the perimeter. Passing through the guards on duty there, the vehicle approached an odd-looking rock formation. One side was a low craggy cliff. Its base was shadowed but as they drew closer, the track suddenly dipped and went under the rock. Down a ramp and an impossibly huge steel door rolled back. One truck remained outside while Finn and Anya's, followed by the UAZ, disappeared into a steep roadway, illuminated either side by small markers that directed the edge of the descending track.

Finn and Anya, sitting opposite one another on wooden benches either side of the enclosed truck, saw none of this, but a glimpse out the partly open rear doors showed that they were underground. The sense of descending was made all the more astounding by the length of time that passed as they wove their inexorable way down and deep into the darkness.

"Into the rabbit-hole," said Finn quietly. Anya caught the reference but was hardly encouraged by it. The Queen of Hearts inhabited such a hole and everyone knew she was mad.

Chapter 42
The Great Sea

As Lebedev and Lander approached the secret base of the United World Soviet, Finn and Anya were being frog-marched into a building constructed several miles below the surface. The vast cavern continued on and down and with lights either side marking the wide road that descended into the bowels of the earth. Around them the sheer scale of excavation and engineering was breathtaking. The actual cavern appeared to be a natural phenomenon; however, it had clearly been developed and shaped by mechanical means over years into a vast subterranean complex of gargantuan proportions. A road system, its direction of travel being only downward, was wide enough to permit passage of the largest possible vehicles. In the centre, dividing the road into two lanes, were a set of rails, the purpose of which, Finn could see, was to transport abnormally heavy loads into the depths below. Heavy cable ducting ran down the sides and a faint hum could be heard coming back up from the abyss under their feet. The whole system appeared to be a series of interlinked caves and tunnels – a fissure in the mantle of the earth that led inexorably down.

They were man-handled into a room and the door locked. Two guards accompanied them. It was made very clear that no communication would be allowed. Finn and Anya were pushed against the back wall and ordered to stand silently, backs to the wall, guns aimed at their torsos.

Less than five minutes passed before the door opened and Gasparov appeared, looking ill at ease. He ordered the guards to bring the two captives. They were roughly handled and made to follow Gasparov as he led them along a corridor.

After a few turns they found themselves standing in a huge control room filled with computer screens and oversized monitors on the wall. A large horseshoe shaped wooden table was the central feature and around it sat several dozen men. Anya gasped when she saw who was sitting at the head. His was the first voice that spoke.

"Nevotslova?" Karmonov turned to the grim-faced men around him. "Now this will be an interesting sideshow." He turned to Gasparov. "You told me you had eliminated her. Either I did not give the order, or someone has lied to me. Certainly someone here is a liar and I know it is not me. Enlighten me Gasparov."

There was a murmuring around the table and all eyes turned to the pale clammy face of the Superdeep director.

"I found them outside the perimeter. This man is British. He says you know him. He... he worked with Nevotslov." His voice was whining, close to pleading.

Karmonov turned to Finn. His eyes narrowed in thought before returning to Gasparov.

"But that was not what I asked you, was it?" he said, his voice low and darkly threatening.

"She... she must have managed to escape. There was a lot of confusion..."

"You told me all my orders had been carried out," interrupted Karmonov. "But they weren't, were they?" He paused, looking at the expectant expressions on the unspeaking committee. Slowly he rubbed a thick finger down the side of his nose. It was like a forewarning of what was coming. The *pollice verso* of Caesar's thumbed fist at the Coliseum.

"Do you know what I am thinking Gasparov?" Gasparov's ashen face found no ally in the eyes coldly fixed on him around the table.

"I am thinking that I do not know if I can trust you, and that unsettles me. There is only room for the wholly committed in this enterprise. I should have hoped you would have known that. There is not room for anything less." He motioned with his hand to a guard standing some feet behind the scientist. "So that leaves us with little choice Ilyich Gasparov."

He gave a single nod to the guard who raised his rifle. Gasparov's eyes opened wide in alarm and shock as he opened his mouth to speak, but the noise that followed was not a human voice, it was the deafening staccato report of automatic gunfire from an AKM assault rifle. As the room echoed with the sudden shots, Gasparov fell forward onto the floor, his mouth still open in unspoken protest, his eyes a picture of terror, blood slowly beginning to form a dark stain on the floor. The room was silent.

As the guards removed the body, Karmonov spread out his hands.

"If a man cannot be trusted, he is of no value to us." It was a statement without any expectation of added comment and the others around the table obliged. Finn noticed one man whose grin indicated an approval for Karmonov's action that was clearly fanatical. The rest of the table was stony faced but Finn detected something else. It was fear.

"Before you... *leave* us," said Karmonov, his attention turning to the young couple before him, "you might explain just why you were caught prying outside this facility?"

Finn felt his own stomach churn with fear. Concentrating hard, he forced down the fatal emotions struggling within. It was a critical moment and how he replied would dictate their survival.

"We got careless I suppose," said Finn, shrugging. "Still, here we are before the great Viktor Karmonov, onetime colleague of Boris Nevotslov." He hoped his evenly delivered comments did not betray just how tense he actually was.

The room broke into a quiet burble of men's voices as the committee digested what had just been said.

"Do I know you?" asked Karmonov, his brow knotted in puzzlement.

"You should," said Finn. "You've been trying to kill me for long enough."

Slow realization dawned upon the Russian's face.

"Nevotslov's experiment!" he exclaimed. He quickly controlled his surprise. "You are very resourceful to have got this far. So it was you who killed Gurevich!"

Finn shook his head. "No, I was not sent to kill. Killers are a different breed altogether. Something you just demonstrated most convincingly."

"Sent?"

"Your whole plan. This facility, all of you. Boris saw further than you thought. He saw what you had in mind, you and this whole twisted room." The noise in the room increased. Voices raised in anger.

"It cannot succeed. It is mass murder on a scale so inhuman that it has destroyed your soul Karmonov. Yours and more." Finn looked at the faces pouring hate in his direction. "For what? A new world? What kind of a world will arise from such ashes, a better one? Death is no giver. It only takes. You are the architects of nothing other than destruction, including your own."

Anya was listening in awe. The voice she heard was Finn's, but the words were someone else's. She recognized the tone, the phrasing. Finn was delivering a message from a man whose words lived long after his death, and that man was her father.

Karmonov held up a hand and slowly the room quietened.

"Words. You sound like the fool Nevotslov himself. But words change nothing. Actions change history." He appealed to his comrades around him, his hands spread in mock acquiescence. "I will be kind to you both and grant you a few more minutes of life. Watch the screens. You are about to see our actions change the world. Three capital cities are about to fall into instant ruin. You shall witness what the future holds. More shall follow, even though you shall not live to see them."

A sequence of pre-arranged orders was given and controllers at the computer terminals began to respond. All vehicles and personnel were accounted for – nothing remained outside. At the entrance tunnel, three sets of mighty six-foot-thick airlock doors slowly slid across. They were spaced one hundred metres apart on the descending cavern and once locked would resist almost any arsenal of military attack. To add to the defence, explosives were set to collapse a kilometre of tunnel after the doors. Even a direct nuclear attack would be ineffective at such depth.

Just before the entombment was initiated, a door burst open and a military officer suddenly entered.

"We have infiltrators!" he shouted. "They are headed down to the docks!"

On the surface, Lebedev and Lander had managed to cut through the perimeter fence, and leaving their vehicle, crawled through the scrub in the fading light. They crept up to a truck that was parked outside a dark slit in an oddly shaped cliff wall. Four or five soldiers loitered about, smoking and kicking the gritty soil. Silently, the Russian and the Englishman sidled up the blind side of the truck. Lander moved forward and looked into the front cab. It was empty and he could see the keys still in the ignition. Silently he opened the door as Lebedev lay on his stomach, training his carbine under the truck toward the small group. They were stamping out their cigarettes and buttoning up their tunics. He nodded to Lander.

In a single movement, Jon was in the driver's seat, turning the key and sinking the accelerator pedal. The engine roared into life, diesel smoke erupting out of the vertical exhaust. Exposed now to the sight of the guards, he shoved the vehicle into gear and released the clutch as Lebedev let loose a burst of fully automatic 7.62mm bullets into the ground around the feet of the open-mouthed soldiers. As they dived for cover, Lebedev leapt onto the back and strafed the ground behind another burst. In front, Jon aimed straight for the entrance while behind him he could see Lebedev firing in his rear view mirror.

As the heavy truck began to pick up pace the soldiers quickly recovered and picking up their rifles, began returning fire at the receding truck. Bullets thudded into the rear of the vehicle and the side window shattered into a flying shower of glass across Lander's face.

Suddenly they were in a descending tunnel. In the jolting, bouncing truck, Lebedev tumbled forward into the seat beside Lander.

"There are crates of high explosive back there!" he shouted. "And I took cover behind them!"

There was nowhere else to go but down and as they hurtled down the smooth floor of the cavern, both men were astounded at the sheer immensity of the engineering project that was incorporated all around them.

There were hub points at different intervals where a choice needed to be taken. Lebedev would select an exit at these points. There were signs on the walls and Jon suspected his colleague was following a route. On a few occasions they would pass groups of men and buildings. They did not wait to see if they were followed, but kept relentlessly following the downward spiral.

"Where are we going?" shouted Lander as Lebedev pointed down a left turn.

Lebedev did not turn and kept looking straight ahead. "Into the Lion's Den my friend. Deep into his den!"

Without responding, Jon kept his concentration on the steeply descending road. Something about the journey suddenly suggested his descent into the Beerenburg. For the first time, it occurred to him to wonder if there might be some kind of a connection with the events on Jan Mayen.

"You seem to have some knowledge of this place Sergei," said Lander suspiciously. "Is there something I should know?"

"There were suspicions," replied Lebedev, checking the mirrors as he spoke. They were driving at breakneck speed, and the Russian was continually looking around as he spoke.

"When you told us about the sounds coming from deep below Jan Mayen," again he looked behind, "it seemed too much of a coincidence."

"A coincidence with what?"

"Information that certain missing naval assets had been taken to Kola. From Kola they disappeared."

"I don't see how..." He was interrupted by Lebedev.

"There was a reason the Americans and ourselves were drilling deep into the Earth Jon Lander."

"Apart from science you mean?"

"You will see if the rumours were true my friend. We will both see."

Suddenly the road split again and Lebedev shouted to him to stop. The one to the left seemed to level out. Lander thought he could see buildings lit up at the far end. The FSB man pointed to the right.

"Take this one, it is still going down. The sign says 'Operating Area.'" Lebedev put his head out the window and craned his neck back the way they had come.

"Go as fast as you can, they are bound to be right behind us." Lander's hand was already on the gearstick. He rammed the truck into gear and slammed his foot onto the throttle. Instantly they were swallowed into the darkness of the right hand tunnel.

The length of the descent was staggering to both men. How deep they were was impossible to gauge, but Lander knew they were miles, many miles below the surface. The deeper they got, the more oppressing became the sense of claustrophobic unease.

Here the tunnels appeared to be more natural. The walls and rock ceiling was a smooth volute, its glassy surface glinting with the truck's headlights. The floor however was clearly engineered; the steeper parts being laid with asphalt.

They drove on and on, the kilometres steadily increasing on the odometer. After what felt like hours, the descent suddenly began to level off.

"Here!" shouted Lebedev, pointing to a dark offshoot. It ran for a hundred metres before coming to a dead end.

"Leave the truck here," said the Russian. "I think we are almost at the bottom."

They got out and started to make their way on foot back to the main route. On impulse, the Russian ran back to the truck, returning half a minute later. He patted his backpack.

"Something that might come in useful later," he replied enigmatically to Lander's questioning look.

Keeping a close eye back up the tunnel, they quickly made their way downwards.

Five minutes later, they arrived and beheld a surreal sight. An unbelievable sight. It was a vast cavern, an odd green fluorescent light illuminating a shallow sandy plain which ended in a flat-mirrored sheet of water a hundred metres away. The water stretched out into the horizon without a visible end. Built on its shore was a huge dock. Along the concrete jetties lay dozens of strange submarine-like vessels. They sat still on the languid water, menacing in their black silence. They were floating on a sea of shimmering iridescent green that provided the eerie light in the cathedral cavern. The underground sea disappeared as far as he could see under the dark roof of the ceiling of rock above. Empty berths in the dock spoke of many dozens more that were gone, out into the world beneath the world above: Sent forth to lie below cities and nations which could not protect themselves from a death that could strike wantonly at any moment and at any place.

Men were milling about on or near the jetties. Others made their way purposefully from block-built buildings set into the cavern walls. Light spilled from windows onto the ground between the buildings and the docks where men were preparing the dark, sleek vessels for their guided journeys in the underground Styx.

They were both stunned by the sheer enormity of it all. Billions of roubles had to have been siphoned into the clandestine engineering feat that lay before their incredulous eyes. These were the wild speculations Lebedev had heard of in FSB headquarters at Lubyanka square. Speculations as secret as they were impossible. The sight before their eyes now made a lie of those impossibilities.

"Now what?" whispered Lander. "This is unbelievable!"

It was, but now he began to make a connection between what he was seeing and the mechanical noises deep below the Beerenburg on Jan

Mayen. His report to the Duma committee had unsettled them and yet at the same he failed to see why. Now the pieces of the jigsaw began to join together and the resultant picture was one of terrible horror. Somehow the Norwegian scientists, deep below the earth, had picked up the sounds of warfare being prepared in the secret caverns of the deep. Suddenly it made sense now why Johanssen and the others had been silenced.

"And the waters returned from off the earth continually... back into the fountains of the deep," murmured Lebedev, a wonder in his voice, He spoke in a voice almost too quiet for Lander to hear.

"What did you say?" he asked.

Lebedev shook his head. "Nothing. Something my *Babushka* taught me when such things were not spoken of."

Not knowing how to reply, Lander only nodded.

They needed some kind of information to know how next to proceed. Lebedev indicated for the Englishman to follow him.

Quietly slipping from shadow to shadow, they made their way toward a sleek hull that seemed to have the least activity about it. Lander's face was grim as he viewed the odd submarines. His recent experiences had not endeared him to such a mode of transport and he hoped Lebedev had no ideas in that direction. The Russian was quickly considering their options. He could not think of many and of those that he could, none had a good ending. He was about to whisper to Lander when suddenly a soldier appeared directly in front of them, his eyes open in surprise.

Jon was already moving. Before the soldier had time to react, Lander's pistol butt slammed across his head and he collapsed, unconscious to the ground. Lebedev quickly grabbed the man's legs and pulled him into the shadows of some barrels. He handed the soldier's assault rifle to Jon who took it while stuffing his pistol into his belt.

The FSB agent searched the man's tunic and among personal items, discovered a simple map. It was a hand-drawn plan of the subterranean complex. Lebedev studied it for a minute and then turned to Lander.

"We passed the Control Room on the way down," he said, pointing at the worn sheet of paper. "It could be where Karmonov and his cronies are." He looked at the map again and shrugged. "Or not."

Lander looked at the huge docks and then back toward the entrance to the tunnel that had brought them here.

"You go back," he said. "I'll check here. We haven't much time."

Lebedev nodded and then suddenly shook his head. "No," he said. "I've an idea. This man's uniform will help. You take the truck back and check where it branched off and levelled. I'll stay here."

"And where will we meet up again?" asked Lander. Lebedev gave a wan smile.

"You assume too much my friend. But we are wasting time. Go, and..." He suddenly grabbed Lander's hand in a firm grip. "May God be with you, Jon Lander."

Jon encountered no one in his furtive return up the steep tunnel. Ten minutes later he was at the truck. Turning it in the wide shaft, he gunned the powerful engine and began the drive back up the underground road.

Lebedev was not a thin man and the soldier's uniform was a tight fit, but it gave him some kind of cover for his next move. Straightening himself, he marched onto the dock and headed for the nearest slender submarine.

~~~~~~~~~~~~

"We must initiate now!" shouted a voice. It was Geim, his eyes alight with fanatical fervour. "Quickly, Viktor – give the command!"

Finn suddenly turned to Karmonov and held out his hands.

"At least tell me how you did it," he asked, "how you created all this..." he motioned around with his hands, "this feat of engineering, without being detected." He was stalling for time, but he gambled that Karmonov's vanity would be piqued.

"We discovered this geo-physical abnormality long ago. Even before we built the Kolskya Superdeep."

"Just kill them Viktor," complained Geim. "They are nothing."

"It amuses me Iosef," shrugged Karmonov, "and do not worry. We cannot be stopped now. I would relish mocking the fool Nevotslov by disclosing our triumph to his daughter and his lackey before having them silenced."

He turned back to Finn and Anya. "When the USSR began to drill, it was partly to discover how widespread was the fissure. It was also to cover our real operation. Over decades we uncovered the route to the hidden sea and made the system of roads and rail. The Superdeep explained the heaps of spoil. No-one thought to ask why so much. With the breakup of our once proud republic, that disaster paradoxically provided the means. The once proud Black Sea fleet of nuclear submarines, now rusting in Ukrainian ports were now able to be transported for decommissioning. The body that organised that was loyal to the United World Soviet. If you haven't guessed it by now, they weren't decommissioned. Along with specially built missile carriers, we are able to strike below the soft underbelly of any nation on Earth. An attack for which there can be no defence."

As Karmonov spoke, Finn suddenly recognised the clearly pre-written patterns in his mind. He turned to Karmonov and raised his voice.
"Boris Nevotslov saw this. He knew the evil you had formulated. He made a weapon to stop you and I will use it!"
Karmonov looked at Finn and grinned. "What have you got you idiot? A nuclear warhead in your pocket?" he laughed a single loud cruel laugh. Others joined in and laughed derisorily at Finn.
"No," said Finn firmly. "*I* am that weapon."
Finn looked toward the large screen and saw that it was operated by some technicians at a large console set apart from the wall and close to his end of the table behind Karmonov. Karmonov gave the order to detonate the three atomic weapons placed months before in the underground sea and miles below the cities identified by red circles on the huge maps on the display. As he did so, Finn narrowed his eyes and concentrated. He fixed upon images of faint neural signals travelling in the synaptic pathways of the two at the console and blocked their activity with a powerful resonance of his own. Immediately they fell forward, heads thumping off the keys on their keyboards before falling sideways to the floor. As the committee members jumped to their feet, Finn turned and saw the room light up with a ghostly dancing pattern of electrical stimuli and pulsating wispy threads in flickering colours indescribable. He was seeing the invisible threads of neural activity; microvolts emanating from the synapses sparking in the room. Caused by a multitude of acetylcholine receptors opening and altering the nerve cell potentials in the brains of the men in the room, Finn's ability to receive and interfere with the incredibly weak voltage was the result of an accident years before in an Irish Sea, defined and enabled by the father of the girl beside him.

"None of you move!" he shouted. "I can short-circuit your nervous systems from here; just I did with those two men. One move, just one move and you will live the rest of your lives as mindless dribbling idiots!" He doubted if he could affect so many at one time, or anyone not close to him. Nonetheless he gambled on their belief that he could.

Everyone froze in uncomprehending torpor. Two men lay on the ground, writhing around and foaming at the mouth. Finn held them in his grip. Suddenly a strangely calm voice spoke.

"You simple fool," said Karmonov, the corner of his mouth a snarling smirk. "Did you think you were the only one?" His eyes rolled back and Finn immediately what felt like a kick inside his head. He reeled back but managed to keep his feet. He looked up and saw Karmonov's eyes return into a vicious stare, filled with detestation for all it beheld.

"You forgot, didn't you, that Nevotslov and I worked together? Yes, I knew about the effects of Ringwoodite, and yes, I too have been exposed to its... *enhancements.*"

As Finn's eyes opened in shocked realisation, Karmonov spread out his hands to the room.

"He can do nothing more comrades," he assured the unknowing onlookers. "He surprised me with his unexpected trick, but with me here, you are all safe. Please, take your seats."

One by one the committee sat down, incomprehension still written on their faces. Karmonov moved forward to the console. The execute order was awaiting initiation on the screen. He leaned forward and went to execute the final command protocol. Suddenly - his finger poised over the keyboard, he paused and turned.

"Destiny can wait for a few minutes," he said to the group. "This man was programmed, to use a blunt word, to assassinate our cause. His neural activity is such that he could create a surge within another's nervous system, a surge that can at least temporarily paralyse. The traitor Nevotslov planned it. When I uncovered his intentions to sabotage our glorious future – though I did not fully know how until now, I had him executed. He thought himself a clever man. I almost wish he could see his pathetic failure now." He put his hand into his jacket and withdrew a stubby revolver. One hand still poised over the console, with the other he raised the gun and pointed it directly at Finn. As the committee began to realise the weight of the danger that had been averted and the supreme pre-eminence of the man before them, a spontaneous applause began to rise around the table. Karmonov basked in his glory, nodding beneficently from man to man. Nevotslov, instead of preventing The Program, had merely cemented himself as the undisputed future head of the certain empire about to be birthed into existence.

"And now," exclaimed Karmonov, "we unleash the gates of hell!"

"Stop!" shouted a voice in English, immediately followed by a loud gunshot. Everyone froze as all eyes looked incredulously to a side door. It was filled by the shape of a man and he was holding an assault carbine in his hands. Smoke seeped from its barrel as the man stepped forward into the room.

Even Karmonov looked shocked.

"Sorry, I will have to kill you if you touch that," said Lander, pointing the gun at Karmonov. He looked toward Finn. "Tell him to drop the revolver old man, will you?" he said, indicating with his weapon toward the Russian. Finn obediently spoke his words to Karmonov who had already understood Lander's English.

"Another British meddler?" he queried, indicating Lander. "This is getting to be quite repetitive."

At that moment there was a mechanical *click-clack* from the main entrance door. The officer who had announced the infiltration had slipped back in, unnoticed and now was standing some twenty metres away, aiming a pistol directly at Lander.

Karmonov, still pointing his firearm at Finn, looked from one to the other and smiled. He nodded toward his officer pointing his pistol across the room at Lander.

"So, now what? It seems we have... what is it called? ...a Mexican standoff?"

"Perhaps," said Lander, "but it's a long shot for him. Either his or your finger so much as twitches and you're a dead man for sure," said Lander smoothly.

"Perhaps," said Karmonov, "Unless he is quicker than you. Either way your death will instantly follow and my deputy will merely complete the sequence, admittedly one I'd prefer to do myself, but one I'm quite willing to die for. After all, we none of us live forever." His finger still hung motionless over the computer keyboard.

There was a silence in the room. The guard had his pistol trained on Lander, Lander his carbine on Karmonov and Karmonov's on Finn.

Geim's eyes were darkly alight with the sudden realisation that greatness was suddenly a possibility being thrust into his hands.

"Finn?" asked Lander, his weapon and eyes still fixed on Karmonov.

Finn nodded uselessly as he replied. His mind was still numb with Karmonov's mental counter.

"Yes, I'm sorry, you must be... *who* must you be?"

"Sort of MI5," replied Lander. He kept his face toward the Russian. "I'm running out of ideas here though. Got any yourself?"

Before Finn had a chance to reply, he felt Anya's hand slip into his own. To his sudden shock, he felt a pulse of neural energy rush from her into himself. What could this be? He probed her mind. He was stunned to detect a heightened level in her own brain activity! He thought quickly. It must have come from handling the Ringwoodite. She had mentioned the Ultra-violet reaction. She was probably unaware of it and the mental stress had released it. His thoughts racing, he did a rapid calculation. The sums teetered on the possible. If he were to fully discharge his own synaptic energy at Karmonov, bolstered with Anya's unsuspecting support, it might be possible...

Finn knew that the phenomenon had allowed his brain to be capable of containing a hugely abnormal charge of neural energy. The surprise of Karmonov's counter had temporarily shocked him. Facing a mind capable of defending itself, it seemed Boris' long laid plans were in tatters, the hope of neutralising Karmonov in ruins. Suddenly another option introduced itself. With the small boost from Anya, perhaps Finn could break through his insulating defence. Karmonov had come closer, now that he was poised at the console.

He also knew that the effort would in all likelihood kill him. He doubted he could survive such a rapid discharge from his brain. It would be like shorting a huge voltage across a thinly insulated wire. The voltage might pass, but not without leaving behind melted plastic and destroying the wiring irrevocably. His was one life however, and millions would die if he did nothing.

He realised then that there was no choice to make.

He turned back to Lander and fixing his thoughts, formed coherent signals within Lander's primary auditory cortex. To Lander, it was as if he was thinking a voice within his head, but not words of his own creation. The voice was without accent or tone, and although his mind was wheeling at the idea, Lander somehow knew Finn was responsible.

"You need to neutralise the guard," said the thought. *"I will take care of Karmonov."*

Lander tried not to look shocked as he faced Finn's meaningful stare. As if to confirm the words, Finn gave a barely perceptible nod.

"Now!" he said suddenly.

It was like slow motion. Lander dropped, spinning as he did so, simultaneously releasing a burst of fire at the pistol toting guard. He went down, releasing two shots into the room as he fell. Karmonov opened his mouth but nothing came out, instead his head jerked back and his body was flung backwards, eyes huge and shocked as he toppled over his chair and landed in a grotesque fashion onto the floor. His revolver spun uselessly onto the floor. Finn immediately crumpled like a puppet with severed strings to the ground. He lay where he fell, unmoving and deadly still. Anya dropped to her knees but stayed conscious. Geim fell forward onto the table, a hole in his head the sign of where one of the stray pistol rounds had found a home.

Quickly recovering, Lander covered the room with his carbine and barked at one of the techs to lock the main door lest other soldiers arrive. He either understood the language of English or that of a pointed gun. Either way he did as he was told. Karmonov was twitching and clearly no more threat. The rest of the room was either paralysed or powerless.

For now.

~~~~~~~~~~~~

The Norwegian survey ship, the M.V. Fugro Discovery was purpose built for the Norwegian Navy to perform various types of hydrological surveys. Being permanently mobilised, it was currently ostensibly completing a hydrographical survey in the inlet of Varangerfjorden at the north of Norway. A mere thirty nautical miles from the Russian border, it had been in the area for almost two weeks and had lost the interest of the Russian observers at Polyarny.

It had been investigating a possible cable route survey for a Norwegian telecoms company across the fjord. Unknown to the company and the base at Polyarny, that survey had finished some days earlier. Also unknown to both parties was what was happening beneath the ship as it made a slow circle in the fjord. Norwegian Navy specialists boarded the ship at night in a silenced rib and sequestered the ship for the Royal Norwegian Navy. The crew were told they were now under naval orders and promised compensation. When they were given certain details of the mission to which they were now part, every man dismissed any need of compensation. All Norwegians, no one complained and as one man, enthusiastically agreed to serve as required. They were proud to do so.

It was a delicate piece of ship-handling, but, like the airborne refuelling of an aircraft, carefully coordinated movements were critical to allow the placement of what it was they were going to hide.

Now lying directly beneath the seventy-metre-long ship was a ninety-seven-metre-long submarine of the Royal Navy. HMS Astute, a nuclear powered attack submarine lay danger-close under the hull of the survey ship. As requested, the M.V. Fugro Discovery's skipper was exactly mirroring the movements being relayed to him of the boat below his hull. As ordered, his Edgetech 4200 side-scanning sonar was active, its purpose no longer to survey, but to mask the movements of the vessel under the ship.

On board HMS Astute, Commodore Legge himself gritted his teeth. He had been involved in more than one covert mission in his life, but this was like no other. He was not commanding the boat, but neither could he expect Astute's captain to shoulder all the responsibility for the hours ahead on his own shoulders. He had made it clear he was only a passenger, but the sub's captain was glad of the Commodore's presence. It was a weight shared.

At the three o'clock point on the survey ship's slow circle, she was no more than five nautical miles from the invisible sea border. In two more circles time, she would head due east and cross into Russian waters. Then the obfuscations would begin.

Lebedev managed to slip back off the slender hull without being seen. A large two-story building at the cavern wall was his next objective. Without attempting to hide, he walked as confidently as he could across to the door. It was unlocked. Inside the entrance was a layout of the premises on the wall. He quickly found what he wanted and made his way upstairs.

Entering the room, three sets of eyes looked up. There was an immediate confusion, made all the more so when Lebedev pointed his rifle at them. One man made to make for a weapon on a rack to his left. Lebedev shot him.

"Anyone else?" he said coldly. There was no reply. He looked at the screens and arrays. Before he went any further, he had a few questions he needed to ask. Before he finally got his answers, another man had to die. He hated killing - violently detested it but he reminded himself, there was a time to kill and a time to heal. The second came after the first, if the latter would ever come again. Still, that knowledge did not take away the unspeakable sorrow a sane man feels when having no choice than to take the life of another.

~~~~~~~

On board Air Force One, the VC-25B was circling out over the Atlantic as the president broke the biscuit containing the Gold Codes. He was about to read and have the launch codes confirmed when a top priority message suddenly came in from the British Prime Minister.
"It's too late now sir," said the Secretary of Defence. "Once we commence this action, the protocol is clear."
The president looked to the Chairman of the Joint Chiefs of Staff. He was holding the phone in an outstretched arm. The Secretary of Defence broke his biscuit. The phone hung between them. Suddenly the president caught sight of his personal secretary. She had her head bowed at a window.
"Give me the phone!" he barked. The Secretary of Defence began to protest but was dismissed by a hand from the president. He listened as the Prime Minster rapidly passed on information that sent a shiver down his spine. Finishing the call, he turned to the room.
"The British know where the attacks are coming from."
"Then let's get this over with," exclaimed the Secretary of Defence.
"No," said the president. "They need us to wait."
"Wait?" cried the Secretary, "Wait for what? The annihilation of Washington?"
The president put the broken tablet containing the codes in his pocket. "I've given him one hour."

Alex Harker-Bell burst into Sir Simon's office. Jonas was there, conferring with his boss.
"What in this world do you think you're doing!" he demanded, his voice filled with anger. "Don't you know what you've done?"
Sir Simon was unflustered. "What do you mean," he asked evenly.

"COBRA," Harker-Bell sputtered. "You've persuaded the P.M. not to capitulate immediately. Are you mad? We have no other option you fools! London, Washington. Millions will die, this is a war crime! We *must* yield!"

Jonas' brow furrowed for a moment. "How did you know the targets Alex?"

"Everyone knows," spat back the older man, "how could I not know?"

"No, not everyone," said Jonas slowly. "Only those few at COBRA and you weren't one of them. So either someone present told you – which was expressly forbidden - or you knew already."

"What are you inferring Smythe?" spat Harker-Bell.

"If you can't explain how you knew at least two of the three targets, then I don't need to infer anything," said Jonas.

As he spoke, Sir Simon was already on the phone.

"Security – my office immediately," he said.

In the control room, Anya knelt down beside Finn. She could not detect a pulse and he was not breathing. Lander was covering the room and could not assist as Anya began CPR on the man she had loved.

There was no other sound in the room but the noise of Anya's efforts, punctuated by her repressed sobs.

"Come on Finn!" she shouted between her tears as she pummelled his chest. "Don't leave me now, don't leave me Finn, don't leave me!"

Suddenly a soldier appeared at the side door behind Lander. Lander swung his rifle around and heard his friend shout out.

"It is me, don't shoot, Jon Lander!"

"I've got a pulse!" shouted Anya.

Lebedev had a jeep outside. He carried Finn as Lander covered their retreat. As they rushed out of the door, Lander saw a movement out of the corner of his eye. The movement was over before he had time to do anything about it. Seizing the moment, a technician had rushed to the main console and executed the launch command. Lander's mind screamed with sudden realisation.

They had failed.

Finn was bundled into the back. Anya cradled his head in her knees as Lebedev took the driver's seat. For Lander there was nothing to do, nothing to undo. He leapt into the jeep and Lebedev gunned the engines and headed for the surface.

It was a long frantic uphill race. There were a couple of attempts to thwart their escape, but it was spontaneous and uncoordinated. After what seemed hours of reckless careering, they came to the first of the blast doors. Lebedev leapt out and operated the unlock panels. Lander took over driving and at each of the following doors, Lebedev, who seemed to have gotten some information on the operation of the exit, punched in the keys to let them through. As they passed, the doors immediately closed behind them. Seconds later they burst out of the entrance into the pallid sunlight.

"Drive as hard and fast as you can!" shouted Lebedev, "There are only seconds left!"

He had no sooner spoken than the earth beneath them rose and flung them, jeep and all, five metres into the air. Crashing to the broken ground, they were flung out as a huge curtain of dust and dirt fell on them like the broken gates of Hades.

~~~~~~~~

"It's Legge," said Jonas Smythe. "There has been an event near the north Finnish-Russian border," he said breathlessly.

He had rushed in from the Thames house communications centre that was patched in to into GCHQ.

Sir Simon looked up, his face expectant and tense.

"An event?"

"A massive seismic concussion concurrent with a nuclear attack!"

"Who, the Americans?"

It was the worst of scenarios; the USA had struck first. Probably the Russian Northern Fleet was their target in Severomorsk or Polyarny. It was the beginning of the end.

"The Americans have denied it," replied Jonas. "It appears to be the Russians themselves."

"The Russians have dropped missiles on themselves? What are you saying Jonas?"

"HMS Astute was shaken. She was about to send the marines ashore when a tidal wave almost turned her over. M.V. Fugro barely made it. It came from near the Kola Superdeep."

"The Chinese?"

"No launches detected sir," replied Jonas. "What about the marines?"

"Tell Legge to proceed. We've gone this far. May as well be hanged for a sheep as a lamb."

Two miles in, the marines, riding their purpose-built raiding quads, came across the jeep and its occupants. Anya was weeping. Finn was held in her arms. Lander was bleeding from a deep gash in his side. Only Lebedev seemed relatively unhurt, though somewhat concussed. The soldiers took the girl along with Lander and Finn at Lebedev's insistence. He assured the captain that he should remain. He was needed in Kola. The others needed help.

So the three were taken aboard the waiting British submarine. With Russian shore and deep sea sensors largely disabled by the massive underground explosions, the captain of Astute was able to slip back into the quietness of the Barents Sea and Norwegian waters. Her presence and action would remain unknown, unrewarded and unspoken of except among a very small group of tight-lipped servants of the crowns of Norway and Great Britain. Certain sailors on board a Norwegian survey ship were to find bonuses in their wages some months later that allowed the older to retire and the younger to pay off mortgages. This too was never spoken of.

On board Air Force One, the president took a further call from the British Prime Minister. He visibly trembled on his knees and then bowed his head as he closed the call. The destruction hour had passed. There was utter silence in the aircraft as a visceral wave of relief crashed across the tangible intensity of the moments before. Suddenly there were cries and shouts of joy. Armageddon was spent on the shores of redemption.

The populations of London, Washington and Beijing carried on their daily lives, unaware of how close to utter ruin they had come. It seemed certain that the explosive event near the Russian border in north Kola had something to do with it. Russian Special forces had arrived and were saturating the area. Moscow assured the governments of the world that they had the crisis under control.

Lebedev nursed the broken jeep the several kilometres to the Kolskaya Superdeep where he was able to make calls to Lubyanka and the Russian State Duma. As he awaited the arrival of the 2nd Spetsnatz Brigade and *Kombrig* Kormiltsev, he slowly exhaled a long sigh before pulling out an old tattered Bible from his inside pocket, a gift of his grandmother from a time long ago. He opened it to the well-worn pages of the twenty third Psalm.

"Yea, though I walk through the valley of the shadow of death," He read aloud to himself, *"I will fear no evil: for Thou art with me."*

He sat with his tired head bowed in the stillness in the complex, accompanied by the cruelly silenced evidences of the evil of that shadowed valley. In the depth of long gone reminiscences, his eyes glistened as he recalled the voice of his grandmother reading the familiar words to him so long ago.

In that sacred silence he sat, surrounded at last by a peace that defied earthly explanation.

Chapter 43
Life after death

HMS Astute's captain had been given instructions by Navy Command to observe and record activities in the area of the Russian Northern Fleet. Doing so under extreme close quarters and in such a technically difficult manner had been the most demanding command of his life. Having a Commodore on board made him feel that his every move was being watched and weighed. Paradoxically, his presence was also reassuring. When the commodore had requested the landing of the party of marines, he had been astounded. When he further explained that it was not an order but a request, his astonishment was compounded by perplexity.

Something about the way he was asked however had convinced the captain that although Navy Command may not have authorised it, someone had. Determining whether to follow orders or to trust the shrouded will of a man he respected above all others finally swung the balance.

When a few hours later the shore party returned with the two men and a girl, he ventured an explanation from the senior officer.

"These people have probably saved the world, captain," was his fantastic reply. "In saving them, you and your crew have done as great a service to humanity as history will never be able to record."

"I don't understand commodore."

Legge looked into the space between them and saw his own memories.

"It is the curse of duty, to be asked to do things we only partly comprehend," replied Legge. "When I was younger, I knew without doubt that deeds done behind the scenes were tainted with duplicity and lacking in honour. Now that I am older, I have learned that nothing is so certain, so simple. I do know this; that the true acts of valour are often done by those who play their part off the stage. That behind those who perform in the spotlight are the unseen others. Men and women who do not play for an audience's applause or a victor's wreath but because there are things that simply must be done. Things without which there would be no stage at all. And so the audience applauds its sparkling heroes, unaware of the true turners of the wheel. The people who allow the rest of us to live without the shackles of daily fear."

"And these three are those others?"

Legge looked up at the younger man. Men like him, like Captain Currie, were his younger self. Men filled with a sense of the noble virtue of unbending duty and obedient service.

"Yes," nodded Legge, "and we may never fully know just what they have achieved, and at what personal cost." He saw the captain slowly nod.

"I asked you to disobey orders today. A captain of the Royal Navy always follows orders. That you did not do so was an act of betrayal." He hesitated for the briefest of seconds before continuing. "It was also absolutely the right thing to have done. When anyone can square that circle then perhaps such acts can be made public."

"But, until then, it never happened," said the captain, a hint of an understanding smile on the edge of his mouth.

Legge out his hand on the young man's shoulder. "You are a good man captain. Better than I ever was."

HMS Astute was back in HMNB Clyde at Faslane four days later. Finn did not recover consciousness during the sailing. His pulse remained weak and the surgeon withheld his opinion that he doubted if he would survive as far as Scotland. Lander was sedated for the first day. He had suffered several lacerations and broken ribs. A long gash in his side took the ship's surgeon several hours to work on. When he was finished he assured Jon that he would have a lifelong reminder of his survival at Kola. There were over two hundred sutures.

Anya was concussed and suffered lacerations and a broken wrist. As soon as the break was set and the plaster dry, she insisted on returning to Finn's bedside. She did not leave him during the entire journey, and remained constantly by his side.

At Faslane Finn was taken by ambulance to Glasgow Royal Infirmary. His consultant was Doctor Robert Jamieson.

Lander and Legge saw little of one another. On the second day out from Kola, the commodore was transferred to HMS Albion. From there he was flown by helicopter to Scatsa Airport on the Shetlands. From there he transferred again to an Islander and flew to Aberdeen. That night he was back in London.

Lebedev was waiting when the 2nd Spetsnatz Brigade arrived. Two days later, he was back in Lubyanka Square. For three whole days he was questioned on every detail of what had been done and seen. The debriefing was rigorous and at the end of it he was invited not to leave Moscow until he was no longer required. He was too exhausted in any case. He had no intention of going anywhere other than his apartment and specifically, the bed awaiting him there.

The Russian President made a glorious speech about the victory of the Federation and the utter defeat of a small group of conspirators who had threatened its democratically elected government. His approval rating soared. There were those in the State Duma however who privately wondered how he might have reacted had the New United World Soviet succeeded. Some envisaged a similar victory speech coming from the same mouth.

There was a purge of senior commanders at Severomorsk and Polyarny. Some were put to public disgrace for failing to act in a moment of national crisis. They were the lucky ones.

Arkhangelsk Technical University was closed. When it reopened over a year later, students were to find that most of the senior faculty had retired or resigned. Certainly they were no longer on campus. The students cared little. Who their professors were was of little importance when their own futures were the main occupation of their dreams.

The natural disasters at Hainan and Indian Springs elicited a multinational aid relief programme. A dual tectonic plate shift was declared to have been the cause. Trusted popular scientists appeared on television, confirming the statements of government geologists from Washington and Beijing. It was a once in a thousand years' phenomenon, they said; a totally unique event. Thus assured, the concerned public gave a collective sigh and moved on.

No one noticed that the main contributors to the massive financial and infrastructural aid came from countries that interestingly, were all nuclear powers.

After a month most of the world forgot about the devastation in places far away and they returned to following the divorces and marriages of the celebrities whose lives were a backdrop to their other preoccupations.

~~~~~~~

Finn lay unresponsive, a patient in the same ward where he had spent eleven years in a coma. Anya visited every day. She was staying temporarily at the home of John and Helen McGregor. Jack was back in Glasgow and his wife instantly hit it off with the young Russian whom she found delightful company even if she spent most of her time at the Royal.

Dr Jamieson had been able to talk with Anya who had told him about the strange substance that had brought about the profound neurological phenomena in Finn. It got him to immerse himself in a particular line of investigations that led to a conversation with the inspector a week later. In the meantime, Finn had opened his eyes and was beginning to respond to external stimuli. When he saw Anya beside the bed, he smiled and managed to squeeze her hand.

"I had understood his abnormal electrical activity would most likely radiate outside the confines of his cerebrum," explained Dr Jamieson, "but it never occurred to me that his neural pathways would be as powerful in acting as receptors as much as transmitters."

"You mean, he could pick up outside stimuli?" asked Jack, hoping he was understanding the doctor correctly. "Mind-reading? Isn't that science fiction?"

"Have you heard of Magnetoreception?" asked the consultant. Jack shook his head.

"It is a sense that some animals possess. Homing pigeons for example. The birds use it to navigate over hundreds and thousands of miles. There was a comprehensive study into the common Robin. It is able to see the earth's actual magnetic field through its eyes. Proponents suggest that the bird is able to visualise quantum entanglement of electron spins. There is a cryptochrome protein in the human eye which has baffled the medical world for years. It could be linked."

"Sorry, lost me at quantum," smiled Jack, "but you think it helps explain Finn's unique ability?"

"What are thoughts?" asked the doctor, "except electrical firing at synapses within the brain. Although the voltage is minute, if Finn could receive the neurotransmissions, perhaps some physical mechanism within his salience network was capable of disentangling the variations of voltage back into coherent thought. A telephone does nothing less. It would explain how he was able to know what someone was reading as they were reading it for example."

Jack thought back to the accounts given to him from the Presbyterian minister. It could also explain how Finn had known his own rank and surname when he purposefully had not supplied it to him.

Dr Jamieson stood up from his desk. "He is sitting up in bed now. I could let you see him for a few minutes?"

When Jack entered, he could see Anya close beside Finn on the far side of his bed. She sat back with a wide smile as the two men entered the room.

"Finn is talking!" she said excitedly. Finn grinned and waved at the doctor and the policeman.

"Sort of," he said thickly. "Anya says I've been asleep for a week?"

"Says the man who can sleep for eleven years," observed Jack drily, but with a large smile on his own face.

"How are you feeling Allen?" asked the doctor.

"Oh, *Finn* is fine doctor," said the patient. "A bit groggy. My head pounds if I try to get out of bed."

"I told him not to!" said Anya quickly.

"Good advice from this very attentive and very pretty young lady," said the doctor with a wink. "So you know who you are and where you are?"

Finn nodded. "Yes, I know who I am. At last, I know who I am."

Dr Jamieson walked with Jack to the main exit. Just he was about to leave, the detective passed on an observation.

"He's got older," he said. "He looks as if he has aged several years."

Dr Jamieson nodded. "I thought so myself," he agreed. "Perhaps time has caught up with him somehow. Another mystery to unravel."

"One you can leave me out of this time!" replied his friend, wagging his finger in front of the doctor's face. Dr Jamieson merely winked and both men stood and laughed.

Some tests followed over the next week. Finn's brain scans did not report any anomalies. His electrical activity was normal. It was conjectured that the trauma of his final effort at the secret base had somehow expended the energy that had resided within his head.

There followed meetings with MI5. Jonas was detailed to debrief his account but Sir Simon Montague himself made the trip up to Glasgow to see the son of Captain Robert Finlay. It was a personal visit and he and Finn met privately in Jack and Helen's front room for a couple of hours. Jonas noticed that when the two men emerged, both bore signs of a wateriness about the eyes that indicated it had been an emotional tête-à-tête.

Legge finally met Lander when he was in Gosport. The commodore was inspecting a new frigate and received a call from the agent just as he was getting into his car. They met in the Isambard Kingdom Brunel pub-restaurant in the centre of Portsmouth. Their handshake was the grip of old friends.

"You're looking a lot better than last I saw you," smiled the commodore. Lander laughed.

"I feel a lot better. I need to thank you. You took a big personal risk in what you did."

"I did nothing," he replied, "Nothing that will be recorded in any case."

"Welcome to my world," smiled Jon. "We'll make a spy of you yet."

They stayed until closing time. They had a lot to talk about.

Jack had one more visit to London. He had to present his final investigative report at Thames House. Afterward, he and Jonas took a walk along the embankment.

"How long until you retire?" said Jonas suddenly. They had been recounting the events that had led to the unmasking of Alex-Harker Bell. The exposed agent was going to go to prison for a very long time. He had fully expected the capitulation of the world governments to Karmonov's demands, and it had explained why he had remained in London. He had been promised the position of regional head of the United World Soviet in what was to have been the British Soviet

Islands.

"Oh... I don't... I'll have the thirty done in under two years. Not sure if I'll hand up the boots or not. I suppose I'll know nearer the time."

"What are you, forty-seven or so? Still a young man Jack." Jonas stopped and addressed his colleague.

"We have a place here for you if you're interested."

"What, me? MI5, in London?"

"We need men like you Jack. Men who tirelessly work the details. You wouldn't have to move you know. A day or two a week here at the most. You could still base yourself at Glasgow if you wanted."

Jack was about to dismiss the offer when he thought for a moment.

"I would need to ask Helen," he said. "She comes before my work."

"Absolutely," smiled Jonas. "There's no rush. Even if it's a year or two away, the offer is still there. Think about it though Jack."

"I will," he replied. "I'll think about it."

And he knew then that he would.

Lander waited at the open air crêperie on the Jardin Des Tuilieries in Paris. The heat made a shimmer of the buildings across the other side of the Seine. Families and young couples sauntered by on the dusty gravel of the park and small birds flitted through the shade of the trees above his head.

He was watching the sun glint off the glass pyramid at the Louvre when a shadow crossed his view.

"I hope you have ordered one for me Jon Lander," said a familiar voice.

"They don't make them in Beef Stroganov," said Lander, looking up at Lebedev. "You're not in Russia now."

Lebedev smiled and sat down. "No, I suppose I'm not. It is warmer here my friend, yes?"

"All the more so for seeing you alive and well Sergei. It is good to see you old man."

"And you my English friend. You did not look so good last time I saw you."

"It's that country of yours. Shooting me was bad enough, blowing me up was quite uncalled for."

Lebedev grinned. He took a seat and they both regarded one another for a moment.

"We did well, did we not?"

"We did Sergei. Not that anyone will know much about it, but yes, I think we did better than we could have hoped."

"The area around the Kolskaya Superdeep will be out of bounds for a long time. There was nothing left of the underground facility. Everything was buried in billions of tonnes of rock.

"How did you do it Sergei?"

"Explosives from the truck. I placed them in a submarine. It must have started a chain reaction."

"One thing I don't understand. Karmonov initiated the warheads. Why didn't they detonate?"

"There was a control hub near the underground sea." His face suddenly darkened. "I had to kill two men to discover how to cut the signals." He sighed. "It does not sit easy with me Jon Lander."

"I know, my friend. I know."

They talked for a while until Jon looked at his watch. "I have someone I'd like you to meet Sergei. Here he comes now."

A large, blond haired giant of a man strode up and stood erect at their table. He grinned and pulled up a chair.

"This is my friend Oversersjant Ari Bjørnson," he said to Lebedev, as the big Norwegian grasped Lander's hand in a fervent welcome. "Good to see you Ari. Meet Sergei Lebedev."

"Russian?" scowled the Norwegian turning toward the FSB man.

"Yes, and my very good friend. *Our* very good friend."

As Ari recounted what had happened after the explosion, Lander was glad to hear that Henrik Jensen had survived. He had a long road of recovery ahead of him, but the prognosis was good. He shook his head in amazement when Jon related some of the history of events from his gunfight at the Beerenburg. As he listened to how Lebedev had rescued him from the rebels, his anti-Russian sentiment dissolved into appreciation.

"It seems to me," he said, catching Sergei's eye, "that this man isn't safe to be let loose on his own. Every time I see him he's either being or has just been, rescued!"

As the three men chatted, talk turned to laughter. The laughter of those who have looked into the face of almost certain death and despite the odds, have together survived.

Passersby heard the laughter and smiled. Men joking about women, or sport or drink. They could not know that they were laughing with joy at the salvation of a world.

Finn took Anya to Northern Ireland at the invite of Alastair & Ruth Boyd. The manse was large and Ruth had prepared two guest rooms for the couple. Finn and Anya stayed for a week and in that time James Kitching, Anne McCracken's brother, came over from Penrith.

The McCracken farm had been willed to their son, Andrew. Following a long series of legal involvement, it became the property of Mr Kitching. He had been considering selling it until he heard of the return of Finn.

Within an hour of arriving at the manse, the old man held out an envelope. It was the deed and title for the farm. The new owner was one Allen Finlay from Ardrossan.

With it came the greater proportion of the money that had been hidden in the wall. James Kitching and his wife insisted Finn have it to keep despite every earnest protestation he made.

The farmhouse was eventually rebuilt and when its new occupiers entered it was as Mr and Mrs Allen and Anya Finn, married some months earlier at Donaghadee Prebyterian by Alastair Boyd himself.

Locals were to talk for years about the guests at the wedding. Strangers from Scotland as well as London, Norway and Russia of all places. Donaghadee hadn't seen anything like it in years and it provided stories that increased in their telling, but never quite surpassing the actual truth, had they but known.

A year after the wedding, the happiest couple in the peninsula had a son. People wondered at his middle name. They called him Tom Rogov Finlay.

Anya would sometimes wonder if her Finn could still read her mind. He told her he couldn't.
She was never so sure.

On Jan Mayen the facilities at Olonkinbyen have been rebuilt. A coronal mass ejection - the Carrington Event, has yet to happen. The scientific consensus is unanimous. It won't be long.

THE TOTAL SUM

Acronyms and Terms used:

CCTV – Closed Circuit Television.

CISS - Communication and Information Systems Specialist.

DV – Developed Vetting. The highest form of security clearance within the United Kingdom. Personnel who have DV clearance have access to TOP SECRET information. The process to vet someone to such a trusted security level is a long and expensive process. It involves a thorough investigation into that person's personal life, including finances, relationships and many intimate details of their lives.

Direction Centrale des Renseignements Généraux – Intelligence section of the French Police, usually referred to as the RG. Now merged with *the Direction de la surveillance du territoire,* and renamed, it had four sub-directorates, one of which was responsible for the prevention of terrorism.

D.O.R's – Duty Officer's Reports – Daily morning briefings on previous day's police incidents.

ETA – Estimated Time of Arrival.

FARC – The Revolutionary Armed Forces of Colombia – People's Army. A guerrilla terrorist grouping in Colombia with its roots in Marxist-Leninism.

FSB – The Federal Security Service of the Russian Federation. Formerly the KGB and based in that organisations former headquarters at Lubyanka Square in Moscow, it is mainly concerned with internal security. It is also considered a military service, though its officers do not wear uniform.

GCHQ – Government Communications Headquarters. The United Kingdom's security and intelligence centre which provides intelligence from signals and communication information to the UK government.

GPS – Global Positioning Satellite.

GRU – Russia's largest intelligence agency. GRU stands for the The Main Directorate of the General Staff of the Armed Forces of the Russian Federation. The GRU is the military intelligence section of the General Staff, tasked with the collation and analysis of foreign intelligence. Although the FSB and SVR are answerable to the Russian president, the GRU reports to the Minister of Defense.

IED – Improvised Explosive Device.

LORAN-C – A low frequency transmitting system in the 90kHz to110 kHz range, first introduced in 1957. It allowed accurate positioning for navigation systems, being long range, accurate and difficult to jam by hostile forces.

HMNB - Her Majesty's Naval Base. The Royal Navy's main base at Devonport.

KGB – The *Komitet Gosudarstvennoy Bezopasnosti*, the Committee for State Security. Dissolved in 1991 with the break-up of the USSR, it had been responsible for internal security, secret police actions and intelligence gathering. It was controlled by the military and its involvement in counter-intelligence and powerful control of dissent are well documented. It was replaced by the FSB and the SVR.

Kulak – Property owning peasants living in the Russian Empire. With Communism, Stalin persecuted them relentlessly, distrusting their loyalty and denouncing them as class enemies. The term became a derogatory accusation against anyone suspected of an enemy to communism because of suspicions of aspired capitalist ideas.

LPD – Landing Platform Dock. Amphibious transport ship, capable of operating several landing craft in an area at the stern which is flooded for the purpose. It can deliver Challenger tanks and has a pad to accommodate two helicopters.

Matushka Rossiya – *Mother Russia.*

MI5 – Military Intelligence, Section 5. Housed in Thames House in

London. It is the United Kingdom's internal counter-intelligence and security agency, also known as Security Services.

MI6 – Military Intelligence, Section 6. Also known as SIS – the Secret Intelligence Service. Based at Vauxhall House in London. Main goal being covert means of intelligence gathering and analysis outside of the U.K.

NATO – North Atlantic Treaty Organisation. Formed in 1949, NATO is made up of forty countries from Europe and North America. Its aims include the collective protection of the member countries and its people.

NIS – The Norwegian Intelligence Services, or *Etterretningstjenesten*. It has several stations, all of
which are north of the Arctic Circle.

NoCGV – Norwegian Coast Guard Vessel.

PIRA - The Provisional Irish Republican Army. Known colloquially in Northern Ireland as 'The Provies'. The PIRA saw themselves as the legitimate successor to the old IRA which had fought against the British in the Irish War of Independence. Seeing themselves as defenders of Republicanism, they ran a campaign of shootings and bombings against police, army and those they saw as enemies of a united Ireland.

PSNI – The Police Service of Northern Ireland.

Rajavartiolaitos – The Finnish Border Guardforce. It is a paramilitary-styled force and is made up of almost four thousand personnel. The border between Finland and Russia is watched and patrolled by the Rajavartiolaitos who are armed and well equipped, including several helicopters, patrol boats and hovercraft.

Rosneft – Huge Russian leader in the oil and gas sector. Largely owned by the Russian state, shares are also held by private oil companies such as B.P. It is heavily involved in oil and gas exploration and employs over 300,000 globally.

RTB – Return to Base.

S.O.E. – Special Operations Executive.

SIS – (See MI6)

Spetsnatz – Special Purpose Military Units. Russian Special forces.

STRAP - This is an agreement between the intelligence agencies of The USA, UK, Australia, Canada and New Zealand. There may possibly be others. It is a commitment only to share sensitive information on a 'Need to Know' basis.

SVR – The Foreign Intelligence Service of the Russian Federation. The SVR's remit lies in gleaning intelligence and performing espionage outside the Russian Federation. It also works in anti-terrorism and reports analysis of intelligence to the Russian president. It reportedly supplies agents working in espionage in several foreign nations and has been accused of arranging assassinations outside of Russia.

UAZ-469 – UAZ (Ulyanovsk Automobile Plant) is a car maker in Ulyanovsk, Russia. The Soviets had various military vehicles made there. The UAV-469 had excellent off-road capabilities and was simple to repair. Sold in over eighty countries, surplus vehicles became much sought after by private enthusiasts.

UVIED - "Under Vehicle Improvised Explosive Device." Home-made anti-personnel bombs, usually attached by magnets to the underside of the victim's car. When the vehicle moved off, a tilt switch would initiate the detonator and set off the device. They were a favourite tactic of the IRA, though Loyalist factions also utilised them to a lesser degree. Members of the Security Forces and civilians working with them were strongly encouraged to be vigilant and make a daily visual check under their vehicles.

ABOUT THE AUTHOR

Ivan Winters is a writer born and raised in Northern Ireland. He is blessed with a wonderful wife and is the proud father of four adult children along with two much-loved grandsons. His home overlooks the Irish Sea with the west coast of Scotland glimmering on the horizon.

Like many, he has always enjoyed the world of imagination animated through the written word. It is a place where adventures can flourish and engage the reader without limit.

The greatest story-tellings for him are ones that recognise the worth of every human being made in the image of God. Ulitmately, it is that story, that narrative that comprises the greatest value and wonder in this world.

Printed in Great Britain
by Amazon